COLD WATER

Also by Dave Hutchinson from Solaris

The Return of the Incredible Exploding Man

The Fractured Europe Sequence

Europe in Autumn
Europe at Midnight
Europe in Winter
Europe at Dawn

Tales of the Aftermath

Shelter

COLD WATER

DAVE HUTCHINSON

SOLARIS

First published 2022 by Solaris
an imprint of Rebellion Publishing Ltd,
Riverside House, Osney Mead,
Oxford, OX2 0ES, UK

www.solarisbooks.com

ISBN: 978-1-78618-722-2

A CIP catalogue record for this book is available from the British Library.

Designed & typeset by Rebellion Publishing

Printed in Denmark

THE PALM HOUSE

ONE

1

In London, if you checked into a boutique hotel, the chances are that it would have been converted out of some seventeenth century pie shop or something, and its dozen or so rooms would be full of odd angles and sloping ceilings and uneven floors and decorated with bits of bric-a-brac carefully sourced by professional designers from high-end junk shops. The last time she'd stayed in London, Carey's room had had a stuffed pike in a glass case mounted on the wall, its blank bead of an eye regarding the room as it swam eternally through a small forest of fake pondweed. There had been a little brass plaque attached to the case, informing the world that the fish had been caught by Mr MJ Harper at Winwood Pond in Middlesex on June 7 1882, and it had occurred to her that Winwood Pond had probably been filled in and had a business park or a housing estate built on it decades ago and this rather inexpertly-mounted fish might be the only evidence it had ever been there. There had been no restaurant or room service, and breakfast had been a miserable affair involving a choice between cereal or a poached egg on artisanal white toast.

In Poland, your boutique hotels came with four hundred rooms, two conference suites, a business centre, a Michelin-starred restaurant, and a roof terrace. Carey was booked into a black-faced cube fronted with small palm trees near the edge of Gliwice, where the town began to break up into detached houses and fields and little bits of forest. It was called Hotel Barbara, after—according to the two-page bio printed in the lunch menu—a previous hotel on the site. She wasn't sure what the point was of demolishing a perfectly good hotel and building another one on the same spot, but she supposed that was how you wound up with two conference suites and a Michelin star.

The hotel sat in a few hectares of grounds a little way off the main road into town from the west, and it was half-empty. Gliwice had its share of little museums and architectural attractions, but it wasn't really a tourist town; most of the people she'd seen at breakfast this morning had been business people, in ones and twos and threes, wearing Nehru jackets and Armani Revival suits and black Jesse Dunn boardroom couture. Jesse Dunn was everywhere in Europe, as ubiquitous as a uniform or a tee shirt with a particularly dull meme. You saw it in Madrid and in Helsinki and the only real variations Carey had ever noticed was a choice of heels.

Breakfast, though, was pretty good, with options to make guests from all over the Continent feel set up for the day, from minimalist Scandi cheese and sliced meat and crispbread to the full bacon, scrambled egg, sausage, hash browns, black pudding and baked beans experience that had been the signature breakfast of the international business traveller for decades. She'd opted for bacon and scrambled egg and toast and coffee, and sat at a table in a corner of the big airy dining room feeling out of place in her jeans and grey sweatshirt and comfortable walking shoes. There had been no time to buy herself local colouration; she'd arrived the previous evening after a four-day train journey from Barcelona and shopping had not been high on her list of priorities.

In the lobby, the business day was just beginning. Groups of business people stood around, briefcased-up, shaking hands with new arrivals as they emerged from the lifts and heading outside as their taxis arrived. Some others sat on the soft furnishings scattered around, consulting pads and phones. The atmosphere was quiet and relaxed; none of them paid her any attention at all. She went into the shop and bought herself a paper guidebook and a map, considered the knickknacks for sale, which seemed to consist mainly of iterations of Gliwice's coat of arms—fridge magnets, decorative spoons, bookends—and little models of colliery winding gear blazoned with the names of neighbouring towns. BYTOM, ZABRZE, RUDA ŚLĄSKA. Upper Silesia, of which Gliwice had spent the past couple of decades aggressively marketing itself as the business capital, was still a heavily industrialised area, even if a lot of the old coal mines and steelworks were now rusting quietly away behind high security fencing because nobody could afford to pull them down and decontaminate the land, if decontamination was even possible after hundreds of years of industrial poisoning. There were no knickknacks associated with Katowice, Gliwice's long-time economic rival. Katowice had the nearest international airport, but Gliwice had better imageers. It was a close-run thing.

She waited for a lull in the to-and-fro of the lobby, then she went to the desk and asked one of the receptionists to order her a cab into town. She wasn't optimistic about getting one in a hurry—the businessfolk seemed to have co-opted every taxi in a ten-mile radius—but the receptionist told her that if she'd like to step outside and wait, one would be along shortly.

So she went out through the big revolving doors and stood to one side of the entrance, a tall Texan woman well into the latter half of middle age, standing outside an hotel in central Europe smelling coal smoke ever so faintly on the breeze and sensing an answering burst of memory in her hindbrain. Her short brown hair was shot through with grey and there was an amused look to her eyes, though she had quite a temper. She was wearing a long black coat whose hem brushed the backs of her ankles, and slung over her shoulder was a scuffed and worn and much-restitched leather knapsack which, when it was new, had been the most expensive thing she possessed.

A city taxi pulled up, detailed with animated adverts for local shops and theatres. Its driver was a brown-haired young man wearing a leather jerkin so voluminous that it looked like it was made from the hide of an entire cow. He leaned over and looked at her through the open passenger-side window. "Tevs?" he called.

"I beg your pardon?" Carey said in Polish.

"Tevs," he said again. He consulted the little paperscreen stuck to one corner of the windscreen like a post-it note. "Passenger called Tevs."

She sighed as she got it. In Polish, *w* was *v*. She opened a door and got into the back of the cab. "That's me," she said. "And it's not pronounced like that."

Hotel Barbara was in a part of town that was almost like a village, but within a couple of minutes they were driving past ranks of apartment blocks that must have been here when the Germans pulled out. They looked like they'd been renovated and cleaned up at some point in the past, but years of Silesian pollution had laid a new layer of soot and grime on them. Interspersed with them were taller Soviet-era blocks, periodically tarted up by replacing their cladding and their windows, little shopping centres that were a dozen small stores built around a dusty paved square, bars, and a big entertainment complex for those who were still Luddite enough to want the cinema experience. The streets were lined with sooty trees in the dappled morning sunlight, and there were lots of people out and about. They all looked relatively prosperous, insofar as it was possible to tell from their clothes, but they were almost all white Central Europeans; even now you didn't get a lot of diversity in Poland outside Warsaw and some of the larger cities up near the Greater German border.

The driver dropped her outside the botanical gardens, a series of massive tessellated glass ziggurats in a big park near the centre of town. There was a sign outside that said PALMIARNIA MIEJSKA, under a banner advertising an arts festival. She went inside, swiped her phone at the front desk to buy a ticket and download a guide, then queued up with half a dozen or so other people to pass through a double set of doors. As she stepped through the second doors, hot humid air slapped her in the face. All around her towered huge primeval-looking plants. She held her phone to her ear and listened to a woman's voice reciting a rather rickety translation—the definite article missing more often than not—about the history and layout of the Palmiarnia. It was divided into a series of biomes. This first one was subtropical, all palms and somehow carnal-looking ferns through which a paved path ran in a series of curves that made the place seem larger than it was. She looked up, past the crowding foliage and a network of pipes and sprinklers, and saw grimy panes of glass. It was very quiet in here; a couple of hundred metres from the park a six-lane urban highway ran past in a cutting, but baffles and soundproofing reduced the traffic to a faint vibration she could feel through the soles of her shoes.

She moved on, through another set of climate-lock doors, to a temperate biome which was really what she could have seen in any forest in the country. The trees were a lot cleaner and healthier, maybe, but it was a bit dull. There were sparrows everywhere, flitting between the trees, hopping around on the path looking for bugs; she wondered if they were part of the exhibit or if they'd got in from outside somehow, maybe through a broken window, and discovered that the place was the Promised Land.

"Well, this is charming," a voice beside her said in English.

She turned her head, saw a tall casually dressed man a few years older than her. He had a very faint Scandinavian accent and a face like the business end of a tomahawk. "Hello," she said.

He took a pack of cigarettes from his pocket, removed one, and said, "I wonder, could I trouble you for a light?"

"You're not allowed to smoke in here," she told him, gesturing at a sign.

He deadpanned her. "You could at least make an effort."

She sighed. "I don't smoke," she said, completing the recognition string. "I gave up on New Year's Eve."

"There," he said, returning the cigarette to the pack and the pack to his pocket. "That wasn't so painful, was it?"

Carey made a rude noise.

He sighed, ever so faintly. "There's been something of a situation here," he told her, and only a Coureur would have examined that statement to detect a capital *S*. "We'd like you to look into it."

"I don't work for you any more," she told him. "You made that very clear."

He looked around the biome. "And yet here you are."

"The message made it sound urgent."

"Not urgent enough to make you fly here. I'll have to have a chat with whoever sent the signal, work on the wording."

She looked at him a moment, then started to walk. He paced along beside her, hands in pockets, completely at ease. "Are you offering me my job back?" she asked.

"Oh, no," he said. "No, I wouldn't dream of being so insulting, unless you wanted it back; you seem to be doing very well on your own. No, we'd like to engage you as a consultant. How do your people put it? A *visiting fireman.*"

"Why me? Is everyone else busy or something?"

"We think you have a certain... perspective which would be useful."

"I don't do Central Europe any more," Carey said. Catalunya, where the crash message had caught up with her, was about as close to Hungary as she ever wanted to be again and still be on mainland Europe. Now she was just over five hundred kilometres from Budapest, as the crow flew, and she was starting to get twitchy.

"That wasn't our fault."

"I don't *care* whose fault it was." She paused as a young couple with a baby in a stroller went past them. "I can't go back to Hungary," she told him. "I'm blown six ways from Sunday there; they'd lift me the moment they realised I was there. And even if I *wasn't* blown, I'm still not going back to Hungary."

"At the moment, that would seem not to be necessary. And if it ever *were* to become necessary, we have resources in Budapest and elsewhere."

She remembered someone telling her that the Coureurs in Hungary were good, but a law unto themselves. She put her foot on that memory.

He looked casually around, a man always aware of the possibility of surveillance, and took something from his pocket. "This is not about Hungary," he said. "It's about here."

She looked down at the photograph he was showing her. In it, a young man and woman were leaning together into the shot, arms around each other's shoulders. They were laughing. In the background was a wall of bodies, the occasional hand gripping a beer glass. In the foreground was a table almost entirely covered in empty bottles and glasses and plates. The look on the woman's face broke

Carey's heart. She looked so young and trusting and happy. The man was blond and handsome and she had never quite got over the suspicion that he looked like the Devil.

"What's he got himself mixed up in now?" she asked.

"We were rather hoping you'd agree to find out for us," he said. "On the face of it, he mostly seems to have got himself dead."

He gave her a moment for the news to sink in, but she realised she had always been waiting for this. It had always been in her future, and in a way she had been prepared for it for a very long time. "People like us, we don't make old bones," he'd told her once, to which she'd replied, "I don't know about you, matey-boy, but I plan to."

"I am," said her contact.

She glanced at him. "That's a place, not a name."

He heaved a sigh. "Yes," he said wearily.

THERE WAS A common agreement that the Baltic peoples were batshit crazy. Part of it was obviously because of decades labouring under German rule or Nazi occupation or Soviet occupation or Russian occupation. That sort of thing would bend the psyche of any nation out of shape, although to be fair one could say much the same about any European nation east of what was now the Polish border. Mostly, though, there was something in the national character. You could poke an Englishman or a Frenchwoman and have a reasonable expectation of how they would react. Do the same to a Lithuanian or an Estonian and it was best to be prepared to run, just in case. Czechs wanted to be Western Europeans but kept being tripped up by a long series of increasingly right-wing governments; Poles were generally quite mad; Hungarians were... well, Carey had certain very strong opinions about the Hungarians; and nobody with any sense messed around in the Balkans because rationality had deserted those countries at least two hundred years ago. But the Baltic states, the old lands of the Hanseatic League, were special. One tiptoed there, if one went there at all.

Maksim had once told her it was the sea itself which drove people crazy. "There's a demon sleeping on the floor of the Baltic," he'd said, and she'd been just young enough and just smitten enough to find it cute, "and its dreams drive people mad."

Well, almost thirty years on and it was her holding his photograph and examining her feelings at the news he was dead, not the other way round. Eventually we all reach an age where the only victory left is outliving our lovers and enemies.

"What happened?" she asked, knowing that even asking the question took her into a territory she was unwilling to visit.

"We don't know," said Kaunas.

"How can you not know?"

They had moved on through another set of doors into a desert biome, although it was not like the desert Carey was familiar with. The air was hot and dry and the soil was sandy and scattered with cacti and scrub vegetation and there were small lizards dozing on flat rocks or darting across the path, but it was not nearly dangerous enough. A long-ago boyfriend, an Englishman, had once told her that Texas was as inimical to human life as the surface of Mars. More so; Mars didn't have rattlesnakes.

"The details are confused," Kaunas said. "We weren't even aware that he was here. Then, three weeks ago, we got word that he was dead."

"Three weeks."

"It took some time for a decision to be made whether to investigate or to leave well alone. Officially, he was involved in a traffic accident just outside town. Unofficially... well, we just don't know. There's a feeling that there was more to it, that the authorities and other actors are hiding something. Does it sound credible that he would have been mixed up with something illegal? I mean, outside his activities as a Coureur."

Clearly, Kaunas knew next to nothing about Maksim, or he wouldn't have asked. Certainly he didn't know about Helsinki. "It would have been in character," she said carefully. "I haven't seen him in ten years, though. He might have cleaned up his act." Although, to be fair, there was more chance of Elvis touring again.

Kaunas regarded a pair of green lizards sitting on top of a saguaro cactus for a moment, then looked at her. "Coureur work can, on occasion, involve an element of personal risk, but the attrition rate is actually very low. Most Coureurs either retire or just drift off into more regular employment. So we do pay attention to fatalities. If Maksim did suffer an accident, that's one thing, one can never adequately plan for accidents. If he was involved in some kind of Situation here, he was off-piste, and that's something else altogether. It would be useful if we knew what it was."

She watched his face. "You're worried about bad publicity."

"The work we do involves a high degree of trust, you know that. Because of our nature, customers can't sue us if something goes wrong; they have to trust us to move their Packages. If word got around that we were *buccaneering*, it would undermine that trust."

"You should have a word with whoever writes those Coureur shows," she said. "They're nothing *but* buccaneering."

He made a sour face and waved the comment away. "Everyone knows they're dramas. Nobody takes them seriously. The people who know us, who use our services, have certain expectations of us. If people started to believe we were nothing more than common criminals… "

Well, there it was. Except Maksim was far from a *common* criminal. She wasn't annoyed that they had called her in—it was logical, if you looked at it from one angle. What did annoy her was that they *knew* about her and Maksim in the first place, and had kept track of her after all these years, even after, on the face of it, they had dispensed with her services. They actually had a photo of them together. That was something she was going to have to deal with, at some point.

"I'm amazed nobody had a word with him years ago," she said. "Told him to straighten out his act."

"You know that's not how it works. He was good at what he did, anyway; it would have been a loss. As it is, he's been doing very little Coureur work at all over the past couple of years, unless he was doing it on the sly. The assumption was that he was winding down to retirement."

Carey shook her head. "Not Maksim."

Kaunas said, "You're likely to spot things that someone who didn't know him would miss. It's been decided that you're more than equal to this."

She thought about it for a little while. Then she handed back the photo. "No," she said. "I'm sorry."

Kaunas raised an eyebrow.

"Actually, I'm not sorry," she told him. "Maksim and I were over a long time ago, and we didn't part friends. I'm not going back there."

He stood very still, watching her. "Well, that's... unfortunate."

"Oh please," she said. "You're not going to *threaten* me, are you?"

He looked surprised. As surprised as a face that inexpressive could, anyway. "Oh. No, no. No, you're a free agent, you're not obliged to take the job. It's just a pity; we thought your involvement might make things more straightforward."

"Maksim doesn't do straightforward," she said. "Didn't."

He glanced down at the photo, and finally took it and pocketed it. "Aren't you curious about what happened to him?"

"I am," she told him. "But not enough to get mixed up in his business again. I'm done with that."

Kaunas thought about it. "I'm sorry," he said. "It seems you've had a wasted journey." He glanced about again, but they had the whole biome to themselves; deserts were dull, even when they were trying to kill you, and there was a sign pointing the way to the aquarium, which promised at least stuff that moved. He reached into an inside pocket of his coat and took out a fat envelope. "This should cover your expenses," he said. "There's a contact protocol in there too, should you change your mind."

Of course, they had been prepared for her to say no. You hope for the best and you plan for the worst. She put the envelope in her pocket. "I wish you luck with this," she told him. "I really do."

SHE GOT A cab back to the hotel. Her first instinct, even though she was booked in for three nights, was to check out right now and put some distance between herself and Central Europe. But she'd missed checkout, and although Kaunas's envelope contained an impressive wad of high-denomination Swiss currency—far more than was necessary to cover her outlays—it went against the grain to just throw away the price of a room if she didn't have to.

A big tour coach was parked outside the hotel and Reception was full of English pensioners and their luggage. What they were doing there was anyone's guess. Instead of going directly to the lifts, she peeled off and headed for the little café tucked away in one corner of the lobby. She sat down at a table and ordered an Americano and a club sandwich and tried to process the news of Maksim's death. What she felt, chiefly, was annoyance at having been dragged across Europe to be told the news. They could have emailed her, if it had mattered that much to them. "Sentiment will kill you," he'd told her once, although she couldn't remember if this was in reaction to a particular event or just one of his endless playlist of homilies, to be shuffled and dropped into the conversation at random for whatever audience was there at the time.

Her sandwich and drink arrived, and she'd just begun to eat when someone pulled out the chair opposite her and sat down. She glanced up and found herself looking at a stout man in his late forties or early fifties, with a shaven head and a big bushy moustache that made him look like a Cossack hetman straight out of Sienkiewicz. He was wearing a well-cut but unremarkable three-piece suit and a wing collar with an ascot, which was a couple of years out of fashion apart from in some of the more distant corners of Europe, and he was regarding her calmly with a faintly amused look in his eyes.

"Do we have some kind of a problem?" she asked him.

He leaned forward slightly in what passed for a bow, then he stood, still with that look of amusement. "My apologies," he said in good English. "I mistook you for someone else."

"Yeah, I get that a lot," she said.

"Do you? That must be terribly inconvenient." And he turned and walked out of the café.

Carey watched him go. Central Europe was a place of craziness: you learned to roll with it or you went home. She looked down at her sandwich, sitting on her plate with one bite taken out of it, and she sighed and pushed the plate away.

* * *

Upstairs in her room, she grabbed her toilet bag from the bathroom, took her travelling bag from the wardrobe—she'd barely bothered to unpack—and went downstairs and checked out.

She took a cab to the station and stood scanning the departure boards for anything that was going West. Operational lore—and the presence of Maksim in this equation, however posthumously, meant operational lore came into effect—dictated that she buy tickets on three separate trains, one by electronic transfer from her phone and two for cash. Then she walked down a platform and boarded a fourth, a rattling little local bound for the Hindenberg border, and bought a ticket from the guard with almost the last of her złotys. Then she sat, watching the countryside go by and getting angrier and angrier, as the train stopped at every little town and pissant station on its route.

It was late afternoon when the train pulled into the border crossing at Strzelce Opolskie along a tunnel of close-woven mesh that entirely enclosed the tracks like an enormous metal cloche. Looking out of the window, she could see places where people had managed to spray graffiti on the mesh, although she couldn't tell what it was supposed to be. The actual physical border was just outside town, but from here there was a train to Breslau, and from there she could catch another train to Berlin and an express to Paris and another express to Toulouse and a local that wound its way patiently up into the Pyrenees and back down towards Barcelona. Four days, if you factored in the time sat waiting at various stations for connections, and waiting on the train while men in various national uniforms came through doing passport and customs checks. An eight-day round trip, just to hear the news that Maksim was dead. That would probably have pleased him.

Her carriage was almost empty. She and the other four passengers alighted and walked along the platform towards customs and immigration. Hindenberg, the ethnic Silesian homeland carved, not without some bad blood, from a number of towns in western Poland, was more than thirty years old, which made it about as stable as a polity ever got these days. She could remember when it had been set up, not long after she came to Europe for the first time. Polish and UN forces had faced off along the border for weeks, taking the occasional pot-shot at each other. The situation had got pretty tense, but somehow it had never broken out into full-scale conflict and there had been few casualties. Poland still regarded the place as an abomination, though; there had been cases in various UN Special Courts ever since, trying to rescind its independence.

She passed through Polish passport control, then down the corridor to the Hindenberg checkpoint. She was travelling on her Texas passport so there was no messing around with visas, although the Hindenbergers got her to open her bags and had a root around, more to be annoying than anything else.

In Breslau, she booked into an hotel near the station so she'd be handy for the Berlin train the next morning. She had a steak and potatoes and a green salad in the almost-deserted dining room, then she sat in her room looking out at the traffic and pedestrians passing by in the street below. She was not, she noted, noticeably less angry than she had been when she left Gliwice. She cursed Kaunas and *Les Coureurs*. She cursed Maksim. She cursed herself for ever having gotten mixed up with either of them. She cursed men and all their works. She cursed Hungary, but that was something she tended to do in idle moments anyway.

Next morning, bleary-eyed over her sausage and eggs, was more businessfolk, more Armani Revival and Jesse Dunne. The faces changed but the clothes stayed the same. Actually, she couldn't be sure the faces changed any more. Maybe she was seeing the same people, over and over again, all over

Europe. If any of those perfectly blameless businessfolk had been granted a glimpse inside her head this morning, they would have evacuated the dining room and called the police.

Some time later, she stood on the concourse of the railway station looking at the departure boards. Bahnhof Breslau was gorgeous, a great echoing space of marble floors and vaulting ceilings, somehow modernistic and fin de siecle at the same time. It had taken on a well-used patina but it had still to achieve the generally run-down and scuzzy atmosphere of most of the big stations of Europe. The whole of Breslau—the whole of Hindenberg—was like that. Greater Germany had funnelled a seemingly inexhaustible line of credit into the fledgling polity, erasing Polish Wrocław and creating a sort of Prussian pocket nation with a financial services sector easily the equal of Frankfurt. Everyone here seemed happy and well-fed. Even the service workers—immigrants from the economically prostrate nations of the European South—seemed content with their lot.

She stood there for a long time. Trains arrived and trains departed. The Berlin train pulled out and she was not on it. Eventually, she found herself on a train back to Strzelce Opolskie.

It was mid-afternoon when she got back to Hotel Barbara. The tour coach was still outside, and the English pensioners didn't seem to have moved from the lobby since yesterday, but now they were leaving.

If the receptionist was surprised to see her return so soon, she didn't say anything. She was very helpful. Carey even wound up back in her old room.

2

Most people's early memories involved a family holiday, a beloved pet, happy moments with grandparents. Carey's was of her father dragging their neighbour out of his house and beating him senseless on his front lawn.

This was when they were living in Houston, a year or so after her baby sister Jennifer died in one of a wave of little measles epidemics which had swept across Texas, which would have made Carey six years old. It took her a long time to understand what had happened, because no one ever sat her down and explained it to her. Jennifer was with them for a while, and then she was not. Her parents became quieter and quieter and her mother withdrew so much that one day she was also not there and then it was just Carey and her father.

The family next door, the Spicers, had two sons a year or so older than Carey, and they had a pet rabbit called Rocky which Carey loved. She liked the Spicers. The boys were polite, Mr Spicer was big and amiable, Mrs Spicer gave her lemonade sometimes. But she loved going round the fence and feeding lettuce leaves and strips of carrot to Rocky. Rocky lived in the house because coyotes roamed the neighbourhood, and the Spicers always welcomed her in for an hour or so. It never occurred to her that they were being kind to the motherless little girl, but her father was becoming distant in a way she vaguely recognised and was afraid of, and the Spicer house was a happy one.

One night, she heard shouting outside. This wasn't unusual; there were a couple of bars round the corner on the main street and sometimes drunks would stagger home past her house. But this was different. It was closer, literally just outside, and one of the people who was shouting was her father.

She got out of bed and padded over to the window and lifted the curtain, and it was some years before she understood what she saw. Her father was dragging Mr Spicer—big, kind, amiable Mr Spicer—onto the lawn next door by the collar of his shirt while Mrs Spicer stood in the open doorway screaming. Mr Spicer's face was distorted and covered in blood which looked black under the streetlights. Her father dropped him on the grass and raised his fist and punched him in the face, shouting, "How many kids have you killed today, Barry? How many kids have you killed today?" over and over again. Carey was too baffled by this scene to be afraid.

The police turned up eventually, by which time Mr Spicer was unconscious, and they took Carey's father away. For Carey there was a spell in the care of Child Services, which was a bit like grown-up school but with a room of your own. Some of the kids in Child Services were not kind. Some of them were, in fact, downright dangerous, and the adult staff carried kiddy-voltage tasers and cans of riot foam on their belts. Carey kept to herself, did her lessons, but when she did get into fights she always won, and she eventually got a reputation as someone best left alone. And then some people claiming to be her mother's relatives arrived and took her away, and she never saw her house or the Spicers or Rocky ever again.

Her mother's relatives were Uncle Byron and Aunt Pru, and they lived in Lubbock. Byron was her mother's brother, and it was quite a long time before it occurred to Carey to wonder why she had never seen or heard of him before. He was a tall, thin, laconic man with long hair worn in dreads and a crinkle of laugh-lines around his eyes. Aunt Pru was small and plump and Welsh. She'd been the singer in a rock band whose tour of the American South had ended prematurely in what she called 'artistic differences'. The rest of the band went home, but Pru had already met Byron, who did sound design for outdoor concerts, and she stayed, although they never quite got round to getting married. Pru had made a new career for herself as a songwriter and backing singer, and she was much in demand. Sometimes a song would come over the entertainment centre and Byron would nudge Carey gently and say, "That's one of Pru's, that is."

Pru was a Welsh-speaker, and Welsh was the first foreign language Carey ever learned. It was still the language she was most fluent in after English, which was a shame because centuries of educational neglect and downright bigotry had rendered it almost extinct apart from in a couple of die-hard Valleys communities.

They were not, it had to be said, natural parents. They'd never wanted children of their own and now here they were presented with this tall, serious-faced little girl, and they were at a bit of a loss. That didn't mean they loved her any less; they threw themselves into their new role, reasoning that eventually they would all get the hang of the situation. They got Carey into a good school and were as kind and attentive as any parents could have been. She thought she detected a certain faint disappointment that she was not remotely interested in music or the music business. Byron tried to teach her piano and guitar, but they didn't take. The piano in particular was a mystery to her; she couldn't get her hands and feet to coordinate. If Byron, who was an outstanding pianist and kept himself limbered up with the occasional gig at a downtown jazz club and the even more occasional performance with the Lubbock Philharmonic, was annoyed by this, he didn't let it show.

One day when Carey was ten, a man came to the door. Pru was in the studio at the back of the house, goggled into a conference space where she was laying down a backing vocal for an album which was actually being recorded in Copenhagen. Byron was in the kitchen cooking dinner, and Carey was helping him. At the sound of the doorbell, Byron turned down the heat under the pan of stew on the range, checked the gate camera, and Carey thought he hesitated for a moment. Then he pressed the button that opened the gate and walked down the hall and opened the door.

The man standing outside was thin and grey and haggard and he was wearing shabby clothes, and he and Byron stood looking at each other, although it seemed to Carey, looking down the hallway, that the man couldn't meet Byron's eyes. He said, "Byron," quietly.

"Mm hm," said Byron, arms crossed across his chest.

"I want to see her," said the man. "You can't stop me."

"I can," Byron said. "We adopted her, all legal and fair and square," and Carey realised with a start that the grey man was her father. "She'd still be in juvenile hall if we hadn't."

"They forced me to sign those papers, Byron," her father said. "I didn't get any say in it." He looked past Byron and saw Carey standing there in the archway leading to the kitchen, and his head tipped over to one side.

"It might be best if you left, Don," Byron said gently without looking round to see what her father had seen.

"You can't do this," her father said without looking away from Carey. "She's my daughter. I've got a right."

"You want to see her, you get in touch with Child Services and we'll arrange a visit for you," Byron said evenly. "You can't just walk in here like this." He looked down at the battered suitcase on the porch at her father's feet. "When did you get out?"

"Last month."

"And it took you this long to come see her?" Byron nodded. "Mm hm."

Her father didn't seem to have an answer for that. He just kept staring at her, head tipped over, as if he was trying to work out where he'd seen her before.

"You got yourself a place?" Byron asked.

"Going to El Paso," her father said. "There's work there. Parole board organised it."

"Mm hm." Byron reached into his back pocket and took out his wallet. He took out a wad of notes and held them out. "Take this."

Her father's attention snapped to the money in Byron's hand. "You can't buy me off, Byron," he said.

"Just trying to be a good Christian," Byron said.

Her father snorted and said, "Christian." But he reached out and took the money. Byron dipped into his wallet again and came out with a card. "And go see this guy, Don," he said. "Get yourself straightened out, maybe then we'll talk about things. State you're in, I can't let you in here."

Her father looked at the card but he didn't take it. "You always thought you were better than us," he said, his mouth twisting. "You didn't even come to their funerals. Just left me to cope on my own."

"I'm going to close the door and walk away now, Don," Byron said calmly. "If you ring the bell again or come back here some other day, I'll call the police. You don't want to see Doctor Moss, fine. But you go to AA, get yourself on a programme, and we'll take it from there. I wish you luck in El Paso." And he closed the door on her father and walked back into the kitchen.

He turned up the heat under the stew, gave it a stir. He didn't say anything for a while, and Carey knew he was waiting for the sound of the doorbell, but it didn't come. Finally, he said, "Did anyone ever tell you what happened?"

Carey shook her head.

"You know what an antivaxxer is?"

Carey nodded.

"Well, that's what your neighbour was. Belonged to one of those little churches, I forget which one. Your daddy blamed him for your little sister's death, and when Ruth—your mom—well, your daddy took it hard and he needed someone to blame so he took it out on your neighbour. Beat him so badly the guy can only see properly with one eye now, I hear. His attorney pleaded insanity, the balance of his mind was disturbed by grief, that kind of thing, and your daddy only got four years. He was lucky." He dipped a spoon into the stew, tasted it, put the spoon in the sink. "Looks like it was hard time, though."

"Why didn't you come to the funerals?" Carey asked.

He looked at her, surprised at the question. "Well," he said, "you're still a little young to understand properly, but families can be complicated things." He stopped, maybe realising that this wasn't good enough for a bright ten-year-old. "Don's a hard man to like," he said. "I'm sorry to say that, but it's true. He's quick to take offence and slow to apologise and he'll let a grudge cook. Some things got said, back before you were born, and I'm not going to repeat them now, but none of us wanted anything more to do with him. That doesn't mean we loved you or your mom or little Jenny any less, but your daddy made sure we knew we weren't welcome in your lives. He told us he didn't want us at the funerals, which was hurtful. We visited the graves later, said our goodbyes."

It was the most she ever heard him say in one conversation, and it raised more questions than it answered, but she stepped forward and hugged him and said, "I love you, Uncle Byron."

"Hey," Pru said, coming in from the studio. "Am I missing a group hug, here?" And she came over and hugged the two of them, and if Carey didn't notice Pru giving Byron a puzzled look, or Byron shaking his head, that was okay, she was safe in the arms of two of the best people she ever knew.

3

It was late when Krista got home, another day of meetings and conferences that had left only a few hours to do her actual job. Unwilling and frankly too tired to cook, she'd picked up a pizza from the takeaway at the end of the street. It wasn't exactly ideal—she was conscious that her life was starting to fill up with junk food of late—but all she wanted was to have something to eat, a long hot shower, a drink, and go to bed.

Going up to the sixth floor of her block, the smell of the hot pizza filled the lift. Someone would complain about it at the next residents' meeting, but screw them.

Juggling the pizza box and her bag and her phone, she managed to unlock the door of her flat and step inside. She flicked the light switch, and for a fraction of a second the light in the hallway blinked on before going out again. She sighed, and there were some moments of low comedy while she transferred everything from hand to hand until she was able to swipe up her phone's flashlight function.

By the light of the screen, she made her way into the kitchen and put the pizza and her bag on the worktop. She tried the kitchen light switch, but nothing happened. The clocks on the microwave and the cooker were blank. Same in the living room; the standby lights on the entertainment set were dark.

In fact, everything was dark, she realised. There was no light coming in from the street outside. Krista went over to the window, lifted the net curtain aside, and looked out. The streetlights had gone out, and there were no lights in any of the buildings she could see. The only light, in fact, was coming from the cars down in the street which had just pulled to a stop, their drivers getting out and exchanging words with each other, trying to work out what had happened.

Darkness in Tallinn, she thought. One of her favourite films. She lifted her phone and started to dial the office, but she'd only entered a couple of numbers when it buzzed and the screen lit up with Markus's caller ID. She hit *answer* and lifted the phone to her ear, but there was nothing, just a strange sense of dead air.

She looked at the phone for a moment, as if that would make it start working again. Then she looked down into the street again. Very distantly, she could hear police sirens. Lots of police sirens. She dithered for a fraction of a second—she was tired and it was a three-quarter-hour walk back to headquarters—and then she picked up her bag again and headed for the door, holding her phone out in front of her like a magic charm to light the way. Before she reached it, she turned and went back into the kitchen and took a slice of pizza from the box and wrapped it in a napkin to eat on the way.

LENNA GROANED AND opened her eyes. For a moment—quite a few moments, actually—she thought she was having another of those hypnagogic dreams where she could see through her closed eyelids but was completely paralysed. She had two or three of these a year, had been having them since university; mostly they were harmless, but every now and again they involved someone standing by her bed.

She'd told her therapist about it, and he had assured her that it was not an uncommon condition—as much as fifty percent of the population had experienced it at least once, and perhaps five percent suffered regular episodes. He said it might be the root of stories of demonic possession and alien visitation—he'd even pulled up Henry Fuseli's *The Nightmare*—a vaguely Goyaesque painting featuring a sleeping young woman sprawled decoratively on a chaise with a small, bestial figure sitting on her chest, while what appeared to be a cartoon horse looked on. It was not remotely what Lenna had experienced, but something about the painting seemed to capture the sensation.

Anyway, this was not one of those times. She could wiggle her fingers and toes and she could blink her eyelids. She wasn't dreaming. She was awake; the heavy, paralysed sensation was because she was still drunk, and the profound darkness was because… yes, *why* was it so dark? Was she at home? Was she in someone else's bed? Someone whose bedroom had thick curtains and no streetlights directly outside? Details of the preceding evening remained elusive.

If she *was* in someone else's flat, that was going to be a problem. Well, it was going to be a number of problems, but the most pressing one at the moment was that she needed to pee and she had no idea where the bathroom might be.

She slowly stretched her arms and legs out to the sides until she encountered the edges of the bed, and established that there was no one there with her, which was puzzling. Was she in some Samaritan's spare room? On previous experience, this seemed unlikely.

Groping around beyond the side of the bed, she encountered a small table, and on it—miracle of miracles—her phone. She picked it up and switched it on, and the light of its screen instantly collapsed the infinite darkness surrounding her.

Oh, so that's where I am...

She spent a few seconds considering the shadows of her bedroom before rolling off the bed and padding unsteadily out of the room and down the hallway to the bathroom. She tried switching on the bathroom light, but nothing happened, so she peed by the light of her phone, balanced it on the cistern while she washed her hands, then carried it down the hall again to the kitchen.

Where all was darkness. No lights on any of the appliances. She lifted the blind away from the window and looked down into the street. All the streetlamps were out, no lights in any of the blocks across the road. It was a moonless, cloudy night, and the sky was a featureless grey only fractionally lighter than the city it covered. Down below, a tram had come to a stop in the middle of the street. Passengers had disembarked and were standing foolishly in the light of car headlamps. There were quite a few people down in the street, considering it was... she checked the time on her phone. Okay, it wasn't that late. Everything was vague in her memory, but she thought she might only have been asleep—if it was sleep—for an hour or so. She couldn't remember when she had left the bar, or how she had got home. *Got to stop doing that.*

Down below, the traffic had come to a standstill, a line of cars and buses and vans. It was interesting how little actual illumination a car headlight actually put out; everything at about knee height was brightly lit, but above that was darkness. Very faintly, she could hear the sound of car horns, and, distantly, the sirens of emergency vehicles.

She tried to call friends to find out what the actual fuck was going on, but there was no signal. The landline phone, which she kept mostly for nostalgic reasons, was similarly dead. Nothing. Not even static. No internet connectivity. Nothing.

In a cupboard in the hall, stuffed in with her camping gear, was a wind-up radio. She located it by opening the cupboard door, pulling everything out onto the floor, and searching through it on her hands and knees. She gave the handle a few turns and switched it on, and the sense of relief when white noise emerged from the speaker almost made her pass out. She settled with her back against the wall and turned the tuning dial, past scraps of music and snatches of conversation in Finnish and Latvian and Russian. So the world wasn't ending. At least not in Finland and Latvia and Rus. Not a lot of Estonian about, though. She found a sport radio station that was based in Tartu, but the studio discussion wasn't about football; instead, the newsreader was talking about a massive power blackout in Tallinn. He actually used the word 'massive'. Then he rode off into the highlands of speculation and started using words like 'cyberattack' and 'invasion' and 'tanks on the border' until someone cut him off. A few moments later, another voice came on, this one fractionally calmer, advising everyone to stay indoors until there was more information. Whether this advice came through official channels or simple common sense was not clear.

Lenna sat where she was on the hallway floor, listening to all this, and thinking that maybe she should be out on the street, gathering material for a story. The problem with that was a) she was still drunk—although it wouldn't be the first time—and b) every other journalist in the city would be doing the same thing. By sunup this would be the only story in Tallinn; anything she could do would just be more background, lost in the noise.

All of a sudden, and quite without warning, the bathroom light came on, and then the living room lights, and then the television. Lenna watched this for a few moments, then got up and went to the living room window. Outside, the streetlights were struggling to life, and the windows in the buildings opposite were starting to come on. As she watched, a glow of reflected light began to spread across the low clouds.

Her phone rang, startling her, and she dropped it and its screen shattered on the wood-block floor.

TWO

1

"WHAT CHANGED YOUR mind, if I may ask?" Kaunas inquired.

"You may not," Carey told him. There was no point trying to explain to him; she didn't even understand it herself.

"Okay," he said. "Well, I'm pleased, obviously."

They were sitting on a bench in Park Chopina, the big park in the centre of town. Over the trees in the distance, Carey could see sunlight glinting on the panes of the Palmiarnia. The park was busy; old folk out for their constitutional, shoppers taking a shortcut home with bags full of groceries, little groups of schoolkids. Kaunas had brought sandwiches and soft drinks as camouflage, and to the casual passerby they were just two friends having lunch in the sunshine.

She held out the envelope with the Swiss francs. "You'd better have this back," she said.

Kaunas looked at it and shook his head. "Keep it; you'll need some expense money."

She thought about it a moment, then put the envelope

back in her knapsack. She said, "What happens when I'm done?"

"I'm sorry?"

"Suppose I find out how he died, what he was up to. Then what?"

She thought she saw Kaunas's body language relax, ever so slightly. He said, "It's quite possible—probable, even—that nothing untoward was going on, and in that case nothing would happen. If you *were* to find something, wiser heads than you and I would take over and decide what, if anything, the response should be."

"Would I be involved in that? If there was a response?"

"Would you want to be?"

"Depends."

Kaunas shook his head. "My feeling is not."

"I might have something to say about that."

He took a bite from his chicken salad sandwich, washed it down with a mouthful of Coke. "Perhaps this is a bridge we should cross when we get to it," he said finally.

She looked at her own sandwich, ham and some kind of mustard pickle. She wasn't hungry. "What kind of support would I have? Operational funds? I'm not doing this on my own dime."

"There is an operational budget, and funds will be transferred into the account of your choice. There's more if you need it, but please try not to be excessive. As to support, there are some Coureurs here and you can make your own arrangements with them, with Central's backing. I have a contact routine for them."

"I want twice my usual fee," she said, more as an experiment than anything else.

"Agreed," he said without seeming to think about it. He blinked slowly at her, and she sighed. He took a little hard drive from his pocket and held it out. "This is all the documentation we have."

That didn't sound very promising. She took the hard drive, closed her fist around it.

"One more thing," Kaunas said, wrapping up the remains of his sandwich and dropping it in the bin beside the bench. "We'd appreciate if you didn't make too many waves."

Was that a veiled reference to Hungary? To her brawling days? "I don't get into bar fights any more," she told him.

"That's good news, obviously. Just... try to keep things low-key. Don't agitate the locals. Things here are volatile enough already."

She was vaguely flattered that he thought she could make that much of a difference. "How long do I have?"

"We're reluctant to put you under the clock, but I'll be in touch at the end of the week to discuss any progress and we'll take things from there."

"I doubt I'll have made a lot of progress by then."

"On the other hand, you might very well have wrapped everything up." He smiled at her. She didn't think he smiled very often; he wasn't very good at it. "Can you think of anything else you might need from me?"

She felt the little square of the hard drive, about the size of a stamp, digging into her palm. "I'll need a photo," she said. She dug a slip of paper from her pocket and handed it over.

Kaunas raised an eyebrow when he read what she'd written. "You can't get this yourself?"

"There won't be anything in public domain, and I don't have access to a pianist." And that was something she was going to have to remedy as soon as she could.

Kaunas shrugged and folded the slip of paper and popped it into the breast pocket of his jacket. "Is this person important?"

"It'd be good to know if he was still lurking around."

"I'll have it delivered to your hotel as soon as I can." He drained his Coke and dropped the tin on top of his sandwich in the bin. He looked at her. "I'm sure this will all go smoothly, and then we can all go home." And with a nod of farewell he stood and walked away. As she watched him go, it occurred to Carey to wonder why, if there were Coureurs in Gliwice, they hadn't been tasked with looking into Maksim's death. And also who, exactly, he had meant when he said *we can* all *go home*.

THE TOWN'S MAIN street was called Zwycięstwa, and it ran, slightly uphill, from the station to the little market square. It was pretty much what you'd expect from a Central European main street; a kind of Austro-Hungarian feel to the buildings, tram tracks running up the middle of the road, fast-food chains, electronics stores, bookshops, drugstores, coffee shops, delicatessens, a couple of hotels. Down side streets, Carey glimpsed more recent buildings, all glass and composite, but if you mentally erased the modern shopfronts Zwycięstwa looked more or less as it must have when it was first laid out towards the end of the nineteenth century. The soil here was poor and sandy and it blew everywhere; the pavements were uneven and felt gritty underfoot.

That was the Central Europe she was used to—solid and no-nonsense and ever so slightly decadent, and more often than not still stained with the soot of the previous century, although a lot of the buildings here seemed to have been recently cleaned. Whether she was prepared to admit it to herself or not, she'd missed this. She'd grown up in a place where an historic building was one which still had its original vinyl siding. Christopher Wren once said that he built for eternity, which you couldn't really say for architects in Texas.

Back in the day, she'd spent a lot of time in towns like this, to the extent that she'd once considered herself more European than Texan, an affectation at which more than one old lover had scoffed. Now, she wasn't so sure that they'd been wrong.

She walked into the first kantor she came to and changed some of the Swiss francs and received a staggering brick of złoties in return. There was a kiosk next door, and she bought a pack of ten disposable phones, each preloaded with ten thousand złoties of credit, which at least cut down the amount of paper money she had to carry. There was a department store across the road, and she spent an hour or so in there shopping for underwear and jeans and tee shirts and a couple of sweatshirts, paying for them with the credit on one of the phones. She'd have to buy more if she was going to be spending any length of time here—she'd only brought a couple of changes of clothes with her from Barcelona—but it would do for the moment.

A little further up towards the market square, she stopped off at an Empik and bought a poster-size paperscreen and some bits and pieces of gear she thought she might need, and then, as camouflage, she splurged on a couple of paperback books, a print edition of the local paper, and a small selection of children's toys. Then she loaded herself and her purchases into a taxi and went back to the hotel.

After a shower, she sorted through the stuff she'd dumped on the bed and put on some fresh clothes. She rang room service for a burger and fries and a coffee, and when they'd been delivered she unrolled the paperscreen and held it to the wall above the writing desk until static cling made it stick.

She sat at the desk eating lunch while she fiddled with one of the disposable phones, trying to get it to talk to the screen. When that was working, she slotted Kaunas's hard drive into the phone, and was rewarded with a menu of four folders.

The screen had a rudimentary gestural interface; you had to move like an angry mime to get it to work. Standing in front of it, she waved her hand up and down a couple of times to catch its attention, then she stabbed her finger emphatically at the first folder and twitched her hand clockwise to open it. It contained a single document, a dump of passport data. Name, Maksim Ilyich Petrauskas; place of birth, Wilno; date of birth, so-and-so, height such-and-such. Photo, biometric data, known identifying marks, etc and etc.

She copied the photo into a new folder and blew it up and sat looking up at it, eating the last of her fries and wondering how long ago it had been taken. In their passport photos, Americans and Brits looked you straight in the eye, as if daring you to refuse them the right to enter your country. Europeans offered you a three-quarter profile, staring off into a misty distance like the members of an old-style German elektronika band. He'd put weight on since she'd last seen him, but so, to be fair, had she. His face looked jowly and his hair, temporarily tamed for the photograph, was receding. At some point in the past decade, his nose had been broken and then not very expertly reset, and it gave him a pugnacious look which suited him, as if one of the major aspects of his personality had finally worked its way to the surface. It was still a handsome face, a face which seemed to have become more itself, a confident joker's face. Once, when they'd been separated for an extended period, he'd asked her to record herself reading a chapter of *Moby-Dick* each week and send it to him, even though he knew she hated the book. He said he liked the sound of her voice, but really it had just been another test, exploring her limits. They'd got a dozen or so chapters into the book and then he'd lost interest, something shinier had come along, she couldn't remember now what it had been.

"He's dead," she said out loud, trying out the concept for size. "He's dead and you're never going to see him again." But there was nothing. Where there should have been grief—and she was not unfamiliar with grief—there was just a blank space, lightly shaded in with the memory of the last emotion she had felt towards him, which had been incandescent rage.

She got to her feet again, closed the photo, and opened the next folder, which turned out to contain the police report of the accident. Whoever had written it wasn't much of a prose stylist; it seemed kind of sparse and perfunctory. Dates and times, GPS coordinates. Maksim had been driving a hire car at high speed away from Gliwice and somewhere out in the countryside he'd failed to see a tractor lumbering out of a junction. He'd T-boned it at around a hundred kilometres an hour, killing himself instantly. According to the first responders on the scene, the tractor driver had survived the crash, but he was dead of his injuries by the time whoever had written the report arrived.

There was a walkthrough of the scene attached to the report. It was of poor quality, stitched together from no more than a dozen images, but it allowed her to zoom and pan around the accident to a small extent by swiping at the air like someone playing handball with an invisible opponent. It was night time and it was raining heavily and the scene was brightly lit by pinpoint lamps on tall stands, casting everything else into impenetrable darkness and making it impossible to get a wider impression of the surrounding area, although there appeared to be buildings of some kind in the background on one side.

The wreckage of the car and the tractor blocked what seemed to be a narrow road. She couldn't tell what make of car it had been; it was completely destroyed. It had struck the tractor with enough force to tip it over on its side, shattering its cab. Carey panned around the scene as much as it allowed. No sign of any bodies. The roof of the car was partially peeled back, but whether that had happened in the accident or had been done later by emergency services trying to get at Maksim, she couldn't tell. A squall of rain was frozen in the act of blowing through the bubble of light.

She flicked back and forth between the report and the walkthrough a few times, then she pulled down a browser and air-typed the GPS coordinates.

The image that came up was of a narrow one-lane country road, little more than a paved cart track, running through farmland and forest on a sunny summer afternoon. It was two years old, which was the last time anyone had bothered to drive a camera car down there. At the spot where the accident had happened, there was a T-junction with an even narrower road which ran off slightly downhill and then curved off out of sight towards a screen of trees. Immediately opposite the junction, what looked like farm buildings lined the road for a short distance. There was a gate a little further along, and just beyond that a bus shelter, then the road disappeared into woodland. In the other direction, the direction Maksim had approached from, there were fields on either side of the road.

After a little trial and error, she tiled the accident scene walkthrough and the street view image up into one corner of the screen and opened the next folder. This contained a death certificate for Maksim. Cause of death, massive non-survivable trauma due to a road traffic accident. She looked at it for a while, but she still couldn't feel anything.

The final folder held a brief item from a local news service, dated just over six weeks ago, and it wasn't any more informative than the police report. Speeding car, rainy night, narrow poorly maintained road, slow-moving tractor. Two dead. The tractor driver's name was missing. There would be a service for the car driver at the city's crematorium. The journalist's name stood out. Robert Wareham. English or American, she thought, not Polish. She made another note. He'd probably just got sight of the police report from a contact, and cobbled the story together from that, she'd done her share of that herself, down the years.

So this was what had prompted Central to bring her all this way, the final documentary moments of Maksim Petrauskas. It seemed insufficient for Maksim, whose death should have been accompanied by the fall of at least one small European nation state. The thought of him having such a mundane end was somehow offensive.

She took out her phone and sent a message. When the response arrived a couple of minutes later, she sent a curt reply and put the phone away again and allowed herself a smile.

She waved back to the walkthrough of the accident, but her arms were getting tired so she just stood looking at it, hands in her pockets. There was no way, these days, to tell just by looking at it whether an image was real or edited or wholly generated. The walkthrough images looked real—there was even a little pile of paramedics' gear discarded by the car, torn packaging, bloody bandages, bits of IV line, disposable one-shot pressure hypos—but she was going to have to find someone who could check.

The police report was interesting for what was missing. It didn't have any of the usual diagrams and speed calculations and impact vectors, and there were no forensic photos of the scene in daylight, no statements from the people who lived at the farm or the car hire company. Either Central had only managed to get hold of an incomplete set of documents, or stuff had been redacted out.

She wondered at the chronology. Three weeks for word of Maksim's death to reach Central, then another three weeks for them to get sight of what documents they could and decide what to do next. It was sloppy, to be honest, and more to the point the trail was cold now.

She'd been working with the documents for almost four hours and she felt tired and sore from using the interface. She copied the photo of Maksim to the phone's memory and sent it to her own phone, then she shut everything down, peeled the screen off the wall, rolled it up, and put it in a drawer of the desk.

Kaunas had sent her the contact protocol for the local Coureurs, which consisted of leaving a line from *The Waste Land* on the message board of a gambling site. She'd snorted a little when she saw this, it sounded so hokey, but the message board turned out to be a frantic unmoderated stew of love affairs, arguments, pleas for money, pleas for drugs, running jokes, bots, trolls, political slogans, and naked selfies, all of it peppered with ads for loans and penis extensions and LARP events. A line about April being the cruellest month simply vanished in the noise.

Robert Wareham was more straightforward. He kept a public address on the news service's site, for people to send him stories and tips. She left him a message and then went to check out the hotel's restaurant, which had very definite ambitions and expressed them in its prices. When she got back, she found that someone had slipped a little white envelope under her door, and she experienced a moment—and it wasn't the first time she'd felt this way, down the years—when she had a sense of being in a bad spy novel.

2

She was in the second year of her journalism degree at Texas Tech when Pru was diagnosed with an aggressive form of pancreatic cancer. She was still living at home—the TTU campus was only a half-hour's bus ride away—and she attended all the hospital consultations and treatments, Byron sitting quietly holding Pru's hand. The cancer seemed, initially, to respond to treatment, but Pru knew it wasn't kidding anyone.

"I used to hate journalists," she told Carey one evening, sitting at home between hospital visits. Byron was in the studio, conferencing with a Finnish folk-metal band about the sound design for their set at a festival in the English Midlands. "My dad said they were no better than parasites these days, telling people what they want to hear instead of what's actually happening." She reached out and patted Carey's hand, and Carey noticed that her palm was fever-hot. "Never thought I'd actually have one in the family. You'll be better than that, won't you?"

"I'll try," Carey told her.

"Promise?"

"Promise."

Pru smiled. "You're a good kid. You've got to watch your temper, though. I heard what happened at the Yellow Cuckoo."

"I'm not sure I can promise anything about that," Carey said. A couple of weeks ago, in a crowded bar just off-campus, a drunk had groped her, and she'd knocked him unconscious with a single punch. The drunk had been making a nuisance of himself all evening and the barman had been winding up to throw him out. Instead, he put the unconscious man in his car, drove him to the nearest emergency room, left him there, and came back and bought Carey drinks for the rest of the night. The boy she'd been at the bar with, yet another generally disappointing man in her life, had made excuses and gone home.

Pru patted her hand again. "Look after Byron," she said. "He doesn't eat enough, never has. Make sure he takes a break every now and then."

"We'll both do that," Carey assured her.

But of course they didn't. The treatments grew more and more aggressive, but the cancer had thrown off secondaries and tertiaries even before it was diagnosed and it was like fighting a prairie fire with a water pistol. There was a brief discussion about trying to get her across the border to Juarez, where it was said clinics working with rogue nanotechnology were curing everything from cancer to male pattern baldness, but Pru just snorted and said she knew what went on in those clinics. High colonics, freaky diets, crystals, drugs made from apricot pits. "If you take me to one of those," she told them, "I will come back and haunt the shit out of the pair of you." Instead, she called a halt to the surgeries and the hospital treatments and she came home to spend her last days with the people she loved most.

Afterward, Carey and Byron looked after each other. She made sure he ate properly and didn't work too hard, and he sat her down now and again for a quiet, level-headed chat about her drinking and her tendency to wind up in fights, and they rebalanced themselves, two where once there had been three of them. They did not put Pru behind them; she was always there, part of the group hug the day Carey's father had come to the house, keeping them on the straight and narrow. Her death rocked Byron back on his heels for a long time; Carey sometimes found him sitting out in the garden, staring into space with a look on his face as if he'd only just realised Pru was gone.

Around that time, news reached her of her father's death. She hadn't seen him since the day he'd turned up at the door, and unlike Pru she *had* put *him* behind her. He was a stranger, someone she had once known in passing.

One afternoon UPS delivered a package which turned out to contain the battered suitcase he'd had with him the last time she saw him, and even before she read the note which came with it she knew he was dead. The note was beautifully handwritten, something you didn't see very often these days, and it told, in brief strokes, the story of someone who had joined the great tide of unemployed who washed back and forth across the southern states in what the pundits were that year calling the Great Economic Overturn. He had tended bar, done manual labour, and none of these jobs had lasted long. He had been running to catch a train in Georgia when he'd slipped and fallen under the wheels. The note was signed 'A Friend'. There was no indication of how A Friend had found out where she was.

The suitcase contained a couple of changes of clean but threadbare clothes, some cheap toiletries, and a handful of old-style paper postcards, the kind of thing you found at little rural truck stops, and that was it. A couple of months later, she embarked on her first ever journalistic investigation, going through Georgia papers and news services and posing as a reporter with one of the Houston services to talk to the press officers of local sheriffs and police departments. It turned out her father had been staying at a rooming-house in Macon, from which he had skipped owing a month's rent, and he had not been running to catch a train. He'd hopped a freight bound for Alabama, and one of the security contractors hired by the railroad company to keep vagrants off their trains had shot him in the chest with a jelly-baton round and he'd fallen off the roof of one of the cars. She entertained a brief fantasy that A Friend was the contractor who had shot him, returning his effects out of a fit of conscience, but she didn't look any further into it. She put the suitcase in a closet and closed the door on it. That, she thought later, was the last time anything was normal, anywhere in the world.

3

It was possible, she had discovered, to interview someone while mildly drunk. Or even quite seriously drunk—there had been that evening last year with the American actor who'd been in town to publicise some short-lived miniseries, she was rather sad she couldn't remember more about it. Alcohol was the great solvent. It relaxed the muscles, loosened the tongue, brought all manner of indiscretions close to the surface.

It was quite another thing, apparently, to interview someone at ten o'clock in the morning while massively hungover.

"You can't keep doing this," Rose told her.

"Won't happen again," she said.

"It will, unless you get a handle on this."

"On what?"

She stared at her. "The drink, Lenna," she said finally.

"What about it?"

Rose tipped her head to one side. She was English, but her Estonian was pretty much perfect, which was a hard trick for the English to pull off. The story around the newsroom was that she hadn't been able to hack it on Fleet Street so she'd come over here and somehow, over the years, worked her way up to editor. Lenna had worked for worse editors. At least Rose didn't shout and throw things or try to grope her.

"You do realise that you drink too much," she said evenly.

Lenna thought about it, shook her head dismissively. "I'm fine, Rose. I was at that Tourism Ministry reception last night, you know what those parties are like."

"Did you get any copy out of it?"

"Some," she said, straight-faced. "I'll have it written up and with you in an hour or so."

Rose watched her a few moments longer, then returned her attention to her desktop, where presumably the email from Byron Stanley's PR was being displayed. "According to this you turned up stinking of drink and you had to excuse yourself several times to go away and be sick." She looked at Lenna and raised an eyebrow.

"Dicky tummy," she said brightly. "Must have had a bad canapé at the reception."

Rose blinked at her. "One of the conditions of being granted this interview was that you'd actually read Stanley's book. His PR said she didn't get the impression that you had."

"I skimmed it." She waved it away. "Come on, Rose, it's science fiction. I got the gist."

"You weren't supposed to *get the gist*," Rose told her. "You were supposed to have read it and you were supposed to have a prepared list of questions. You weren't supposed to wing it with the press release and the back cover blurb. They're saying you were grossly unprofessional."

She snorted. "Writers. Itchy little prima donnas."

Rose sat back and crossed her arms. She glanced across at Marit from HR, who was sitting in an armchair in the corner of the office and so far had not said a single word. She looked at Lenna again. "We keep having this conversation," she said. "Everyone in the office went out on the night of the blackout and managed to file copy when the power came back. From you, nothing."

"I was ill," Lenna said.

"Dicky tummy?" Marit said quietly. Lenna didn't give her the satisfaction of responding.

"Your timekeeping's appalling," Rose went on, consulting another document on her desktop. "You haven't been in the office on time in... eighteen months. For the past three months you haven't come in once before lunchtime."

"I work late. Come on, Rose, you know that."

Rose looked at her. There was no spiel about how Lenna was a talented journalist with a problem and there was no way she could be protected for much longer so she'd have to get a grip somehow. She just looked at her. Blinking slowly.

Finally, she seemed to come to a decision. "You've had enough last chances, Lenna. You're fired."

"Now just a damn *minute*," she said. She felt, rather

than heard, Marit getting to her feet, behind and to one side of her.

"You're a drunk, Lenna. You're barely producing any work and you're starting to damage the reputation of this organisation. I don't have any choice."

Marit's hand landed on her shoulder, a little harder than was strictly necessary. Lenna felt a wave of panic going through her. "You can't do that," she said to Rose. "If I'm a drunk I have an illness, and you can't fire me because of illness. I'll take this to a tribunal."

"Come on," Marit said. "Let's go."

"Go ahead," Rose told her. "Take it to a tribunal. You've had three verbal and two written warnings in the past six months; it's not like we haven't given you a chance to clean up your act."

Marit's hand moved down and closed on her upper arm like a vice. "On your feet," she said.

"No," Lenna said, trying to become heavier by willpower alone. "Rose, I'm sorry, okay? I promise you it won't happen again. I'll be in tomorrow at eight in the morning. I won't drink on the job any more."

"Not good enough," she said.

Marit got her hands under Lenna's armpits from behind and tried to bodily lift her out of the chair. "Up," she muttered. "Come on."

"I promise, Rose. I'll do anything. Let *go* of me, you bitch." She squirmed in her seat to dislodge Marit's grip. "You're *hurting* me."

"If you don't go quietly I'll call security to throw you out," Rose said. "Your choice."

"This is ridiculous, Rose," Lenna said reasonably, her heart and mind racing. "Can't we talk about this like adults?"

"We *have* talked about it. And you promised it wouldn't happen again. But it did. We can't keep carrying you, Lenna. This is a newsroom, not a crèche."

It was a pretty good line, she had to admit, and that was probably why it hurt so much. She said, "I've worked my heart out for this paper. You'll regret this."

"No, you haven't," Rose said sadly. "And no, I won't. So, shall I call security?"

For a moment it occurred to Lenna to sit where she was and call her bluff, but a distant and increasingly rarely used rational corner of her mind suggested that would only make things worse. She grabbed her bag from the floor beside her chair and stood, glaring at Rose. For some reason, she couldn't think of any famous last words, no exit line that would rock the editor back in her seat and leave her speechless, so she settled for a final glare, turned on her heel, and marched out of the office, Marit right behind her.

"Where do you think you're going?" Marit asked as they pounded down the corridor.

"I've got some things in my desk," Lenna muttered, planning the scene she was going to cause in the newsroom. "Personal things."

"Oh no you don't," Marit said, taking her arm in that death-grip again and hauling her to a stop. "Your belongings will be forwarded to you."

"I'm not having you going through my stuff."

"You don't get a choice."

Lenna tried to shake free, but Marit kept hold of her, and for a few moments they stood there like that, Marit with her feet solidly planted while Lenna struggled ineffectually. Finally, Lenna stopped trying to free herself.

"That's better," Marit said, but she didn't let go. "Now, let's go, please."

Without releasing her, Marit marched Lenna down the stairs to the front desk, where the receptionist was pointedly busying herself with some paperwork or other. "I've been fired," Lenna told her as they passed, but the receptionist didn't look up. "Bitch."

Marit actually escorted her out onto the pavement before letting go. Then she turned and, without a word, went back inside. Lenna tried to follow, but her access had already been cancelled and her phone wouldn't unlock the door. She pressed it against the sensor plate over and over again, feeling numb and unreal, but the door remained shut. She glanced up at the little black golf ball of the security system over the door, imagined Rose and Marit and the rest of them gathered around a monitor sniggering at her attempts to get back into the building. Well fuck that. She flipped a finger at the camera, slung her bag over her shoulder, and stomped off.

The Penultimate Bar was a serious place for serious drinkers. There was no pretence, no fashionable food—no food at all. There were no comfortable furnishings, no candles on the tables, no paintings or moodily black and white photos on the walls, no quiet Euro-muzak. It was not trendy. It did not attract hipsters or students or tourists. It did not serve coffee or provide free internet. Its ambience was regularly described as 'threatening', in the city guides that could be bothered to mention it at all. It was Lenna's favourite bar.

She finished her third vodka and supposed she should try to take stock, but taking stock seemed, at the moment, an insurmountable achievement. She had no idea what state her bank account was in, from day to day, because actually finding out how little money she had was too scary. She'd somehow relied on momentum to carry her from paycheck to paycheck, and that had worked so far, by luck or a miracle, but now there was no paycheck in her immediate future. It all seemed too complicated, so she ordered another drink.

She'd rung everyone on her phone's contact list—except

Rose and the HR department—and no one had responded. People who had, just yesterday, been bombarding her with messages and emails and press releases were now mysteriously unavailable. It seemed a bit soon for news of her sacking to have spread quite so widely, but she presumed that was what it was. All of a sudden, she had nothing these people wanted, and so they didn't want to know her.

That triggered a slow welling of angry self-pity, in which she allowed herself to wallow. Bastards. All those people who had pretended to be her friends while she was useful to them and now turned their backs when she needed a favour in return. It didn't have to be much; a bit of freelance work to tide her over until she found something more permanent. But no, they couldn't even do that, couldn't even have the decency to answer her calls. All she'd ever done was have a couple of drinks. There was no law against that; hell, it was practically part of the job description if you were a journalist. It wasn't as if Rose and everyone else was exactly teetotal, although she couldn't imagine that dried up bitch Marit drinking anything stronger than coffee. Hypocrites, all of them.

She waggled her glass at the barman for a refill. She needed it; she'd had an upsetting day. Best to take the rest of the day off to recover. She could face things with a clear head tomorrow.

OF COURSE, THERE was no clear head the next day. She struggled awake midmorning, half-convinced that the events of the previous day had been a terrible dream, but as she stumbled around the kitchen she remembered that it was not. She really had been fired.

A thought crossed her mind, like a ship sailing along a distant horizon, that now everyone had had a night's sleep and time to consider and tempers had cooled, she might approach Rose. Not to beg—she wouldn't give them the satisfaction—

but to discuss the situation rationally. She should give that a try today sometime. Maybe in the afternoon.

The thought sailed away for ever as she found a bagel in the bread bin. She pinched the spots of mould off the surface, cut it in half, put it in the toaster while her coffee brewed. There was remarkably little to eat in the flat; she could have sworn she'd shopped recently. She ought to do something about that. Maybe in the afternoon, after she'd had a bit of a nap.

AND THAT BECAME the shape of her days. Late at night, over a few drinks, she made plans which seemed clever and guaranteed to succeed, but the next morning, bleary and achy, they seemed absurdly complicated. She went out to the Penultimate occasionally, but it was cheaper to buy a bottle and drink at home. She had to watch the pennies now, she kept reminding herself. The growing stack of bills stuffed unopened into one of the kitchen cupboards—she would get round to doing something about them but for the moment she just had too much on her mind—suggested she was running low on funds. She had elected to have paper bills rather than receiving them electronically because she was aware just how easy it was to hack someone's online accounts. Also it was a lot easier to claim something had gone missing in the post.

So, that was the bills taken care of. She shopped, every now and again, when she realised there was no food. She tried phoning her contacts but she still seemed to be persona non grata, which occasioned quiet evenings of righteous rage while she binge-watched old television series and occasionally dipped into the news, just to keep in touch with the outside world.

One afternoon, at the checkout in the supermarket, she swept her phone over the reader to pay for her groceries and the device made a beeping noise. She tried again. The same beeping noise. It seemed very loud. She looked round and attracted the attention of an assistant, who came over and watched her swipe the phone again.

"Account declined," he said, pointing to the words on the checkout's screen.

"What's that supposed to mean?" she said, a numb sensation gathering in her feet.

"It means your account's been declined," he said with the air of someone who has seen this happen too often. "Usually it means you've got insufficient funds to pay for your purchase."

"That's ridiculous," she told him, the numbness spreading up her legs. "There must be something wrong with the machine."

"Ah, that's not possible," he told her with a sad little smile. "The machines are checked daily; it's part of our compliance."

Lenna could not have cared less about the supermarket's compliance. "The phone, then," she said. She slapped it against her palm a couple of times and tried it again, was rewarded with the same beep, which seemed to be increasing in volume. "Ridiculous," she muttered.

"Perhaps you should call your bank," the assistant suggested.

"Yes," she said. "I'll do that when I get home; I don't have the number with me." The assistant nodded soberly and neither of them mentioned that it would have been the work of a few moments to look up the number of the bank. "Now, I'll have to pay for this in cash, I suppose..."

THE SHOPPING MORE or less cleaned her out of available cash, but she hadn't been about to admit defeat and just leave her stuff at the checkout. She had flashed on an image of everyone watching her walk out of the supermarket, unable to afford a basket of groceries, and she wasn't going to let that happen.

So she had a little over a hundred kroons in paper money and some coins. On the bright side, she had food and a couple of new bottles of vodka so things weren't desperate yet. She made a plan to call the bank, but they would probably mention the letters she hadn't responded to, and she didn't feel quite up to dealing with that, so she didn't bother.

The inbox of her phone started to fill up with messages. After a quick glance she didn't bother to open it any more, just watched as the number of messages climbed into treble figures. People started to knock on the door and ring the bell, but some sixth sense told her they weren't here to offer her a job, so she sat very still and very quiet, and at night she didn't put any lights on. Perhaps they'd stop coming to the door if they thought no one was here.

She retreated to bed, sitting up late at night swiping aimlessly through news sites. One night, she happened upon a blog she hadn't seen before. *JUSTICE FOR SERGII!* ran along the top in screaming red capitals. The author of the blog bemoaned the death of Sergii, an Estonian of Russian ethnicity, at the hands of the Tallinn police. It was a tale of woe and righteous despair, a little man against the might of Estonian authority. No one listened, the author said. No one cared. The media did not want to know.

Lenna read, scrolling through older posts. Some of them were very old indeed, in blogosphere terms, where something written a year or so ago might as well have been pressed into clay tablets in cuneiform, and they were utterly inept, as if whoever was running the account had not only never used social media before but had never even encountered the concept. Even her grandmother, whose total witlessness with modern technology precluded anything but the most basic of phones, could have made a better job of this account.

But the author had not given up; they had kept going in the face of official indifference, because Sergii's life *mattered*. It was important to those who knew and loved him, if not to anyone else. Lenna reached out to the bedside table for her glass, but she didn't pick it up.

One of the early posts was an appeal for help. Donations, administrative aid, more practical things. The author was not, they said, media-savvy—which would have been obvious to a four-year-old—and any advice in that area would be well-rewarded. There was a phone number at the end of the post, for anyone who felt moved to make contact and offer what they could.

Lenna looked at the number for a very long time. Then she copied the number into the phone's address book and pressed 'call'.

"Mr Reinsalu is a busy man," said Dima. "You will meet him soon."

"Is Mr Reinsalu in charge of your campaign?" Lenna asked.

"In charge of everything," Dima told her. "He does the thinking, I do the street stuff."

Lenna sighed inwardly. She had wanted to meet her contact from the campaign at a bar, but he had insisted on a Starbucks. Probably because he wouldn't have been able to get served in a bar; he looked about twelve, a scruffy young man in jeans and a heavy leather jacket. He was wearing a dazzle scarf round his neck; tied around the face it would camouflage the wearer from the facial recognition algorithms of surveillance cameras. Or something. Lenna was vague on stuff like this. Anyway, most students had them; they were as much a badge of resistance as Guy Fawkes masks had been for an earlier generation.

"So, you want to join our group," he said, trying to look tough with a chai latte and a sticky bun on the table in front of him.

"I think there are some skills I can bring to the campaign," she said. She took out her phone and beamed her CV to his. She'd sat up with it last night, polishing and embellishing. "I'm an experienced journalist and I've run a number of media campaigns." This last part was only fractionally true; she'd been a team member on one campaign, for a new brand of detergent. She'd quit after two days because it was beyond dull and she felt destined for better things.

Dima picked up his phone, swiped up the CV. He looked impressed. "Are you security conscious?" he asked.

"Excuse me? Am I what?"

He put his phone down again. "I'm under surveillance all the time," he said, lowering his voice until she had to lean across the table to hear him. "We're up against the police, right? The police don't like it when people stand up to them."

Lenna glanced around the coffee shop, but no one was obviously watching them. "Right," she said.

"I have to be a ghost or I'd wind up under a tram or something. They've killed people already; that's what this is all about."

"Okay," said Lenna.

"Get yourself one of these," he told her, waggling the end of his scarf. "You're on the street? You put this on and you're invisible."

Well, not really. The scarf might render the wearer's face unrecognisable to cameras, but to the naked eye it was printed with a wrenching jagged pattern of black and white with occasional flashes of brilliant colour. It would be like walking around wearing a migraine.

"Yes," she said. "So, when do I meet Mr Reinsalu?"

"When I say you can," he said. "The police would *love* to find him and make him disappear. I'm the cutout. I meet you; if I get a bad feeling about you, you never hear from us again."

"Surely you can't think I'm the police." It was absurd, but faintly flattering.

"Maybe you're not. Maybe you're just a snitch."

"I see." She was starting to get a *bad feeling* about this whole thing, but the state of the campaign's website and social media convinced her they needed her, and she had a sense that they were not short of donations. Inept people with lots of money didn't drift through her life very often; she might not get a second chance. She said, "And what sort of *feeling* are you getting from me?"

He sat back and made a show of giving her an appraising look. "You don't look like a cop," he allowed.

"So that leaves... snitch."

He thought for a moment. "What I can do," he said, picking up his phone, aiming it at Lenna, and capturing an image, "is ask some of my contacts if they recognise your face."

"Hey!" she protested. "You're supposed to ask permission before you take my photo. I could have you arrested."

"They'd have to find me first," he said, waggling the scarf again while he typed with his thumb. "There," he said, laying the phone down. "Now we wait."

"You're a dick," she told him. But she sat where she was. "How long is this going to take?"

He shrugged carelessly. "Shouldn't be long. My contacts are good."

"Dick," she said again, crossing her arms across her chest.

They stared at each other for a couple of minutes, until Dima's phone buzzed. He picked it up, looked at the screen, and nodded. "Looks like you're clean," he said.

Lenna thought of her image on all Dima's friends' phones and said, "I'm not sure I want this job any more."

"Yes you are," he said, putting the phone down. He looked at her and smiled.

Maybe he wasn't such a dickhead after all. "I can help you," she said.

"What makes you think we need help?"

"I want to see Mr Reinsalu," she said.

He looked at her for a few moments more, then he took out a pen and a crumpled bit of paper. He smoothed out the paper on the tabletop and scrawled on it, then handed it over. Written on it in a childish hand was an address in Pärnu. "Be there tomorrow at ten o'clock," he told her.

She put the bit of paper in her pocket. "How will I recognise him?"

"He'll know you," said Dima. "From your photograph."

"It is, of course, an absolute scandal," Mr Reinsalu finished. "A man is dead, a family has been denied justice. Meanwhile, the real criminals walk free."

"It's awful," Lenna agreed, putting as much sincerity into her voice as possible. She had put some effort into this meeting, only having a couple of drinks the previous night, getting to sleep early, showering and washing her hair and putting on her smartest outfit. She was, she thought, the image of the concerned professional journalist, a crusader for truth and justice.

"No one has helped me," Mr Reinsalu admitted sadly. He was a small, compact man with a fuzz of grey hair and an untidy goatee. His suit had seen better days. "I kept asking, making appeals, but no one came. No one wanted to know."

"Someone wants to know now," Lenna assured him, cringing inside at how corny she sounded.

Mr Reinsalu didn't seem to notice. "What I lack is any

expertise in the media," he told her. "I'm a simple country lawyer. It's all a bit of a mystery to me."

"You don't have to worry about that any more," Lenna said, and cringed again.

They were sitting in the dining room of a small hotel in Pärnu. In order to ensure that no one was lurking outside her door with a writ or some other legal inconvenience, Lenna had slipped out of the flat at five o'clock in the morning, sat nervously in a café near the station while she waited for the first train of the day. She was battling not to yawn, and she really wanted a drink, but all Mr Reinsalu had provided was a hotel breakfast. At the prospect of so much free food, Lenna had piled up her plate.

"Did you have many responses," she asked, carefully offhand, "to your appeals for donations?"

"Oh yes," Mr Reinsalu said, mopping his plate delicately with a wad of bread. "Many responses. Funds are not a problem. The problem is practical expertise."

Lenna tried not to show the relief she felt. She had spotted something in Mr Reinsalu's blog. On the surface, it was the blog of a man who had single-handedly taken up a hopeless cause, battling the indifference of the entire Estonian establishment. But what Lenna had seen was a desperate man with, quite possibly, a large amount of disposable cash and no one to spend it on.

She said, "If I *were* to take on the job, it would have to be a salaried position. It will take up quite a lot of my time, time I could otherwise use to write for the papers."

Mr Reinsalu was nodding as he chewed the piece of bread. "Oh, absolutely. That goes without saying."

It was perfect. The cause was already hopeless; if she failed, it wouldn't be her fault. And in the meantime she would be pulling down a salary.

Mr Reinsalu took a delicate sip of coffee. "How much were you thinking of?" he asked. "Salary-wise?"

Lenna mentally took a deep breath. Here was the moment of truth. She named a figure half again as large as her old salary at the paper. "Plus expenses," she added.

Mr Reinsalu nodded. "Yes, we can manage that," he said.

"Really?" Lenna blurted before she could stop herself. She'd expected him to haggle, to laugh in her face, to get up and walk out.

He smiled. "Really."

Emboldened, she said, "I would need the first month's salary in advance. And there may be some… legal matters which need settling before I'm able to give my full attention to the work."

Mr Reinsalu dabbed his lips with his napkin. "Oh, I'm sure I can help you with those," he said with a smile. "I am a lawyer, after all."

THREE

1

THE SKY ABOVE the Old Town was full of swifts, and she took this as a good sign. Swifts were cool. They spent the majority of their lives on the wing, and she knew how that felt.

There wasn't a lot to Gliwice's Old Town; it mostly seemed to be a warren of winding little streets surrounding the Rynek, at the top of Zwycięstwa. The Rynek itself was somehow comfortingly bijou. It would have fitted into one corner of Kraków's enormous market square—one of the largest in Europe—and disappeared. It was quiet and lined with little cafés and restaurants and art galleries, and this evening the little ratusz in the middle was lit up with multicoloured spotlights.

Carey found the pizzeria easily enough, in the top corner of the square, and when she went in she found it was half empty. A waiter seated her at a table by the window and left her a menu and a carafe of water. The menu was long and extensive, which was a relief because dinner at the hotel, exquisitely good though it was, had been nouvelle cuisine on an almost microscopic scale. She ordered a small deep-pan margerita and a side order of garlic bread and some chicken wings, and the waiter had just left the table when her phone rang.

"Hello," said a deep brown voice in English. "My name's Robert Wareham. You left me a message."

"Hi," said Carey. "Thanks for calling. I was wondering if you could help me. I'm in town working on a story." She named an Austin news agency for whom she tried to file at least one piece a week. "I'm kind of flatfooted at the moment and I could use some brains to pick."

Wareham thought about it. "Which story did you have in mind?"

"There was a car accident about six weeks ago. Name of Petrauskas. You did a piece on it."

"Yes, I remember that." He had a West Country accent, but there was something else in there, as if he'd lived somewhere else for a long time. "I'm not sure how much help I can be, but I'm happy to have a go. Why not pop over to the office tomorrow? Say around lunchtime?"

"That would be great. That's very kind of you."

"Nonsense," he said cheerfully. "Always good to meet a fellow journalist. Even if I can't help, we can still swap war stories. See you tomorrow." And he hung up.

As she put her phone back in her pocket, a short, fat, middle-aged man in jeans and a denim jacket and a black sweatshirt walked up to her table and sat down opposite her. He clasped his hands on the tabletop and said, "You can call me Stefan." No recognition string, not even a hello.

Theoretically, there was no pecking order in *Les Coureurs*, everybody was equal, but Carey didn't respond well to people being brusque with her and sometimes you just had to put your foot down and establish yourself right from the off. "I can call you anything I want, my friend," she told him.

That just bounced right off Stefan. "What are you doing here?"

"You know what I'm doing here. You know who I am, you know where I'm staying because I didn't tell you where to deliver that note, and you know what I'm doing here."

He had a plump, florid face and big brown eyes, and sparse strands of hair straggled across his scalp. "Tell your masters we want nothing to do with this."

'Your masters' was an interesting choice of words. "You can tell them yourself. I was told I could rely on you for support."

He shook his head. "Not from us. We want no part of anything to do with him. He almost ruined us. We just want to be left alone."

"Well, that's not really an option, is it, Stefan," she told him. "Either you cooperate with me or you lose any support you get from Central."

He snorted. "Americans," he said. "You think you're all *spies*. You think you're all James Bond. We're not spies. We're *Les Coureurs des Bois*."

"You need to get a life," said Carey.

"We've lost half our best people," he told her. "He came in here like a Medici prince and just recruited them out from under us. I don't even know where they are now."

"You should take that up with Central."

He made a rude noise. "If he's dead, good. So long as he's out of our town. Go home, if you have one." And he got up and walked out, almost colliding with the waiter who was bringing Carey's starters.

"Your friend isn't staying?" he asked, putting the wings and garlic bread down in front of her.

She watched Stefan stomp out into the square and out of sight. "He's got some kind of intolerance," she said.

THE OFFICES OF Nowa Gazeta were in a business park set in a few hectares of trees and lawns on the fringes of a big out-of-town shopping mall on the northern edge of the city. It shared its building with a medical supply company and a workshop that printed designer shoes, and there was a pervading smell of chemical feedstock.

"You never really get used to it, I'm afraid," Robert Wareham said apologetically as he led her from the reception desk and through Gazeta's newsroom, which was about the size of a bus, to a little interview room on the other side. "Can I get you something to drink?" he asked. "The coffee's indescribably bad but we've got some bottles of fizzy mineral water in the fridge."

"I'm good," she said, sitting in one of the room's comfy chairs. Through the window, she could see a small jungle of vines and spiky bushes. "Thanks."

"Okay." He settled himself in the other chair and crossed his legs. He was about her age but a couple of inches shorter, rangy and in good shape with neatly barbered grey hair and a goatee that didn't really suit him. He was wearing a good suit, not expensive but well-cut. "So, you want to know about our mystery man."

"Anything you can tell me, yes."

"I'm sorry," he said, tipping his head to one side, "who did you say you worked for again? Your message didn't make it quite clear."

She named the Austin news service again, adding, "I'm freelance. I've been doing the tour for a year or so, filing stuff for a bunch of services in Austin and Houston. Lifestyle pieces, local colour, arts, restaurant reviews."

"Are people in Texas interested in reviews of restaurants in Poland?"

"You'd be surprised."

He smiled. They were both journalists, they knew the score. The only thing you could be certain of about the business was that there was never enough content. You went out and scared up copy anywhere you could find it.

"So, what can I tell you about Mr Petrauskas?"

Not as much as I could tell you, I'll bet. "How did you first hear about the accident?"

"We subscribe to a daily digest from the police. Mostly it's drink-driving and fights and domestic abuse. Every now and again a nice juicy murder."

"Thin stuff."

"Things have been getting more lively lately." He saw the look on her face. "With the government?"

Carey shook her head. "I've only been here a few days."

"Oh. Well, you should look it up. It's a *lot* more interesting than a car crash."

Now he mentioned it, there *had* been something on the news the evening she arrived, but she'd edited it out. It was a rare day when there *wasn't* some sort of row in the Polish parliament and she'd had other things on her mind. She said, "So, what happened to Mr Petrauskas?"

Wareham tipped his head to one side and regarded her calmly. "You know," he said, "I have a hard time believing a competent journalist would think a story about a car crash in Poland would be of any interest at all to news agencies in Texas or California or the United States."

Well, it hadn't been much of a cover story to start with. They looked at each other for a while, then Carey said, "I'm a private detective. I've been hired to investigate the death."

Wareham thought about it. "That sounds more plausible at least," he said. If he was angry at being lied to, he gave no sign. "Although I have a feeling it's still not the whole truth. Hired by whom, may I ask?"

"I can't tell you that."

"Your client only has privilege if you've been hired by an attorney on their behalf," he told her. "Isn't that how it works?"

"It's how it worked in Marlowe's day maybe," she said.

"It's more complicated now. And I have professional standards."

"Well, thank the gods someone does, these days. Do you at least have credentials?"

She had an Austin PI's licence, which she kept current by going down to Police Plaza every three years and filling in a form and handing over a thousand bucks. It had been of limited use in Europe, down the years, and it was annoying to have to keep going home to renew it, but Coureurs collected backstops the way oil tankers collected barnacles. You could never tell when one would come in handy. She showed him the little laminated card, and he read it front and back and flexed it between his fingers before returning it.

"You're a little out of your jurisdiction," he said.

"That'll be the police you're thinking of. I just go where the work is."

"Hm." He frowned at her. "And you can't go directly to the local police about this?"

"I'm still trying to get a handle on what happened before I approach the authorities." Which had the advantage of being at least eighty percent true; she had no intention of going anywhere near the police if she could avoid it.

"Hm," he said again. Then he smiled brightly. "I've never met a real-life American private eye before. This is exciting."

He didn't believe a word she'd told him. Mr Wareham did that old Hugh Grant floppy-haired-Brit schtick very well, but he was going to bear watching. She said, "It's really not."

He thought for a few moments, then he said, "How would you feel about going for a bit of a drive with me?"

IT WAS A nice day in the place where Maksim had died. The sun was bright but not too hot, and there was a bit of a breeze driving fluffy clouds across the sky and rustling the tops of the trees nearby. Carey walked up to the junction and stood there, hands in the pockets of her coat, turning slowly.

Wareham stayed beside his car, a hydrogen-cell Audi which had been a very nice automobile when it was new, about thirty years ago, but was now spotted with rust. She watched him light a cigarette and lean against the side of the car, then she went back to examining the scene.

They were about half an hour's drive outside Gliwice, twenty minutes or so on a main road southeast in the general direction of Kraków and another ten minutes up a narrow, winding country road that took them through an arm of dense birch forest and out again into farmland in the direction of somewhere called Sierakowice.

She turned slowly in place, taking it all in. The road, the trees, the fields, the farm buildings lining the road. The road was even narrower than it had looked in the images she'd seen at the hotel, and they hadn't given an adequate sense of how badly maintained and bumpy it was. The surface was crumbling away in places, particularly at the edges, where it looked as if something large and patient had been nibbling away at it. The road leading off the T-junction was, if anything, narrower and in worse condition than the one she was standing on. It wasn't signposted; there was nothing to say where it went, or even if it went anywhere at all. There were faint, fat skid-marks where the car's impact had driven the tractor a short distance before tipping it over, but apart from that there was no sign that anything had ever happened here.

Her phone rang. She looked at the screen but there was no caller ID. She thumbed *answer* anyway and said, "Hello?"

"Who are you?" asked an unfamiliar woman's voice in impeccable BBC English.

"Who are *you*?" she asked, and the connection went

dead. She swiped to the call log, but there was no sign she'd received any call in the past couple of days. There was a particularly pernicious phone advertorial doing the rounds in Europe at the moment; time to update her security again.

"Hey," said a voice, and she turned and saw a little old man leaning on the gate of the farm on the other side of the road.

"Michał, my friend!" Wareham was in good-natured motion, leaving the car and crossing the road to the gate. "How are you today?" He shook the little old man's hand, and then the two of them embarked on a conversation in Polish too rapid for Carey to follow.

"No marks," she said, nodding up the road as she joined them. "There are marks where he hit the tractor, but not further back. He didn't even try to brake. Hello," she added to the little old man.

"This is Michał," Wareham said, smiling. "He's the closest thing we have to an eyewitness."

"He says you're a private detective," the little old man said in good but heavily accented English. "Like Kojak."

The old shows never went away. "Kojak was a police lieutenant," she told him. "I'm more like Rockford, but less Californian."

He grunted to show he got the joke. He was thin and wiry, with a shock of dirty white hair and a deeply seamed face. He was wearing a sheepskin-lined denim jacket over a filthy pair of dungarees and a grey tee shirt which might once have been white. "What's your interest in this?"

"I'm being paid to investigate."

"Who by?"

The problem with a legend, she had found, was that you spent more time having to defend it than you ever did defending your real identity. She never had to explain herself when she was interviewing a restaurateur or an actor. "I can't tell you that," she said. "Client confidentiality."

"Is your client a criminal?"

She glanced at Wareham for help, but he seemed to be too busy enjoying the exchange to step in and help. She said, "No, I don't believe they are."

Michał gave that some thought, then he said, "I'll tell you what I told the police. I was in the kitchen making my supper. It was about eight o'clock and it was raining heavily. I heard the sound of a car engine and then a loud bang. My son and I came out here to see what was going on and we saw a tractor lying over on its side over there," he gestured at the junction, "and the wreckage of a car. We checked the car but the driver was obviously dead. The driver of the tractor had been thrown from his cab and he was unconscious but alive. My son called the police and they arrived about five minutes later, took statements, then told us to go back inside. I came out the next morning and everything was gone. End of story."

So there had been statements. She wondered why they weren't attached to the report. "Are you sure the car driver was dead?" she asked, feeling a distant numbness.

"His head was crushed," said Michał mildly. "That will usually do it."

Carey was aware that Wareham was watching her carefully. She said, "What about the tractor driver?"

"He was over there." Michał pointed along the wall that bordered his property. "Head injuries, his right leg was bent the wrong way, but he had a pulse."

"Do you know who he was?"

Michał shook his head. "Never saw him before."

"You said the police turned up five minutes after your son called them. Is that normal?" She looked at Wareham, then back at Michał. "Are they usually so quick?" Even if they'd been on patrol in the area, it would have taken them longer than that just to get here from the main road, particularly if the weather was bad.

The two men exchanged a satisfied glance, as if she'd correctly identified the false proposition in some fantastically complex equation, which was irritating. "It was unusually prompt," Wareham told her.

She sniffed and turned to look at the junction again. "Did you hear the tractor?" she asked.

"I don't remember," Michał said behind her, after a few moments' thought.

"You heard the car, you heard the crash." She turned back, saw that Michał and Wareham were exchanging glances again. "What about the tractor?"

Michał thought about it a moment longer, then he shook his head. "I don't remember."

"There was a lot happening," Wareham said reasonably. "And it's not as if tractors are an unusual thing round here; it would be easy to overlook a familiar sound, especially if it happened just before something completely out of the ordinary."

She looked at him. "Yeah," she said. "Yeah. Well, thank you," she said to Michał. "I'm sorry to have bothered you."

"No bother," he told her. He nodded to Wareham, then walked back across the farmyard to his house.

"So," Carey said when he was out of earshot. "What do your police contacts tell you?"

"Not very much more than Michał just did," Wareham said. "The car was going too fast, it hit the tractor. The driver was killed instantly; the driver of the tractor died on the way to hospital."

She put her hands in her pockets. "That's kind of *light*."

Wareham turned and started to walk back to the Audi; Carey fell into step beside him. "Reading between the lines, this was a police pursuit that went terribly wrong," he said. "That's why they arrived so quickly; they were already chasing him. It would be an embarrassment for the police, causing two deaths like that. It wouldn't be a surprise if they wanted to keep any details out of the public eye until an official inquiry could take place."

Carey nodded. "Yeah, I figured that." It didn't *quite* scan, though. The timing didn't feel right—if you added the time it must have taken for Michał and his son to get outside and take in the scene before calling it in, the police could have been as much as ten minutes behind the car. What sort of chase was that? She looked up the road past the farm, thinking.

"What about him?" she asked, nodding at the farmyard gate as they reached the car. "What's his story?"

Wareham opened the driver's door. "Story?"

"How long's he farmed round here? How likely is it that he didn't recognise the other driver?"

"Oh. Well, I can't help you with that, but Michał doesn't farm here; the farm belongs to his son, he just lives here. Michał was Emeritus Professor of Mechanical Engineering at the Jagiellonian University in Kraków until he retired. One of the top men in his field, I'm told. He still does a couple of guest lectures at the university here every year." He grinned at the look on her face. "Appearances can be deceptive, can't they?"

2

As Carey and her graduating class—one of the last classes to physically graduate from TTU for several years, it turned out later—were stepping on the stage in their gowns to collect their degrees, the authorities in Xian were struggling to contain an outbreak of flu. It had started small—no more than four or five cases scattered around the city—but it was spreading quickly; ten cases, twenty, fifty, a hundred. By the time the number of cases had reached a hundred and fifty the first deaths were happening, and scientists realised that the mortality rate was horrifying.

Carey was finalising plans for a trip to Europe when news of the outbreak reached the West. She'd discovered she had an ear for languages; like pretty much everyone in Texas she spoke Spanish, but her French was good too and she could get along in German and Dutch, and she had an idea to do a year-long post-graduation tour of the Continent filing lifestyle pieces for news agencies back home to build up her portfolio. She particularly wanted to do something on the Trans-Europe Rail Route, which was patiently extending itself, kilometre by kilometre, from Portugal towards the Russian Far East. Stories of flu cases popping up in England and France and Czechia seemed distant and unimportant.

Two weeks later, she was sitting watching the news and seeing her plans going down in flames. The flu had boiled out of control out of China. Hotspots in Europe grew and joined up. The members of the European Union hardened their borders in an attempt to slow the spread, but it was too late; it was already there, sweeping like a shadow across the Continent. Towns, cities, nations went into lockdown as the death figures rose into the hundreds, then the thousands, then the tens of thousands.

In Texas, as in the wider US and quite a lot of the rest of the world, the first announcements of lockdown were broadly ignored and people went on with their lives as before, as much as they could when businesses were closed and there was nothing in the shops because panic buying had emptied them. It was only the flu, and many thousands died every year of the flu and nobody paid them a moment's attention. Individual liberty was more important than the risk of spreading the disease, which was probably a hoax designed to take away people's rights anyway.

The President went on television and said, "Don't be so fucking stupid. Stay home."

Actually, he didn't use those words. He gave an address which invoked the spirit of the first settlers on the North American continent, the fallen in all of America's many wars, the names of former Presidents—with some notable exceptions. He begged his people to listen when he advised them not to go out. He didn't quite make it a direct order from the Commander In Chief, but he sailed close to it.

Most listened, many didn't, and a lot of them died. The death toll rolled lazily over into six figures and showed no signs of slowing down, let alone stopping. "Darwin Awards are going to be busy this year," Byron grunted.

He and Carey locked themselves down. They were fortunate; they were well-off, they had a big house with big grounds and a lot of supplies laid in. A lot of people weren't so lucky. Byron could work, remotely, until it became obvious that there were going to be no live gigs this year and probably not the next either and the work dried up.

He wandered around the house for a couple of days, then he got a bunch of his friends together in a conference space and they recorded an album to raise funds for local Lubbock emergency services. Carey saw the track listing and saw the names of some people she would, if she had still been inclined to think that way, have thought of as musical megastars, including the last surviving member of U2, who must—she did the sums—have been well over a hundred years old.

Byron nodded when she mentioned this. "Back when my daddy was a boy, it was unusual for someone to reach a hundred. In Britain, the Queen would send you a postcard or something if you managed that. These days, a hundred and twenty's no big thing. Better medical care, if you can afford it, I guess. Things always go better if you're rich."

A few days later, when the album was mixed and about to go on sale, he said, "I did the orchestration and played piano on his last-but-one solo album. That must have been before you were born; he doesn't record much any more, so I'm grateful to him for joining our project. They sent a private jet and flew me to Dublin to lay down my track. They had this concert grand that was…" he looked away into a great distance. "It was a work of art. I never played a piano like it before or since. It was like the piano that all pianos dream of being. I almost waived my fee, just for the honour of sitting down at it." He shook his head. "It was a crappy song, really hokey, but there hasn't been a day passed since then that I haven't thought about that piano."

She nudged him. "Why didn't you say you were connected? I thought you were just a gnarly old jazzman."

He chuckled. "Because that's what I am."

Decades later, no one could give an accurate number for the dead. More than fifty million in Europe, they said, at least twice that in the United States. India was a mass grave. In China… nobody knew. Carey and Byron sat in their living room and watched it all on the news, and their life, their own little life, seemed dull and completely divorced from what they saw on screen. Things were becoming *millennial* out there, and the highlight of Carey's day was discovering that her sourdough starter hadn't died during the night. "Never thought the end of the world would be so fucking tedious, excuse my French," Byron mused. "I also thought there'd be toilet paper."

Debate would still rage, almost half a century later, over where it had started in the first place. The media dubbed it the 'Xian Flu', and the name stuck, even though some studies suggested that it had travelled west to east rather than the other way around. A small cluster of very early cases around Heathrow might have been the result of a contagious traveller from Xian, but it was hard to be certain; it seemed to erupt in dozens of places around the world simultaneously.

It was impossible to think in terms of numbers like that. Fifty million dead was a figure so horrific that it became an abstraction. Unable to encompass the larger catastrophe, one found oneself focusing on familiar faces, on individual tragedies.

Byron died six months into the pandemic. He'd made a run to the store to see if he could pick up some groceries; he'd worn a mask and stayed a good distance from anyone else, but he still picked it up. By then, order had very nearly broken down in large areas of the country. Hospitals were overwhelmed, food was scarce, looting was widespread. In Texas, the Governor had mobilised the National Guard, the Texas Rangers, and anyone else she could swear in, and had locked the state down in all but name. Quarantines and curfews were strictly—and in some cases fatally—enforced, looters were shot. For a while, the neighbourhood had rung with gunfire almost every day, but now it seemed peaceful again; the only sounds she heard were helicopters passing overhead and public health trucks going by in the street as they collected bodies, and even they were growing fewer and fewer. *It's very quiet, as America gets on with dying*, she wrote late one night in a piece for one of the *NYT*'s satellite agencies. Then she deleted it.

One morning, Byron complained of chills and a headache. Carey dosed him with aspirin and antibiotics against secondary infections and put him to bed. By the evening, his temperature was spiking and he had a chest infection. They still had some medical gear left from Pru's illness—gloves and masks and gowns Byron had somehow never managed to throw away—so barrier nursing was not such a problem. Carey sat up all night with him, and it was like sitting next to a campfire.

By the next morning, his fever had broken and he was strong enough to take a few mouthfuls of soup. The temperature and chills had returned by the evening, and he began to cough up blood, and by midnight he was dead.

Carey washed him and sat beside him, staring at nothing, for the rest of the night. As the sun came up, she unzipped one of the body bags the public health volunteers had delivered to every house in the street and rolled Byron into it. She wrote out a label with his name and address and dates of birth and death. She left the space for religion blank, slipped it into the holder on the front of the bag, and then dragged him as gently as she could out of the house, down to the gate, and out onto the pavement. And then she sat beside him, she was never sure how long for, until she heard the motor of the public health truck coming down the street.

She knew one of the volunteers, a short, fat man who sometimes played sax with Byron on his jazz nights. He was wearing a disposable biohazard suit and he pulled down his mask as the truck pulled to a stop. His face crumpled when he saw her sitting there beside the body bag.

"Ah, Jesus," he said, getting out of the truck and coming over to her. "I'm sorry, kid."

Carey got stiffly to her feet and backed away through the open gate and up the drive until they were standing ten feet apart, and they looked at each other with shell-shocked eyes. "You be gentle with him," she said as the other two members of the truck's crew got out and lifted Byron off the pavement.

"I have to ask," said the sax player, "have you had symptoms?"

She shook her head.

"You're required to isolate for two weeks following the death of a..." His voice tailed off.

"I know," she said. She'd read all the PSAs posted by the authorities.

"We'll be taking him to Freemont once we've finished this morning's tour." Freemont was the big new cremation facility outside town. "His ashes will be stored there until..." His voice tailed off again.

"It's okay," she said, watching the others slide the body

bag into the back of the truck. There were three others already in there. "I know the routine."

"I'm supposed to tell you this stuff, but..." He looked at the truck. "*Dammit*, Byron," he said. He looked at her. "Will you be okay?"

She nodded. "Just do right by him." She watched the crew get back in the truck and prepare to drive off. "And put your fucking mask on, Frank!" she yelled.

3

IT WASN'T THE end of January yet, and already Christmas felt a long, long time ago. Conscious that this would be her first Christmas without her father—her first Christmas without any family—Markus had booked them a room in a little boutique hotel in Helsinki and they'd spent the holiday there. Krista's heart hadn't been in it, though. She appreciated the thought—Markus was one of the kindest people she had ever met—but when he'd sprung the trip on her she hadn't been able to tell him that she would rather have spent this Christmas alone with her thoughts, letting the memories settle before going on to make new ones. But she'd sensed that this trip was more important for him, that he desperately thought he needed to do something for her, so she'd gone along with it, even though it wasn't necessary.

She'd taken a few days' leave for the trip, even though she was never properly on leave these days, and had tried to put everything—work, her father, all the external stuff—out of her mind for Markus's sake. He too, she knew, was mourning the old man.

So here she was, hitting the ground running on a bitterly cold Tuesday morning, the entire country under fifteen centimetres of snow and capped by sallow, boiling, yellow-grey cloud. On the tram into town, everyone took up two times as much space because of all the warm clothing they were wearing. Krista strap-hung and watched the morning news on her phone. Three months on, the blackout was no longer the top item—that space was occupied by some boyband announcing they'd split up—but it was bubbling under at number two, the investigation into the forty-minute-long interruption of Estonia's infrastructure still grinding along, angry questions and accusations flung across the Parliament.

Conventional wisdom was that they had been lucky. Though there had been injuries—mostly traffic accidents when the lights suddenly went out—no one had actually died. Airliners on approach to Lennart Meri Airport had been diverted down the coast to Riga, emergency generators had cut in at hospitals and emergency services. There had been some wobbles, and a few fires—the server room of a company in a business park on the edge of town had gone up like a firecracker when the power came back on—but the city and the country had come through it as well as could be expected.

As for the cause, everyone looked east to the old enemy, currently staging a small military exercise a few kilometres the other side of the border. That it had been a cyberattack was not in question, and it was generally agreed that unless some non-state actor had suddenly acquired hackers of genius and a hatred of Estonia, Rus was the prime suspect. It was the sort of mischief they were good at.

The Russians, of course, denied it. The Russian ambassador, a man with a twinkly sense of humour and a taste for garish cufflinks, had stood up in front of the cameras with a straight face and reminded the world that Rus did not have a monopoly on hackers. It could, he said—and he reminded everyone that outside interference had not been proven yet—just as easily have been some teenager sitting in a bedroom in Auckland or Detroit or Berlin with a laptop and a surfeit of testosterone. He looked genuinely hurt that anyone could suggest his government might have been responsible.

Everything seemed to have stalled. Krista was not privy to the investigations of KaPo, Estonia's Internal Security Service, but her work with the Gangs Taskforce sometimes brought her into contact with their officers, and from them she picked up a sense of frustration. The whole police force was feeling the political pressure to identify the culprits, but KaPo felt it more keenly.

It wasn't as if she didn't have pressures of her own, although the rest of her team, already in the squad room when she arrived, didn't seem to be feeling them. One of their number—she'd never found out who—had dubbed them '*The Untouchables*', although they were more like Charles Martin Smith's accountant than Kevin Costner's Elliott Ness. They were young—the majority of them were under forty, except for Kustav, who was in his fifties and therefore inevitably known as 'Paps'—and bright and eager, graduates of university and the police school, experts at paper trails and unknotting offshore accounts and hedge funds.

Krista hung up her coat and said good morning to everyone and began summarising where they were at in their current investigation. Before Christmas, word had started going round Tallinn that a Chechen warlord who styled himself 'Tamburlaine' was looking to invest in businesses and property in the city, presumably looking for a beach-head for future operations. Tamburlaine himself was based in Hamburg, but had obviously felt himself moved to expand his operations up the coast, because individuals identified as his representatives—honest-to-god mob lawyers—had been seen in town scoping out potential business opportunities.

This was clearly not an optimum outcome for anyone. Tallinn was not short of home-grown thugs, and didn't need to import them from elsewhere. There was also a counter-terror aspect to the business; Chechen separatists had been blamed for a string of recent bombings in Moscow and St Petersburg, and though Tamburlaine had not previously shown an interest in politics or indeed Islamism, his supposed interest in Estonia was less than welcome.

Which meant that, in addition to her own investigations, Krista was liaising not only with the Estonian counter-terrorist unit but her opposite number in the Hamburg police, a working group within EuPol which had somehow shouldered its way onto the scene despite there being jurisdictional questions, and a bluff and amiable detective named Sidorovich from the Moscow police. The rumour in the squad room was that Sidorovich was really Security Services, but Krista had grown up among cops and she knew the real thing when she saw it. Which did not, of course, preclude the near certainty that Sidorovich was reporting everything back to an intelligence handler. Krista tried not to take it personally; it was just the way things were.

None of this made her job any easier, though; even at the best of times one had to wade through thickets of bureaucracy in order to get anything done. At the moment, it was sometimes difficult to even see the job in the distance. She tried to insulate her team from this, keep their eyes on the prize.

She waited for the team to settle, then took a breath and prepared to begin her briefing, when the door at the back of the room opened and her superior, Politseikolonelleinent Tamm, looked in. "A moment of your time, major," he said to her.

Everyone turned to look. It wasn't unusual for Tamm to pop down for informal briefings and pep-talks—he liked to stay hands-on as much as possible—but nobody could remember him running his own errands before.

Krista was momentarily flustered, as if she'd been

running up a flight of stairs only to find the top two or three missing. She looked around the room, and her gaze settled on Kustav. "Could you handle the briefing, please?" she asked.

"Of course, boss," he said, standing up while Krista gathered her bag.

As she passed him on the way to the door, she murmured, "Keep them busy. I won't be long."

"Got it," he said.

Outside, Tamm was standing in the corridor running a hand through his already permanently tousled hair. He was a tall, rangy man with old scars on his hands and bags under his eyes. As Krista closed the door behind her, he said, "A situation has come up."

"What kind of situation?"

But Tamm was already striding away from her down the corridor. "Come with me," he said.

He led her up the stairs—to discourage conversation, she thought later—to one of the upper floors of the building. Executive country, a place she only visited when giving presentations to senior officers and visiting dignitaries. He stopped at a door, opened it, and motioned to her to go ahead of him.

The room was small and cosy, more an informal breakout room than an office. Two sofas faced each other across high-quality carpeting. There were prints on the walls—etchings of the high town—and the windows looked down into the town square. Sitting on one of the sofas were two women and a man. Krista knew one of the women by sight, a Colonel from Internal Affairs named Jakobson. The other two were strangers.

As she entered, Jakobson and the others got to their feet. Hands were shaken and introductions made—the other woman was a Major named Nurmsalu, the man a Lieutenant Vainola—and when that was all over Krista was invited to sit on the unoccupied sofa while Jakobson and Nurmsalu and Vainola sat on the other, looking at her. There was an awkward atmosphere in the room.

"Major," Jakobson began. "My office has received an allegation."

It had to be Tamburlaine. Somehow his people had got wind of the investigation and he'd decided to throw a spanner into the works. Krista said, "I'm sure it's groundless."

Nurmsalu and Vainola were looking everywhere but at her. Jakobson took a slim briefcase from the floor by the sofa and opened it on her lap. Krista said, "My investigation is at an advanced stage; it would be counterproductive to—"

Jakobson looked at her. "Oh, it's not against you."

Krista found herself performing a furious mental algorithm to decide which of her team might have been careless enough to allow Tamburlaine to slip the end of a crowbar into the investigation.

"It's your father," Jakobson went on.

Krista's mind went blank, all of a sudden. "My father's dead," she said automatically.

"We know," Jakobson said. She seemed, if anything, faintly embarrassed. Standing beside the door with his arms crossed, Tamm looked furious.

"He died last February," Krista said to no one in particular.

"We know," Jakobson again. She took a cardboard folder from the briefcase, flipped it open, and glanced at whatever it contained.

"What's he supposed to have done?"

Jakobson looked down into the folder for a moment longer, then looked Krista in the eye. "He's accused of being involved in one, and perhaps several, murders."

* * *

ONCE UPON A time, almost twenty years ago, there had been a man. Sergii N, Jakobson called him, an Estonian national of ethnic Russian and Ukrainian heritage. Sergii owned a business in Tallinn, and in the course of conducting this business he had come to the attention of the police. Jakobson kept the details vague.

At some point during the investigation into his activities, Sergii had been brought in for questioning. There had been a scuffle, and one of the arresting officers was injured, not seriously. Sergii was charged with assault, found guilty, and spent three months in jail. In the meantime, Sergii's business was found to be blameless of any criminal activity and the investigation was wound down.

Sergii left prison a deeply unhappy man, and he settled down to devote his life to making life difficult for the Tallinn police. He launched a number of lawsuits alleging wrongful arrest and police brutality—he, he said, had been the victim of assault, not the police officer in question. He was being targeted because of his ethnicity, the actions of the police had put his business in jeopardy, and so on and etcetera. He actually became quite the minor annoyance.

Until one night he was discovered down by the port, unconscious, severely beaten. He lingered in a coma for several weeks, until medical opinion led to life support being withdrawn. He survived forty-two minutes after the plug was pulled.

In the wake of his death, his family accused the police of being responsible. The police, for their part, were more inclined to blame some of Sergii's associates—the investigation had turned up no evidence of criminality on Sergii's part, but that didn't mean it wasn't there. There was an investigation into his death, but it went nowhere. It all petered out, in the end, but every now and again in the following years there would be a suspicious death in the Russian community, and Sergii's family and supporters would resurrect their complaint. There were years of them on file. The Tallinn police had murdered Sergii. The Tallinn police were operating death squads targeting ethnic Russians.

In due course, these complaints grew fewer and fewer, and then stopped altogether. There had not been one for fifteen years or so, until a few weeks ago, when the death of Sergii had been anonymously brought to the attention of Jakobson's department and she realised with horror that the allegations of police involvement had not been investigated at all. Had, in fact, been completely ignored. Going back through the original complaint, she discovered the names of several police officers who had been involved in the arrest of Sergii, names which resurfaced again and again in the allegations of brutality and death squads. Among them was Krista's father.

THEY KEPT HER in the comfy little room all morning, then stopped for a break for lunch—coffee and sandwiches brought in by Tamm's secretary—then continued in the afternoon. Night had long since fallen, and the lights of the square filled the windows, when Jakobson finally sat back and took off her reading glasses and rolled her shoulders. Beside her, Nurmsalu and Vainola, who had barely said a dozen words all day, seemed to slump on the sofa in relief.

"Fine," Jakobson said, putting her spectacles on again and leafing through the sheaf of written notes she'd accumulated.

"It's not fine," said Krista, who was fuming about too many things to count. "It's not fine at all."

"No," Jakobson said absently, making a note on one of her sheets of paper. She looked at Krista. "From this moment, you're on leave," she said. "You're not to discuss this conversation with anyone. You're not to approach any former or serving police officer for any reason, but *particularly* about this conversation. You are absolutely *forbidden* from approaching any Russian citizens of Chechen origin, or their representatives." Quite early on in the proceedings, Krista had floated, rather strongly, the theory that the whole thing had been cooked up by Tamburlaine to derail her investigation into his activities. "Don't leave the city, please. We'll want to speak with you again."

Krista glared at her.

Jakobson sighed and took off her glasses again. "We're all professionals here, major," she said. "It's not my job to take a *view* on your father's guilt or otherwise, it's to gather evidence in the case. If that evidence were to prove that this is a malicious accusation—say on behalf of your Chechen friend—and any action you took jeopardised subsequent court proceedings, well, that would be unfortunate, wouldn't it." Ignoring the look Krista gave her, she stood. Her colleagues stood, too, and Tamm, who had remained by the door all day except when he had escorted Krista down the hall to the lavatory, began to stir. Jakobson glanced at Nurmsalu and Vainola and nodded briefly. The two officers left the room. "Paavo," she said to Tamm. "Give us a moment, please."

Tamm looked at her, then at Krista, and he scowled, but he too left the room and closed the door behind him.

"Right," Jakobson told Krista, who had not budged from her sofa. "This is off the books, but this business has the potential to blow up in everyone's face. The original complaint was made almost twenty years ago, which means that one of my predecessors was either staggeringly negligent or wilfully buried the whole thing. But the point is that there are documents on file which support the fact that the complaint was made. You know how it's going to look if this is allowed to become common knowledge."

Krista said nothing.

"I can guess how it must feel, hearing this news, but this

fiasco already looks like a cover-up. My investigation has to be seen to be fair and open and above board. If you interfere in any way you can only make things worse, and I need to know you understand that."

Krista thought about it, then she nodded.

"Okay," Jakobson said. She went to the door, paused with her hand on the handle. "I knew your father," she said. "Not well—I was a young officer and he was..." She held her hand up above her head. "Up here somewhere. But I knew him, and I liked him. That doesn't mean I'm going to cut him any slack, but I promise I will treat him fairly."

"I'd expect you to do that anyway," Krista said stiffly. "Whether you knew him or not."

Jakobson nodded. "Go home, major. Sit tight. We'll be in touch."

"We're not supposed to be having this conversation," said Oskar Kross. "As I'm sure you were told."

"They're saying my father killed a man," Krista said. "Maybe more than one man."

They were standing in front of a glass case containing a display of quite hideous candlesticks. Around them tourists moved quietly through Tallin's City Museum, some of them listening to audio commentary beamed to their phones, others content to read the little liquid paper descriptions mounted at the base of each display. There was the low, respectful buzz of conversation one gets in museums and no one paid Krista and Kross any attention at all, although that did not mean no one was paying them any attention.

"You're probably not under surveillance," said Kross. "Not yet, anyway. You will be, if they find out you've been talking to me."

"I need advice," Krista told him.

Oskar Kross was a small, wizened man in a superb suit. He was quite bald and in one hand he clutched a big fur hat. He said, "I haven't been here in ages, you know."

"Oskar," she said.

"Yes." He looked grave. "The police were in touch with me this morning. All my records pertaining to your father have been ordered sealed pending their removal. I should really be at the office in case someone turns up to take them away."

"You're a busy man, Oskar. You have lots of appointments."

"Hm." Kross turned away from the candlesticks and they walked through into another room, this one dominated by a hologram of a magnificent sailing ship, emblematic of the city's Hanseatic past. Some children were playing with the controls, making the hologram twirl and tilt in thin air as labelled red tags appeared and disappeared here and there around the superstructure.

"Did my father *ever* say anything about this to you?" she said.

Kross sighed. "You know you can't ask me that, Krista. Lawyer-client privilege. The only reason the police can requisition my records is because of anti-terrorism legislation." He saw her raise her eyebrows. "There's no suggestion of a terrorist connection; it's just a tool they use."

"What should I do?"

"Do?" Kross tilted his head and looked up at the ship hanging over them. "I would cooperate fully. Have they given any sign that they think you may be involved?"

"No. Not so far, anyway."

Kross nodded. "Then I would say your best course is to cooperate. You know nothing, so it can't hurt, and you may learn something. The alternative is to refuse and be entirely isolated."

"I know nothing because there's nothing to know," she said. "The whole thing's insane."

Kross said, "Are you *sure* there's nothing to know?"

"Oh, don't you start, Oskar. I've had a whole day of this from Internal Affairs."

He turned to her, hat clutched in both hands. "It's important, Krista. Something he said, some mood he was in one day. Something you may have overlooked. If you don't tell Colonel Jakobson about it right now you'll appear complicit."

She shook her head. "No, Oskar. There's nothing. My father is innocent."

"Good." He went back to watching the ship, but the children had grown bored and wandered off into another room, and the hologram hung motionless.

"Should I instruct you to act for me?" she asked.

He glanced at her. "You could," he mused. "It wouldn't hurt, necessarily, although some might see it as an admission that you have something to hide. Have you spoken to the police union?"

"They're on my list. Jakobson told me not to speak to any serving police officer about it, though. I don't know if they count or not."

"I don't see how they can object to you consulting your union rep. I would certainly have words with them if they did."

Krista looked around the room, her mind reeling. It was as if real life had suddenly been replaced by a series of tableaux that she was passing through, although unlike the museum there was no handy audio commentary to tell her what things were.

"What's the worst-case scenario?" she asked.

Kross thought about it. "The worst-case is that the allegations are true and your father *was* involved with some kind of vigilante squad within the police force. The investigation proves this beyond any reasonable doubt and your father's name, and the name of anyone else involved, is blackened for ever. If any of the officers involved are still alive, they are tried and convicted. The name of the Tallinn police force is tarnished. The government has to be seen to be tough. There is a high-level investigation into the whole force, perhaps into the whole Estonian police service. There are retirements and resignations and sackings. The force is in disarray for a generation." He nodded to himself. "Basically the worst parts of the Bible."

This was more or less how Krista saw it, but it seemed worse, coming from someone else. She said, "It's not true."

"Of course it's not," said Kross. "Your father was a tough guy but he was one of the straightest police officers I ever met. I'm sure he was quite capable of killing to protect himself or his family, but in cold blood? The way this accusation is presented?" He shook his head. "No."

"Could this Sergii have threatened us?" Krista asked, thinking aloud.

"Not as I understand it. He was a small-time hoodlum, and a barely competent one at that, according to Internal Affairs. And even if he had, your father would have gone to his superiors rather than taking matters into his own hands; you and your mother would have been taken into protective custody until everything was safe again."

Krista raised a hand up to touch the illusory hull of the sailing ship, but it was just out of reach of her fingers.

"You can't touch it," Kross said. "It isn't really there."

Krista lowered her hand. "Yes," she said. "I know."

The next room was given over to a huge diorama of the city as it had been in Hanseatic times. This was definitely real, hand-made in the 1990s, when 3D printers and fabbing weren't even plotlines in science fiction novels. It sat on a waist-high table and was covered with a transparent dome to keep it clean and stop people stealing the model buildings. Kross and Krista stood looking down on it for a while like glum gods.

"You can see my flat from here," Kross said, pointing.

You could also see the town square and the location of the police station which, until a few hours ago, had been Krista's place of work. She said, "Thank you for agreeing to meet me, Oskar. It was good of you."

He inclined his head. "You'll be getting my bill in due course." Krista narrowed her eyes at him, and he smiled. "That was a lawyer joke."

"It might be best if we left separately," she said. "Just in case someone *is* watching."

"I doubt that will fool anyone."

He was right; it wouldn't have fooled *her*.

"If you do need my help, in a professional capacity, don't hesitate to get in touch," he told her. "In the meantime, I'm required to cooperate with Colonel Jakobson. It's nothing personal."

She nodded. "I understand, Oskar."

He looked at her. "I took care of your father's legal matters for almost thirty years," he reminded her. "*I* know he didn't do it. There will be no evidence to support this ridiculous claim."

"I should go," Krista said, checking her phone. "I'm meeting Markus."

Kross nodded. "My advice? Stay home, keep your head down, do what Internal Affairs tells you. I'll be in touch."

They walked to the entrance, said their goodbyes, and then Kross went out into the evening while Krista retrieved her coat and hat from the cloakroom. By the time she stepped out onto the street Kross was gone and it was snowing again, big fat slow flakes.

FOUR

1

SHE'D THOUGHT, AFTER five years of steady work and steadily increasing success, that Coureur Central were going to welcome her back into the fold. If they'd just wanted to give her a final warning to pack up and go back to Texas, they wouldn't have dragged her halfway across Europe; someone would have had a quiet word with her in Spain and she would have told them to fuck off and they would have taken things from there.

She hadn't been sure how she felt about the prospect of coming back into the Coureurs. In a lot of ways, it would have been merely symbolic, after so many years working freelance. There were some areas of support which might have been useful, but she'd done without them for so long that it was hardly a strain. She was doing okay on her own. Really, she thought, she'd only come to see what their terms might be.

Whatever happened, she'd expected to be back in Barcelona by the weekend, so she hadn't bothered to do a lot of homework on Gliwice, which had been sloppy of her.

Polish politics were a mystery to her. On the rare

occasions when it had been relevant to pay any attention at all, it had seemed that their governments oscillated between being somewhat right of centre, solidly right, and so far to the right that US Republicans' jaws dropped in amazement. The current one was definitely the latter and it had somehow—the details were obscure and seemed to rely as much on body language as politics—managed to anger Gliwice's city authorities so much that they had threatened to declare independence and secede from the Polish Republic.

This was quite a trick. In normal circumstances, she'd have expected the city's authorities to go along with Warsaw, but once they'd actually said it, there was no going back without losing face. There had followed a period of negotiation which basically boiled down to the government saying, "You wouldn't dare," and the city replying, "Just try us," and then, the week before Carey's arrival, they had finally gone ahead and published a set of articles of secession.

The city was plastered with posters, some animated, some not, for one faction or another—in true Polish fashion there were more than two—but Carey had tuned them out. One did in Europe, these days; it was the only way to make your way down the street with your wits intact. Paying attention now as she walked around town, she saw posters for Loyalists, Secessionists, Communists, Anarchists, Social Democrats, Trotskyites, Fascists, Actors, Writers, the Police, Crypto-Anarchists, Crypto-Fascists, Neocons, Libertarians, Crypto-Libertarians, Anarcho-Libertarians, Neolibertarians, something which styled itself—with admirable if rather alarming directness—The Gun Party, and any number of other groups which had self-assembled for the occasion like scratch baseball teams. One poster she saw a lot featured a stern-looking pope and the single word *Nie!* blinking slowly on and off at the calming rate of a resting heartbeat. She'd assumed it was something to do with reproductive rights.

If one judged by the tone of the posters alone, one might reasonably have expected the city to be in a state of some ferment, but by and large everyone seemed to be ignoring it. The streets were full of people shopping and going to work and visiting restaurants and cafés and generally just getting on with their lives, and if one just ignored the political goings-on, as she had, it would be possible to believe that nothing out of the ordinary was happening. The mainstream media was all state-controlled, and discussion shows were full of talking heads pushing their own agendas. Footage from the Sejm, the Polish House of Representatives, was just a lot of people arguing and making angry speeches, which wasn't exactly unusual. Hindenberg, still an open wound for most Poles, was virtually next door. Carey didn't give much for Gliwice's chances.

"They can't hope to get away with it, can they?" she said, watching buildings and people going by.

"They think they have a good case," Wareham said, stopping the car at a roundabout. "The government doesn't see it that way, of course." He moved off again.

"I was in Nord-Rhein when they declared independence," she recalled.

"Was that in your capacity as a journalist or a private investigator?" he asked amiably. She gave him a hard look and he smiled. He was in casuals today, jeans and a grey polo shirt and an old suit jacket with baggy pockets. Oddly, it made him look a little older than he had in a suit. "What was it like?"

How long ago was that now? Twenty years? Twenty-five? She'd made a lot of money that month; all the agencies she filed for had wanted copy, and she'd even had the *New York Times* yelling down the phone to her. That was probably the nest-egg which would have enabled her to buy that ranch-house outside Austin. If she'd ever bought it. "It was lively, for a while."

"I missed that one," he said. "I was here for Hindenberg, though. Speaking of *lively*."

"You've been here that long?"

"I came out not long after the flu," he said. "Never quite went home again. I like Poland and the Poles, although they don't always make it easy."

She grunted. She'd arrived in Europe around the same time. The whole continent had seemed to be in the process of losing its mind, borders being hardened, cities still in lockdown, economies on their knees. The place had seemed haunted, back then, and not just by the fifty million or more dead. She couldn't remember, now, whether anyone had ever come up with an accurate body count. Certainly they hadn't in the States.

"I hear things are about to get lively again in your country," he said.

"Beg pardon?"

He thought about it. "Sorry. I still find it hard to think of Texas as a country. I meant the United States."

"Oh." He was talking about Montana, which had been rumbling along for almost as long as she could remember. "No, Washington won't ever let *that* happen." Texas was a republic, California had embarked on a long leisurely examination of alternative political systems, and Hawai'i had dug deep into its genealogy, reinstated its royal family and turned itself back into a kingdom—but Montana was a nightmare scenario, a state full of heavily armed militias. If they ever became independent, Idaho and probably one or both the Dakotas would go with them, and nobody knew what would happen after that, although there was general agreement that it wouldn't be good. "The UN threw their proposal out, anyway."

"Can anyone stop them?"

"What are they going to do, fence off the whole state? Sure, they have a beef and they have lots of guns, but the feds are always going to have more of everything."

He thought about that. "What a time to be alive," he said.

"Amen to that."

"Here we are," he said, slowing and then making a left-turn onto a side-road that curved around in front of a group of four identical high-rises.

Here, according to the police report, was where Maksim had been living, in an old martial law-era block a little way out from the centre of town. Its windows and cladding had been replaced sometime in the past, but it looked grimy and run-down and there was a solid band of graffiti twice as tall as her around its base. There was some scruffy parkland around the blocks, and a one-storey flat-roofed supermarket next door to a shisha bar over to one side. Looking up from ground level, she saw a cliff-face of balconies festooned with aerials and dishes and washing.

It was a public address, the place where everyone would have known he lived—he would have been keeping somewhere more covert as a base of operations, if he had been involved in something—but she went there anyway. She'd called Wareham and got him to go with her as cover; a local journalist poking around would cause fewer waves than someone flashing a Texan investigator's licence, and he'd already been there anyway, doorstepping the neighbours.

"It's mostly student accommodation these days," Wareham told her as they rode up in the lift. "But there are still some private lets. It's relatively cheap, and there are worse places to live. How long do you think you'll be staying?"

Thinking about Maksim, she almost missed the question. "As long as I have to," she said. "Why?"

"I was wondering how you'd feel about having dinner one evening."

"Are you trying to pick me up?"

He gave a half-smile. "The romantic nature of the situation has quite overwhelmed me."

That made her smile, too. "Yeah, okay. Let's do that."

The lift bumped to a stop and the doors opened, and they stepped out into a well-lit corridor lined with the heavy security doors favoured by European apartment-dwellers. There was a smell of cooking in the air, and Carey could hear music coming from one of the flats further along. Looking in the other direction, she saw a stout, well-dressed woman standing in the corridor. Beside her, she could almost hear Wareham putting his bonhomie into gear.

"Iwona," he said, walking towards the woman. "How splendid to see you. Thank you *ever* so much for letting me do this."

Iwona was in her mid-fifties and her short hair was nicely styled and streaked with copper and pink highlights. She allowed Wareham to bestow a chaste kiss on either cheek and gave Carey a territorial look.

"Iwona," Wareham said, "this is Petula, one of my colleagues." Carey had to work hard not to glare at him. "Petula, this is Iwona, from the letting agent."

Iwona favoured Carey with a limp, bone-dry handshake, then ignored her. "This is irregular, Robert," she said. "I'm not supposed to let anyone in until the apartment has been cleared."

"Oh, Iwona," Wareham said, doing the Hugh Grant thing again. "The police have already been here, haven't they? How can it hurt? Come on, there's a slap-up dinner in it for you."

Iwona made a little show of thinking about it, then she dipped a hand into her shoulder bag and came up with a bunch of keys. "Just this once," she said, starting to work on the column of mechanical locks lining the door. "And just because it's you. But please don't take anything away with you. We're still waiting for the gentleman's estate to contact us."

They were going to be waiting quite a while for that. Carey supposed that she probably represented Maksim's 'estate', as much as anyone did, but she didn't say anything.

The final lock turned, and Iwona opened the door and led the way down a short corridor with a bathroom opening off to the right. Carey glanced in as they passed, saw a toilet and a washbasin and a shower with a single bottle of shower gel sitting in the tray.

The police had tossed the place and hadn't bothered to tidy up afterward, so it was indistinguishable from the aftermath of a burglary. In the main room, cupboards and drawers had been opened and their contents tipped out onto the floor, although there wasn't much, and what there was was carefully generic. Printed magazines, entertainment drives, some stationery still sealed in its packaging. There was a little tangle of cables in one corner where an entertainment centre had been; they'd have taken that for a forensic check of its drives. On the other side of the breakfast bar, the cupboards of the kitchen area were open and packets of cereal and loaves and crockery and pots and pans were piled on the worktops. All the drawers had been taken out, to check whether anything had been taped to their backs or undersides, and then stacked on the floor. The fridge contained a single shrink-wrapped steak which had turned green, and a bag of swampy liquid which had once been salad.

The bedroom was the same. They'd upturned the mattress and looked under it, although they hadn't cut it open. The bed itself was an open wooden frame and there were plenty of places to hide something within it, but the police didn't seem to have checked and neither did Carey, under the watchful eye of Iwona, feel any need to. He wouldn't have left anything here.

Piles of clothing on the floor in front of the open wardrobe. Jeans, tee shirts, outdoor gear, underwear, a lot of it still in its bags and packages. Carey stirred a toe through it while Wareham schmoozed Iwona. Under a black hoodie, a paperback book lay open face-down on the woodblock floor, a nearly-new Polish edition of *Moby-Dick*. Carey picked it up and casually flicked through it looking for dog-ears or notes, and a little postcard, the size of a credit card, fell out. On the front was an image of the Danish island of Sylt, part of a commemorative set issued to mark the independence of the Wadden Islands Federation. She remembered there were a lot of cards in the set, because there were a lot of Wadden Islands. The back was blank. She palmed the card and slipped it into her pocket, put the book back where she'd found it before Iwona had a conniption fit.

Back in the main room, she stood at the window. The view looked out across trees and apartment blocks and, far away, what might have been the open countryside, it was hard to tell. She still hadn't managed to get a handle on the geography of the place.

Wareham came over. "All right?"

She nodded. The place was a prop; Maksim might have slept here a few times, just to establish himself, but he'd been doing his business somewhere else, and if there had been any clues to where that was, they were in the hands of the police now.

They did another circuit of the flat, for appearances' sake, and Wareham took some photos and dictated some notes, then Iwona led them out and locked up and took the lift back downstairs with them. She didn't pat them down to make sure they hadn't stolen anything, but she looked as if it had crossed her mind.

Outside on the pavement, the estate agent let Wareham give her three pecks on the cheeks, reminded him about dinner, and with a final hard look at Carey she walked off in the direction of a nearby tram stop.

"That woman doesn't like me," Carey said as they headed back to the Audi.

"Oh, Iwona's all right," he said. "So. What did you think?"

"What did *you* think?"

He smiled. "It doesn't look as if anyone had been doing a great deal of living there, even allowing for the brief time Mr Petrauskas seems to have been here."

She nodded. "And the police didn't bother to search properly. They just did it the way they've seen it done in the movies; a professional would have stripped the place down to the brickwork."

He glanced at her. "You think the police are mixed up in… whatever you think is going on here?"

"You'd think if they were interested enough in him to chase him to his death, they'd have been interested enough to search his flat properly." It still didn't scan, somehow. Why had the police turned up at the crash so quickly? Why had Maksim been belting along that crappy road in the first place?

"Just out of interest, what *do* you think is going on here?" Wareham asked.

"I don't know. That's what I'm supposed to be trying to find out."

"You knew him, didn't you. Mr Petrauskas."

"Why would you think that?"

"I saw the way you were looking around the flat. You looked sad."

"I always look sad. Sad's my default setting."

They'd reached the Audi. Wareham blipped the doors open. "Are you going to tell me about it?" he asked.

Carey got into the passenger seat. "No," she said.

* * *

SHE GOT WAREHAM to drop her near the market square, after promising to get in touch about dinner, and watched him pull away into the maze of little narrow streets before turning and walking away.

It had occurred to her that the political situation in Gliwice cast the local Coureurs' unwillingness to help in a different light, so more out of a sense of experiment than anything else she'd run the contact routine again and the following day she'd received a message telling her to be at a basement pierogi bar off Zwycięstwa at such and such a time.

Inside, it was small and cramped, the furniture rickety. Paperscreens on the white-painted brick walls showed happy harvest scenes from the foothills of the Tatras down south. Rolling hills, smiling apple-cheeked peasants in traditional dress, horse-drawn carts piled high with hay. More smiling costumed peasants, working in what looked like a suspiciously antiseptic rustic shed to make oscypek, a cheese made of a mixture of sheep and goat's milk. Cute, but kitsch. There was no footage of Nowy Targ, the regional capital, which the last time she had been there had been neither kitsch nor cute.

She ordered a portion of ruskie pierogi, filled with potato and cream cheese, and they arrived boiled and then lightly fried in pork fat. They were pretty good, but twenty minutes later her plate was empty and the Coureurs hadn't showed, unless they were among the lunchtime crowd starting to make the restaurant uncomfortably busy.

Screw 'em. She paid for her pierogi and went back upstairs and onto the street. Her phone rang, and when she answered it a woman's voice said, "Who are you?"

"What?" she said, feeling herself starting to get annoyed, and the connection was cut.

She was checking the call log when the phone rang again. "Who is this?" she barked testily.

"More to the point is *where* I am," a man's voice said. "And *where* is not where *you* are. I'm at the hotel and you're not."

Scowling, she looked up and down the street until she saw a Starbucks in the distance. She gave him directions and set out that way herself.

So the local Coureurs were assholes. She could put up with being unpopular, her life had not been one of uniform popularity, but she drew the line at childish phone stunts and not turning up for a meet. She was going to have to teach them some respect.

Maybe it really was a cultural thing. The Europeans were the heirs of Alec Leamas and George Smiley and Harry Palmer; the Americans had... who? Jason Bourne? Matt Helm? A few years ago the Coureurs had been a pop culture thing; you couldn't change channels without coming across some Coureur adventure show, and most of them, now she thought about it, had more of an American sensibility than a European one. The few Coureurs she knew had affected a public disdain for the shows, but more than one had admitted privately to her that they were rather tickled to find themselves the subject of mass entertainment. The experience, she supposed, was somewhat akin to being an MI6 officer reading le Carré. There weren't all that many of the shows about these days, anyway. Fashions changed. People seemed to be in the market for teen musical dramas at the moment, which she found vaguely enraging.

So, where did this leave her? In Carey's experience, Coureurs tended to be solitary types—you could wind up being sent who knew where at a moment's notice—but it wasn't unusual for a group of Coureurs in the same town or city to form themselves into an informal crew, pooling resources and sharing out jobs. Which was great for them, obviously, but not so convenient for a *visiting firefighter* who needed, say, new papers or some arcane item of technical support. The local Coureurs would naturally have the best people on retainer, and when it came to false documents second best could often get you arrested.

Coureurs also loved to gossip among themselves. There was a vasty undertow of rumour, hints, tips, libel, slander, misinformation, operational lore, myth, legend, outright lies, and sometimes genuine news which comprised the nearest thing they had to a handbook. Carey had not heard, in her travels around Europe, that the Coureurs in Gliwice were assholes, particularly. She had not, she realised, heard anything about them at all. That wasn't necessarily significant; all it probably meant was that they were a competent crew getting quietly along with their stuff.

All of which begged the question, just what the hell had Maksim *done* to them to make them behave this way? Notwithstanding Kaunas's worthy sentiments about client confidence, she suspected this was the real reason she was here. Not to clear up the circumstances of Maksim's death, but of his life.

It was a little too cool today to sit outdoors, so she settled down in the coffee shop, at a table with a good view of the door, and she was just finishing her latte twenty minutes later when Anatoly walked in, a rucksack slung over one shoulder. He spotted her and came over and sat down.

"Is that all your luggage?" she asked, nodding at the rucksack. "We might be here a while."

"I left the rest at the hotel," he said. "Do you know there's no airport here? I had to fly to Katowice and get a taxi."

"It's not even Katowice," she told him. "It's almost as far from there as it is from here." She took a sip of coffee. "You want one of these?"

"Tea," he said. "Black. With lemon. Not Earl Grey."

When she came back from the counter, he had taken

a packet of sandwiches from his rucksack and was unwrapping them. Anatoly had a phobia about flying. It was better than it had been when they'd first met—she'd arranged therapy for him—but he was still too nervous to eat while in the air. He'd fallen into the habit of buying sandwiches on board and eating them when he was safely back on the ground. It was by no means the weirdest behaviour she'd ever encountered.

"How was the flight?" she asked.

He glared at her, then looked at his sandwich. He peeled back the top slice of bread, revealing a soggy landscape of salad and tomato and something resembling meat. "Does this look like chicken to you? I asked for chicken."

She looked, and to be honest it was hard to be sure. "It won't kill you. Probably."

He replaced the slice of bread and mashed it down with the flat of his hand. "Perhaps you should tell me what this is all about," he said. "Before my tranquilisers wear off."

She sat back and watched him take a bite of the sandwich. While they were on the subject of le Carré, Anatoly had something of the look of a young Smiley, if Smiley had been written by Chekhov. He was plump and sandy-haired and owlish behind round-lensed spectacles. He was the type of young man that certain women like to mother, but he was a Moscow-trained hood, the estranged son of an extended family of Russian espiocrats. She'd met him in London a few years ago in the middle of a Situation neither of them entirely understood, the collision of two—and perhaps more—intelligence ops. She'd never been able to get to the bottom of it; the people she'd been hired to jump at the time could only provide her with a few paragraphs of a story which she suspected ran to many convoluted pages.

"We're looking for a Coureur named Maksim Ilyich Petrauskas."

He grunted. "*There's* a collision of cultures. Lithuanian?"

She nodded. "Mother from Kursk."

"He's got a Russian patronymic."

"After his grandfather."

Anatoly considered this. "Okay. Do you know him?"

"We've got history. Does the name ring a bell?"

"I'm not on first-name terms with every vaguely Russian operative in Europe, you know. And you could have emailed me, if that was all you wanted."

It had been worth a try. Sometimes, very rarely and entirely at random, the gods did smile briefly on one. "He's dead," she told him.

Anatoly looked at her for a moment, then tore open a couple of sugar sachets and dumped them into his tea. "You're sure?"

"I saw his death certificate."

"Well," he said, stirring the tea, "that shouldn't make him hard to find. I don't know what I'm doing here."

"There's a doubt."

"There always is." He tasted the tea, winced slightly, and added more sugar.

"We can't rely on local talent."

"Unfriendly?"

"Resentful, more than anything, I think. Maksim had some scam going here and that stirred everybody up. Then he gets himself killed and everything settles down. Then I turn up and start lifting stones. I had a meet; they're not going to cooperate. Basically, they're assholes." She didn't mention the earlier abortive meet; it was still irritating her too much.

He sat back and looked around the coffee shop. "This is a lot closer to Rus than Edinburgh, you know." As a result of his adventure in London, Anatoly had been declared persona non grata by his family. Maybe one day they'd let him come home, but that hadn't happened yet and there were no signs that their attitude was going to soften any time soon. She'd resettled him in Scotland under Hungarian papers, which had been the best she'd been able to do in a hurry. At the time, she'd thought she was being humane, but she did wonder whether she hadn't done it out of some subconscious urge to keep him handy in case of need. He was field-trained and he had a good operational eye, and he'd been useful now and again.

"I figure this will go quicker if there's two pairs of feet," she told him. "Sooner it's over, sooner you can go home."

He sighed. "Okay. So, where do you want to start?"

"If the locals aren't going to be any help, we'll have to scare up our own resources," she said. "We're going to need a pianist, at the very least."

"That should be straightforward enough." Anatoly had a different idea of 'straightforward' from most other people.

"Without making waves."

"Well, that goes without saying." He tried his tea again.

"And there's him." She took from a pocket a printout of the image she'd asked Kaunas to source for her, and put it on the table in front of him. A stout, angry-looking middle-aged man in dress uniform glared up at them. "Yegor," she said, and she sat and watched as Anatoly recognised the uniform and boggled slightly. "He was a colonel with the FSB, back when the FSB still meant something."

"The FSB still means something." Anatoly picked up the photograph and frowned. "How old is this?"

"About twenty years."

"So he must be, what, in his eighties now?"

"About that, yeah."

"Then this image is next to useless. I can't just shove it in people's faces and say, 'Try to imagine him twenty years older.'"

"I'm going to see if I can find an artist who'll mock us up something that looks more recent."

"You've met this Yegor?"

She nodded. "A long while ago. Maksim and Yegor are a package. If Maksim was here, Yegor will have been too."

"But now Maksim is dead, there's no need for Yegor to remain."

"He's still here," she said. "I can feel a disturbance in the Force." She saw Anatoly narrow his eyes at her. "Old joke."

"Any other names? Aliases?"

She shook her head. "Not that I know of."

"Well," he said. "This is a good start. All we have is an out-of-date photograph and your intuition. It's a good thing I have a lot of holiday saved up."

"Don't be snarky, there's a dear."

Anatoly popped the last bit of sandwich in his mouth and washed it down with tea. "What are we supposed to do, if it turns out that Maksim is alive?"

That was, of course, a good question, and it was one reason why she liked having Anatoly around. She'd seen *The Third Man*, too. In fact, now she thought about it, the first time she'd seen it had been with Maksim. "We'll worry about that down the line," she said. "First steps first."

2

IT TOOK ALMOST two years for scheduled flights to Europe to resume, and even then a lot of nations, looking with horror at what had happened in the United States, had closed their borders to Americans. In retaliation, the State Department had issued an advisory listing which European countries were considered safe to visit. If you combined the two, the possible destinations for the American traveller dwindled to the high single figures. Carey had wanted to go to Spain; she wound up in Luxembourg.

Which was not, in all honesty, such a bad thing. Luxembourg had aggressively closed its borders in the very early days of the pandemic and was only now cautiously opening them again. It was one of the wealthiest countries in Europe, and its healthcare was second to none. It had survived the Xian flu better than most.

That was not to say that it was untouched. Carey had her temperature checked three times between getting off the plane and finally emerging into arrivals, and she had to give a nasal swab before she was allowed through passport control. She was told to quarantine in her hotel for three days in case she became symptomatic, and given about two dozen phone numbers for doctors, hospitals, Infection Control, the Health Ministry.

The interior of the cab which took her from Luxembourg-Findel into the centre of town smelled of alcohol-based disinfectant, and the driver was separated from her by a perspex screen and didn't seem inclined to make conversation. It was a grey, drizzly day, and though people were out and about the streets seemed quiet. Everyone was wearing masks, and she kept seeing uniformed officers making random temperature checks. Everything—the buildings, the clothes, the weather—seemed exotic.

At the hotel, there were signs everywhere telling guests to wear masks and maintain a two-metre distance. She held her passport up to a camera to check in, submitted to another swab, was issued with a key-card for her room, and carried her own bags up three flights of stairs.

Her room was small and comfortable and smelled of having been deep-cleaned after its previous occupant. Its window looked down into a little courtyard at the back of the hotel, where widely spaced tables stood under big umbrellas and heaters. There was another prominent notice on the back of the door telling guests to wear masks unless dining in the restaurant and to maintain distance. There was a list of phone numbers to call if one felt symptoms coming on, and when she turned on the television she was presented with a five-minute video about local regulations, including information about the temperature spot-checks she'd seen driving in from the airport.

She ordered a meal from room service—fried potatoes and ham and a green salad—and tried to write a piece about the American Experience of arriving in post-flu Europe, but every journalist was doing that these days and there wasn't much new one could say about it. Around five in the afternoon, jet lag sat down on her like a huge soft friendly giant, and she climbed into bed and slept for eleven hours.

SHE WAS THREE years too late. American correspondents who had been trapped in Europe when the pandemic hit were like rock stars now, the ones who had survived. When infection rates plateaued and then began to fall, journalists had set out to report on the shell-shocked Continent. This was not as easy as it sounded; global air travel had more or less ground to a halt, and all but two or three US airlines had briefly sucked billions of dollars of aid from the federal tit before going bust. Some journalists had themselves smuggled across the border into Canada and flew from there. One had talked her agency into hiring an ocean-going yacht, sailed to the Azores and then on to the coast of North Africa, and from there had made her way to Greece with the help of people smugglers. Another, a man named Ralph Meyer, had stepped into legend by embarking on an extraordinary odyssey via Alaska, across the Chukchi Sea in a fishing boat to Chukotka, and then a stupendous cross-country journey, filing articles the whole way. He had only arrived in Western Europe earlier that year, where the French had promptly arrested him for visa irregularities and deported him back to San Francisco.

There was no way Carey was going to do anything like that. She was well-off, by general American standards—

Byron had made her sole beneficiary in his will, and he had not been poor—but she couldn't afford a yacht and a crew, and she lacked Ralph Meyer's resources; there were those who muttered that he'd only managed to get into Russia because he was ex-CIA, and maybe not so ex at that. So she had to do it the easy way.

And that would have been okay; she was contracted to do some pieces about Luxembourg's recovery after the pandemic and if she'd been the only US journalist there it would have been a nice place to sit and work and range further and further as Europe began to open up again. The problem was, she was not the only US journalist in Luxembourg. As one of the few European destinations currently open to them, it was knee-deep in American correspondents, and more were arriving on every flight. Every other person in her hotel had an American accent, and they were all writing articles about Luxembourg's recovery after the pandemic.

When she was finally allowed out of the hotel, she set out into the city on foot, recording interviews with shopkeepers and businessmen and financiers and passersby. More than one of them said, "What are you doing here? Is there not enough grief in your own country?" to which the only sane answer was, "Well, *yes*."

"It's a fair question," Raphael mused one evening in a bar in Hollerich, on the edge of Parc Merl.

Carey finished her beer and signalled for another. "I know. It just makes me feel kind of stinky. Like a disaster tourist."

Raphael sat back. He was a local journalist, a fixer one of the agencies she was working for had put her in touch with. He was in his thirties, a tired-looking man with a cowlick of black hair and a baggy suit. He said, "First job I ever did—the first *real* job—was a steelworks explosion near Charleroi. Twenty men dead. The paper I was working for got hold of the names and addresses and sent me out to their homes to see if I could source photos." He took a sip of red wine, put the glass back on the table. "It's the kind of thing you give to the newest journalist in the newsroom. So there I was, doorstepping the families of the dead men a couple of hours after the accident. Things were kind of chaotic, the authorities dropped the ball over and over again. In a few places, I rang the doorbell before the families had had official confirmation." He shrugged. "I got all the photos, went out that night and got drunk, went back to the office the next morning."

The waiter brought Carey's beer and another glass of wine for Raphael, left them on the adjoining table, and went back to the bar. Carey collected them. The bar was almost empty. Partly because it only had about a third of the tables it should have, to leave plenty of space between customers, and partly because even two years on Luxembourgers still didn't go out much unless they had to. Walking around town in the evening gave Carey a spooky feeling, as if she was walking through the set of a disaster movie.

She said, "I need to get out of here, Raphael."

"Well, quite," he said.

"I'm serious," she told him. "I'm just doing the same stuff everyone else is doing. Some of the people here have been interviewed so many times they've got themselves media managers."

He laughed. "Where would you go?"

"Spain," she said. "I want to go to Spain."

"Ah." His smile went away and he looked grave. "Spain." He drank some more wine. "Spain's not even a Schengen country any more." Spain and Greece had chosen to leave the European Union the year before the pandemic, and were currently struggling to negotiate terms for their future relationship with a European Parliament which was still barely functioning. Some of the smaller, newer members around the Adriatic were showing signs of having second thoughts about having joined. "Germany is not impossible, but Spain..." He shrugged.

"There are three flights a day from Luxembourg-Findel to Madrid," she told him. "I saw the boards when I arrived. There are two expresses, morning and evening. Don't tell me it can't be done."

"Oh, *physically* it's possible, obviously. *Physically* it's easy. It's a matter of papers; you wouldn't even be allowed on the plane or the train with an American passport."

Carey sat back and crossed her arms and stared levelly at him. They sat looking at each other for quite some time.

Finally, Raphael said, "It wouldn't be cheap."

3

The sainted Sergii had not, in fact, been a saint at all. The files Mr Reinsalu gave her painted Sergii as an honest businessman, but Lenna smelled the small-time hood beneath the retrospective paint job. In the few photographs they had of him, Sergii looked like Nikita Kruschev, if Kruschev had had hair. He was a small, annoyed-looking man with piggy eyes. Lenna didn't think she would have liked him, but she didn't have to. Sergii was dead.

That he had served a brief spell in jail was impossible to gloss over. He had been under investigation for handling stolen goods—which was barely a crime at all, as far as Lenna was concerned, if you didn't know they were stolen—and he'd defended himself when a policeman struck him. He'd kept his head down during his subsequent prison sentence, and when he got out he began trying to get his unfair conviction expunged, as any honest businessman would.

He was still campaigning to clear his name when his body was found near the port one morning with massive multiple injuries, broken bones, a shattered skull, a burst spleen. The official conclusion was that he had been the victim of a traffic accident, the driver in question having fled the scene

His wife, Sofia, knew who had really been responsible. She filed a complaint with the police, and received no response. She tried to contact them again, and again there was no response. She bombarded them with phone calls and kept being handed off to lackeys rather than the senior officers she wanted to speak to. She went down to police headquarters a couple of times and raised her voice, and for her efforts was escorted out of the building with a gentle warning that if she persisted she would be charged.

Then on a visit to family in St Petersburg, Sofia and her son Alexei were killed, ironically enough in a car crash, although this time there was no ambiguity; the other driver, roughly eighty percent alcohol by body weight, also died in the crash.

After that, The Case of the Mysterious Death of Sergii puttered out. He had no family and few friends, and Sofia's relatives had despised him. There was no one to speak for him until Mr Reinsalu came along, almost two decades later.

Mr Reinsalu had come to the case quite by chance, a half-overheard conversation between two men in a busy restaurant. Curious to know what they'd been talking about, he'd looked it up and found a tale of injustice that offended his sensibilities. He couldn't articulate quite why it had struck such a chord with him, except that he thought Sergii had deserved better, petty criminal or not, than to be beaten to death in an alleyway and have his murder simply ignored. If the police *were* going around killing people, something ought to be done about it.

And he painted a compelling picture of why it was so important. His investigations around Sergii's case had turned up the deaths of several other ethnic Russian men, all of them involved in low-level criminality which had brought them into contact with the police. Mr Reinsalu theorised a *death squad*, a group of vigilantes within the police force who had grown impatient with the slowly grinding and sometimes counterintuitive wheels of justice and decided to take matters into their own hands.

He had already been in touch with the police to revive the complaint about Sergii's murder, and he had received what he considered a lukewarm response. Initially, they had asked him to hand over all documentation he had about the case, but since then his inquiries had been met with a polite response. The investigation was ongoing and the police could not discuss it with him, but he would be informed of the results in due course.

This was all of vaguely academic interest to Lenna. With a salary coming in and the tricky negotiations with the bank and the utility companies taken care of by Mr Reinsalu, she felt as if a great cloud had lifted from her life. The flat felt like a home again, rather than a prison. She could afford to go out to eat, and she did so regularly, making sure that she would be seen by her former friends and contacts and they would get the message. *I'm doing quite all right without you, fuck you very much.* None of them tried to get in touch, but that was all right because she had nothing to say to them.

The work itself was quite straightforward, and if she had had any self-awareness at all Lenna would have been faintly embarrassed by how much she was being paid for it. She was basically writing press releases from twenty-year-old material, cutting it up and rejigging it for different sites and news organisations. She made the occasional phone call, but all the principals in the case were dead, so there was nobody to interview. Mr Reinsalu was handling all contact with the police, such as it was. She could work from home, wearing only her pyjamas. Nobody cared. The English had a phrase, *money for old rope*.

Having said all that, there was something very satisfying

about watching the story spread, first from obscure websites, then to social media, then to the mainstream media, then to a whole raft of comment blogs. *I did this*, she thought. *I made this happen.*

A few days after this realisation, she was watching streaming footage of a demonstration outside police headquarters. It wasn't a very big demonstration, a dozen people wrapped up against the cold and holding banners which bore slogans like JUSTICE FOR SERGII and POLICE MURDERERS. Someone with a loudhailer was shouting at the building in Russian. Facing the demonstration, a handful of slightly bemused-looking police officers stood outside the doors of the building.

The doorbell rang, followed by a firm knock. Lenna looked at the door. Since the normalisation of her relations with the financial institutions which dogged her life, she had ceased to fear the doorbell, but Mr Reinsalu was the only person who visited her, and she wasn't expecting him today.

She got up and went down the hall and peered through the door viewer, was rewarded with a fisheye view of a tall middle-aged woman in business clothes. As she watched, the woman rang the bell and knocked again. There was a strong temptation not to answer, to tiptoe back into the living room and wait until the woman grew tired of knocking and went away, but she could hear the sound of the entertainment set from here, the Russian man shouting at the police, and if she could hear it anyone standing outside would probably be able to hear it too.

She opened the door and found that, in addition to the tall woman, two police officers had been flanking the doorway, out of sight of the viewer. Her heart thudded in her chest. "Yes?" she said.

The woman held up a laminated card identifying her as a member of the Tallinn police force. "Lenna Rüütel?"

"What's this about?"

"Are you Lenna Rüütel?"

The temptation to deny it was very strong, but she hesitated for too long; she'd never get away with it. "Yes," she said finally.

"My name is Jakobson. Could you get dressed and come with us, please?"

"What? No, I'm busy at the moment."

Jakobson glanced past Lenna and down the hall, at the far end of which she could see into the living room and the screen of the entertainment set. "Yes," she said. "So I see." She looked Lenna in the eye and said, "Please get dressed and come with us. I'd prefer not to have to take you into custody; the paperwork is tiresome and I already have more than enough to do."

"You're arresting me? For what?"

Jakobson sighed. "No, I'm trying *not* to arrest you, Ms Rüütel. I'd much rather you came with us voluntarily."

"Is this about Sergii?" Lenna said.

Jakobson narrowed her eyes at her. "I won't say 'please' again," she said. "It's your choice."

It was, of course, no choice at all. "Wait here; I'll just put some clothes on." She went to close the door, but Jakobson stepped smartly inside and closed it behind her.

"I don't think so," Jakobson said.

Lenna looked at her for a few moments, then said, "Fine. Fine. Make yourself at home." She turned and headed for the living room, Jakobson at her heels. "I haven't done anything wrong," she said, taking her phone from the coffee table on the way to the bedroom.

"Oh, I think you'll find that everyone's done *something* wrong," Jakobson told her, looking around the flat with a lack of enthusiasm. "It's quite dispiriting, if you let yourself dwell on it. Please put that down."

Lenna looked at her for a moment, then left the phone on the bookcase.

She took her time getting ready, partly to annoy Jakobson and partly because if she *was* going to be dragged down to police headquarters she at least wanted to look good while it was happening. When she emerged from the bedroom wearing her best interview suit, Jakobson was standing in the middle of the living room holding her phone.

"You won't be needing this," the police officer said. "I'll look after it for you. Keep it safe." She dropped the phone into her coat pocket.

Lenna thought of complaining, but it would only make things worse. "Shall we go then?"

Jakobson glanced at the entertainment set as Lenna went to wave it into sleep mode. The screen was still showing the feed from outside police headquarters. The Russian man was still shouting. "I suppose you think this is funny," she said, half to herself.

THEY DIDN'T TAKE her to police headquarters, but to the police station on Raekoja plats. She was issued with a visitor badge and taken upstairs to a small, comfortable room equipped with a table and two chairs. Jakobson sat her down on one of the chairs and took the other, facing her across the table.

"So," Jakobson said. "Firstly, I'm required to notify you that you are not under caution and that this conversation is being recorded. Secondly, thank you for agreeing to come down here."

"I wasn't given any choice," Lenna said for the benefit of the recording devices.

Jakobson let this go. She said, "Could you tell me what your connection is with Sergii N?"

"There is none," Lenna said. "I never met him; I'm just running media affairs for the campaign."

"The campaign," Jakobson nodded. "The campaign which consists of you and the lawyer Reinsalu."

"Mr Reinsalu is my employer. Perhaps you should be speaking to him if there's a problem."

"A problem," Jakobson said, nodding again. "Well, yes, there is a *little* problem. Your campaign is standing outside my police headquarters with signs accusing the police force of being murderers. Yes, that is a bit of a problem."

"They're nothing to do with us," Lenna protested.

Jakobson gave her a Look. "Seriously," she said.

"We didn't organise it, they didn't contact us and let us know it was going to happen or ask our permission. I have no idea who they are."

"They're *very* irritating, is who they are."

"A group of concerned citizens," Lenna said, using a phrase she thought Mr Reinsalu would approve of.

"Don't be so smug and self-righteous," Jakobson warned.

"You can't talk to me like that." Although clearly she could, and not worry that the conversation was being recorded. "I suppose a police force that would kill citizens wouldn't be too bothered about being disrespectful."

Jakobson's eyebrows shot up. "You know," she said, "I didn't think you had that in you. But don't do it again. Tell me how you got involved in this thing."

Lenna told her story, glossing over her firing from the paper and subsequent descent into penury, and when she'd finished Jakobson sat back in her chair and said, "Yes, well, I have no idea how much of that to believe. Your former editor tells a *very* different story."

Lenna sat where she was, unable to think of a single thing to say.

Jakobson rubbed her eyes. "You see," she said, "I can't tell whether you're the drunken little airhead you seem to be, or whether you're really very smart and just *pretending* to be a drunken little airhead. I have to admit, if it's the latter it's a very good act."

Lenna stood up. "I don't have to sit here listening to you insulting me."

"No, you don't," Jakobson agreed without moving from her chair. "Perhaps I should have arrested you, after all. You'd have had to sit there then."

Lenna glared at her.

"Oh, sit down," Jakobson said tiredly.

Lenna sat.

"Your employer isn't a lawyer, you know," Jakobson told her. "Oh, he was, but he was caught embezzling funds from his employers. They didn't want the scandal of a court case, but he was quietly disbarred." When Lenna didn't respond, she crossed her arms. "So here you are, this strange pair. A disbarred lawyer and a journalist whose personal life is so chaotic that nobody will employ her. And you are, quite genuinely, causing all kinds of trouble for me and the police force. Personally, I think that's remarkable. Nothing to say now? Hm? Okay. How about some coffee?"

She got up and went to the door, opened it a few inches and spoke to someone in the corridor outside, then returned to her chair, where she regarded Lenna for a long time.

"The police force is not perfect," Jakobson told her. "I'm with Internal Affairs, so trust me, I know. But it doesn't go round murdering people. You're making trouble, whipping people up, for no reason at all. Right now you might issue a press release or have a quiet word with the organisers of that little mob outside headquarters and they might pack up and go away, but eventually—sometime quite soon—you're not going to be able to control them any more. That's why I'm talking to you now, while people are still listening to reason, to see if we can defuse this."

Lenna thought about it. "May I have my phone back, please?" she asked. "I should be recording this too."

* * *

"She seemed quite genuine," Lenna said.

"Well, of course she did," said Mr Reinsalu. "It's part of her job."

They were sitting in a McDonalds not far from her flat. She thought this was not the time or place to raise the subject of Mr Reinsalu's status as a lawyer. In fact, she thought there would never be a time and place to do that. She liked him, thought he was a genuinely kind man, and if he had chosen to take up the cause of Sergii's death as some route towards redemption that was none of her business.

She said, "She asked us not to inflame things further while her investigation is going on."

Mr Reinsalu shrugged. "That demonstration was none of our doing."

"Yes, I told her that."

Mr Reinsalu grunted and popped a couple of french fries into his mouth. He had not been pleased to learn that she had been taken to the police station, but his displeasure was balanced by the fact that they were now in contact with the person running the investigation. Just having confirmation that there *was* an investigation was quite a step forward.

"You asked her to share the products of her inquiries, of course."

Lenna nodded. "And she said she'd keep us up to date, as much as she's able."

He shook his head. "That's meaningless, I'm sorry. She's not obliged to tell us anything. All she's done is warn us to keep our mouths shut."

"I believed her. She doesn't want this thing to escalate."

"Oh, I don't doubt that at all."

"Well, none of us do. Do we?"

Mr Reinsalu looked thoughtful. "Did you notice that for months I have had very little response from the police, but the moment someone protested outside police headquarters they actually did something?"

"Yes," Lenna said. "They arrested me, as good as."

"I don't *want* to make trouble," he said, continuing the thought, "but perhaps we *should*, you know. Perhaps we've just been too polite up to now."

The problem was that they were not activists. They were amateurs. How had Jakobson put it? *A disbarred lawyer and a journalist whose personal life is so chaotic that nobody will employ her.* The only knowledge they had of campaigns was from watching them on the news. "I don't think just posting 'A March Is Happening, Come Along' on social media will end well," she said cautiously.

"No," Mr Reinsalu said, shaking his head. "That's a flash mob you're thinking of. No, there needs to be an *intelligence* behind this. Let me talk to some people."

COLD WATER

FIVE

1

First steps first. While Anatoly went off to discreetly find them some support, Carey took a bus out to the city's main cemetery.

How do you find a dead man? Well, one advantage of the dead was that they tended to stay put. In Maksim's case, his notional final resting place was an immense acreage of gravestones and tombs lined with trees near the edge of Gliwice. There were kiosks at the gate selling flowers and votive candles in little glass vases. She bought a bunch of tulips and walked down the main path of the cemetery towards the large old brick-built chapel at its heart. Poles took their dead seriously; everywhere she saw people tending the graves of relatives and friends, pulling up weeds, cleaning headstones, picking up wind-blown rubbish. On All Saints', this place would be as full as a football stadium. As it was, it was busier than any graveyard she'd seen in Texas.

Away to one side of the chapel, screened by a row of trees, was a smaller, newer building, stark and austere.

She pushed through the door and found herself in a little reception area panelled with pale wood and lined with pots of freshly cut flowers. There was a reception desk, but nobody about. Carey stood looking about her for a few moments, then she pressed the bell-push mounted on the desk. She didn't hear a buzzer or a bell, but after a couple of seconds a tall young man wearing a sober dark suit emerged from a door to one side of the reception area and bowed slightly and shook her hand.

"My name is Mazowiecki," he told her. "May I help?"

"It's a little difficult," Carey said, loading her body language with what she thought was the right amount of mourning sorrow. "A friend of mine was cremated here a month and a half ago. I've only just heard and I'd like to…" she held up the flowers and contrived to look a little helpless.

Mr Mazowiecki smiled. He had a nice smile. He seemed like a nice man, and Carey felt momentarily guilty for lying to him. "Certainly," he said. "What was the name?"

"Petrauskas. Maksim Petrauskas."

Mr Mazowiecki nodded. "I remember. A Lithuanian gentleman, I believe."

"Yes, that's right."

"Could you follow me, please?"

He led her through another door which opened into a little stone-flagged room, again lined with flowers. Two walls were given over to stone shelves, on which were arrayed a couple of dozen crematory urns, all of them the same fake-bronze design. Mr Mazowiecki walked up to one of the shelves and indicated an urn on a shelf at about chest height.

"Wait," Carey said, confused. She'd been hoping for a quick look at the documents pertaining to the cremation, not to stand here looking at Maksim's ashes. "He's still here? I thought you'd…" she mimed scattering.

"No arrangements were made for the disposal of the gentleman's remains," said Mr Mazowiecki. "It can sometimes take a little while for family or friends to come to a decision, and in those circumstances we retain them."

She looked at the rows of urns. "Who arranged the service?" she asked.

"An old gentleman," he said. "Very gruff. Excellent Polish, but I thought I detected a Russian accent."

So at least she had eyewitness testimony of Yegor's presence in the city. "Did many people turn up?" she asked. "It was very sudden."

"Yes, so I believe. No, perhaps half a dozen people. All men, all very well-dressed. Most of them about your age, if I may make so bold."

Mr Mazowiecki had a good eye and a better memory. She decided to push it a little further and said, "He had friends from many countries."

But Mr Mazowiecki wasn't about to be drawn on that. "Indeed," he said. "Would you like to spend some time alone?"

Would she? "Yes, that would be very kind."

"Take all the time you need," he said. "I'll be out in reception."

When he was gone, she looked at the urn. Well, there he was. Presumably. *Maksim Ilyich Petrauskas* and his dates engraved in a nice unassuming font on a little plate attached to the front of the urn. She noted that the birth date was wrong, five years younger than on his death certificate, which was a typical piece of Maksim vanity.

The question, really, was—if he'd been up to some sort of mischief here, as Kaunas and Stefan seemed to believe—why he'd been cremated under his own name. Why hadn't he been under false papers? Or had he simply had the misfortune to have been killed while he was carrying his own passport? She couldn't recall if he'd even *had* a passport in his own name. He was calling himself 'Konrad' when they first met. He spoke beautiful hochdeutsch and he'd been spending a lot of time with the anarchic little Coureur groups working out of Berlin. It was more than a year before he told her his real name and where he was really from, but by then she was incapable of surprise at anything he did.

She took a couple of photos of the urn, laid the tulips on the flagstones in front of the shelves, and went back to the reception area. Mr Mazowiecki was at the desk, arranging a pile of little books which set out the order of service for mourners. He looked up and smiled as she approached.

"Is everything in order?" he asked.

"It is, yes, thank you," she told him.

"Will you be taking the remains with you?"

"I'm sorry?"

He laid the last book on the pile. "Your friend's remains. Will you be taking them with you? Or shall we send them on to you?"

Well, she hadn't been expecting that. She briefly entertained an image of herself lugging Maksim around in her baggage, blinked it away. "Isn't that a matter for his next of kin?"

"He seems not to have had any. And the gentleman who arranged his funeral is now unavailable."

That was no great surprise. "I'm in transit at the moment, Mr Mazowiecki," she told him. "It's not really convenient for me to take the... right now. Can I get in touch later and let you know where to send them?"

He looked sad. "The other lady said that. Yes, of course. Please, at your own leisure."

"Someone else was here?"

Mr Mazowiecki narrowed his eyes at her fractionally, perhaps sensing a personal drama about which it might be better not to know. "Last week," he said guardedly. "A lady somewhat less than your height, perhaps some years younger. Very civil." In contrast to Carey, of course, who was not in the least bit civil.

"Did she say who she was?"

"A friend." He smiled. "Like yourself. She spoke no Polish, but her German was good, although I got the impression she had a hint of a Baltic accent."

Carey shook her head. "She doesn't ring a bell, I'm afraid. I didn't know all his friends."

"Indeed," he allowed, not seeming terribly convinced.

"I wonder, Mr Mazowiecki, if I could sign the book of condolence?"

He thought about this, for perhaps a little longer than was necessary. "Certainly," he said. "This way."

He led the way to another little side-room lined with flowers, where a large paper book lay open on a plinth. Lying on the pages of the book was a cheap ballpoint pen, shackled to the plinth by a long chain. Carey looked at this and considered the story it told, and found it unutterably sad, for some reason. She said, "Would it be possible for you to let me have a business card, Mr Mazowiecki? So I can call you later to make arrangements."

"Of course. I have some in the office. If you'll excuse me?"

When he was gone, she flipped back through the book until she'd found the day of Maksim's cremation. She didn't bother looking at the names, just photographed the pages, and by the time Mr Mazowiecki returned with his card, she was signing a name that she'd made up off the top of her head.

"Would you like to see the chapel?" he asked, handing her the card.

"Um," she said, surprised. "Yes, sure. Why not?"

The chapel was just as austere as the rest of the crematorium; the only outward sign of religion was a modest crucifix mounted on the front wall above the curtained dais where the coffin would rest before being rolled out into the cremation area beyond. There were two rows of pews, enough space for about thirty people, and a wooden lectern to one side of the dais.

Mr Mazowiecki had brought the pile of little books with him, and now he started going along the pews, leaving a copy every couple of feet. He said, "We don't conduct many services. Cremation has never really caught on in Poland, culturally. Except during the flu, of course."

Carey had thought the crematorium seemed unusually small. "You look too young to remember," she said.

He smiled. "My father worked here before me, and he told me stories. The government built a big facility outside town, and the flu victims were cremated there; we could never have coped here."

This seemed quite an unusual conversation to be having with someone who presented as a grieving friend. Carey watched him patiently laying out the books.

"Your friend," he said. "A car crash, yes?"

The penny finally dropped. "Mr Mazowiecki," she said.

"Witold," he said. "Witek."

"You knew who I was the moment I walked in here."

He straightened up and held the service books to his chest. "I'm sorry," he said. "That was cruel of me. Stefan said you'd probably come here."

She sighed. She really was getting sloppy. She thought of his brief visit to the office. "Does he know I'm here?"

He shook his head. "I'll mention it to him, at some point. Maybe in a few days. Stefan doesn't speak for all of us."

"He seems to think he does."

"He's very angry about what happened. We all are, I suppose, but he's letting it blind him, at a time when we need clear heads."

"What *did* happen?"

"You don't know?"

Carey shook her head. "Stefan just blurted out some confused stuff about Maksim causing trouble for you."

Witek looked at her a few moments, gathering his thoughts, then he went back to laying out the books. "He arrived about three months ago," he said. "At least, that's when we first became aware of him. There's a gang here who call themselves Rocketman. They're not very big and they're not very ambitious, but they are very smart. Technical boys. That's how they've managed to survive without the other gangs rolling over them, by offering a very high grade of technical services. We've used them ourselves, on occasion. The first we knew about your friend, he was involved in some kind of negotiation with them. We don't know what he wanted from them, but after he'd been here a week or so some of the other gangs started attacking each other for no reason we could discover. Some restaurants were torched, there was a gas explosion at a language school. It all got a bit exciting. There were a lot of deaths."

Starting a gang war seemed a bit of a stretch, even for Maksim. She said, "Stefan said something about him recruiting your people."

"That's Stefan's obsession," he said. "We can't be certain. But yes, some of our people have gone dark. They've taken holidays and not left contact procedures, stuff like that. Nobody knows where they are." He finished one block of pews, moved over to the other. "I wasn't here when all this happened. I had a Situation in Hindenberg. Just a milk run, some corporate data needed moving to Kraków, but I've got a Greater German passport so it made sense for me to go. When I got back, everything was in an uproar."

"So you just heard about it second-hand," she said. "You don't know for sure."

"The deaths and the property damage are real enough," he told her. He'd run out of books. He stood at the front of the chapel and looked at her. "And then it all suddenly stopped, and a couple of days later we conducted his service."

"What about the mourners? Were any of them local?"

He shook his head. "I heard a couple of them talking and they sounded Estonian, or maybe Finnish. Somewhere up at that end of the Baltic, anyway. They all looked as if they were ex-military, though, even the old Russian. No matter how you dress people like that up, the muscle memory never forgets."

"And the woman who turned up?"

"You don't know who she was?"

"I still haven't got a handle on how many people are involved in this, let alone who they all are."

"Not military, but not a civilian, either, I think. I thought at first she might be another Coureur, but now I wonder. She asked the same questions you did, though."

"Any name?"

"No."

"But another Balt, you thought."

"I thought so, yes."

She tried to make it all fit together in her head, but she was still missing too many pieces. "I could use some support," she said.

"Ah, no." He shook his head regretfully. "No, I'm sorry. Some of us disagree with how Stefan is handling this, but we all just want to be left alone. We're a small crew and all we've ever done is move corporate Packages. We're not into *excitement*."

They would also be watching to see how the independence thing shook out, and trying to prepare for the aftermath. "Aren't you at least curious?"

"I know enough to know this is out of our league, whatever it is."

It was unusual, and somewhat refreshing, to encounter a Coureur who knew their limits. Most of them maintained kudos by taking insane risks. "How about if I just called you if I needed something mansplained to me in the future?"

He shrugged. "You have my number."

He walked her to the exit. At the door, he said, "Was he really your friend, or was that just a story?"

She felt sorry she wouldn't be working with this kind, gentle young man. He seemed more than capable. She said, "I hadn't seen him in a long while, and we weren't friends by then, but yes, we were close once."

He inclined his head. "I'm sorry for your loss, then," he said. "And whatever it is you're doing here, I wish you luck."

BACK AT THE hotel, Anatoly reported that he had recruited a computer expert, a *pianist* in Coureur operational jargon.

"She's good," he said over dinner. "You'll like her."

"We'll still need a cobbler," Carey said. "And maybe a blacksmith too."

Anatoly nodded. "It's not difficult to pick up someone who's good with networks; all you have to do is a bit of research on the message boards. It's a bit harder to find forgers and artificers, especially if you don't want me to make waves." He sliced a piece off his steak. "Do we have an operational budget, by the way?"

She looked at him. "What have you promised her?"

"There are some hardware upgrades she's had her eye on. I have a list."

She thought about it. "Okay. Well, price it up and I'll take a look at it. All spending goes through me. And get receipts where you can; let's try to run this thing as shipshape as we're able." Ideally, for an op like this, she would also have had access to a stable of stringers to do the footwork, but she was just going to have to wing it.

"How did you do?" he asked.

"There's an urn with his name and dates on it," she said.

"For all I know, it's full of cigarette butts. About half a dozen mourners turned up for his service. One of them was probably Yegor, but no ID on the others. I photographed the condolence book, for whatever that's worth; one joker signed himself 'Rupert of Hentzau.'" She told him what Witek Mazowiecki had told her, and he thought about that for a while.

"And this was all, what, three months ago?"

"About that." Carey ate some of her bigos.

"I suppose the question is what all those military-type people have been doing in the interim," he said.

"It's certainly one of the questions." What she was hoping was that, shorn of their leader, they would have scattered and removed themselves from the equation. It would simplify things some.

"Could this actually have been a bona fide Situation?"

She'd been wondering about that herself. Kaunas had implied that it wasn't, but she wasn't inclined to trust him. Right about now Anatoly was the only person she knew for certain she *could* trust. She said, "Let's keep an open mind, for now."

They ate for a little while in silence. When they'd finished, the waiter cleared their plates and presented them with the dessert menu, which was basically a checklist of all the worst things for someone trying to watch their weight. Carey settled for a lemon sorbet; Anatoly spent a long time gazing longingly at the menu and then weakened and ordered a slice of chocolate torte.

"We're going to need somewhere else to stay," she said, watching the waiter heading to the kitchen for their orders. "Everybody and their dog knows we're here. And the restaurant bills are obliterating our budget."

He nodded. "I have that in hand. I'm going to look at somewhere tomorrow."

"You've been busy."

"Yes," he said. "Yes, I have." He looked at her for a few moments. "You know," he said, "eventually someone's going to notice we're asking about Maksim."

"I sure as hell hope so," said Carey. "I'm making enough noise."

2

A WEEK OR so after her chat with Raphael, she got a message telling her to be waiting outside Fort Thüngen, in Les Troi Glands, at a certain time. She got to the park early, found the squat little fortress, and stood near the bridge that led over the empty moat to the entrance. The fort was up on a hill, looking out across the Alzette valley towards Pfaffenthal and the High Town, a wooded vista of buildings and church spires, and it was breezy up here. There was not a soul about.

The rendezvous time came and went. Carey paced slowly back and forth in front of the fort. She walked over to the brow of the hill and looked at Luxembourg City. She went back to the little bridge. Ten minutes. Fifteen. Thirty. She called Raphael, but there was no answer. She left him a curt message.

Finally, cursing under her breath, she stomped off around the fort to the glass-and-steel edifice of the Museum of Modern Art behind it. She bought an open roast beef salad sandwich and a coffee in the museum's almost-empty restaurant, sat in a corner eating. She left Raphael another curt message.

Two men approached her table. They were both blond and of medium height, but one was stocky and the other was thin and gawky, all knees and elbows. They were both wearing masks.

Carey looked at them, standing side by side on the other side of the table. "What," she said.

The stocky one's eyes crinkled in a smile. There was something amused about his body language. He said, "I used to date the Rokeby Venus."

"Fuck off," she said, and went back to her sandwich.

"You're not really getting into the spirit of this, are you," he said.

"Put your mask on," the skinny one said. "You have to wear a mask indoors."

She gave him a hard look. "I'm eating."

"There's a thousand euro fine," the stocky one said, putting a hand in his pocket. For a moment, it seemed to Carey that she was surrounded by thousands of mosquitoes, then the noise rose beyond the range of human hearing. "And they also stop people reading your lips."

Carey laid down her knife and fork, dug a disposable mask from her bag, and put it on. "I don't like being stood up," she told them.

"Who does?" asked the stocky one cheerfully. "May we sit?"

"Would it make any difference if I said no?"

"None at all." They sat. "I'm Konrad," he said. "This is Oskari." He seemed to be finding the whole thing very amusing. "You want to go to Spain."

"I did when I got here this morning. I'm not so sure any more."

"Spain's tricky," he went on. "There's freedom of travel between the Schengen countries, but of course it's not Schengen any more. Also, they're having problems with the Catalonian separatists and the Basques again." He looked at her thoughtfully. "It would almost be easier to make you Spanish. You don't look Spanish, but Oskari doesn't look Finnish and I don't look German, so who knows?"

"You do look German," Oskari told him.

She looked from one to the other. "Is this some kind of performance art?" she said.

Konrad narrowed his eyes. "There is a performative aspect *to* it," he allowed. He turned to Oskari. "Fair?"

"There doesn't *have* to be," Oskari mused.

"Aw," said Konrad. "Sometimes you have to be a bit rowdy." He looked at Carey. "Was that right? 'Rowdy'? I'm still working on my English."

His English was fine. Oskari sounded vaguely Scandi, but Konrad only had a faint accent, although Carey didn't think it was German. She looked at her sandwich; she'd only eaten about half of it. She sat back and clasped her hands on the tabletop and looked at the two men.

"Who the hell are you guys?" she asked.

They performed a take so perfect it might have been rehearsed, looking at each other then looking at her. "We're *Les Coureurs des Bois*," said Konrad.

"Never heard of you," she said.

THEY DELIVERED MAIL. Which, in post-pandemic Europe, was not as straightforward as it sounded. Schengen, the borderless Europe of the EU's glory days, was quietly fracturing, bits breaking off around the edges. Nations found that border wire, erected to choke off freedom of movement and the spread of the flu, was actually rather moreish. Nation states were a big thing in Europe, that year. It was one of the reasons Carey wanted to go to Spain; as well as Catalunya and the Basque country, a handful of other regions were lobbying for autonomy or complete independence, and there were similar places in France and Germany. Europe was like an ice floe that was breaking up.

Konrad was coy about how many Coureurs there were. Carey suspected he just didn't know. "Less than a million," he said. "More than fifty." He didn't know how they'd come into being, who was running them. He spoke vaguely of Coureur Central and Founding Fathers.

Sometimes, they delivered people.

Two weeks after her meeting with Konrad and Oskari, there was a knock on her door. When she answered it, she found a scruffy youth in jeans and a long black coat standing outside in the corridor. He handed her a small envelope and walked off without saying a word.

The envelope contained a little booklet with carmine covers embossed in gold with the words Unión Europea ESPAÑA above a complicated coat of arms, and below it the word PASAPORTE. Inside was her own passport photo and her own date of birth, but apparently she had been born in Legazpi and her name was Verónica Torrejón Hernández and she had a husband named Miguel. The passport was well-used—it had been renewed before Spain had left the EU and it still had a couple of years left to run—and it had a current Luxembourg visa.

She was paging through the entry-exit stamps when her phone buzzed and she found she had received an e-ticket for the morning express to Madrid the next day, in the name of Verónica Torrejón Hernández. The ticket was followed by thirty-odd pages of regulations and restrictions and advisories.

Her phone rang. "Have the materials arrived?" asked Konrad.

"I have questions," Carey told him.

"And you wouldn't be human if you didn't," he told her. "But they can wait for now. I'll see you tomorrow."

"You will?" But he'd hung up.

THE NEXT MORNING, she tried to time things so she wasn't standing around Gare Lëtzebuerg for too long attracting attention. The morning rush-hour, such as it was, was over and when she arrived most of the people in the station were queueing for the Madrid express, and there were no more than a couple of hundred of them.

She joined the queue, checked in her ticket, had her temperature taken, and gave a swab and the name and address of the hotel she'd booked herself into in Madrid. She went through security, succumbed to a pat-down and a search of her bags when the detector gate gave her one of those annoying false positives, and she was almost at the back when she got to passport control. By this time, nerves were starting to get the better of her. She didn't know the exact procedure for what would happen if she was caught using false papers, but she assumed it would end with her being deported and banned from visiting Luxembourg—and possibly Europe—ever again. She tried to keep her breathing slow and even and remain casual at the same time. She had a very strong urge to step out of the queue and walk away, maybe feign illness to get back through security. She thought that would work; she was close enough to passing out as it was.

At the desk, the officer took her passport, typed its number into a terminal, checked the screen, glanced briefly at her, then stamped her exit visa and, lightheaded and stiff-legged, she walked out onto the platform and boarded the train. Just like that.

She found her seat. She had the carriage almost to herself, just a couple of people further along near the front. She put her bags in the luggage racks at the end of the carriage, sat down, and took a long, slow, shaky breath.

"Hi," said a voice.

She looked up. A stocky man with mousy brown hair was putting his hand luggage into the overhead rack. He took off his mask, and she saw a young, kind-looking face. She said, "Please, put your mask back on."

"The train's deep-cleaned at both ends of the journey," he told her, slipping into the seat beside her. "It's sealed until we reach Madrid. We're well outside minimum distance from other passengers and we've all been tested. And we're married, so we're exempt. I'm Miguel, by the way."

She'd only ever seen him wearing a mask, but she recognised his voice. "Why's your hair brown?"

"That would be a long story," Konrad said.

"What are you doing here?"

"That also would be a long story, but I have some business on the coast." He didn't say which one. "I thought I'd kill two birds with one stone. A moment, please." He put his hand in his pocket, and there was that momentary insect-whine again, rising in pitch until it was impossible to hear it.

"What's that?" she asked.

"Something that confuses microphones." He saw the look on her face. "Don't worry, nobody's onto you. A lot of businesspeople go back and forth on this train; you sort of take it for granted that someone's slipped the cleaning staff a couple of hundred euros to plant a few bugs in every carriage, see what they pick up." He settled back in his seat. "I was a few people behind you going through the controls. You did okay."

The way he said it made her feel as if she'd passed some obscure kind of test, and that made her feel grumpy. "You didn't give me a lot of time to think about it."

"Second thoughts," he said, shaking his head. "To be avoided, if at all possible. But you did okay, for your first time."

"How do you know this is my first time?"

"Oh," he said mysteriously, "you learn to tell."

The train manager came through the carriage, making one last ticket check. "Please put your mask on, sir," he said to Konrad.

"But we're married," Konrad protested, indicating Carey, who tried to look married. "There's nobody within…" he craned his neck to look over the seat in front, "… at least five metres of us."

"Regulations, sir," the train manager told him. "Please put your mask on, or I'll have to ask you to leave the train."

Konrad dug his mask out of his pocket and put it on unwillingly. The train manager gave them one last look, then moved on along the carriage.

"Told you," Carey said quietly.

IT WAS AN eleven-hour journey from Luxembourg to Madrid, the majority of it with France blurring past the window at several hundred miles an hour. The towns they passed through were quiet; the countryside seemed deserted and overgrown. Konrad made small talk for a while, then he put on a pair of goggles and an earbud set and embarked on what sounded like a long and dull conference with someone. Carey tuned him out, read for a couple of hours, then pulled up her notes and started to cut together a couple of articles. Konrad might have wanted to leave her no time for second thoughts, but she'd had some interviews lined up for the rest of the week, and she'd had to cancel them at short notice so she needed to file something in a hurry.

Her mind wasn't on it, though. She nudged Konrad, who lifted his goggles and blinked at her. "I'm going to have something to eat," she told him. "Want me to bring you a sandwich or something?"

He shook his head. "I'll go later."

She took her bag down from the rack and walked two carriages back to the dining car, where they were only allowing ten people in at a time. The food was airline stuff on disposable TV dinner trays. She picked at dim sum and sweet and sour pork, drank a glass of beer. Looking out of the window, she saw the view was blocked in the middle distance by a high fence, its mesh so dense that she could barely see through it. She watched it go by for quite some time; it just kept coming, mile after mile of it.

Back in her carriage, Konrad was still on his conference, or maybe it was another one. She tapped him on the shoulder to let her back in her seat. "How's the food?" he asked.

"Harmless. What's that?" She nodded out of the window, where the fence was still going by in the distance.

"What's what?" He squinted out of the window, eyes still adjusting from being goggled into a conference space. "Oh. That's the Line."

"What line?"

"The Line. The Trans-Europe Rail Route."

"Oh." She settled into her seat and looked again. "*Oh.*" It hadn't occurred to her that she'd actually see it. "Where's the other end now?"

"Chersky," he said without seeming to think about it. "Sakha Republic. They're already running services, to take workers in and out. That's how that guy got out. The journalist."

She frowned at him. "Meyer? He never said anything about the Trans-Eur—the Line."

Konrad snorted. "I know a guy who was mixed up in that. He bribed a port official at Ambarchik to let him ashore, then he got someone to drive him out to the railhead west of Chersky and he got on a train with a bunch of Line workers and just rode all the way back to Paris. Took him six weeks."

Carey thought of all Meyer's dispatches from the various stops on his journey. "He said he did it mostly by car."

Konrad chuckled. "He rented himself a farmhouse outside Meaux and just wrote all that stuff from what he'd seen from the train and people he'd talked to on the way. Then the stupid bastard went into town one day and a drunk drove into his car and when the Gendarmerie checked his papers there was a discrepancy between the address on his visa and the place he was actually living and they just booted him out."

"They gave him a Pulitzer," Carey said, half to herself, watching the fence finally dwindling into the distance as their train angled away from it.

"Journalists," Konrad said. "Can't trust any of them. No offence." He pulled the goggles down over his eyes again. "Still," he said thoughtfully as he tapped his pad to reopen his conference, "hell of a trip, that. Six weeks on a train."

THEY CROSSED THE border at San Sebastian in the early evening, and a couple of hours later they pulled into Estación de Atocha. Carey felt cramped and stiff after so long on the train—designers never thought about tall people when they were coming up with public transport. Konrad, on the other hand, had slept from around Bordeaux and he seemed fresh as a daisy, which was irritating.

The international platforms at the station were screened off with fencing that looked as if it had started out as temporary but was now starting to look permanent. They queued up to have temperatures and swabs taken again, and somehow she and Konrad got separated as the passengers funnelled towards the passport desks. Carey handed her Spanish passport over, got another brief look, and passed through. Same story at customs, no one paid her any attention, she just walked through; she thought she caught sight of Konrad at one of the customs tables, his suitcase open in front of him and a uniformed officer going through its contents.

She waited outside in the concourse. It was a lot busier here than Luxembourg had been; Spain had not had a case of the flu for over a year and people seemed to be coming out of hiding. It was a long time since she'd seen this many people in one place and it made her feel a little claustrophobic.

"Well," Konrad said, emerging from the arrivals doors, "that was fun."

"Smuggling something, were we?" she asked.

He grinned. "Nah. Spot check."

Someone jostled past Carey, and a moment later she realised that her bag, which she'd put down beside her feet, was gone. "Shit!"

"What?" Konrad asked, concerned.

"Some bastard's stolen my bag."

Konrad swore in a language she didn't recognise. "Did you see who took it?"

"No," she said, looking around the concourse. "Someone bumped into me and it was gone." Over on the far side, she thought she caught sight of a shock of blond hair, gawky elbows shoving people out of the way, but a moment later they were lost among the crowds. "Shit!" She gathered herself. "Right. Let's find a cop."

"You can't do that," he said.

"The hell I can't."

"You're here on false papers," he said calmly. "You don't even know how to find the address you're supposed to be living at. If you give a statement to the police you'll last about ten minutes."

She glared at him. "I'll wing it," she said.

"No," he said, taking her arm gently, and she had to physically restrain herself from decking him. "Think about it. All they have to do is ask you a few routine questions and you won't be able to answer any of them. You'll be in jail by this time tomorrow; the Spanish take this kind of thing *very* seriously."

"The guy at passport control hardly looked at my passport, that's how seriously they take it."

"What was in the bag? Anything valuable?"

"Just clothes. Everything valuable's in here." She hefted her shoulder bag.

"So, is it worth risking jail, just for a bag of clothes?" he asked reasonably.

"It's my clothes, dammit," she said. "It's *all* my clothes. I don't have anything else to wear. Let go of my arm."

He let go. "Listen," he said, "it's up to you, obviously. But this little adventure has cost you a lot of money and no small amount of risk, and a lot of people have put a lot of time into it." He was talking quickly but calmly, keeping his voice pitched just loud enough for her to hear. "You're going to throw all that away within an hour of setting foot in the country, for a bag of clothes."

She kept glaring at him. Thing was, he was right. She'd been expecting to be arrested at any point between Luxembourg and here, and instead it had worked perfectly. She was where she wanted to be, and attracting the attention of the authorities could only jeopardise that.

She said, "Dammit."

Konrad took a half-step back and it was only when he relaxed that she realised how tense he was. "Good." The laugh lines around his eyes crinkled up. "Look, I have to be somewhere in an hour, but how about dinner later? I'll call you at your hotel."

She nodded, already thinking about how much it was going to cost to replace her clothes, and then justifying it by telling herself she'd packed for Central Europe and she'd have had to buy lighter clothes for Spain anyway. "Okay. Yeah, I'd like that, I think."

He smiled again and started to walk away. "And try to stay out of trouble," he said as he moved away into the crowd.

And she did, mostly, but it was almost a year before she saw him again.

3

THE FIRST THING Krista did, on leaving the museum, was stop off at a kiosk and buy a five-pack of preloaded disposable phones. She did this almost on autopilot, knowing that Jakobson would be having her phone monitored, barely aware that she was already creating a secret life for herself, a place of safety.

For a moment, stepping away from the kiosk into the snow and the crowds on the town square, she experienced a dislocation so profound that she was unsure where, and who, she was. She was still young, kept herself in shape, but for that brief moment she thought she might be having a stroke.

Then it passed, and she was looking across the square and everything was familiar and her father was under investigation for murder. The two things refused to butt together.

She turned and looked in the direction of the police station. She couldn't see it from here, but from the outside, it looked no different from the other buildings on the square, a Hanseatic frontage indistinguishable from its neighbours save for a discreet sign by the front door. Behind the façade, though, was a state-of-the-art facility, a series of nested cubes that went several floors beneath ground, connected by a maze of corridors and blast doors. It was a product of its time, of the war on terror, which had been going on for as long as anyone could remember. She'd liked the place; it had a quiet sense of purpose, of putting one's shoulder to the wheel and getting the job done. She'd spent an appreciable part of her professional life there. But now it seemed unfamiliar, like a faintly sinister illustration in a child's book of fairy stories.

This was how life changed, without warning or time to prepare. One moment you were doing your job, unaware that catastrophe was barrelling towards you from decades before. The next moment, you were in an interview room being grilled about your father. And the moment after that you were standing outside in the snow, wondering if you would ever set foot inside your place of work again, and if you would recognise it if you did.

Did I brief the team? she thought. She couldn't remember. There was a blank spot somewhere between arriving at work that morning and sitting down in the interview room with Jakobson. Tamburlaine was still, as far as she was concerned, in the frame for this outrage. It was his style; he fancied himself a Machiavellian, a manipulator of people and events, although he was also quite content to employ a fantastic amount of violence when it suited him. And even if he wasn't responsible, it would be unforgivable if this ridiculous accusation against her father resulted in the Chechen mob gaining a foothold in the city.

There was too much to think about. She took out her phone and dialled a number.

"It's ridiculous," Markus said. "Isn't it?"

For a fraction of a second, she had the strongest urge to slap him, but it passed. "Yes, Markus," she said tiredly. "Yes, it really is."

They were sitting in a café not far from the university. Her call had caught him working late and they'd decided to meet here rather than at his place or hers because she didn't think she could face public transport right now.

"There was something on the news about some sort of demo outside police headquarters earlier," he said. "Was that something to do with this?"

She felt cold. "I don't know. Did they mention my father?"

He shook his head. "I don't think so. Just something about police brutality."

Krista rubbed her eyes. It was only a matter of time before her father's name was mentioned, and then everything would just get out of control.

He said, "So, what happens now?"

"Now? Well, I'm unofficially suspended while the investigation continues. They say I'm on leave, but they'd have me escorted out of the building if I tried to go to work. I'm not allowed to talk about it to anyone."

"You're talking about it to me."

"You're not anyone."

He sat back and looked at her. He was a big, untidy man, his university security pass still hanging on its lanyard round his neck. He was smart enough and secure enough in his own ego to understand that she wasn't here for a hug. Hugs never actually solved anything, just put off the moment when you had to face things. What she was really here for was to vent at someone, and for the moment Markus was the only person she trusted.

"What about this journalist? The one who contacted the police?"

"I'll probably be arrested if I go within a hundred metres of him," she said. "Anyway, I don't know who he is."

"He's not going to publish?"

"Jakobson's managed to convince him to sit on it, for the moment, but that's not going to last long. You know what the media are like; it's a miracle it hasn't leaked already."

"Is there anything I can do? Nobody's told *me* to stay out of it."

Bless him. "You're a geography teacher, Markus, not an investigator."

"Geography *lecturer*."

She smiled and shook her head. "I don't want any collateral damage. But if I think of something, I'll let you know." She looked round the café. "I should go."

"You sure you want to be on your own right now?"

"Yeah. I want a long hot shower and an early night." She gathered her things together. "Call you tomorrow."

"Sure." If he was hurt, he didn't show it. They were both adults. He did, in the end, give her a hug. "Sleep well."

* * *

AND SHE DID, almost. Back home, she left a trail of discarded clothing across the flat and stood for a very long time under the shower with the water dialled up as hot as it would go. Later, she microwaved the leftovers of a Thai takeaway from a couple of days ago, sat curled up on the sofa in her thick fluffy bathrobe and flicked through the channels on the entertainment set. The news, as it had been for some weeks, was more or less evenly divided between the upcoming parliamentary elections and the ever-evolving soap opera that was the rest of Europe. Estonia, Latvia, and Lithuania had never fallen for the wider European fashion for Balkanisation; unlike other nations, they had thrown off no statelets or polities or communes, and they displayed a sturdy confraternity which had led some to suggest throwing wire around their common border and declaring a Baltic federation. Elsewhere, there seemed to be, scanning through videos and presentations, a lot of anger out there, and she wondered how it had passed her by. She'd been more focused on the Tamburlaine investigation than she'd realised.

Her phone rang, and she cursed herself for not switching it off. She sat where she was and waited it out, and presently it stopped ringing. And a few moments later started to ring again.

She sighed and got up from the sofa. It was probably not Markus; he'd got the point that she didn't want to be disturbed—although with Markus you could never be sure. He might just be making a quick check that she was okay, and if she didn't answer it wasn't beyond him to turn up at her door. It could conceivably be Kustav wondering what the hell was going on, or Tamm, or Jakobson. None of these were people she could just ignore. Well, maybe Tamm.

As it turned out, it was none of them.

"Krista?" said a familiar voice. "It's Erik Lill."

She scowled. "We shouldn't be talking to each other, Erik," she said.

There was a pause. "So you know about it?"

"I spent most of the day with Internal Affairs."

"Jakobson?"

"And a couple of wingmen. She's spoken to you?"

"They just left. They gave me notice of a formal interview tomorrow."

"Then we definitely shouldn't be talking to each other."

"Fuck 'em," Lill growled. "What did they say to you?"

"That *Paps* is implicated in a suspicious death twenty years ago. Maybe more than one."

"This is... *insane*," he said. Lill had been her father's secretary, sidekick, aide de camp, confidante, driver and general bagman for the final five years or so of his career. Krista was amazed that Jakobson hadn't hit him first. "He's barely cold in his grave."

"Erik," she said, "we have to stop talking now; you could be arrested just for calling me."

"You think I *care*?" Lill was on long-term sick leave, crossing the days off his calendar as he approached retirement. "Did he ever talk to you about this?"

"How could he? It never happened. You don't *believe* it, do you?"

"No, of course I don't. Do you really think the police service could keep something like this quiet for so long?"

"It looks like someone tried. According to Jakobson the original complaint was just... ignored. Not even buried, just ignored."

Lill snorted. "A bunch of police officers going round murdering Russians? That would have stayed secret for about five minutes. It's ridiculous."

"They have to investigate, whether it's ridiculous or not," she reminded him. "To find out why nothing was done about the complaint in the first place, if nothing else."

"Are you going to do anything about it?"

"Like what?"

"He was your *father*, Krista."

"Yes, thank you, Erik, that had slipped my mind."

He was silent for a few moments, getting control of his anger. "I'm sorry; that was awful of me."

"There's nothing I *can* do," she told him in what she hoped was a kindly tone of voice. "I've been put on leave and told not to go anywhere near the investigation. If Jakobson finds out we've even been talking to each other about it the most optimistic thing I can expect is demotion."

"This is a matter of principle."

"It probably wouldn't matter too much to me, but you could lose your pension," she pointed out. "It's all very well having principles until you can't afford to feed yourself."

He thought about that. She almost heard him straightening his shoulders and tucking in his chin. "We must fight this, regardless," he said.

Yes, she thought. *We must*. She said, "Let me think about this. Don't call me again. I'll call you."

"What should I tell them tomorrow?"

"Jesus, Erik, have you listened to nothing I've said? Tell them the truth. There's nothing to be afraid of."

"There's always something to be afraid of," he said, and he hung up before she could ask him what he meant.

SHE WAS WOKEN by her alarm the next morning. She stumbled cursing into the bathroom and had been standing under the shower for at least five minutes before remembering that there was no reason for her to be up this early. She wasn't going to work; she'd forgotten to switch off her alarms.

"Idiot girl," she murmured to herself, resting her forehead against the tiles of the shower.

Well, she could either go back to bed or she could carry on getting on with the day. The shower had brought her back to consciousness and she didn't think she'd be able to go back to sleep, so she dried herself and dressed in a tee shirt and yoga pants and went into the kitchen to stand in front of the fridge. Lately, breakfast had consisted of a cup of coffee, lunch had been a sandwich and a piece of fruit at her desk, and dinner had depended on which takeaway she passed on the way home, so there wasn't much to choose from, but there were a couple of eggs and some bacon that was only a day or so past its use-by date, so she used those to make herself some scrambled eggs and sat watching the dawn trying to fight its way through the clouds, forking food into her mouth without tasting it. She made a mental note to go food shopping later.

When eight o'clock rolled around she took out one of the disposable phones and called Kustav. The first thing he said was, "Are you okay, boss?"

"I'm fine," she said. "Do you know what happened?"

"I know you spent the day with the vultures," he said. The older generation of officers—and quite a few of the younger ones—had a very low opinion of Internal Affairs. "What's it about?"

"I can't talk about it," she said. "I'm not under investigation, but I've been put on leave until IA have finished, so you're going to have to stand in for me."

"Okay. How long do you think you'll be gone?"

"I don't know. Not long, I hope. Don't let the investigation slump, Kustav. Keep on pushing. Whatever's going on, we can't let it distract us from Tamburlaine, understood?"

"Understood."

"When I do come back, I want to find everything in good order, okay?"

He was quiet a few moments. "Is this about the colonel, boss?"

She felt a cold finger trace its way down the back of her neck. "Why?"

"IA went to see Erik Lill yesterday evening."

That was the police grapevine for you; faster than the speed of light. You could use it to transmit messages to civilisations orbiting distant stars. One more reason to believe that this whole thing was a mistake. As Lill had said the previous evening, it would simply have been impossible to keep a death squad secret.

She said, "I can't talk about it, Kustav. Maybe when it's all over."

"Okay." He sounded doubtful. "If there's anything I can do, let me know."

"Thank you," she said. "Just keep on top of everything there and I'll be back as soon as I can."

"What should I tell the others, boss?"

"Tell them I've been called away for a while," she said. It was true enough, as far as it went. "Tell them if I find out they've been fucking around while I'm gone heads will roll."

He chuckled. "Will do. Boss?"

"Yes?"

"Take care."

She smiled. "Thank you, Kustav. You too. I'll be in touch."

She hung up and sat staring at the window. Fat flakes of snow were drifting past beyond the glass.

Is this about *the colonel*? She should, she supposed, address the elephant in the room. The near-legendary thirty-six-year veteran elephant in the room, lavishly decorated and universally adored.

He was a hard act to follow, if you wanted to be a police officer in Tallinn. His public profile had receded into a great multimedia pile of yellowing press clippings and forgotten web pages, but he still stood tall in institutional memory.

He'd come late to the force, in his late twenties, after university and a string of short-lived, unsatisfactory jobs.

In one address to a class at the police school he'd said that policing had never previously occurred to him, that it had been a spur-of-the-moment thing, but Krista thought he was being disingenuous. Nothing was ever left to chance—the man she remembered would have made a list of jobs that interested him and worked through them. Looked at from that perspective, the police force was about a third of the way down the list.

Still, he'd been an exemplary cadet, close to the top of his class. His probationary period had been exemplary, too, a string of glowing assessments. A couple of years on the street and he'd been fast-tracked out of uniform and into a new Criminal Intelligence unit. CI eventually span off a whole organisation chart of smaller units—the Gangs Taskforce was one of them—but for quite a while it had belonged to her father, and he had brought it to bear on the many facets of the city's organised crime.

It was not admitted to the general public, but it was axiomatic that you could not break organised crime, just as you could not win the war on drugs—one might as well try to defeat the weather. It was, however, possible to win significant victories, and significant victories was what her father achieved. "We put them on *notice*," her Uncle Märt—not really her uncle, just one of the extended family of cops who had decided to take over her upbringing after her mother died—told her once.

No one lives for ever, of course, and as the colonel's career entered its final laps before retirement he moved, increasingly, towards administrative roles. He did not always do this willingly; he was a street cop by nature, and he chafed at office work—had, in fact, declined multiple promotions in order to remain at the sharp end of things.

My father the murderer. For a brief, transgressive moment, she tried the idea on for size before dismissing it once and for all. The colonel had been tough, but he had been straight. He'd seen too many cases falter and fall in the courtroom because someone had done something they should not, or had neglected to do something they should have. He had drummed this into her over and over again during her time at the police school, and during her probation, and her time on the beat, and her slow rise from the ranks. There were few things in this life worse than watching some lowlife you'd spent months building a case against walk free because you, or some subordinate, had not followed, for example, the proper protocol for a chain of evidence. There were no shortcuts in the law, and those who tried to take them were doomed to fail. Her father wouldn't have allowed it. It was that simple.

So what the fuck was going on?

SIX

1

"Have you any idea," asked Carey, "what a Fujitsu-Cray nitrogen-cooled mini-supercomputer actually costs?"

Magda sat primly in the room's other armchair and blinked slowly at her from beneath long eyelashes.

"The peripherals we can do," Carey went on, scanning down the pianist's wish list. "But we're not made of money."

"He wants me to hack the police," Magda said, nodding at Anatoly, who was perched on the edge of the bed.

"I've seen people hack the local law with their *phone*," Carey told her. "You don't need a freaking supercomputer."

Magda shrugged. She was tall and slim and she had long hennaed hair. She was wearing a long black and purple velvet dress, which set off her pale skin and huge kohl-rimmed eyes. She claimed to be twenty, but Carey thought she looked no more than fourteen. "If it's that easy, get him to do it." Nodding at Anatoly again.

Carey shook her head. "No supercomputer." Reaching the bottom of the list, she said, "What the hell is a *cloth laptop*?"

"It's a Russian thing," Anatoly said uncomfortably. "The FSB developed them. Back when the FSB meant something."

Carey raised an eyebrow at him. She looked at Magda, who said, "Souvenir."

"No souvenirs, darling."

"I can find you a... what do you call it? A *cobbler*." The girl's self-possession was startling. She was going to be quite scary when she grew up, Carey thought.

"I think I can source one," Anatoly offered. "A cloth laptop." He didn't sound particularly happy at the prospect.

"How?" asked Carey.

"Best you don't know."

Carey looked at him a moment longer, then she looked at Magda again. "Okay. No supercomputer, but you get the rest of the shiny. How does that sound?"

"I want him," Magda said, looking at Anatoly. "He's cute."

Anatoly blushed, but Carey smiled. Magda was feisty, and she had a twisted sense of humour, and she liked that. What kind of pianist she was remained to be seen. Carey said, "You'll have to audition if I'm going to spend all this money on you."

The girl looked around the room, then pointed at the paperscreen on the wall. "Can I use that?"

"Sure, go for it."

Magda looked at Anatoly. "Give me your phone, cutie."

Looking bewildered and annoyed in roughly equal measure, he handed his phone over, and Magda took it over to the wall and made a connection with the screen. Then, with a series of moves more elegant than Carey could ever have managed, she swiped and air-typed and pasted through a sequence of browsers and menus and dialogue boxes, and after about ten minutes she had a pair of documents side by side on the screen.

Carey got up and went over to look. One of the documents was the record of her entry into the country from Greater Germany almost a week ago, a complete dump of the data from the false passport on which she was travelling. The other document was from Anatoly's passage through immigration at Bydgoszcz airport on his Imre Kovacs passport. She scrolled up and down through it, reading the codes and notations the passport had picked up since she'd had it made for him two years ago. He'd made a couple of visits to England, which she hadn't known about, but he was over eighteen and he could go where he wanted. If he felt like getting himself arrested, that was his problem.

She turned to Magda and nodded. "Okay, honey, we'll be in touch. We've got to do a bit of due diligence now."

"And how do you plan to do that without my help?" the girl asked.

Fair point. Carey narrowed her eyes fractionally. "We'll get by for now. Go home, but keep yourself handy."

Magda attempted to win a staring contest with Carey, but that was never going to happen, and in the end she just nodded, collected her cloth shoulder bag from the floor, and left the room.

Anatoly stood next to Carey and looked at the passport data on the screen. "Well, *I'm* impressed anyway," he said.

Carey snorted. "She's probably been wandering around in the Immigration Service database since she was old enough to buy her own Doc Martens; she had a backdoor already set up so she could put on a show for us. But yeah, it's promising. Does she check out?"

"As far as I can see."

"Okay, let's put her to work then." She looked at the screen again. "You really think you can lay your hands on one of these cloth laptop things?"

"Yes."

Something in his voice, a sort of stoic misery, made her glance at him. "You're not planning on doing something stupid, are you?"

"We just hired a teenage goth to wrangle our network needs," he said. "I'm not sure where 'stupid' even begins on this job."

"ARE YOU SURE you need to recruit all these people?" asked Kaunas.

"I know some people in Madrid who could do the job, but they'd be off their home ground," Carey told him. "Plus, they wouldn't come. And you and the locals don't seem inclined to help."

"Yes," he said thoughtfully, looking out into the distance. "The locals were a surprise, I will admit."

They were back on their bench in Park Chopina. Today it was Carey's turn for the chicken salad sandwich. She said, "How much do you know about what was going on here?"

"Very little, as I said. Word reached us that Maksim had been here and that he'd subsequently been killed in an accident."

She didn't believe that for a moment. If that was all it was, they wouldn't have sent for her. "And you didn't try to find out, yourself?"

"That's what we're doing now," he told her. "Finding out."

Carey took a bite of her sandwich. It was pretty good; better than the ham and mustard option. "I think you're right about the accident," she said. "There's something else going on there, but I won't have any better idea until I can get a proper look at the police documents; stuff seems to be missing from the material you gave me. It sounds as if he was trying to set something up with one of the local gangs, though." She didn't mention the gang war; it might have had nothing to do with Maksim, and anyway, if Kaunas had done his homework he'd already know about it. "He seems to have had a crew of his own, though. At least half a dozen, maybe ex-military. That's enough to cause some trouble, if he was of a mind."

Kaunas sighed. "Did he have any connection with Gliwice? Business interests?"

"Not while I knew him." Although that, of itself, was not definitive. She hadn't known about Helsinki until it had been too late. "It's been ten years, Kaunas. For all I know, he was running half of Europe's organised crime."

"We'd have heard about that," Kaunas said absently. He tried his own sandwich, but it didn't seem to give him any great pleasure. "There has been something of a breakdown of communication with the local Coureurs."

Tell your masters. "Yeah, I kind of figured that. You might have mentioned it earlier."

"I didn't want to colour your judgement. Do you have any sense of what we've done to offend them?"

"I got the impression they think you sent Maksim in here to piss them off."

He sat for a while, watching a young guy in shorts and a tee shirt throwing a frisbee for a quite enormous German Shepherd. The dog seemed to be having the time of its life, which was good because it looked as if it could tear someone's leg off if it got annoyed. "So," he said finally. "What's your reading of the situation? How serious would you say it is?" What he really meant was *how does this affect us?*

"He came in here and started throwing his weight around, and that upset the locals, but that was Maksim. He was talking to one of the local gangs, but again, that was Maksim." She shrugged. "The thing with the police is unusual, though. They *could* be covering up for a botched pursuit, but I think there's more to the story, and I'd like to know what that is, at least."

Kaunas said, "I have to be somewhere else tomorrow."

"Fine. I don't need my hand holding."

He looked at her. "I know it's none of my business," he said, "but perhaps you should consider working on your people skills."

"People skills are wasted on people."

He looked at her a moment longer, then got up to leave. "I'll be in touch."

MAGDA'S COUSIN BOKSI—Carey never found out his real name—looked, if anything, younger than her, but that might just have been something to do with him turning up wearing his school uniform. Anatoly was out on some unspecified errand, so it was left to her to do the boggling for them both.

"Boksi doesn't talk much," Magda told her.

"No kidding."

Boksi was short and pale, with a great mop of black hair. He reached into his schoolbag and handed over a plastic card and a little green booklet. Carey turned them over in her hands. The card was a New Zealand passport in the name of Anna French. It had her photo embossed on the front. The little booklet, an Irish passport, also had her photo in it and the name Mary White. She couldn't tell how good the New Zealand passport was without a little widget to read its data, but it looked kosher. The Irish one, though, was a work of art. It looked as if Mary White had been doing a lot of travelling since it was issued five years ago; it was a bit worn and creased and its pages were full of different visa stamps. Carey leafed through it and gave Boksi a level look.

"You did this?" she asked, holding the passport up.

Boksi nodded.

"Can you do driver's licences?"

Boksi nodded.

"I'll have a licence to go with each of these passports," she told him. "And you're on the payroll."

"We know a blacksmith, too," Magda said.

THE HOUSE ANATOLY had found was on a street called Zimnej Wody, tucked away between the polytechnic and the canal about twenty minutes' walk from the market square. The street was busy with students during the day and quiet at night. The house stood on its own at the end of a long block of apartments, and it looked like an architectural experiment, three stories of wood and brick and glass with a little walled garden at the back.

Inside, it was all polished wood floors, white walls and minimalist furniture. The kitchen resembled a 1950s vision of the future and there was a big studio on the top floor lit by big windows and skylights.

"It was built as a show-house," the letting agent told them. "A proof of concept. It's actually quite famous, in certain architectural circles."

Carey looked around the big ground-floor living room. "I never lived in a famous house before," she said.

The agent, a young man who had introduced himself as Bogdan, was wearing a dove-grey three-piece from the Armani Revival and a collarless black shirt done up at the neck. His shoes were works of art. He said, "Its security system is state-of-the-art."

"Well, you wouldn't want anyone breaking into such a famous house," Carey said. She smiled at him and walked to the back of the room, where sliding glass doors led out onto a patio and steps down into the garden. Above the wall, she could see the long monolithic block of the main polytechnic building stretching into the distance. She wondered who in their right mind would want to live here, notwithstanding the house's fame. She turned and beamed at Bogdan. "We'll take it."

THEY WALKED BACK into the centre of town. At the top of Zimnej Wody was a big, busy intersection. Left to right ran Częstochowska, and diagonally off that ran Konarskiego, both of them four-lane roads. Straight ahead was Kłodnica, a narrower, bumpy street that ran along the canal towards the town centre.

Kłodnica came out on another wide, busy road, this one with tramlines running along it. On the other side of the road was an enormous brick-built church. Carey thought she was starting to get her head around the place; there was a scruffy pedestrian walk beside the church, alongside the canal, which led to Zwycięstwa. So long as she had some idea where she was with relation to that, she figured she'd be okay.

They crossed the road and walked past the church. There was a little group of people outside with placards carrying that *Nie!* poster of the grim pope. One of them stepped forward and thrust an animated flyer into Carey's hand as she went by. She glanced at it, saw the beatific face of Christ drifting among the clouds over a united Poland, and folded it up and stuffed it in her pocket. "This country's going to drive me out of my mind," she said.

"One would hope not," Anatoly told her.

"Is Rus like this?" She'd never visited, either for work or pleasure, although Maksim had had a lot of Russian contacts. He'd also had a lot of Ukrainian contacts, courtesy of some familial connection of his mother's, and every now and again he'd talk about 'doing something' about the country, although he'd never said what.

"Oh, it's worse," said Anatoly. "But in different ways."

"You know we're being tailed?"

He nodded. "The young couple with the baby in the pram." Carey remembered them passing by at her first meeting with Kaunas in the Palmiarnia. "And the kid on the skateboard on the other side of the road," Anatoly added. "And the older gentleman up ahead of us, the one with the green coat and the hat. And the businessman looking in the window of the chemist's shop."

She'd missed the older guy, but it was obvious now he'd been pointed out to her. She was getting too old for this shit. "Stefan's people," she said. "Coureurs."

One of them, at least. Anatoly wasn't so sure they all were; they didn't seem to be working as a team, although you could put that down to amateurishness. "They're not very good, whoever they are. They're attracting more attention than we are."

"That's probably deliberate," she said. "To remind us we're not welcome here."

Anatoly thought about it, shook his head. "No," he said. "No, I think they're just not very good."

It would be fairly straightforward to shake them off, but it was going to be annoying if she had to do that every time she wanted to go somewhere. She wondered if it was worth having a word with Witek Mazowiecki, see if he could get Stefan to see sense.

"We should give them a slap," she said. "While we're here."

But Anatoly wasn't worried about the Coureurs, or whoever the other tails belonged to. What he was worried about was the unassuming little middle-aged man who had been walking his wire-haired terrier under the trees beside the canal on Zimnej Wody when they left the house. He'd gone off in the opposite direction to them, but there he was now, a little way ahead on the other side of the road, and he'd somehow managed to find the time to dump the dog and change his clothes.

* * *

Magda's cousin, Boksi the boy cobbler, knew someone who knew someone who knew someone who knew someone named Romek. To Carey's relief, Romek was at least an adult, if not by much. He was a stout, sad-faced boy in his twenties and he wore a long black overcoat and biker boots. His head was shaved and there was a row of little silver rings decorating the rim of his right ear.

He'd said to meet him at a church on the edge of the Old Town. They spent a leisurely hour or so shaking off the Coureur tails following them from the hotel, but as they approached the church Anatoly spotted the unassuming little man he'd seen the previous day, standing in a bookshop perusing a big hardcover art book. He was standing by the window, tilting the book to the light so he could appreciate its colour plates better, and also so that he could keep an eye on the street without seeming to.

"There's something I forgot to do," Anatoly said without looking at the bookshop as they went by.

"What?" Carey said. "What did you forget to do?"

"Something important," he told her, starting to peel away. "Carry on with the meet; I'll see you back at the hotel." And with that he crossed the road and disappeared up a side street.

Carey watched him go. "You asshole, Tolya," she muttered, then she turned and carried on. She didn't notice the unassuming little man leave the bookshop behind her and set off almost, but not quite, in the direction Anatoly had taken.

"There were supposed to be two of you," Romek said when he sat down beside her in the church.

"Yes," Carey agreed heavily. "Yes, there were."

He thought about it. "Maybe we could do this another time," he mused. "When your companion can come with you."

She looked at him. There were some situations you didn't go into singlehanded, but she suddenly thought this was not one of them. There was no sense of threat from this sad-looking boy. "Nah," she said. "Let's see what you've got."

He had a car outside, a little Fiat that must have been almost a century old but seemed to be in mint condition. Carey folded herself uncomfortably into the passenger seat and Romek drove off, the engine sounding like a huge hairdryer.

"I'll have to take the long way round," he said, guiding the car along the Old Town's narrow streets.

"Yeah, I figured," she said. There was a big pro-independence march down at the railway station end of Zwycięstwa, blocking the whole street, and it was messing traffic up all over the town centre. She had a sense that the mood in Gliwice had darkened since she arrived. Certainly her own mood was darkening. "You pro or anti?"

"I don't care," he told her. "I just wish it would stop."

Once out of the town centre, Romek turned the car south on the main road towards Rybnik, but he'd only driven a couple of miles before turning off onto a secondary road and then pulling in on what seemed to be a farm track. He reached across into the glove compartment and took out a thick cloth hood.

"What," said Carey.

Romek looked genuinely apologetic. "It's secret," he said. "Please, wear it and don't try to work out where we're going."

"I'm already lost," she told him.

Romek waggled the hood at her. "Please. Or I'll take you back into town and we can forget about this."

She put the hood on, and Romek reversed back onto the road and then drove around for about an hour. Carey thought they hadn't travelled more than five or six miles as the crow flew when she felt the car bump down another farm track, but by then all the turns and intersections had thoroughly confused her. Quite what any pedestrians thought when they saw a tall woman go by in a little Fiat with a bag over her head, she didn't like to think about.

When the car finally stopped and she was allowed to remove the hood, Carey saw they were parked beside a ruined old farmhouse, its roof missing and most of its ancient stucco cracked off the brickwork beneath. It looked as if it had been in this state ever since the Germans left. There was no point trying to take a sneaky photo or even memorising what it looked like; she had a sense that this was one of those rare places that had never found its way into the online world, a blind spot in the global village.

Romek led the way around the farmhouse and towards a rickety-looking barn that stood behind it, half-hidden in a little wood. The door was open, and inside smelled faintly of old manure. In one corner a discarded armature of rusty metal rods might once have been a piece of farm machinery, it was impossible to tell for sure. In another corner, Romek clicked a key fob and a little section of the littered wooden floor, about as big as a couple of packs of cigarettes, popped up. Underneath was a tiny keypad. Romek knelt and, with a pen and the confidence of long familiarity, picked out a twenty-digit code, and a moment later there was a hiss of hydraulic rams and a much larger section of flooring hinged up in the middle of the barn.

The trapdoor—it was six inches thick, original planking over a slab of concrete—hid a dozen or so steps that led down to a metal door and another keypad. Another twenty-digit combination opened the door to bright light and a breath of cool air. Romek motioned to her to go through, but Carey wasn't going to fall for that. She waved him inside, then stepped into the doorway behind him.

"Oh my," she said.

The room was about half the size of a basketball court. It was painted white and lit by bright LEDs set into the ceiling. Carey felt the breeze of a ventilation system brush her cheek as she walked along the workbenches that lined the walls and looked at the racks of tools. There was an industrial printer in the middle of the floor, next to a big computerised lathe. Over in one corner, she could see a little electric forge beside an anvil and a rack of blacksmith's tools.

She turned and looked at Romek, who was leaning back against one of the benches, arms crossed over his chest. "I don't mean to be rude," she said, "but where did you get all this stuff?"

"It's from the flu," he said. "When things got very bad, the government started to set up regional command and control centres, workshops, armouries, stockpiles of vehicles and petrol. Then the flu burned itself out and when they decommissioned all those places, they forgot about this one."

Carey raised an eyebrow.

"They really did," Romek told her. "But when we found it, Magda went into their records and erased any mention of it. Just to make sure."

She saw a stack of big duffel bags against one wall, walked over to them and opened the top of one. "And these?"

Romek looked faintly embarrassed. "There was a delivery error."

She gave him a hard stare.

"Polish Coureurs are pricks," he said. "They're so..." he searched for the word. "*Precious*. There was a guy in Kraków, people say he was pretty cool, but he's supposed to be retired now. The rest..." He made a rude noise.

"Wouldn't let you join up, huh?"

"We all wanted to," he said. "Me, Magda, Boksi. We're good, we know we're good. But they just patted us on the head and told us to go back to the playground. They said we were too young, but they're just snobs. They don't want anyone muscling in on their private club."

"Yeah," she said, closing the duffel bag. "Yeah, I met some of them." The thing was, Stefan's Coureurs were right; these were children, wannabes looking for a bit of adventure. On the other hand, she hadn't been much older when she first came to Europe. Romek was right too, they were really talented; Boksi was a genuine artist, and he was going to be a menace when he got older. And she couldn't afford to be picky. At the very least she needed Magda, and the girl and Boksi and Romek seemed to come as a set.

She slung the bag over her shoulder and picked up one of the others. "I'll take these two for cash," she said. "For the rest, I'll put you on a retainer." She handed him a slip of paper. "Can you get me these?"

He looked down the list. "Not even a problem," he said. "I'll call you later about delivery."

She looked around the workshop. "You know, being a Coureur's really dull, most of the time. That stuff you see in the shows, it's just fiction. Not even very good fiction. All you do is carry parcels from one place to another."

"Magda and Boksi say that's not what you're doing."

"This is nonstandard," she allowed. "That doesn't happen very often. The guys you talked to, they want to make out it's too exciting to share with you, but what they're really doing is sitting on their asses for months on end waiting for someone to pay them to move a package of corporate data from here to Berlin or Prague. They spend most of their time on trains and nobody cares about them because they're not doing anything illegal. They're not big and they're not clever, okay?"

He smiled and nodded. He had a nice smile, when he made the effort to use it. "Okay."

"I can't promise you thrills and spills, but we're going to get along just fine."

2

It was a busy year, much busier than she'd anticipated. There were very few American correspondents in Spain, and those that were had been there when the pandemic hit; they had the story sewn up and she had to be careful she didn't tread on any toes. Journalists tended to be territorial, and her legal status in the country was precarious at best.

So she put some effort into becoming Verónica Torrejón. She rented an apartment some distance from the centre of town, where property became affordable for someone on her limited budget. She made sure she was seen in the neighbourhood, got to know her neighbours and local shopkeepers. If anyone commented on her Texas Spanish she explained it by saying she'd spent a long time in the US when she was growing up. Her Spanish improved, but she never lost the accent. She cautiously opened bank accounts, but she needn't have worried; the Spanish economy had been bumping along the floor even before the flu and they were keen on investment, however small. She gradually accumulated utility bills and friends and all the everyday things that form a life. With some trepidation, she changed the address on her papers, cutting Verónica off from the paper-thin story Konrad had given her, but all she had to do was fill in a couple of forms online; nobody even asked a supplementary question.

She wrote reviews of gallery openings and fashion shows and film premieres. She interviewed industrialists and politicians. After months of trying, she wangled herself a visit to the far western end of the Line, an enormous fenced compound on Portugal's Atlantic coast. By then, she was so used to being Verónica that she didn't think twice about the border crossing. A group of a dozen correspondents from all over Europe—Germans, French, Italians, one Brit wearing cargo pants and a Union Jack tee shirt—were shepherded around the site by a representative of the Trans-European Rail Company, a blandly charming Hungarian woman in a lightweight suit and a panama hat. The Line had built a terminus, which looked to Carey like a much larger version of the old Union Station in Los Angeles, and there were dozens of administration buildings and big maintenance sheds and a complicated network of tracks and turntables and switches. They weren't allowed to take photographs, but they were given flash sticks full of images and text and data compiled by a PR firm in Antwerp. The whole thing made Carey feel uncomfortable in a way she couldn't quite quantify.

As her confidence in Verónica grew, she increased her range. She took a train to Barcelona, where relations between Catalunya and Madrid had grown complicated and frosty again. She went up to Bilbao, which was starting to style itself as the capital of Euskal Herria, and she had a couple of clandestine meetings with Basque separatists. She had to publish the articles she wrote about these under a pen name, in case the Spanish authorities took offence and put her under the microscope.

She flew to Paris for a few days, visited the Line station at Paris-Savigny, and got that odd feeling of disquiet again. It seemed unusually fortified, more like a secure compound than a station. It was the same story at the Belgian station outside Charleroi, although here the company owned a number of office buildings in the town as well.

From Belgium, she took a train to Berlin for an interview with a minor Bundestag official about the general state of European politics. It was not, she could tell, a subject which made him particularly happy. He stood at the window of his office and reeled off a sorry list of nations and autonomous and semi-autonomous areas and regions which were getting a taste for independence. "I give the EU five years," he told her glumly. "Schengen is dead. The Belgians will wait and see what the Dutch will do, and the Dutch will leave, and once they go everyone else will follow. Eventually it will just be us and the French." He heaved such a huge sigh that she thought his heart was breaking. "It was a beautiful experiment, but it's over."

Somewhat taken aback by the tone of the interview, she went to a bar a few streets from the parliament building, got herself a beer, and sat at a corner table going through her notes and wondering how she could write them up in a way that wouldn't trigger a wave of suicides across the EU.

At one point she looked up and Konrad was sitting at the next table. Later, she thought about how matter-of-fact it had all been. He hadn't been there when she came into the bar, and she hadn't seen him arrive. He was just there, a glass of beer in front of him, looking at her and smiling. Like a magic trick.

After a little while, he got up and came over, still smiling. "I owe you dinner," he said.

"I RAN INTO a bit of a *situation* after I left you," he said, and he put an odd emphasis on 'situation', as if it should have had a capital 's'. "That happens, sometimes. You get a call and you have to drop everything and just *go*."

"And you couldn't have got in touch and let me know?" she asked.

"It was a bit urgent," he said. "Sorry."

"You could have called me when your *situation* was over," she said. "You've got my phone number."

"It's been one of those years," he said. "And please, don't ask me to tell you about it. Operational security."

They were sitting in a restaurant that styled itself like an old-fashioned bierkeller in Friedrichstadt, not far from the old site of Checkpoint Charlie. Panelled walls, waitresses in dirndls and blouses, a menu packed with various wursts, potatoes, dumplings, sauerkraut. The place smelled of beer and food and old tobacco smoke, which probably came out of a can like that leather smell they sprayed inside new cars because it had been decades since the EU had allowed diners to smoke in restaurants. Carey knew a tourist trap when she saw one. Still, the beer was good.

"It sounds as if you've done well, anyway," he said, dissecting the meat off his eisbein. "Very impressive, the way you built up the legend we gave you."

"If you had time to spy on me, you had time to get in touch and tell me why you abandoned me like that."

"It's not spying," he said mater-of-factly. "More protecting an investment. We might be able to use Verónica Torrejón again, if you ever decided to move on."

"I think I'll hang on to her," she said, tucking in to her wiener schnitzel. "For the moment."

"You're pretty good, actually," he went on. "Not everyone could arrive in a strange city on false papers and build a new life for themselves like that."

She hadn't thought of it as building a new life, more adding an annex to her own. "I didn't have a lot of choice. Nobody was going to help me."

He sat back and beamed at her. "How would you like to do something like that for a living?"

"I already do something for a living."

"Well," he said, going back to his meal. "How about another revenue stream, then? Something you could do alongside your journalistic work."

"Like what?"

"Admin, mostly," he said. "Paperwork."

"You want me to do your typing?"

He laughed. He had a nice laugh. "We'd bring someone in, to show you the ropes. Just to get you started. After that, well, we might not be in touch for months."

"Is it illegal?"

He thought about it a moment, and she noted that. "Nah," he said. "Not really. It's nothing the authorities would pay attention to, anyway."

"Why in the blue blazes would I want to work for you?"

He grinned a buccaneering grin. "Because you're curious about us."

That much was true. She'd done what research she'd been able to do on *Les Coureurs*, and either they were criminal human traffickers or they were latter-day knights in shining armour or they were a shadowy band of freelance superspies.

"Look," he said seriously, "five years ago you could drive all the way from the Atlantic coast to the northern end of the Baltic without having to stop once at a border. Now you can't even drive from Portugal to Spain without going through passport and customs controls. And it's only going to get worse."

She thought about what the German politician had told her earlier.

"It's..." he searched for the word. "It's *uncivilised*. Borders are primitive, mediaeval. They promote division and nationalism. They're offensive, frankly."

She'd formed a lot of opinions about Konrad in the brief time she'd known him, but idealism wasn't one of them. "It's also a great business opportunity."

He gave her that piratical grin again. "That too," he allowed. "Come on, how about it. Give it a try; if you don't like it, you can walk away. Nobody will blame you, it's not a life for everyone."

That sounded like a challenge. She knew it, and he knew she knew it.

"Sure," she said. "Okay."

* * *

SOMETIME LATER, SHE woke up and felt him snuggled up beside her. She lay for a while looking up at the ceiling of her hotel room, thinking back over the past few hours, the past few days, the past year.

"By the way," he murmured sleepily, "my name's not Konrad."

3

KRISTA WAS ON her third or fourth circuit of the supermarket. She wasn't sure how long she had been here; she paused periodically to consider the shelves, grabbed something, and dumped it in her trolley. It looked as if she was preparing for a siege.

Her phone rang. She took it out, saw Markus's caller ID, put her thumb over the answer icon. "Hi," she said.

"Where are you?" he said.

"Supermarket. Why?" And then her phone buzzed to tell her she had another incoming call. She checked the ID, and felt her heart sink all the way into the floor. "I'll call you back," she said. She hung up, opened the second call, and said, "Hello."

"Did you go to the media?" asked Jakobson.

"No."

"Because if you did, your career's over."

"No, I didn't." All of a sudden, the supermarket seemed simultaneously too large and too small. "What's happened?" But she already knew.

"The story's loose," Jakobson told her. The phone buzzed again; Krista looked at the screen and watched the incoming calls mount up. Four, five, seven, ten, fifteen. When they reached twenty, she put the phone back to her ear. "—about twenty minutes ago," Jakobson was saying. "Hello? Are you still there?"

"Yes, colonel," she said, feeling tired and heavy. "I'm here."

"In an hour, your father's going to be the most famous man in Tallinn," Jakobson said. "Half an hour after that, he'll be the most famous man in the country. Don't go home; the media will be there. Where are you?"

Krista heard herself telling the colonel. "I was shopping," she added.

"Shopping," Jakobson muttered. "All right. Leave your groceries where they are and go outside. There will be a car there in five minutes. Don't talk to anyone, but in particular do *not* talk to the media; they'll have your number soon."

"They have it already, judging by the number of people trying to get through to me."

"Take the SIM and the battery out of your phone and dump it, right now," Jakobson told her. "If they have your number the next thing they'll do is run a geotrace on your phone." It was against the law to do that, but of course there were any number of pop-up electronics shops where, for a few kroons, someone would hack the cell network to locate a particular phone.

Krista suddenly felt unwilling to move. She was perfectly comfortable where she was, leaning on the handle of her trolley in the frozen food aisle. She couldn't see any reason why she should go anywhere else. She said, "Is all this really necessary, colonel? I'm tired and I'm upset and I'm actually quite hungry. No one's going to hurt me and I'm not going to give any interviews. I'd like to go home."

"Do as you're told, major," Jakobson said. "That's an order." She hung up, leaving Krista standing there in the middle of the supermarket, phone still held to her ear.

It was, she thought later, the *that's an order* which did it. Nobody had said that to her since she was promoted to lieutenant, and she'd given them precious little cause to say it even before that. She turned and abandoned her trolley.

Instead of heading for the exit, she went towards the back of the supermarket, where a set of automatic doors opened and closed in response to RFID chips mounted in the semiautonomous stock pallets used to stack the shelves. Someone, probably in defiance of regulations, had wedged the doors open, but she could see stickers that read WARNING! AUTOMATED MACHINERY. Removing the back of her phone as she went, she stepped through.

The space beyond was larger than she had expected, larger than the supermarket itself. Aisles of shelving almost eight metres tall, packed with products, ran away into an ill-lit dimness. Here and there were the shiny metal sarcophagi of freezers and fridges, and stacks of goods on old-style inert pallets. Orange light blinked across the walls and shelves where freight-handling robots rolled across the cement floor, following tramlines of conductive paint. There was not a single person to be seen.

There was still time to change her mind, and for a moment she actually thought of turning on her heel, going back into the store, and going out on the street to wait for Jakobson's car. But she'd had enough of the colonel interfering in her life.

One of the robots was coming towards her down the aisle, a machine almost as tall as she was and as long as a car, with a telescoping platform on top fringed with stout hydraulic arms. The platform was loaded with packs of kitchen paper, and as it went by Krista stripped the SIM and battery out of her phone and reached up and shoved it between the packs. The machine came to a sudden stop as she breached its safety perimeter, then started up again as she moved away further into the storeroom.

For such a large space, it was claustrophobic in the store. The shelves were packed solid with products and the machines took up much of the floor space, endlessly rolling and pirouetting as they moved stock, lasers blinking red as they read barcodes on the shelving and matched them to the goods they were carrying. There was a narrow path right down the middle of each aisle—space, she presumed, for engineers to carry out emergency repairs—and she trotted down this, robots passing by on either side.

At the far end of the store were big doors leading to the supermarket's loading dock. She hit the fat red button beside one of them and the door started to concertina up, admitting a wave of chilly air. When it was high enough for her to pass beneath it, she ducked through and out into daylight. Behind her, she thought she heard an alarm, but it could have been anything.

Out on the loading dock, there was more handling machinery—autonomous forklifts and loaders—all of it parked for the moment, waiting for deliveries. It went without saying that she had been on camera from the moment she stepped into the supermarket, but there was nothing she could do about that and if she moved quickly enough it wouldn't matter. She hopped down off the dock and walked across the yard behind the supermarket to a high chain-link fence. There was a rolling gate in the fence large enough to admit a truck, and beside the gate was a kiosk, in which stood the first human being she'd seen since she stepped into the storeroom.

He was in his fifties, of North African appearance, one of the wave of immigrants Estonia had taken in before the EU had finally hardened its southern borders against refugees. He was wearing a uniform in the colours of the supermarket's logo and he looked up from his phone as Krista knocked on the side of the kiosk.

"Could you let me out, please?" she asked.

"I'm sorry, miss?" he asked in almost accentless Estonian. "You should use the employees' entrance."

"Yes, but it's over there," she waved vaguely behind her, "and I need to catch the tram over there." She pointed through the fence. "Go on. *Please.* Just this one time? I'm late for a job interview." She didn't quite bat her eyelids at him, but it was a close thing.

As it was, she didn't have to. That bit about the job interview swayed him—obviously nobody liked working here. He nodded and pressed a button and the gate started to roll aside. "Good luck!" he called as she slid through and out into the street. She waved without looking back.

She turned left and walked at a brisk pace down the street, not so fast that she would attract attention, but as she reached the main road a car pulled up and stopped across the junction, to a symphony of horns from the drivers behind. The passenger door opened and Vainola stepped out and stood looking at her, hands in his jacket pockets. He wasn't quite smirking. Krista sighed and walked to the end of the street.

"That was a really good try," Vainola said in a tone of voice that was almost not patronising.

"A bit obvious, though," she said.

"A bit, yes," he agreed. "Get in, please."

She got in the back of the car. Vainola closed the door and got into the passenger seat and the car pulled away.

"If you do that again, I'll be forced to arrest you," Vainola told her as the car slowed and took a right.

"If you're insubordinate like that again, I'll have you back on the beat, lieutenant." She tried to put as much force as possible into the threat, but it wasn't much.

Vainola laughed. "For the purposes of this investigation, I outrank you."

"You do for the moment, lieutenant," she told him, settling back with her bag on her knees. "But it won't last."

* * *

Jakobson glowered at her when Vainola delivered her to the safe flat, but didn't make a comment. It was as if she had expected Krista to make a break for it and was just wearied by being proved right.

The flat was out on the edge of town. It was larger than hers but felt shabby in a way she couldn't quite put her finger on. It felt as if there were long periods when it was unoccupied, like a flat used by visiting businessmen, and the rest of the time it was looked after by a housekeeper who only visited a couple of times a week. The furniture was clean but vaguely out of date, ditto the fridge and cooker.

"So," said Jakobson.

"So," said Krista.

"I pulled the girl who's supposed to be running this thing into Raekoja plats and had a harsh word with her," Jakobson said, holding out her phone. "She's a smudge, though. I'd be surprised if she can wipe her own backside without a drink in the other hand. This will be the lawyer, turning up the pressure."

Krista took the phone, found herself looking at a Russian-language website that called itself *Ultimate Truth!* With an exclamation mark. The story was pretty much as Jakobson had told her yesterday, only with even more exclamation marks. Ethnic Russian person beaten to death by police in Tallinn. There was a rather lurid account of Sergii N's autopsy. About halfway down the page was an image of her father in full uniform, at some official event or other, followed by a long and heartfelt diatribe on the subject of the racism of the Tallinn police force and the years-long cover-up of the death of Sergii N. Near the bottom of the page there were hints of other attacks by the Tallinn police on ethnic Russians.

"That's where it started," Jakobson said. "It's everywhere now. It was always going to break; I was hoping we'd have more lead time."

"Why didn't they go public straight away?" asked Krista. "I don't understand. Why wait?"

"I thought they were being reasonable. Obviously I was wrong." Jakobson stood and walked over to her. "I know you think we're *not* being reasonable, but you're at ground zero in this. You're not a suspect, as yet, but you were standing next to the suspect, and everyone wants to talk to you." Krista let that *as yet* pass. "Anything you could say to the press can only make things worse. Perhaps you can make a statement in due course, but it will be a statement we write."

"At least you didn't tell me this is for my own good."

Jakobson smiled sadly, and Krista suddenly realised how tired she looked. "Well, that too," she agreed. "But mostly it's for *our* own good. You're an adult and you've been a police officer for a good long while. You know how these things work. Now, may I have my phone back?"

Krista took the phone from her pocket and handed it over. It had been worth a try. "Can you get word to my boyfriend?" she asked. "I promised I'd call him."

Jakobson nodded. "Any message?"

"Just tell him I'm okay and I'll be in touch when I can."

"Okay." Jakobson walked to the door. "I can't order you not to look at the news," she said. "And I'm going to treat you like a grown-up and not take the entertainment set away. But it might be advisable if you kept your head down. It will be upsetting."

"It's a bit late for that. Like you say, I'm standing beside ground zero."

Jakobson gave her a long, level look. "Right. Well, make yourself at home. I'll be back presently and we'll talk further."

"Right."

Jakobson left, and Krista heard the door being locked from the outside. It had not escaped her notice that

Jakobson had not asked for Markus's phone number or address.

KRISTA WAS SITTING watching the Russian ambassador giving a press briefing. The ambassador was not twinkling today. Today he was solemn. Even his cufflinks were small and discreet.

"I'll be honest with you," he told the press room in his flawless Estonian, "this is an outrage. We will be meeting with the President and Prime Minister shortly to demand a full investigation into this terrible murder, and if guilt is found we will be demanding full reparations."

"What kind of reparations?" one of the journalists asked.

"We'll decide that in due time," the ambassador told him. "Next question."

"They want to send us one of their detectives," Jakobson said from the doorway. "To make sure the investigation is handled properly."

Krista looked over her shoulder. "How do we feel about that?"

"We feel unhappy." Jakobson walked over to the sofa and sat next to Krista. "How are you holding up?"

Krista muted the sound on the press conference. "Climbing the walls."

Jakobson nodded. "The press have your flat staked out."

Krista sighed, even though it wasn't a surprise. "Bastards."

Jakobson took a phone from her bag and held it out. "This is to replace yours."

"It's a cheaper model," Krista noted.

"Don't push it," Jakobson told her. "The code for the front door's on here. Can I trust you not to do anything silly?"

"That depends on what your definition of 'silly' is at the moment."

"If you want to go out, don't go alone. My number's in the contact book. Call me and I'll assign someone to keep you company. The chances of bumping into the media are fairly slim, but you never know and I don't want any unpleasantness."

Krista took the phone. "Where would I go? I can't go home. Did you speak to Markus?"

Jakobson shook her head. "He's smart," she said. "He left town yesterday. Left a message for Colonel Tamm saying he's checking into a hotel somewhere and he'll let us know where he is when he's settled. Tamm says he sounded angry."

"I can't blame him." Everything had moved so quickly, and she'd been so mired in her own misery, that she hadn't thought about how it would affect him. "Did he say where he was going?"

Jakobson shook her head. "But he said he'd be in touch."

"How long is this going to last?"

"At least until the investigation makes its final report. And probably for a while after that. Then they'll lose interest. Something else will come along." She paused. "It could take a while."

"I'm not used to just sitting on my hands like this."

"I know. But I can't let you get involved in the investigation. You're his *daughter*, major. How would it look?"

And for all anyone knew, she was mixed up in it. She saw the colonel's point, but she didn't like it. "I could use some new clothes, and the food here's awful. Can you arrange a shopping trip?"

"I can do that right now." Jakobson took out her own phone and dialled a number. "When would you like to go?"

"Soon as possible; these clothes are starting to stand up on their own. You'll have to lend me some cash as well. I can't walk into a bank and get them to transfer my details onto this phone."

"There's a line of credit on there already," Jakobson said. "From the witness protection budget. Try not to go mad, th—get over here," she said into her phone. "Dress for shopping." She hung up. "Yes, don't go crazy. You've run your own ops; you know what the paperwork's like."

"Who was that on the phone?"

Jakobson smiled. "Babysitter."

THE BABYSITTER TURNED out to be named Ivari, a large, affable young lieutenant in jeans and work boots and a puffa jacket, his ensemble topped off with a peculiar orange knitted cap with long earflaps. If he felt at all awkward about bodyguarding a superior officer, he hid it remarkably well.

He had a car parked two streets away, and he drove them to a big shopping centre on the outskirts of Tallinn, on the grounds that they would be less likely to bump into someone who knew Krista there than in the centre of town.

"I'm not so sure," she told him, starting to feel uncomfortably warm in the long two-storey mall. "Everyone I know shops here."

He shrugged. "We could go to Pärnu."

"We're not going all the way to Pärnu just for some fresh underwear," she told him. Anyway, this was so obviously a test. Jakobson wanted to see if she would try to contact someone, or bolt altogether, and she wasn't going to give the colonel the satisfaction. "How long have you been with IA?"

"Two years," he said, stuffing his hat into a coat pocket. "I was with Diplomatic Protection before that." He smiled at her.

"What's Jakobson like to work for?"

"What you see is what you get. She's not afraid of taking a bullet for the team."

Krista had known senior officers for whom responsibility was something to be avoided at all costs. She said, "Are you allowed to talk about the investigation?"

"I wouldn't be, but I'm not involved in this case anyway, so it's academic. I'm just a spare body to go shopping with you. I know the broad details, though." A sour look crossed his face, betraying what he thought of the whole thing.

"You do know my father's innocent, though."

"I don't know any such thing," he told her. "One thing you learn in IA is to go into each job with a completely open mind, no preconceptions at all. That's one of the reasons people don't like us. They think we should be protecting the reputation of the force. Which we are, just not the way they'd like. You know what they call us."

"Vultures, yes."

He nodded. "It's inevitable, really. Cops investigating other cops are never going to be popular. Not if they do their job properly, anyway." He paused while Krista stopped to look in the window of one of the shops. "I saw your father lecture once, at the police school. He was intense."

She grunted. Intense. That was her father.

"Anyway," he added. "Let's not talk about this. Let's shop."

Ivari turned out to be an ideal shopping partner. He didn't get bored or whiny, knew when to offer an opinion and when to keep his mouth shut, and he was a good conversationalist. Krista found herself beginning to relax for the first time in what felt like days. She hadn't realised just how wound up she'd been.

It seemed as if he had been right about the shopping mall, too; Krista didn't see anyone she recognised. It was a weekday morning and everyone would be at work, which helped.

Finally, both of them weighed down with shopping bags, they adjourned to a Starbucks for coffee and pastries.

Krista guarded a table while Ivari went to the counter. They'd chosen a place near the back of the café but with a clear view of the doors, and where she was sitting Krista could see across the big central atrium of the mall. On the opposite side was an electronics store, its window stacked with the screens of entertainment sets. A crowd had gathered in front of the window, and as she watched more people joined it. All the screens were showing the same footage, but from this distance she couldn't quite make out what it was. A close-up of a termite colony? A pitch invasion at a football match?

"Something's going on," she said to Ivari when he returned with a tray laden with cups and plates.

"Sorry?" He put the tray down on the table, then squinted in the direction she was pointing. "Oh," he said, and at that moment his phone rang. "Yes? Yes. Really? Right." He hung up. "We're going to have to postpone lunch, I'm afraid," he told her. "The colonel wants you back at the flat as soon as possible."

"Why?"

He glanced across at the electronics shop again. The crowd outside was almost a hundred strong by now. "Just to be on the safe side," he said.

THE THINGS YOU *miss when you go shopping*, Krista thought. The protest march was three or four hundred strong, which wasn't a bad turnout considering the general grotty subzero state of the weather. It wound through the Old Town, a sea of chanting heads and bobbing banners, towards police headquarters. Tourists and locals alike stood watching it pass by, curious but passive. It was on all the news channels, hurriedly drafted correspondents giving a moment-by moment narration from the scene. Occasionally the cameras cut to one studio or another, where talking heads ventured their opinions. Krista heard her father's name several times, and muted the sound.

She turned it back up when she saw a photo in the studio background of Maart Sálumäe, Estonia's popular young Prime Minister. One of the newsreaders read a statement from Salumäe's office, something bland calling for calm and promising that the death of Sergii N was receiving the utmost attention and the investigation would report in due course. Then the camera cut to another press conference with the Russian ambassador, and Krista muted the sound again.

"Well," Ivari said, with what Krista thought was admirable understatement in the circumstances, "this is a hell of a thing."

She watched the cameras cut back to the march. It was starting to get dark, and the crowd outside police headquarters were holding up their phones to record the wall of police officers standing between them and the building. If this really was some sort of ploy by Tamburlaine to get her off his back, it was running way out of control.

Krista got up from the sofa. "Sod this," she said. "I'm going to have a shower. See if you can cobble together something to eat; I didn't have my lunch."

He checked the time on his phone. "I should be going," he said.

"You can hang around long enough to have dinner with me," she told him, going into the bedroom.

When she came out, with an armful of new clothes still in their packaging and her shoulder bag clutched to her chest, he was clattering around in the kitchen trying to find pots and pans and utensils.

She turned on the shower, then changed quickly into jeans, sweatshirt and hoodie, and stepped out into the hall. The sound of clattering from the kitchen had been replaced by the smell of cooking. Krista dithered for a few moments, then she grabbed her coat from its hook in the hallway, opened the front door, and stepped out into the corridor. She held her phone over the sensor and heard the lock click, and a moment later the handle waggled as someone tried it from the other side.

Krista stood, almost hypnotised. There was a mechanical override to allow the door to be unlocked from the inside, to prevent accidents and allow the occupant to escape in case of fire and power outages, but it seemed that it had been disabled, and clearly nobody had thought to give Ivari the key code, because he was unable to open it. That was very poor, not health and safety conscious at all.

The handle stopped waggling, and she heard a muffled "For *fuck's* sake" from the other side, then she turned and was gone.

SEVEN

1

THEY MOVED INTO the house on Zimnej Wody on the evening of Carey's ninth day in town, then Anatoly took a train out to Bytom, one of the neighbouring towns, and collected a knapsack from the left luggage at the station there.

The knapsack was a delivery from Romek, and it contained a toilet bag, two changes of clothes and a packet of roast beef sandwiches for camouflage, and three dozen surveillance cameras tucked away at the bottom, each of them a little larger than a cube of sugar and covered with a mimetic coating that made it disappear into whatever background it was stuck to.

In the living room, Carey opened one of the big duffel bags she'd taken from Romek's workshop and took out what seemed to be a baggy coverall made entirely of rags. "Ever used one of these?" she asked.

Anatoly shook his head.

"They're absolute bastards," she said, struggling into the coverall and doing up the fastenings on the front. "They trap body heat so you warm up very quickly." She reached into the duffel again, came up with a lightweight motorcycle helmet, put it on, seemed to *shrug*, and suddenly where she had been was an indistinct blurry figure.

"I can still see you," Anatoly said.

"You're standing too close," she told him. "It's not perfect."

He moved away to the other end of the living room, and from that distance there was only a faint roiling in the air that would be easily missed if you didn't know it was there. "It's not bad," he said. "When can I try it?"

Carey *shrugged* back into visibility and took off the helmet. "When I say you can." She started to fill the suit's kangaroo pocket with cameras.

"When are we going to talk about what you think you're doing here?"

She glanced at him. "What's that?"

"Since you got here you've been blundering around bumping into things, pretending to be a journalist."

"I *am* a journalist."

"Pretending to be a private detective."

"I *am* a private detective. I have a licence, anyway."

"Now you've moved us into what must be one of the most *obvious* houses in the city."

"I like it," she said, putting a last handful of cameras in the pocket and sealing its flap down. "It's famous."

He said, "If you're staking us out, it would be courtesy to let us know."

"Staking us out?"

"Like goats."

She picked up the helmet again. "Where did you go yesterday?"

"I thought I spotted a tail."

"We dropped them all."

"Not one of the Coureurs, or whoever they are. Someone else."

She stood looking at him. "Who else?"

"I'm not certain. They're good, though. Professional." So professional that he thought he had been meant to spot the tail. It was a message, and he had sinking suspicion that he knew who it was from.

Carey gestured at him with the helmet. "You tell me about this stuff, okay? You don't go off on your own and play *Tinker Tailor*. I need to know these things."

They had a brief staring contest. "Seriously, Tolya," she said. "I need to know." She put the helmet on and disappeared. "Now open the door for me; it'll only confuse the neighbours if they see it opening itself."

Carey spent two hours sticking cameras to trees and walls and lamp posts in a ragged perimeter around the house, all the way up and down the street, and on Konarskiego and Częstochowska. Clumsy in the stealth suit, she clambered up a fire escape on the side of the polytechnic building and stuck a couple up there to overlook the area. It was a mild evening and the suit's systems were allowing quite a lot of body heat through to match ambient temperature, but she still had to stop a few times and open the front and let herself cool down. Smaller Central European towns tended to turn in early, and there weren't many people about.

It was after midnight by the time she got back to the house, and Magda, who had spent the evening sticking paperscreens to the walls of the studio upstairs and setting up her gear, had made contact with the cameras and tiled their views onto a single big screen.

"A couple of them aren't working," she said. "But we have plenty of redundancy."

Carey nodded. "They print these things for, like, a nickel apiece; you expect some duds in a big enough batch." She looked around the studio, the screens, the neatly arranged modules and tapboards on a worktable in the middle of the room. "Okay," she said. "Let's get this show on the road, then."

SHE'D THOUGHT THE Gliwice police had been slipshod in their investigation of the accident, but she'd been wrong. They'd done a thoroughly professional job. The problem had been hers; she'd only been given a fraction of the available information. The full report on Maksim's death ran to almost fifty gigabytes. There were accident simulations, diagrams, impact models, animations. There were full autopsy protocols complete with video—which she looked at once and then never opened again. Pages and pages of written reports, folders of audio testimony, high-definition walkthroughs of the scene on the night of the accident and the following day. It confirmed something Carey had been suspecting for a while, that the report Kaunas had given her had not come directly from a police source but from a stringer who had been told about it by a police source, or possibly at an even greater remove; it wasn't much more than hearsay.

"Was this stuff hard to get at?" she asked Magda. "Not for you, obviously, you're a star. For ordinary people?"

The girl shook her head. "Just the usual security. Took me twenty minutes."

It wasn't just sloppy; it was almost criminal. Central certainly had access to pianists at least as able as Magda; they could have got hold of the report and handed it over to her, rather than giving her a hurried one-page précis, they'd had plenty of time. They'd sent her into the situation with what amounted to some back-of-an-envelope calculations.

They had a name for the tractor driver. Zbigniew Karski, identified from his driving licence, and an address in Gliwice. "Do you know where that is?" Carey asked, pointing.

"Yes," said Magda. "But that whole block's condemned, it's waiting to be demolished. The only people living there are a few squatters."

Carey pouted. "Okay, see what you can find out about Mr Karski."

The body in the car had been identified by one YG Iyeguda, a citizen of Yaroslavl. Yegor's little joke, she presumed. 'Yenokh Iyeguda' was the birth name of Genrikh Yagoda, one of the early heads of the NKVD. According to Mr Iyeguda, he and Mr Petrauskas had been in Gliwice on business, finalising a deal to supply tractor parts to a firm on the outskirts of town. The deal had hit a snag—something to do with intellectual property rights, Mr Iyeguda was a little vague—and Mr Petrauskas had got frustrated and drunk one night and driven off. He was a man, apparently, of strong passions. Reading this, Carey couldn't quite suppress a little smile. Yegor had a good poker face, and she could imagine him saying all this stuff and the officer interviewing him swallowing it whole.

The story had checked out—toxicology showed three times the legal limit of alcohol in the deceased's bloodstream, as well as signs of long-term amphetamine use—and Maksim's remains had been signed over to Mr Iyeguda and the file closed.

"Ever hear of a gang called Rocketman?" Carey asked.

"They're not a gang, really," Magda said. "Just a bunch of *boys*. They hire themselves out to do tech stuff."

"I heard them described as a criminal gang."

Magda shrugged. "Sure, they do some criminal stuff. How else is anyone supposed to make any money these days?"

"I hope *you* haven't been doing criminal stuff." Magda sat back and gestured at the accident report, spread over half a dozen screens on the wall. "Apart from that."

Magda snorted.

"Do you know anything about their setup?" Anatoly, who had been sitting in a corner paging through a printout of the report, glanced up. He looked at Carey, then at Magda, then back to Carey. "Could you get into their system?"

"They don't have a *system*," Magda said. "Everything's done on separate pads and laptops and phones, it's all compartmentalised. All the important stuff's kept offline. There's no one thing you could break into and have access to everything."

Carey sniffed. "Okay." She looked at the screens again. "Can you work up a go-to on them for me? History, biographies, MOs, capers they've been involved in?" Anatoly opened his mouth to say something, thought better of it.

"I know one of them," the girl told her. "Andrzej. He's a creep; he wanted to be my boyfriend."

Carey thought about that. "Okay. Well, let's keep Andrzej at arm's length for the moment. Just see whatever you can scare up about his pals."

She went into the kitchen to get a coffee, and Anatoly went with her. "Do we have a problem?" she asked.

"I don't know," he said, leaning against the worktop. "Do we?"

Carey put a cup in the coffee maker and pressed the button. "We need to know what the Rocket boys were doing for Maksim," she said. "They're not going to just volunteer the information and I'll be damned if I'm going to wind up beholden to them for it. We need a way in."

"There are better ways," he told her. "More discreet ways. Let me do it."

"There isn't time for discreet," she said. She let the last drops of coffee drip into her cup, took it out, dropped a sugar cube into it, and stirred. "In a few days the Sejm is going to vote on whether Gliwice can become independent, and when they do this town's going to go bang, whichever way the vote goes. I've seen it before. We might as well give up when that happens, because nobody's going to want to talk to us."

"We could pull out," he suggested. "Wait it out somewhere, come back later."

She shook her head. "We already lost too much time recruiting the kids. We need to make some progress, shake the tree and see what falls out. How are you doing with the photos?"

Anatoly had been doing a round of bars and clubs with photos of Yegor and Maksim, so far with no result. He thought it was a waste of time, but he kept it to himself. "It's a big town," he said, "for one person."

"Do your best," she told him. "If Magda doesn't come up with anything, we'll try things your way."

PEOPLE, ON THE whole, preferred to think of life as a straightforward, uncomplicated matter. One thing led to another and loose ends got tied up, and frankly incomprehensible shit which tipped your life off its axis only happened to others.

Anatoly had felt that way until not long after his tenth birthday, when frankly incomprehensible shit had invaded his life and refused to leave. After his mother's death, his father, not one of the world's natural parents, had been inclined to send him off to one of Rus's many military academies, but that was never going to end happily for anybody, so his upbringing had instead been farmed out to an extended family of aunts and cousins.

This was not, in itself, unusual or perhaps even noteworthy, except Anatoly's father was a colonel—and more recently a general—in Rus's security services and the aunts were all still involved with various branches of intelligence, some of them impossibly obscure and arcane. They had taken one look at the sad, gentle, plump boy in their care and set about turning him into an operative.

The extent of their success was not for Anatoly to judge. Certainly, he had a lot of tradecraft, and his operational awareness was good, and when they judged he was ready the aunts—and occasionally his father—had sent him out into the secret world on jobs which were notable for their informality.

By then, he had somewhat surprised himself by also becoming a moderately successful novelist, although that success was waning when, two years ago, his father had sent him to London on what was presented to him as a perfectly simple mission, little more than the delivery of a message.

What Anatoly—and the colonel, it transpired—did not appreciate at the time was that he had walked right into the middle of some frankly incomprehensible shit involving several other parties, the aunts among them.

Carey had scooped him up from that situation—*rescued* was not too strong a word—and deposited him, somewhat improbably, in a new life in Scotland. He had not had any contact with his family since then, although they had posted some veiled messages to the effect that he was, essentially, dead to them now.

Which was why the presence of the unassuming little man, patiently trailing him wherever he went, was unsettling. It must have been obvious to him by now that Anatoly knew he was there, but it was impossible to shake him. Everywhere Anatoly went, there he was, a patient plodder, calm and implacable.

He was there now, a good hundred metres or so back on the same side of the street, almost lost among the shoppers on Zwycięstwa. He seemed, as far as Anatoly could judge, alone, although if he was carrying out the surveillance without backup he was basically a magician. There were also a couple of the Coureurs on the street, horribly obvious and amateurish. Anatoly had started recreationally dropping them and picking them up again, tailing *them* for a while, walking them round town on pointless errands, and they were starting look a bit ragged. He wondered, in an academic sort of way, whether it would be possible to simply burn them out if he kept at it long enough.

There was another demonstration on Zwycięstwa—there was one, for one faction or another, most days now, and they were becoming increasingly bad-tempered—and he pushed through the crowd, taking off the rather shapeless felt hat and sunglasses he was wearing as he went. On the other side of the street, he slipped into a department store, walked straight through and out again through a side door. He wandered along side streets for half an hour or so, working his way gradually towards the Old Town, and when he got to the ice cream shop fifteen minutes early for the meet he wasn't terribly surprised to find his father and one of his aunts already waiting.

They were sitting at a table by the window, huddled up in their coats, glass bowls before them. The café was packed with families and older folk, and his father looked intensely irritated at having to mix with normal people. For the barest moment, Anatoly hesitated. Then he went to the counter and queued for an espresso, a little bit of professional etiquette so they could see he was here and the situation was secure.

He carried his cup over to the table and sat down. "I was expecting someone else," he said, by way of greeting.

"So I gather," his father said. "Fortunately, your contact is more intelligent than you, and brought your request directly to me."

"And congratulations on your recent promotion; I'm sure that was very gratifying."

There followed a brief staring contest, during which Anatoly crossed another name off the list of people he could trust. It hadn't been that long a list to begin with.

"We were passing," his aunt told him pleasantly. "We thought we'd see how you are."

"How do I look?"

She regarded him soberly. "Tired," she said. "You put weight on."

"Thank you."

"That haircut doesn't suit you."

"Yes," he said. "Thank you. Have you been having me followed?"

"Of course we have," said his father. "Do you take us for fools?"

Anatoly took his father for many things, but a fool was not among them. He sighed. "So, since you seem to have taken over this matter, can you help me?"

The upper reaches of Europe's espiocracy were as scornful of borders as any Coureur. While they guarded their own frontiers as jealously as an abusive lover, they prided themselves on being able to pass beyond them, spirits in the wind, whenever they wished. It was a contradiction which had nagged at Anatoly, like a faint headache, for quite some time, although it had clearly never troubled his family, who sallied forth from Moscow whenever the whim struck them. It was an absurd thought, of course, but he had on occasion wondered what Carey would think if she met them.

"I'm curious why you think I should consider helping you," said the general.

"Because it's your fault that I'm in this farcical situation?" Anatoly suggested. "Because I'm your son?"

"This situation is none of *my* doing," the general told him.

"What *are* you doing here, actually?" Anatoly asked. He looked at his aunt. "Come to admire your handiwork?"

"Petulant boy," his aunt said, dipping her spoon into her ice cream. One of the kids at the table behind her jumped up and down in his chair, jogging her arm, but her face never lost its beatific calm. "Are you enjoying your new life?"

"My days are filled with unicorns and rainbows," he said deadpan. "I am experiencing unprecedented personal growth."

"You're working as a tax inspector in Edinburgh."

"I'm a data entry administrator," he told her, annoyed but not surprised that they had tracked him down.

"A son of mine..." his father muttered.

His aunt laid down her spoon, plucked the wafer which had been stuck in one of the scoops of ice cream, and nibbled a corner while she watched him.

"I'm not going to ask what happened in London," he said.

"Good," said his father. "Not even you would be so foolish as to expect an answer."

It was something of an effort to keep a lid on his anger. "We'll leave that for another family reunion." He sat back and looked around the café. The classic scenario would have been to pack the place before he even got here. Irregulars, not toughs from the embassy, because he'd have recognised the type and bailed the moment he saw them. Full sound and vision, tiny cameras stealthed with mimetic coatings stuck to the walls. Back in Moscow, analysts would go over the footage again and again, studying his breathing, the dilation of his pupils, the faint tremor in his hands. Three separate snatch squads waiting in unobtrusive vehicles parked in nearby streets.

Or maybe they'd come alone after all. His family were omniscient and omnicompetent. The only places safe from them were the places they weren't interested in.

"Why do you want this thing?" his father asked.

Because a Polish teenager with the brain of Alan Turing wants it as a toy. "It's obsolete," he said. "A museum piece. Like a poisoned umbrella. How can it hurt?"

"That's not what I asked."

"Your father and I," his aunt said, stepping in smoothly, "would like to know what you can offer us in return."

He took a breath. "If you do this for me," he said, "I'll come back to Moscow."

His father gave him a stony look. "You seem very certain that we want you back."

His aunt was watching him with her head tipped a little to one side, the wafer forgotten between her fingers, an unreadable look on her face. "You must feel you're very invested in this situation," she said.

"Nonsense," said the general. "He's trying to manouver us into a position where we take him back."

"No," she said, "I don't think so."

This sort of double-act just bounced right off Anatoly. He said, "Well, this has been fun." He drained his cup and made to stand. "Have a safe journey home."

"Sit down," his aunt told him, while the general did his best to stare a charred hole straight through him. When Anatoly was sitting again, she said, "We'll want an overview of whatever it is you're involved in. It doesn't have to be any more complicated than that. A *precis*."

"A running *precis*," his father grumbled.

"You're asking me to blow my own operation."

His aunt returned the wafer to the melting ice cream in its dish. "We're asking for a *view*. Something's happening here, and we don't know what it is."

This was quite an admission from another member of his family. "If you don't know what it is, how do you know something's happening?"

"There's a blind spot," she said, "and you seem to be inside it. We'd like to know what's in there with you."

"It's nothing earth-shaking."

"It's *earth-shaking* enough for you to approach us for the device," the general grumbled.

"It's a means to an end," he said. "It's not the end itself." He thought about it. "I'll have to discuss this with other parties. Can you source me the item or not?"

"Of course we can," said his aunt. She lifted a huge leather shoulder bag onto her lap, rummaged about in it for a moment, then put what appeared to be a small travel pillow on the table.

They all sat looking at each other for a while. His aunt nudged the pillow fractionally towards him.

"It's customary to say 'thank you'," his father told him stonily.

Anatoly reached out and took the pillow. "Thank you," he said.

"He always was ungrateful," his father told his aunt.

"Oh, I think he'll be grateful this time," she said, smiling at Anatoly. "Won't you?"

He stood up, the pillow clutched in his hand. "I'll be in touch," he said.

His aunt inclined her head. His father looked as if he wanted to hurdle the table and carve out his heart with his ice-cream spoon.

"Right," he said. "Good to see you again. Love to everyone at home."

As he left the café, he saw the unassuming little man standing on the other side of the street, hands in pockets, watching him quite openly. They looked at each other across the traffic for a little while, then they nodded, one professional to another, and walked away in opposite directions.

"It's a towel," Carey said when Magda opened the pillowcase and removed its contents.

"It's a very sophisticated cryptanalytical tool," said Anatoly.

"It's the printer," Magda said, laying aside what looked like a rather washed-out hand towel. "*This* is the tool." She took from the bag what looked like an embroidery sampler, as if someone had decided to stitch an old-fashioned computer tapboard. She held it up, examined both sides. She looked as if Christmas had arrived early.

"I don't understand these things, really," Anatoly went on. "But I gather it's rather esoteric. It would probably be worth a lot of money, if you could find the right collector."

Carey lifted a corner of the towel. There was no visible way in which it could be a printer. She wondered if this wasn't all some kind of joke. Something *esoteric*. She said to Magda, "You're not planning on selling this thing on, are you?"

The girl looked solemnly at her. "No. I'm not."

Carey nodded. "Okay. Well, now you've got it, see what dirt you can dig up for me on Rocketman." She looked at Anatoly. "You. Coffee."

They went into the kitchen and Carey started to fiddle with the coffee maker. "You should have told me before you arranged the meet."

"You wouldn't have let me go."

"Damn right. Suppose they'd snatched you out of there? I'd be here on my own."

"It's the only way we could have got that thing," he said. "You can't find stuff like that on the internet."

"We could have bargained Magda down."

Anatoly wasn't so sure about that. He lit a cigarette. "They're interested in whatever's going on here," he said. "That's useful to know."

"They're interested because they don't know *what's* going on," she told him. "People like that, they hate not *knowing*, Tolya. It doesn't mean anything."

"I disagree. They came here in person, and it wasn't just to see how much weight I've put on. They came here in a hurry. *And they brought it with them.* I don't think you understand how unusual that is. They were making a point. Whatever it is, it's important to them."

She sighed. You could go clean out of your mind trying to unpick the doublethink necessary to deal with the intelligence services. She found herself wishing she'd caught that train in Breslau; she'd be back in Barcelona by now. She liked Barcelona.

"I forgot to ask how things went with Kaunas," said Anatoly

"He says I need to improve my people skills."

"You have people skills?"

2

SHE'D ALWAYS THOUGHT Dutch place names sounded like they should be on one of those maps you got at the beginning of a fantasy novel. Zaandam. Castricum. Alkmaar. *Fabled Alkmaar, City of Glass*, she thought, looking out of the train window. It didn't look very fabled. She could see some office buildings. Sleet blew across the platforms of the little station. The North Sea was only a few miles to the west and there was nothing much stopping its weather scouring across Noord-Holland. As the train pulled out again, hail rattled against the windows.

There were only two trains a day between Amsterdam and Den Helder, but even so she had the carriage almost to herself. The pandemic had almost brought the Netherlands to its knees; almost half the population had died, and even now there was a haunted, sober quality to the country. In Amsterdam, tourism was slowly recovering, but out in the countryside everything seemed to be sleeping under a magic spell, flat fields and lowering skies and hardly any people to be seen. As the train rolled north, she saw buildings in the distance which seemed to reflect the light with a flat grey sheen, entire villages mothballed under layers of spray-on plastic, waiting for the people to return. Some of the fields were neatly cultivated, but many of them were growing wild, and a lot of the canals and drains that divided the landscape looked dangerously close to overflowing their banks. Looking at that, you could see just how much institutional knowledge the country had lost, how close the infrastructure still was to collapse.

It seemed to Carey that Europe—the whole world—was like one of those 3D puzzles that looked like a cube or a house or a puppy or something but when you took them apart you found it was impossible to put them back together the same way again. You'd see news shows about how the population was booming again and economies were starting to pick up, but the place had grown strange and just continued to get stranger. The EU seemed all but finished as more and more member nations split away, and many of those were throwing off progressively smaller and smaller independent states of their own. She'd heard of an Albanian colonel who'd set up his own country somewhere in the Balkans, four or five square kilometres of hillside and woodland, ruled under the divine right of kings, and he wasn't alone. It was as if the flu had brought with it a need for national identity, no matter how small the nation happened to be.

Things weren't much better in Spain. The economy was back on its feet, relatively speaking, and you saw lots of people about and things were starting to look prosperous again, but the Basques and the Catalans were still lobbying for statehood, and Galicia and Andalusia were looking as if they were thinking seriously about following suit.

As travel restrictions began to relax, US citizens were once more allowed to roam unhindered about Europe. Madrid was suddenly ankle-deep in American correspondents and political commentators, and Carey and the others who had been there for years found themselves regarded almost as tribal elders, wise folk much in demand for advice and contacts. Carey avoided this as much as possible, mostly because she was still in the country under false papers and she was eminently deportable—although that wasn't the problem it might once have been because she now had Mad Skillz—but also because she'd served her time as a stringer and she wasn't keen on doing it for a new set of clients.

She'd wound up extending her stay in Berlin, first for a week, then for a month. She and Maksim played games in the streets. How to tail someone. How to shake a tail. How to pick one up. How to set up and service a dead drop. Brush-passes, double-passes, fake passes, escape and evasion, comms protocol, crash contacts, Situations, jumps, dustoffs, pianists, cobblers, blacksmiths.

Evenings, they went to parties. Maksim seemed to know everyone, actors and artists, writers and politicians. They went to parties in Kreuzberg where serious people read serious poetry, and parties in Wedding where anarchists got wildly drunk and plotted the overthrow of the German State. They moved hotels every few days.

She kept seeing the same guy around, sometimes chatting with Maksim, sometimes just standing in the crowd at a party, smoking cigarettes that smelled as if they'd been rolled from a substance used to fumigate mattresses. He was fiftyish and tubby, with a face like an angry potato, and he wore shabby old suits and a beret.

"Yegor," Maksim told her when she asked. "Yegor's ex-FSB, he's an absolute star. I'll introduce you." But somehow he never quite got round to it and she and Yegor never really spoke, he just came into her life by osmosis.

Eventually, a Situation came up for Maksim, something in the East. They parted with a hug on the platform at the Hauptbahnhof, and over Maksim's shoulder Carey spotted Yegor waiting beside the train with a battered suitcase at his feet. "I'll be in touch," Maksim told her, although of course he never was.

Meanwhile, there was work to do in Spain. When she finally got back to Madrid, she found a shaven-headed little fireplug of a man wearing dungarees and a heavy metal tee shirt waiting outside her apartment.

"I am called Luis," he informed her solemnly once they'd got the recognition string out of the way. "I'm here to instruct you."

"Maksim's taught me all that," she told him.

Luis smiled sadly. "No," he said, "he has not."

And he was right. For Maksim, being a Coureur was wild and crazy, a romp, constantly winging it and taking risks. For Luis, it was austere and correct and almost courtly. They went back over all the things Maksim had shown her, and this time, it seemed to Carey, they did them right.

"Maksim wants adventure," Luis told her, as if that was somehow distasteful. "We do not."

"Don't we?" she said.

"No," he said. "We don't."

So it was another round of tradecraft, but this time there was a slow elegance to it which she hadn't appreciated before. Luis bird-dogged her first live Situation, a milk-run carrying a pouch of data from a corporate office in Zaragoza to its headquarters in Toulouse. There was nothing remotely illegal about it, but Luis got her to treat it as if she was carrying contraband, sourcing false papers for France and Spain and travelling by car and on foot through the Pyrenees via Andorra. "You never look in the Package," Luis told her. "If the client wants to tell you what's in it, that's their business, but you never ask."

Along with tradecraft, he brought her homework, a series of tasks in support of false identities. She rented flats under false names, applied for passports and driving licences using names and biometrics he provided. She ate meals at restaurants and handed over the printed receipts to Luis, hired cars, argued with lettings agents and utility companies. Once, she spent a day in a flat in Lisbon sitting beside an old landline phone. When it rang, a woman identifying herself as Officer Pereira of the Lisbon police asked if a man named Anton Blum lived at that address. Carey said he did, and Officer Pereira thanked her and hung up. What that was all about, she never found out, and she never asked. Sometimes she wondered who Anton Blum was, and what he had got himself mixed up in.

Her induction into *Les Coureurs* never officially ended, there was no formal graduation ceremony. She simply saw less and less of Luis and one day he just nodded and shook her hand and walked away.

Maksim wandered back into her life shortly afterward with a bunch of flowers and a bottle of vodka from some country she'd never even heard of before, but he only stayed for a week or so before there was a new Situation for him and a new Situation for her and they were off in opposite directions again.

And that seemed to set their relationship. They travelled all over crumbling Europe, sometimes together, more often separately. They moved a lot of Packages. Sometimes they managed as much as a month together in Madrid or Berlin before they were called away again. It was not the most satisfactory of relationships, but it seemed to Carey that, in these post-EU days, it was a peculiarly European one.

DEN HELDER WAS the end of the line, literally as far north as you could go on the Noord-Holland peninsula without being in the sea. Sleet lashed the bus on the short ride from the railway station to the ferry terminal. Looking out of the window Carey saw neat, tidy, empty streets, but the town was actually doing okay, relatively speaking; half an hour later, as the big car ferry left the terminal for the twenty-minute crossing to Texel, she saw a couple of destroyers and a frigate in port at the naval dockyard on the other side of the harbour.

She seemed to be the only foot passenger; the only other people she could see in the big lounge appeared to be employees of the ferry line. She poked around in the gift shop, resisted the many Texel sheep-themed toys and mementoes, bought a couple of paper maps and guidebooks of the island instead.

"We were busy over the weekend," said the cashier when Carey mentioned how quiet it was. "All the young EU going to the festival."

"Yeah, I'm going to cover it," Carey said.

The girl snorted. "I heard the EU was over."

"They're not going down without a fight."

The cashier slipped Carey's purchases into a brightly decorated paper bag. "You're sure you don't want one of these?" she asked, holding up a plushie sheep. "My cousin makes them."

Carey wavered, then bought the sheep, and when they docked she marched down the ramp with it tucked under her arm.

There was a hurriedly installed passport control booth at the foot of the ramp, but it was empty and she walked past it. Over on the other side of the terminal's car park, she could see buildings going up, more permanent passport and customs control facilities. There was a bus to Den Burg waiting. She was the only passenger. She sat and looked out of the window. The landscape was grassy and bleak and flat and whipped by winds and rain and sleet. She felt as if she had arrived at the edge of the world.

The EU roadshow had set up a number of white marquees and a large temporary building in Den Burg's little market square and then surrounded it all with linked crush barriers manned by sodden security staff. Walking miserably through the rain from the bus stop, sheep under her arm, Carey barely spared them a glance.

The hotel was on one side of the square, a charming white bar/restaurant with a residential annexe built onto the side like a small block of flats. She checked in, went to her room, dumped the sheep on a chair, kicked off her shoes, and lay down on the bed and closed her eyes. She'd been travelling for ten straight days.

It was not the first time the EU had chosen to stage a festival in this peculiarly out-of-the-way and nearly inaccessible place, but this year there was a particularly political message to it. The legal and administrative status of Texel and all the other islands of the Wadden archipelago, which straggled in a broken line up the North Sea coast, was vague at the moment. The islands had declared themselves to be an autonomous region a couple of years earlier and the various ethnic groups who lived there—Dutch, Germans, Frisians, Danes—were still trying to work out between themselves and their parent countries a viable framework for full independence. It was all dragging its way, calmly and unhurriedly, through courts and parliaments and local assemblies, and nobody expected a decision any time soon. No one could even agree on a name for the new polity.

You could drive from Texel to Wangerooge, off the German coast near Wilhelmshaven, along the Wadden causeway, a series of bridges and dams linking islands like Norderney, Juist, Terschelling and Vlieland—more names out of a fantasy novel—and then take a series of ferries, island-hopping until you reached Esbjerg. The EU had put a lot of money into the Causeway, in the years just before the Xian flu, and were not inclined to let it go without at least making a point, so Den Burg was full of young EU representatives—and they *were* young, Carey didn't see anyone who looked over thirty—standing in their tents in the market square and trying to attract miserable-looking tourists with pens and mugs and tee shirts bearing slogans like WE LOVE EU TEXEL and OUR UNION, *YOUR* UNION. Carey interviewed a few of the delegates, all of them annoyingly upbeat, and sat in on a couple of discussion sessions in the temporary building, and concluded that this passive-aggressive love bombing was doomed to fail. The thing was, she suspected the EU folk knew it too.

On her third night in Den Burg, sitting in the hotel's frankly excellent restaurant and eating dinner, Maksim came over to her table and sat down opposite her. "Hi," he said. "What are you eating? It looks good."

"Lamb stew," she said. "And yeah, it's terrific."

He attracted a waitress by force of personality alone. "I'll have the lamb stew," he told her. "And a glass of Amstel. Brandy and coffee to follow."

"You want all that on the same bill?" the waitress asked, glancing at Carey's meal.

"I don't see why not," he said. He beamed at Carey. "My treat."

When the waitress had gone, he reached over and gave Carey's hand a squeeze. "How've you been?"

"Busy," she said, squeezing back. "You?"

"Non-stop," he agreed, giving the menu a once-over and putting it back in its holder in the middle of the table. It was a month or so since they'd last seen each other, and it had been a bit of a slog for Carey.

"I missed you," she said.

He beamed at her again. "Are we all set at this end?"

"I guess," she said, going back to her food.

Maksim glanced around the restaurant. It was packed with young people wearing EU Festival lanyards and badges, all of them talking far too loudly. "I thought maybe we'd have a day at the beach tomorrow. How do you feel about that?"

"Only the truly crazy would go to the beach in weather like this," she told him.

He laughed. "It's bracing."

"It *snowed* this morning," she said. "It's *April* and it snowed."

"Some sea air will do you the world of good," he said.

"It's all sea air here," she said. "The bits of it that aren't sleet."

He gave her that old Maksim grin. "Five bucks says the weather's better tomorrow."

She looked at him. The problem was, she thought, she really liked him. "Make it Swiss francs and you're on," she said.

IRRITATINGLY, THE NEXT morning dawned bright and clear under a blue sky streaked with high cloud. "That's five Swiss you owe me," Maksim told her with a grin.

The beach at De Koog was about twenty minutes from Den Burg on the bus. Pretty much everywhere on the island was twenty minutes from Den Burg by bus. The little town sat behind a pair of high embankments and a dry moat that stopped the North Sea from inundating the area. Walking from the bus-stop, Carey saw bars and restaurants and cafés and gift shops, most of them still shuttered until later in the season, and a couple of biggish hotels sheltering behind the inner embankment. There were a few people about, but not many. Carey recognised a few of the EU delegates.

On the other side of the outer embankment was a promenade overlooking the beach. The sea was slate-grey and calm, but an offshore breeze was lifting white spray from the tops of waves. There was a signpost on the promenade with arms pointing to various places—Amsterdam, Berlin, Copenhagen. One arm pointing out to sea was marked *Boston UK 175 sea miles*.

"Is a sea mile longer or shorter than a real mile?" Carey asked.

"I don't know," Maksim said, hands in pockets, staring out to sea. "Let's get something to eat."

A line of houses and apartment blocks had been built along the crest of the embankment, their patios and verandahs protected from the wind by tall perspex shields. There was a café with an outdoor seating area, similarly shielded with perspex. They sat at a table and ordered toasted cheese sandwiches and tea and looked at the horizon, beyond which lurked *Boston UK*. It was the closest Carey had been to England. She closed her eyes and tilted her head back and felt the miniscule warmth of the sun on her face.

At one point, a woman walked past the café. She paused at the crest of the embankment and took out her phone and took some pictures of the sea. She was tall and she had short brown hair, and if you gave her a quick glance in low light you might reasonably mistake her for Carey. Carey suddenly realised she knew the woman, though. She'd been in Copenhagen for a gallery opening the previous year. The agency she was working for had booked her into a boutique hotel in the centre of town, and she'd wound up having her breakfasts at a McDonalds near the Tivoli. The tall woman had been at the opening, but then her hair had been long and blonde and she'd been wearing a long blue evening gown and she'd been on the arm of a much older man, the pair of them flanked by gigantic security men in excellent suits.

"That's Marthe Schiller," Carey said as the woman set off again down towards the beach. It had never occurred to her—why should it have? She had short brown hair and she'd never worn an evening dress in her life—that they looked alike.

Maksim pursed his lips.

"What's going on here?" she said.

Maksim gave her a look. *You don't look in the Package.*

"If she's doing what I think she's doing, her husband's going to want her back and he's going to be coming after whoever jumped her out," she told him.

Maksim took a sip of tea and looked seriously at her. "We do not ask," he said. "We do not question. We move the Package. She's been at a retreat on Rømø; she snuck out and took a ferry to Sylt yesterday and came down the causeway from there on these papers." He took a passport from his pocket and handed it over. It was Belgian, made out to someone called Sophie van Ost, whose photo was so poor it could have been of either of them. The photo in the passport Carey had travelled from Antwerp on was almost identical. "She'll be going to the mainland this afternoon and you'll be driving back up to Denmark."

"This is never going to work," she said. "Someone will have missed her already. Henning Schiller will have people looking."

He shook his head. "It's not that kind of retreat. Nobody knows she's gone yet, but when they do they'll be checking on ferry passengers and they'll see Sophie van Ost among them, so she has to be seen to go back. That closes the loop. It's foolproof, trust me. Sleight of hand."

She stared at him. "You can't ever just do something simply, can you," she said. "It's always got to be bells and whistles and as complicated as possible."

He grinned. "Complicated," he said, picking up the remains of his toastie, "is what fools people."

Back in Den Burg, the Euro-folk were packing up their show. The tents in the square were coming down and riggers were dismantling the temporary building. The next couple of ferries back to Den Helder were going to be busy; Marthe Schiller would just disappear in the crowd.

Walking back to the hotel from the bus stop, Carey glanced to one side of the square, where the town's little main street curved off in the distance. She thought she caught sight of a figure in a shabby suit and a beret emerging from one of the houses, but she couldn't be certain.

Back in their room, she packed. "Tell her not to go in the gift shop on the ferry," she said. "I talked to some of the staff in there on the way out." She gave him the plushie sheep. "And tell her to carry this."

Maksim gave the sheep a suspicious look. "Okay." They stood looking at each other. "So, I'll see you soon, then."

"Yeah, right." She hugged him and gave him a kiss. "You mad bastard."

MARTHE SCHILLER'S CAR, a hired hydrogen-cell Audi, was parked behind the hotel. Maksim had the keys. Carey put her bags in the boot, got in, and drove away from Den Burg.

The sleight of hand relied on the uncertain administrative status of the Wadden Islands. At one end, they were in the Netherlands, at the other they were in Denmark, but for the moment at least there was no passport control and therefore no record of border crossings.

The drive up the causeway to Wangerooge was uneventful, and she made the ferry to Sylt with time to spare. She ate dinner in one of the boat's dining rooms, kept to herself, but made sure she was seen. She thought of Marthe Schiller, who was probably already in Belgium by now.

From Sylt, it was a short ferry-hop to Rømø, and then a drive across the causeway to Skaerbaek on the Danish mainland. She checked into a motel for the night, and the following morning she returned the car to the hire company at the local station where it had originally been hired from, and she got on the express to Copenhagen.

Around Odense, she made her way to the dining car and

had a cheese and ham omelette and a beer for lunch. She felt grimy and travel-weary. Maybe once she was back in Madrid she'd log out for a while, concentrate on local journalism. She'd covered a lot of ground lately and it would be good to stay put for a few months.

A young man sat down opposite her. He was wearing a plaid shirt over a black tee shirt, and a combat jacket over them both. He had fair hair and an old-fashioned hipster beard and a kind face. They sat looking at each other for a while.

"I'm not going to ask where she is," he said finally. "Even if you know, you wouldn't tell me."

"I have no idea what you're talking about," she said. "Who are you?"

He bowed his head slightly. "Peter Schiller." Carey felt a wave of goose pimples go up her arms.

"I still don't know what you're talking about."

Peter smiled. He had a nice smile. "My stepmother thinks she's sort of frail," he told her. "But she's not. My father's a monster; frail people don't survive long around him. Eventually, it got too much for her, and I don't blame her for leaving." He clasped his hands on the table between them. "I don't know who you are, and I don't want to know. But I wanted to thank you, on her behalf." He took a card from one of the breast pockets of his jacket and put it on the table. "If you ever need anything, get in touch. I hope it won't ever come to that, but just in case."

Carey looked down at the card. Europeans still favoured physical calling cards. This one just had a phone number on it, not even a name. She thought of Maksim saying, "It's foolproof," and was suddenly overcome with a powerful urge to find him and punch him in the face. She looked at Peter and said calmly, "I think you've got the wrong person."

He smiled again and got up. "I don't think so," he said. "Have a good journey." And he walked off down the aisle and out of the carriage. A few minutes later, when the train stopped at Odense, she saw him walking down the platform, apparently without a care in the world, heir to one of Europe's great criminal empires, if you believed what you saw on the news.

3

KRISTA WAS IN a cab when the phone rang.

"Turn around and go back and we'll pretend this never happened," Jakobson said.

"If I'm not under arrest you have no right to hold me," Krista told her. She saw the driver glance at her in the rear-view mirror, but that was all right. She wanted him to remember her.

"This really doesn't make things look good for you," Jakobson said. "It makes you look guilty."

"You already think I'm mixed up in this, colonel. That's why you put me under house arrest, not because you were worried about the papers catching up with me." She heard Jakobson sigh. "You went out *shopping* today. Do you really think I'd have let you do that if I thought you were involved?"

"I was under guard the whole time."

"Yes, well, I'll be having a quiet face-to-face with Lieutenant Käsper about that in an hour or so."

"It wasn't his fault," Krista said. "I tricked him."

"He's supposed to be better trained than that."

"You disabled the override on the door so I couldn't get out," Krista told her. "Does the key code in the phone only open the door during the daytime, when there's someone available to babysit?" Silence, at the other end of the connection. "Fine. Well, this is me officially withdrawing my cooperation."

"Major," said Jakobson. "Listen to reason."

Krista hung up. "Pull over here," she told the driver, rummaging in her bag as if to put her phone back in it but in reality shoving it down the back of the rear passenger seat.

She paid with cash she'd withdrawn at the mall earlier in the day, walked off slowly until the cab had vanished into the evening traffic, watched it carry her phone off into the distance, presumably to an appointment with Jakobson's people when they finally tracked it down. It probably wouldn't buy her a lot of time, but it was a breathing space.

So, here she was. Night in Tallinn, snow on the ground and snow swirling in the light of the streetlamps, a fugitive from the police. What she'd done was enough to put a serious reprimand on her career, at the very least. It might very well have ended it. And she had no idea what to do next.

One step at a time. She stopped at a kiosk and bought a cheap phone, slotted in the expansion card onto which she'd copied her old phone, and walked to the nearest bank cashpoint while it took over the new one. She withdrew four thousand euros in cash—almost everything she had in her current account at this point in the month—and took another cab to the other side of town. All these things were trackable, but it would take time and she planned to keep moving.

In a run-down café, she wolfed down a sandwich and a cup of coffee and dithered over whether to call Markus. She decided against it. Things were already bad enough for him; making contact right now could only make them worse.

There was, she thought, really only one place she could go, and she realised she had been trying not to think about it.

* * *

THE MAJORITY OF people, if asked what the most important part of a surveillance state was, would probably say 'cameras', but that wasn't quite true. The most important thing was forgetting that the cameras were there at all.

If mass surveillance had arrived all of a sudden, fully-formed, a camera on every building and in every public vehicle, there would have been an outcry. But it hadn't happened like that. It had happened gradually, a camera at a time, and people had got used to them to the point where they didn't notice them any more. Down the years cameras had become smaller and the software behind them more sophisticated, but they were invisible, just another part of everyday street furniture. It was only when you thought about them that you noticed just how many there were.

The trick, with surveillance, was to move quickly and to keep moving. There was no central control room monitoring all the cameras in Tallinn; the street cameras belonged to the traffic authority, every store had its own system, each of the four bus companies, and so on. The authorities could tap into these any time they wanted, but civil rights legislation meant they had to produce a warrant first unless there was a massive emergency, and that took time. At this time of night it would mean trying to find a judge who was home to sign the warrant, or failing that rousting one from a restaurant or a theatre. Krista figured she had maybe half an hour.

She spent a few minutes of that half-hour buying two overcoats in a rundown little secondhand shop not far from where the taxi had dropped her. They were tatty and smelled peculiar, but they were warm and had hoods, and they altered her profile, which was important. Wearing one and with the other in a carrier bag, she left the shop and walked down the street.

Next, she caught a tram. It was cold on the tram; half the passengers were wearing hats or had their hoods pulled up. She found a seat in the final carriage, and kept her head down while she typed inconspicuously on her phone. A review of any footage might fail to spot her among all the other people in cold-weather gear.

The tram took her across the city. Surveillance was thinner on the ground the further you got from the centre of town, until the only cameras were on main roads and on streets patrolled by private security firms, which handily advertised their presence by means of warning signs bolted to lamp-posts.

She made her way from the tram stop, down lanes and side streets. At one point, feeling reasonably comfortable that she wasn't in range of a camera, she changed coats and stuffed the old one into some bushes. She found a pebble by the side of the road and dropped it inside her right boot, where it was just annoying enough to alter her gait. The trick was to walk differently enough to spoof the recognition algorithms, but not so much that you looked like someone deliberately walking with a stone in your shoe, which the algorithms were also written to look for. It was surprisingly tough to pull off.

In a new coat and with a new walk, she made her way to a shabby-looking car hire firm which had come to her attention during the investigation into Tamburlaine. The team hadn't so far been able to prove any connection, aside from rumour, but it was definitely a low-level criminal enterprise, and they had chosen to keep an eye on its affairs, just in case. When she walked into its offices at eight o'clock on the evening of the protest march, she found the owner, a middle-aged man wearing a shabby three-piece suit, sitting at a desk and pecking tentatively with two fingertips at the keyboard of a battered old laptop.

Krista didn't have time for small talk. She told the owner of the firm that she wanted to hire a car on the quiet, something without tracking devices, and she wanted to pay cash.

He had no idea who she was, of course, so he had no idea that she knew a lot more about him than he would probably have felt comfortable with, from the details of his bank accounts to his browsing history. He was so relieved to make at least one hire tonight that he gladly agreed to do the transaction in cash and he didn't look too closely at the ID she'd mocked up on her phone during the tram journey, which was good because it was paper-thin, not much more than a false name and address and an electricity bill she'd created using the phone's text editor and a cut-and-pasted letterhead. He didn't even bother to ask for her driving licence. She'd been reasonably sure she would get away with it—the firm was far from the centre of town, and it didn't pay a lot of attention to annoying things like legality. All you had to do was appear confident, seem as if you knew what you were doing, and have the bare minimum of ID and a wallet full of kroons.

But she was still willing her heart rate to return to normal as he led her out to a compound at the back of the office and showed her a car that was so old it had an actual physical key. She took a few minutes to familiarise herself with the controls and then she drove out of the compound and onto the street, and turned northeast.

THE CAR WAS a wreck, probably as old as she was, which was good because it was unlikely to have a tracker fitted as standard, and bad because most of the way to the coast she expected the engine to just give up and drop onto the road, which would have been problematical because any half-competent traffic cop coming to investigate why she'd come to a sudden stop would blow through her false ID as if it wasn't there.

The village was an hour or so's drive from Tallinn, straggling along a little bay nibbled out of the coast by the

Gulf of Finland. To get there you had to turn off the main road and onto a minor road, and then you had to turn off that and drive along a narrow, bumpy road—a cart track, basically—through dense forest that suddenly opened up into a vista of rocky beach and abandoned dinghies and wooden houses. It was quite some time since she'd last been here—since not long after her father's retirement, she realised—but the scene was as familiar to her as if she'd only seen it yesterday. Years ago, when she was a little girl, the village had briefly become notorious as the scene of a multiple murder, but that was probably the most interesting thing to have happened here in a thousand years.

She drove past a modest bungalow in the crook of an arm of the forest which stopped just short of the shore. She could see no signs of surveillance, but that was the point of surveillance; you weren't supposed to see it. She supposed she'd find out in the next few minutes.

She parked on a flat grassy area a few metres further on, walked back to the bungalow. Its boards were weather-beaten but it was neat and well looked-after and the garden seemed regularly tended. The lights were on, inside, behind thin curtains. She walked up to the front door and knocked.

It took a minute or so for him to answer; she heard the sound of his chair before he opened the door. Then she was standing there looking down at him and he was sighing.

For almost twelve years, Erik Lill had been her father's closest confidante in the Tallinn police force. Aide de camp, partner, all-purpose gofer, if not keeper of her father's secrets then at least party to many of them.

"They were here again yesterday," he told her, driving his chair back into the living room. "They seemed angry."

"They don't want to upset the Russians," she said.

"Tempers are starting to get frayed; all it would take is one unwise word."

"Russians," he snorted. He stopped in the middle of the living room, spun his chair round to face her. "Have you done something to your hair?"

"Apart from not having time to wash it for a couple of days?"

He nodded. "That's it." He gestured at a sofa which stood against one wall. "Please, sit."

She sat. "I probably shouldn't stay here long," she told him. "They'll be looking for me."

"Yes," he said. "Yes, I did wonder about that. Did they take you into custody?"

"Protective. They said."

Lill rubbed his eyes. Krista noticed his hand was shaking. "Well," he said.

"What did they want to know?" she asked.

"Well, obviously they wanted to know if your father murdered Sergii Volkov."

Volkov. So that was his name. "What did you tell them?"

Lill looked at her. "I told them what I told them before. It's ludicrous and it's offensive; your father wasn't that kind of man, he wasn't that kind of police officer. We should be arresting and prosecuting whoever's spreading this absurd story, not wasting time and effort persecuting your father."

"You have to be careful with them, Erik. Suppose they withdraw support for your treatments?" He was undergoing a strenuous programme of treatment intended to encourage the myelin sheaths of his central nervous system to regrow; there were those who said the treatment was almost as bad as the MS.

He snorted. "Let them. How much worse off would I be?"

She sighed. "Did my father *know* Sergii Volkov?"

Lill was silent for a few moments. "He arrested him a couple of times."

Krista felt her heart sink. Any kind of connection between her father and Sergii N only strengthened Jakobson's case. "Who *was* he?"

"Sergii?" Lill looked thoughtful. "Sergii was a shit. Small-time criminal and wife-beater. Ran an import-export business. He was an absolutely *terrible* criminal, no aptitude for it at all. It made us wonder why he bothered; he'd been in and out of prison since he was eighteen or so, and every time, he went straight back to it. Never learned his lesson. Some of us sort of admired that, in a twisted kind of way. The rest of us found it a bit pathetic."

"Did my father arrest him, that last time?"

Lill shook his head. "No, that was someone else, I can't remember who. It'll be in Records. We thought he was handling a bunch of high-end watches—Patek Philippes, Breitlings, Jaeger-LeCoultres from a robbery in London. It turned out we were wrong, but he was being interviewed about it and he lost his temper and punched an officer, stupid bastard."

"And he tried to sue the force when he got out of jail."

Lill nodded. "Half-heartedly. His lawyer knew it was never going to work; he just went through the motions and then gave up."

"So he wasn't making trouble?"

"No; he was just trying to see if he could wangle some compensation. Like I said, he was useless. And his lawyer wasn't much better, now I think about it."

"You seem to know a lot about him."

"Everyone knew Sergii. He was sort of a bad-luck mascot. You'd pick up bits of gossip about some harebrained scheme or other he'd got himself arrested for. Also, I was the officer who investigated his death."

"Oh." Krista sat bolt upright on the sofa.

Lill nodded. "There was no mystery about it. He had three or four times the legal driving limit of alcohol in his blood. He was blind drunk, stepped off the kerb without looking, a car clipped him, he cracked his head on the pavement, and goodbye Sergii."

"Everyone's saying he was beaten to death."

"He was in a punch-up earlier that evening. Got drunk in a bar and started annoying the wrong people. A couple of guys took him outside and roughed him up a bit. It was hard to tell which injuries were which, from looking at him, but the autopsy report said it was a hit-and-run that killed him. Now, whether it was an *accident* or not..." He shrugged. "We could never prove it, so we left the file open. It's probably still open."

"The wife thought he'd been murdered," Krista said. "She said he'd been hassling my father and my father killed him to shut him up."

"I don't know about any of that." He moved the chair back a few centimetres and squirmed to try to get more comfortable. "Jakobson had all this documentation I'd never seen before. Complaints by Sergii about your father, complaints by Sergii's wife alleging we'd killed him. All of it new to me."

"Surely you'd have seen it when you were investigating his death?"

"You would think so, wouldn't you?"

"You think someone buried it?"

"I don't know. Jakobson said her office never logged a complaint from the wife, but when they went looking for it, there it was."

For the first time, Krista began to appreciate the true scale of the disaster which was overtaking the Tallinn police. At the very best, they looked criminally negligent. At worst? She closed her eyes and tried not to think about that.

"Jakobson says they found details of three other

complaints, while they were looking for Sergii's documents," Lill told her. "Three more cases where the police were accused of killing Russians. All of them apparently ignored or deliberately covered up. She's got her people going through Records to see if there are any more."

Krista put her hands to her face. It wasn't a simple disaster; it was a catastrophe of Biblical proportions. It was Revelation and Ragnarök combined.

"You look tired," he said. "You shouldn't drive tonight."

"I can't stay here, Erik," she told him, opening her eyes. "I'll be fine."

"I really don't think you need to add a car crash to your list of woes," he said with a sad smile. "They won't come out here at this time of night."

"They'll know I'll come to see you. It'll just be a matter of time. Best if I leave now."

He nodded. "Where will you go?"

"I was thinking maybe I'd go down the coast, into Lithuania, maybe, or Poland. Give myself time to think."

Lill pulled a face. "Oh, please," he said. "Jakobson's never going to believe that so there's no point in lying to me about it."

"I don't want to get you in trouble, Erik. If they pull the plug on your treatment..."

"Then they pull it."

She got up from the sofa, knelt beside the wheelchair, and hugged him awkwardly. She had never exactly *liked* Lill, but she could still feel sympathy for him. "I'm sorry this has happened," she said.

"That's kind of you," he told her, "but it's not your fault."

"Well," she sat back on her heels, balancing herself by holding on to one of the chair's armrests, "*someone* needs to apologise, and it might as well be me."

He thought about that. "All right, then." He patted her

shoulder. "Thank you." As she stood, he added, "But even if you don't stay tonight, I don't think it's a very good idea to go back to Tallinn. It would be unfortunate if you got caught in the riot."

She found herself actually doing a comedy double-take. "The what?"

EIGHT

1

She was early for the meet. Partly it was just basic operational procedure, partly it was because she'd expected to have to spend half an hour shaking off Stefan's people, but either they'd suddenly developed unexpected tailing skills or they'd just given up and gone home, because she didn't spot any of them. She spent fifteen minutes on evasion procedures anyway and then she headed for the church.

According to the guidebooks it was variously the Church of St Barbara or the Garrison Church of St Barbara, but the locals just called it 'Barbara'. She wondered who Barbara was, and why Gliwice seemed so taken with her.

It was a huge neo-Romanesque brick structure with a tall brick tower topped with a spire set off to one side, and the *Nie!* demonstrators were outside again this bright breezy morning. They'd set up a table and they were selling posters and tee shirts and mugs and signing people up for newsletters and direct action events. Carey managed to dodge past them without attracting any more leaflets, and pushed open the heavy door.

Inside, the church was cool and quiet and smelled of incense. It was more austere than she was used to, for a Catholic church; she'd been expecting something more ornate. A handful of old ladies were scattered around the interior, either kneeling at prayer or just sitting. The only man in the place was sitting over to one side, by the wall. He had a shaven head and a bushy moustache and he was rocking that wing collar and ascot look again. Carey went over and sat next to him.

They sat there in silence for a while, then Carey said quietly, "Do you want to explain any of this to me?"

He smiled. "I understood you were the one who wanted to explain things to me."

"This isn't funny."

"It is," he said. "A little."

"You already knew who I was," she said. "When you sat down across from me at the hotel. You knew I was here before I'd even decided to stay."

"I didn't know what was on your mind, of course," he said. "I'm technical, not psychic."

"How did you know who I was?"

"Our mutual friend told me. He said you were coming."

"How did *he* know?" Maksim had been dead for six weeks before she'd even heard of Gliwice.

He shrugged.

"And you decided you'd take a look at me? Is that it? Just for laughs?"

He smiled again and watched a young priest fiddling about with something on the altar. "I was sorry to hear about his accident."

"You don't sound sorry, particularly."

He shrugged. "He was a recent acquaintance; our relationship was a business one." He smiled at her. "I barely knew him."

"What kind of business were you doing?"

He gave her a wry look. "Client confidentiality is of the utmost importance to us."

"You're a crook, Jerzy. You don't have clients, you have accomplices." She said it loudly enough for the old ladies in the pews nearby to hear, but nobody paid any attention and he just smiled again.

"We're a small group," he told her. "The only way we can survive is if everyone trusts us. It's a tricky path to walk, but we manage, day to day. If word got out that I was betraying the confidence of a *client*, everyone else we deal with would start to wonder how secure their business is. That kind of uncertainty can easily lead to bloodshed."

"Well," she said, taking a folded sheet of paper from an inside pocket of her coat, "if it's *trust* we're talking about..." She laid the paper on the pew between them.

He didn't touch it; he barely even glanced at it. That faintly amused look didn't falter. "Are you trying to threaten us?"

"Nope," she said brightly. "Just you."

He looked at her for quite a long time, then without taking his eyes off her he picked up the paper and unfolded it, glanced at the strings of figures printed on it, a list of the sums he'd been skimming off the gang's profits, and the bank accounts where he'd squirrelled them away. Then he folded it again and put it back on the pew.

"He hired us to conduct an electronic surveillance on a business address in the Old Town, the Diana Academy of English." His expression hadn't changed, but there was a faint snap of distaste in his voice. "It was perfectly routine, nothing he couldn't have done himself, but he said he wanted to remain at arm's length."

"Did he say why he wanted them watched?"

"No. And there was no product; the premises were empty and they stayed that way. No one ever visited."

"Didn't that strike you as odd?"

"It's hardly the strangest thing we've been hired to do."

"And that's it? That's all he wanted?"

He glanced down at the sheet of paper and smiled tightly. "All this unpleasantness," he mused, "for so little return." He looked at her. "He said you'd be angry."

That was hardly a feat of prescience. "Did he say anything else about me?"

Jerzy stood to go. "He said you wouldn't stop."

"HE CLOSED THE accounts," Magda said when Carey got back to Zimnej Wody. "The money's gone."

Jerzy, hiding the evidence. She grunted. "No great surprise. Could you find it again?"

The girl thought about it. "Maybe," she said. "Eventually. He won't make it so easy, now he knows I'm looking."

"Cool. Just in case we need to squeeze him again."

"Yes," said Anatoly. "Blackmailing one of the city's organised crime bosses. Very cool."

"They're not organised crime," Carey told him. "They're just a bunch of pianists. What are you looking at me like that for?"

Instead of answering, he went out into the hallway, and when she'd followed him into the kitchen and he'd closed the door, he said, "I wish you'd tell me what we were doing, because I thought we were looking into the death of your friend and so far all we've done is stepped on the toes of everyone who could do us harm."

"Says the man who dragged Russian Intelligence into this."

"We're talking about you, not me." He pulled one of the kitchen chairs away from the table and sat down. "Are you okay? Really?

"I'm fine."

"You're not fine. You're blundering around provoking people."

"I'm fine," she said again evenly. "And if you want to go back to Edinburgh I can book you a flight right now."

He looked at her a moment longer, then he rubbed his face. "What did the Rocketmen tell you?"

"He didn't have a scam going with them; he'd hired them to do some surveillance. Nothing properly criminal."

"So that was a waste of time."

"No," she said patiently. "It wasn't a waste of time, because we didn't know about it before. Maybe it's important, maybe it's not, but at least we know now."

He blinked at her. "I don't like being so *noisy*."

"You're a spy, Tolya, you hate attracting attention, and that's fine, covert is good." She smiled. "Sometimes you've just got to get rowdy, though."

SHE THOUGHT ABOUT getting old, sometimes. She thought it was inevitable. You hit sixty and you wouldn't be human, you wouldn't be *normal*, if it didn't cross your mind now and again that there were more years behind you than there were ahead of you, especially after some of the things she'd lived through. She'd stopped drinking and she thought she was better for it; she'd stopped getting into fights and she was sure she was better for that, but she got tired more easily and there were aches and pains she hadn't had before. She was still in pretty good shape, considering—she found herself taking a depressing array of supplements these days—but she didn't know how much longer she could go on taking trains and planes and crossing and re-crossing borders. It had ground her down, over the years. She could feel it.

She could just stop. She had an apartment in Austin and an apartment in Madrid and half a dozen or so safe houses scattered around Europe and she was not badly off. She'd made a good living from *Les Coureurs*, down the years, and she'd made a good living as a journalist, and Maksim had introduced her to a firm of accountants in Jakarta who had turned out to be the best thing he had ever brought into her life. Indonesia was constantly on the edge of armed revolt, but her accountants were always correct and scrupulously straight with her and down the years they had made wise investments using her money.

Les Coureurs were a narrow fraternity. Most of them never met. Most of them made peanuts. Some did it for nothing more than bragging rights. A few, a very few, were legends. There was Leo, who wound up having his head cut off and left in a luggage locker in Berlin. There was a crazy Englishwoman named Faye Ostler, who had walked an entire cell of anarchists out of some short-lived fascist state in the Italian Dolomites by disguising them as a church choir from Cardiff. There were vague and *very* weird stories about some guy in Kraków, none of which she believed. There was Maksim, although his legend had waned. You heard people talking about Maksim less and less these days, and if you did the stories were usually wrong. About herself, she had heard nothing. No stories, no wry anecdotes. Nothing. She felt as if she had passed through her life without leaving a mark, a professional who had done her job and then got off the stage. It was as if she hadn't been there at all, and sometimes, in idle moments, that really *really* fucked her off.

She wondered if Maksim had felt that way, as she used one of Boksi's fake driving licences to hire a car at the station and drove out towards Sierakowice. He was a couple of years older than her, had been a Coureur since he was in his mid-twenties. Had he been conscious of his waning legend? Was that what Helsinki had been all about, a demonstration that he still had the moves? And when that had ended so disastrously, had he come up with whatever he had been doing here? Was this supposed to have been his last great score, his swansong? It seemed skewed, to her. It stank of desperation.

What it did not stink of was improvisation. She had a sense of something intricate and planned down to miniscule tolerances, and a sense that it involved her somehow. If Jerzy had been telling the truth, Maksim had known she would be here, had *planned* for her to be here. So what had gone wrong?

The narrow road seemed, if anything, in even worse condition than it had a few days ago when Wareham had driven her along it, and she kept her speed down. At the junction, she drove on a little way past the farm and turned onto a forestry road that cut deeply into an arm of woodland. She parked the car and walked cautiously back to the junction, but there was no one about to see her.

She tried to imagine what it had been like, night-time, raining, the tractor lumbering up the slight hill to the junction. Visibility probably wasn't that great, the sound of the rain and the engine would have masked all other sounds. With the turn onto the main road almost complete, Mr Karski wouldn't have been paying much attention to what was happening to his left; the first thing he knew that anything was wrong was probably the sudden illumination of the car's headlights as it came up the road towards him at better than a hundred kilometres an hour, and by then it would have been too late to do anything at all about it.

She looked at the marks on the road again, where the impact had occurred. Then she walked back a hundred metres or so, just to satisfy herself there were no skid marks. Maksim hadn't touched his brakes at all. Further back, though, there *were* marks, a pair of fat hyphens barely visible on the asphalt, as if someone had spun their tyres briefly. She looked at these for a while, took a couple of photos, and walked back to the car. On the way past, she looked at the farm. None of the buildings lining the road—barns and equipment sheds, from the looks of them—had windows on this side. She couldn't see where the main farmhouse was, but it seemed to be set some distance back, invisible from the road. Michał and his son had had a little walk to get to the accident, and she mentally added another minute or so to the time before they had called the police.

Back in the car, she took out her phone and read the report again, thinking about that time lag before the police had arrived; not long enough for them to have got here from town but too long for them to have been in pursuit.

What if, she thought, they hadn't been chasing him at all? Suppose he hadn't been running away; suppose he'd been running *towards* something.

She backed the car onto the road and drove on north, keeping an eye out for anything unusual at the side of the road and knowing that, if it was there, it would be too well-hidden to see. A kilometre or so from the junction, the sound of the tyres on the road surface changed momentarily, a fraction of a second of silence and smoothness under the car. She'd driven a couple of hundred metres before it even registered. She pulled in to a passing spot and walked back.

It was easy to find; a section of the road maybe three metres long and extending all the way from one side to the other had been repaired. It was a good, professional repair, and it looked almost brand new. She knelt down and brushed her fingers across the surface. Minor road repairs, these days, were a piece of cake; you cut out the damaged section and poured a mixture of crushed stone and ground-up asphalt and some sort of nanotechnological bonding agent into the gap and smoothed it out. It set solid in a few minutes, even in the rain. A couple of guys with jackhammers could have done this repair in about half an hour. On either side of the road, bushes had been cut back a few feet to allow the road team to work, although they were starting to grow back. She poked around in them for a while but didn't find anything. She went back to the car.

Further on, there was a junction with a stop sign. She

turned left and a minute or so later the road surface improved again and she was in a village. She missed the sign with its name, but it wasn't much more than a wide spot in the road; a few newish-looking houses, what looked like some light industrial units, and a little general store, all set well back. She pulled into the store's car park, went in and bought a can of Coke, stood by the car drinking it in the sunshine while she looked at the fields and woods on the other side of the road. A bus went by, followed by a couple of cars that couldn't pass until it pulled in at a stop somewhere.

Back inside, she showed Maksim's passport photo to the woman behind the counter.

"What did he do?" the woman asked.

"Ran off with his girlfriend," Carey said.

The woman pulled a sour face. She was short and stout and her hair was pulled tightly back and tied in a ponytail. "He looks the type. Are you sure you want him back?"

"She's welcome to him," Carey told her. "I just want the car."

The woman chuckled and shook her head. "I haven't seen him here."

"How about him?" Carey said, holding up the photo of Yegor. The woman narrowed her eyes. "His uncle," Carey added. "If the bastard was in trouble, that's who he'd run to."

The woman looked at her, an uncertain expression on her face. "I don't know these men," she said evenly. "I don't know you, either."

"That's okay," Carey told her, putting away the prints. "I was never here. Thank you."

Anatoly would have handled that better, she considered, driving back the way she had come. He'd have managed to ask the questions without the woman ever knowing they'd been asked, and five minutes later she'd have forgotten he ever existed. Either way, it was going to take days, weeks maybe, to check all the little villages in the area. And that was if she was right and Maksim's bolthole, the place where he was doing his real business, was somewhere in the area.

She drove back towards Sierakowice, and this time when she reached the farm she took the turnoff and bumped down the narrow road, retracing the route the tractor had taken. About half a mile from the intersection, she came to a spot where the ground on both sides of the track was churned up. She stopped the car and went to look. A lot of people had walked about here when the ground was muddy. She saw what looked like toolmarks, spades and rakes maybe, and off to one side a single short mark of a fat tyre. She took photos, stood a while thinking.

Another half-mile or so along, she spotted another repair on the road. It was identical to the first one, a stripe of new macadam about nine feet long. An idea forming in her mind, she found a broad spot, performed a ten-point turn—there was nobody about to see her so what the hell—and drove back to the intersection and from there to the junction with the main road.

And there it was. She'd missed it when Wareham drove her out here, there had been too much on her mind, but there was a third repair, a few hundred yards before the junction. Same size as the other two, but someone had driven over this one before the surface had quite finished bonding and there were a lot of overlapping tyre marks in it. She took out her phone and dialled Magda.

"Do me a favour and check if there were any roadworks around Sierakowice around about the date of the accident," she said. "Anything at all, scheduled or unscheduled." She hung up and photographed the tyre marks, and then she stood there in the middle of the road, looking about her and thinking about timing.

* * *

"A LOT OF the gangs are new. Ish," Wareham told her. "Oh, there's always been crime here, it's like any city, but a lot of them came in after the flu. It was a strange time; looking back, we were very vulnerable."

They were sitting in what from the outside presented as a rancho-style roadhouse a few miles to the northeast of Gliwice, on the road to Tarnowy Gory. Inside, it was full-on hunting lodge. Everything was rough-finished wood: the furniture, the walls, the floors, the ceiling. There were wild boar heads—fake, Carey hoped—on the walls, and the waiting staff were dressed in some sort of peasant costume she didn't recognise. The lights were turned down low and the place was mostly illuminated by candles in glass holders which sat in the middle of each table. She'd opted for the venison stew; Wareham was tucking into a steak and fries with the happy abandon of a man who's given up bothering to watch his weight. He was wearing slacks, an open-necked shirt and a blue blazer.

"I heard you had a gang war," Carey said.

"Who told you that?"

She shrugged and took a sip of mineral water.

He looked around. They were sitting in a corner of the gallery that ran around the first floor of the restaurant, by a window that looked out across the car park to a wall of trees on the other side of the road. "I think it's probably a bit extreme to call it a 'war'," he said. "You know what gangs are like. Someone says the wrong thing or jostles someone else in a bar and then honour has to be satisfied." He went back to his meal. "There was some low-level stuff a little while ago, but it's settled down now."

"I heard there were some deaths."

He looked at her. "Organised crime has quite a high attrition rate. These things come in waves, I've found down the years."

She tore a bread roll into pieces and dipped one in her

stew. "You've heard of Rocketman?" She popped the piece of bread in her mouth.

He considered that for a moment, then he laid down his knife and fork and sat back. "You know," he said, "we could have done this at the office. Then I wouldn't have had to pay for the meal."

"I'll pay, if it means that much to you."

They looked levelly at each other for a little while, then Wareham took up his cutlery again. "According to the police, they're what we used to call 'white-collar crime' when I was growing up," he said. "They do embezzlement, mostly. They hire themselves out to other gangs who need some technical problem solved. I've never met any of them. They sound rather prosaic, from what I understand. Black-hat hackers, hardly a new story."

"Maksim had something going on with them."

He raised an eyebrow.

"He paid them to carry out surveillance on a language school."

"The Diana Academy?"

It was her turn to raise an eyebrow.

"It burned down," he told her. "A couple of months ago. The police suspected arson."

Carey suddenly recalled Witek Mazowiecki saying something about an explosion at a language school. "A gas explosion," she said.

Wareham nodded. "Not a very big one. It blew out the windows and set the place on fire. The building's boarded up at the moment."

"Could it have been a front? For something else?"

He thought about it. "I suppose that's always possible," he allowed.

"Did you cover it?"

He put his knife and fork down again. "All right," he said with a sigh. "I thought we'd have a pleasant evening and a nice meal. I wasn't expecting the third degree."

She looked at him for a long time. "Maksim was a Coureur," she said finally. "I'm a Coureur. Maksim was my boyfriend, off and on, for about twenty years and Coureur Central have asked me to find out what he was up to here because they think it might represent a public relations problem for them." She blinked. "Happy now?"

Wareham rubbed his eyes. "Not a Texan private investigator, then."

"I'm from Texas and I have a PI's licence," she said. "What more do you want?"

Wareham sniffed. "The Diana Academy was set up here five years ago. Five years this month, actually, if memory serves. As far as I was ever able to discover, it was completely kosher. You don't get actual physical language schools much these days; years ago every other house was an English school, but nowadays they're mostly online. But the Diana Academy was a proper school. I spoke to some of its former students and they were more than happy with their time there. The school had five tutors, all native English speakers, and an administrative staff of four, again all native English speakers. I've never been able to find out who owned and ran it; it seems to have belonged to a hedge fund based in Ireland, but they never replied to any of my requests for information. A year ago, the school closed. There was no fuss, no hint of scandal, they just graduated their final intake of students and locked the doors and everyone went away. I tried to track down the teachers, but there was only the vaguest of personal information about them. The building's still being leased by the hedge fund, but it's been empty ever since."

She said, "You didn't believe I was a journalist—which I am, incidentally—and you didn't really believe I was a private investigator, but I tell you I'm a Coureur and you just swallow that without any questions at all?"

He shrugged. "I've found that in any given situation, the maddest explanation is often the right one."

She looked down at her meal. "I didn't want to do this," she said. "I told Central I wanted nothing to do with it and I left the country."

Wareham crossed his arms. "Why did you change your mind?"

"I don't know," she said. She looked at him. "I really don't. I wish I'd just kept going."

He thought about that. "I've never met a Coureur before," he said. "Although I've heard of you, obviously. Would you be up for an interview?"

"You can fuck right off."

He chuckled. "Are you all so bad-tempered?"

"Yes," she said. "And it's no fucking wonder, the shit we have to go through."

Wareham picked up his knife and fork and went back to working on his meal. "While we're in a confessional mood, I should tell you that I've had dealings with the English Intelligence Services down the years."

"You're a spy?"

He shook his head. "More of a… what do you call it? A *stringer*. Sometimes they ask me to keep my eyes open for one thing or another. It's never anything ground shaking, or at least it never seems to be. It's rather a giggle, actually."

"And you're telling me this why?"

"I'm wondering whether they should know about you and Maksim. It's starting to sound less and less like a traffic accident and more like some kind of operation. They have resources that could be put at your disposal, if you needed them."

It was such a blatant pitch at recruitment that she didn't even get annoyed. "I'd rather you kept it to yourself. Can you do that?"

He nodded. "As I said, I'm just a local source, I'm not

obliged to make reports on my own initiative, although they would expect me to let them know about anything important. Do you really not know what Maksim was doing here? Really?"

There was no record of Maksim Ilyich Petrauskas entering Poland. He'd just suddenly appeared in Gliwice using his own name. She said, "Whatever it was, he wanted me here. He told Rocketman's boss I was coming."

"How could he have known?"

She shrugged. "Beats the hell out of me. Maybe he planned to get in touch and ask me to come." She looked out of the window. A big black SUV with smoked windows was pulling into the car park. The lights shone on its wax job. She said, "Wild horses couldn't have dragged me back into his life, though."

"But here you are," Wareham said.

"Yeah," she said. "Yeah, here I am." The SUV pulled into a parking space near the restaurant. Its lights went out and the doors opened and a man in a business suit and a woman wearing a short fur coat over a long grey dress got out. They seemed a little overdressed for this place, but each to their own. Carey started to turn back to look at Wareham, but sudden motion caught the corner of her eye and she looked back through the window and saw two figures in motorcycle suits and helmets approaching from either side of the car pointing accusingly at the man and the woman. She heard no sound, but the man and woman fell down and the two dark figures walked off out of sight. A moment later a motorcycle with two people on it roared out of the car park and took off up the road in the direction of Tarnowy Gory. By that time people were running out of the restaurant and gathering around the two fallen figures by the SUV. She sensed Wareham getting out of his seat and coming round the table to look out into the car park.

"Well, shit," she said.

* * *

"THE POLICE ARE calling it a mob hit," Anatoly told her.

"Yeah," Carey said, "no shit." It was gone midnight; the police had kept everyone at the restaurant while they took statements and then Wareham had hung around for a while chatting up material for a piece about the shooting before driving her back to Zimnej Wody. One of the staff said the victims were the underboss of some minor German gang and his wife. They ate there a couple of times a week, regular as clockwork, which was terrible security but it was too late to tell them about that now.

Magda pretty much owned the local police database by now, and all their comms. The cloth laptop was cabled into a bunch of little black boxes on one of the tables in the studio. It was doing about a dozen pieces of heavy processing at once; one of the paperscreens on the wall showed the results of an ongoing trawl of Poland's Immigration Service records using Maksim and Yegor's photographs. They'd gone back almost a year now and there was still no sign of them. On another screen, the laptop was running facial recognition on Gliwice's traffic camera database, again without success.

"I checked for road repairs," Magda told her. "There's no record of anything in that area for the last eighteen months."

Carey nodded. She felt drifty and a little shivery and she wondered if it was delayed shock coming on. It was far from the first time she'd seen dead people, but it was the first time she'd seen anyone killed right in front of her. It had all seemed so matter-of-fact and unhurried, just two guys walking up and pointing at them and then they were dead. She hadn't even been able to make out the guns.

"How much capacity does that thing have left?" she asked, nodding at the cloth laptop.

"As much as you need," said Magda. "It was developed to handle massive amounts of parallel decryption; it'll just keep on doing stuff for as long as you ask it."

"Okay. See if you can work up a go-to on Robert Wareham." She spelled the surname. "Anything you can find, doesn't matter how small."

"Is he mixed up in all this?" Anatoly said.

She couldn't see how. She'd been the one who had approached him, and all their contacts since then had been initiated by her. "He came out to me as an SIS zero-hours man tonight," she said. "He offered me *resources*. Can't hurt to know a little more about him." Anatoly scowled. "Remember what I told you about espionage, once upon a time?"

He nodded. "Nothing but grief," he said.

"Damn right," she said, looking from screen to screen. "Nothing but grief."

2

"TEXAS HAS BEEN an independent nation for almost two years," the man behind the desk told her. "We've opened embassies in Paris and London and Milan. You never thought to visit one of them?"

"I've been busy," Carey told him.

"Mm hm," he said. The little plaque on his desk identified him as JE Brookshire, and he was smooth and bland in a summer-weight business suit.

"I'm a freelance journalist," she said. "I need to work; I can't just take off across Europe when I want." Most of this was, of course, a barefaced lie. She'd been doing little else but taking off around Europe for the past few years. In the wake of the Line's sudden and unexpected declaration of statehood, she had spent almost eight months following it across the Continent from the station in Portugal—now redesignated as an embassy—all the way to the Russian border, interviewing officials and politicians and locals as she went.

Brookshire knew all this, of course. It was in the inch-thick printed dossier of application forms sitting on the desk in front of him. "But you *can* take off and fly across the Atlantic," he said.

"I had some time, there's some things I need to do here, and I thought it would be better to deal with the Texan government direct rather than embassy staff." She had also wanted to wait and see if Texas could actually make a success of nationhood, but she thought it better not to mention that.

Brookshire said, "It's usual for there to be a certain degree of *residency* involved, in the case of citizenship." He paged through the dossier. "According to this, you haven't lived here for ten years."

"I still own property here," she pointed out. "And I pay all my taxes."

Brookshire turned another couple of pages. "That is true," he said. He looked at her. "Are you planning to move back here permanently?"

Nothing could have been further from Carey's mind. She said, "I can't rule it out." She already had Spanish, German, Belgian and Dutch citizenship, under various identities, but it seemed important for her to have Texan nationality under her own name.

"Hm." Brookshire closed the dossier and clasped his fists on top of it. "Ms Tews," he said seriously, "have you ever thought of being of service to your country?"

"HE SAID WHAT?" said Frank.

"They want me to be a spy," she said.

"Licence to kill? Like that?"

They were sitting in a bar in downtown Lubbock; it was early in the afternoon and there was almost nobody else there. She said, "Well, I don't think they want me to kill anybody. He was kind of vague about it."

"What did you say?" She hadn't seen Frank since she left Texas; he'd lost weight and all his hair, and his bald scalp was dotted with the angry little carmine pits of skin cancer treatment.

She shrugged. "I said I'd give it some thought."

"Wow." He topped up his glass from the pitcher in the middle of the table. "I never met a spy before."

"It's irksome, is what it is," she said. "If they make it a condition of citizenship." It was almost part of Coureur body language to be scornful of national security services; they were commonly regarded as being hidebound and monolithic and slow to adapt, but the infant Texan Foreign Intelligence Bureau could cause her real problems, if it put its mind to it. It was no good withdrawing her citizenship application and just walking away; she was on their radar now, and in her experience the intelligence services of young nations were usually eager to prove themselves. She could go back to Europe and change all her identities, which was going to be really annoying and wouldn't work anyway; they'd spot an anomaly and dog her footsteps for years, and they'd queer her status in every nation where she had residence. All because she'd wanted to be a good citizen. "Bastards."

Frank was staring at her. "You okay?"

She sighed. "Just thinking." She drained her glass, refilled it from the pitcher, nodded to the waitress for another one.

"I shouldn't be drinking so much," Frank said. "They say it contraindicates with my meds."

"How's that going?"

He raised a hand, almost but not quite ran it over his scalp. "I've got another six weeks of treatments," he said. "They say we'll see then."

She touched her glass to his. "Here's to you, Frank."

"Yeah," he said. "Amen to that." Carey had leased the house out for a peppercorn rent to a local musicians' collective, and down the years it had grown in reputation. Now there were moves to turn it into a proper arts centre, and Frank, somewhat to his own bafflement, had been put forward as administrator. This was all to the good, as far as Carey was concerned—Byron and Pru would have been quietly thrilled, she thought—and her main reason for returning to Lubbock had been to tidy up the legalese involved, touch the pen to various documents. She could have done it at a distance, but she thought it was important to be there. Applying for Texan citizenship had almost been an afterthought, and now that had turned out to be a mistake.

The city hadn't changed a whole lot since she'd last seen it. A lot of businesses had gone bust during the flu lockdowns, and others had upped and left when the state seceded from the union, but new ones had come in to replace them, and if Lubbock was still not as busy as she remembered when she was a girl, it was a lot busier than when she'd left for Europe.

"I read your stuff, now and again," Frank told her. "You're good."

She raised her glass to him.

"How long are you going to be here?"

"Just as long as it takes to finalise the paperwork for the centre. I've got to go back to Austin and see this pencil-neck about my passport. A week, maybe. Ten days." Back in Europe, it looked as if Russia might be the next nation-state to fracture, and oddly it seemed that they and the Siberian separatists were approaching the matter like adults rather than pointing guns at each other. She didn't want to miss that.

"I got a letter from an attorney says he represents someone called Rae-Lynne Sampson. That ring any bells?"

"My dad's sister," Carey said with a sinking heart. "What does she want?"

"The attorney says Mrs Sampson is part-owner of the house. Wants a share of the arts centre and about a million bucks."

Carey sat back and stared at him. "That is just so much bullshit," she said. She'd only ever met Rae-Lynne a couple of times. She remembered a small, skinny, pinch-faced woman in bell-bottom jeans and a batik blouse. "Byron and Pru owned the house free and clear, and Byron left it to me in his will."

Frank nodded. "I guess she heard about the centre on the news and decided she'd try and get a piece of it."

"Frank," she said. "Why didn't you tell me about this right away?"

"It's under control," he said. "I got Byron's attorney on it."

Byron's attorney was a smooth-talking predator called Taylor Voss, a forty-year veteran of the music business. He would walk over Aunt Rae-Lynne as if she wasn't there. "She doesn't want anything to do with the arts centre," she said. "She just wants to make a nuisance and delay things until she gets a payoff."

"That's about what Voss said." Frank took a sip of beer. "He did cuss some, too, though."

Carey sighed. Rae-Lynne had no claim on the house or the centre, but if she had a smart lawyer she could keep it in the courts for months, and in the meantime the centre couldn't open. It would be easier to give her what she wanted just so she'd go away. "Let me think about it," she said.

* * *

BROOKSHIRE FOUND HER sitting on a bench in Emma Long Park, eating an ice cream and watching people canoeing on the lake. "You couldn't have come to the office?" he asked, sitting down beside her.

It was a hot, bright day. Carey had bought herself a hat with a big floppy brim to keep the sun off. Brookshire was wearing a panama that went well with his cream linen suit. She shielded her eyes with her hand and looked out across the water. "I want a quid pro quo," she told him.

"You'll get a passport," he said. "Isn't that quid pro quo enough?"

She reached into her bag and took out a little envelope containing a flash card. "I'm having a bit of legal difficulty," she said, putting the envelope on the bench between them. "Make it go away by this time next week, and I'll work for you."

Brookshire glanced down at the envelope, then he sat back and tipped the brim of his hat down over his eyes. "And that's it?"

"That's it. You scratch my back, I spy for you. Take it or leave it. I'm sick of driving back and forth between here and Lubbock."

Brookshire scowled. "We don't like to say 'spying'," he said. "You'll be working in Human Intelligence."

"Mr Brookshire," she said, gathering her things and standing up. "In my experience, human intelligence is rare as hens' teeth these days."

A WEEK LATER, Frank called to tell her that Aunt Rae-Lynne's attorney had been in touch to formally drop all claims on the arts centre. A day or so after that a brand-new Texas passport in her name was delivered to the hotel where she was staying. The following day, she flew to Madrid.

When she got home, she sent Brookshire an audio file of their conversation in the park, the one where she asked him to bend the law to get her to spy on Texas's behalf, and a video clip of their meeting filmed by Frank from a canoe out on the lake. It wasn't a very good clip—the distance was extreme and Frank was a terrible cameraman—but she and Brookshire were easily identifiable and there were a couple of moments where it was possible to read their lips. She attached a note from Turner Voss detailing Rae-Lynne's sudden withdrawal of her legal case following Brookshire's intervention. She didn't make any threats, just sent the files.

A few days later, she got a message from Brookshire. It said *Bravo. Be seeing you.*

Not if I see you first, matey-boy, she thought, but of course when he did come back into her life she didn't see it coming.

3

"I THOUGHT WE had an understanding," said Jakobson.

"We didn't tell them to riot," Lenna said, and she was able to say it truthfully. The word 'riot' had never been mentioned.

"Can you stop them?" Jakobson watched her face and nodded stonily. "Thought not."

"I might be able to do something, but not while I'm in a cell."

Jakobson glared stonily at her and shook her head.

"Are you going to charge me?" Lenna asked.

"Haven't decided yet," Jakobson said. "Thinking about it. Under the Terrorism Act, I can hold you for forty-eight hours without charge, and right now that seems like an attractive prospect."

"That's not going to help anyone. We didn't want this, but emotions are running high."

"You see?" Jakobson said, nodding. "I told you it would happen. I told you it would get out of control, and you just carried right on doing what you were doing." She actually wagged a finger at Lenna. "This is your fault."

Lenna tried to load her body language with reasonableness. It was a trick which had worked in the past with difficult employers and boyfriends who had started to grow tired of her drinking. "It's really not," she said, conscious she was starting to whine and not caring. "They came to us and said they wanted to hold another march. We thought it would be like last time, just a few people standing outside police headquarters with banners."

"You know," Jakobson said wearily, "I thought after our last conversation we had agreed to be professional."

"We're still waiting to hear from your *liaison*."

"And you couldn't have called me and *talked* to me about that? You had to put people on the streets instead?"

Lenna pouted.

"I mean, are you *actually* running things at the campaign, or does it just say that on your paycheck?"

"That's not fair," Lenna snapped. "I'm not involved in policy decisions."

Jakobson snorted. "Policy decisions. Your precious campaign's two men and a dog." She shook her head. "I've got more important things to do tonight. Hold out your hand."

"What?" Without thinking, she put her hand out. Jakobson seized her wrist, turned it over, and pressed something cold to the inside of her forearm. There was a snapping sensation against her skin, then the spreading feeling of a bruise. "Ow!" There was a fat inflamed circle on the skin, with a tiny red dot in the middle. She pressed her arm to her mouth.

"Get out," Jakobson told her. "Don't leave the city; I'm

going to want to talk to you again. If you think you can do anything to stop this fiasco, by all means feel free to do so, but I won't be holding my breath." And with that she turned and left.

An officer came along to escort her along the corridors and back upstairs to the front desk of the police station. At the desk, a sergeant made her sign half a dozen forms, in triplicate, then handed over her bag. She took her phone out and looked at the time. Almost two in the morning.

THE POLICE STATION they had taken her to was some distance from the centre of town, and even further from her flat, which was a problem at this time of the morning; public transport wouldn't start running for another couple of hours. It was biting cold outside, and she wondered if she shouldn't go back in and ask if she could wait for a taxi, but she wasn't going to give them the satisfaction. She felt tired and panicky, and in the distance she could hear the sirens of emergency vehicles.

She tried the numbers of a couple of cab companies, but nobody was answering their phone tonight. She was just trying to work out what to do when she saw a bus coming up the street towards her. Without thinking, she stepped out in front of it with her arms raised. The driver mashed his hand on the horn, but he still pulled to a stop, although he didn't open the doors.

"Where are you going?" Lenna shouted. The liquid matrix display on the front of the bus said *KADRIORG*, but that was ridiculous. Kadriorg was kilometres away and the bus was going in the wrong direction. The driver shrugged helplessly.

"Let me on!" Lenna yelled.

The driver shook his head.

"I have money! I can pay!" It never for a moment occurred

to Lenna that she was trying to hijack a bus metres from the front door of a police station.

The driver thought about this for a lot longer than Lenna felt comfortable with. She could smell smoke in the air, and the sirens were getting closer. Finally the driver heaved a huge sigh and opened the doors.

Lenna ran round the front of the bus and climbed aboard. "Where are you going?" she said again.

"You're welcome," the driver said.

Lenna took a breath, willed herself to slow down. "Thank you," she said.

The driver nodded. "Okay."

"Where are you going?" she asked again. "Not to Kadriorg, surely?"

He shook his head. He was in his mid-thirties, tall and broad-shouldered, and he looked terrified. "I was heading for the bus station in Juhkentali but someone's overturned a bus there and set it alight; the whole area's full of crazy people."

"So where?"

The driver looked out at a little group of officers who had gathered on the front steps of the police station to watch the bus. "I might stay here for a while," he said.

"Oh no you don't," she said. "I have to get home."

"Where's that?" She told him, and he groaned. "I just came from there. It's madness; the streets are full of people throwing things."

Lenna felt her heart sink. "So what are we going to do?"

"We could get out of the city, park up somewhere, wait for daylight."

"You're not serious."

"The trouble's only in the city centre and in a couple of other places." Lenna could see him coming up with the plan as he went along. "I've got friends in Jüri; they'll let me park on their farm."

"That's crazy." It was as if she'd fallen into a zombie apocalypse movie. "I'm not going to Jüri."

He shrugged. "That's where I'm going."

Lenna thought about it. "You don't have to go south from here; you can go past Juhkentali and drop me there, then head down past the airport."

"Juhkentali." The sucked his teeth. "Okay, we'll try that. Better find a seat."

She looked down the length of the empty bus. "Yes," she said.

"And you said something about money."

THE BUS DROPPED her on the edge of Juhkentali half an hour later and several hundred kroons lighter. The driver didn't bother saying goodbye, just closed the doors and drove off into the night, leaving Lenna standing on the pavement wondering if she had lost her mind. All of a sudden a night on a farm out in Jüri didn't seem so bad, but the bus was already heading off down Peterburi tee towards the southbound junction by the big shopping centre.

The streets were deserted. No cars, no people, but in the distance she could hear shouting and more sirens, and what sounded like quite a crowd somewhere beyond the buildings behind her. She moved quickly away from the sound, making for her flat in Raua. It was only a couple of kilometres or so away, on the other side of Gonsiori; she'd be home in a few minutes.

Everything went well for the first couple of minutes, but then she became aware of the sounds of shouting and things breaking ahead of her, and when she emerged from a side street onto Tartu mantee she saw, a few hundred metres further on towards the city centre, a group of maybe fifty or so people gathered outside a department store. The huge windows of the store lay in a glittering carpet on the pavement and the road, and people were going in and out through them. The ones going in were empty-handed; the ones coming out were laden down with boxes and bags. As Lenna watched from the corner of the side-street, half a dozen police vehicles came screaming up, lights and sirens turned off so as not to alert the looters. Officers in riot suits spilled out of the vehicles and started to lay into the looters with batons and tasers and shotguns firing beanbag rounds. At least, Lenna hoped they were beanbag rounds. The police weren't messing about; Lenna couldn't tell whether they were putting down the crowd as efficiently as they could, or if they had entirely lost control. Another police car came roaring up and struck one of the looters, scooping him up and carrying him a few metres before braking and tumbling him across the glass-strewn road. An officer jumped out and struck the prostrate looter twice with his baton, then waded into the fight.

Lenna took a couple of deep breaths, then hurried across the main road and down the side streets on the other side. No one noticed she was even there.

The sounds of the fight carried a long way on the cold night air, but she didn't see any more trouble. At one point she passed a young man sitting on the pavement outside a Japanese restaurant. He was smoking a cigarette and he seemed perfectly calm, but as she went by Lenna saw that the side of his head was slick with blood. She kept going.

A few minutes later, she came to her street. It seemed deserted and she stumbled as far as her building, held her phone against the sensor, and all but fell into the lobby when the door clicked open. She let it close behind her and leaned back against it, breathing hard.

SHE FINALLY MANAGED to contact Mr Reinsalu around eleven o'clock that morning. She told him about being arrested, about her journey home from the police station. For once, she didn't embellish much. Last night was beyond embellishment. She kept seeing that one looter, scooped up onto the bonnet of the police car and then shot off into the road like a bag of bedding. And then the policeman hitting him.

Mr Reinsalu made sympathetic noises and said he'd call her later. Lenna wondered where he had spent the night of the riot; she'd forgotten to ask.

At lunchtime, she made herself an omelette, sat eating in front of the news with the plate on her knees while she watched scenes of people clearing up after last night's disturbances. Various government ministers gave press conferences condemning the violence and restating the Prime Minister's determination to get to the bottom of the murder of Sergii N. Salumäe himself had given a short press briefing earlier in the day, with a promise of a more substantial statement later.

The people in the footage from Tallinn looked shell-shocked, baffled by what had happened. The snow had turned, briefly, to rain, and everything looked dreary and horrible. The news networks were running their own investigations into Sergii's death now, rolling reports that repeated every half hour or so. They didn't seem to have managed to dig out much more than the basic facts.

The inbox on her phone was full of messages. She'd block-deleted the whole thing during that unpleasantness with the bank and the utilities, but now there were dozens again. She opened the folder and found message after message from papers and media outfits asking her to get in touch and discuss the prospect of interviews or commissions for articles. All of a sudden, she had something everyone wanted, and now they wanted to be her friend. There was even one from Rose, a breezy hi-how-are-you suggesting they get together for a drink and have a chat about her returning to the paper.

Well. They could all fuck off. For the moment, anyway. Let

them wait until *she* was ready. Rose could fuck off completely and carry on fucking off until she was somewhere outside the solar system; there was no way she was ever going back there, no matter how much satisfaction it would give her.

NINE

1

"It's really quite impressive," Kaunas said. "You've been there a little over two weeks, and so far you've recruited technical support, taken a *very* expensive lease on a house, and found yourself in the middle of a gang war."

"I didn't start that," Carey said. They were in a blandly generic conference space, a white room with a conference table and comfortable-looking chairs. They were both using off-the-shelf avatars; Kaunas looked a bit like a slimmed-down Father Christmas, while Carey, who had just stabbed at random at the menu without looking properly, was presenting as a giant sunflower. "Things are getting a bit rowdy here, though. It's hard to see how much more progress I'm going to be able to make until they calm down again." For a Coureur, chaos was normally great camouflage. It wasn't so useful to Carey, who needed to talk to people who were suddenly unwilling to speak to outsiders. Rocketman were nowhere to be found, having no doubt decided it was prudent to leave town until everyone stopped trying to kill each other.

"Do you know who *did* start it?" The avatar was

cheerful, everyone's favourite grandfather, but Kaunas's voice was cold.

"No, and that's not my job." The truth was, *nobody* knew how the mess had started. The assassins at the restaurant were still unidentified and no one had claimed responsibility, but it was as if everybody had taken it as the signal to revisit old grudges and enmities, and an accelerating wave of murders, bombings and kidnappings was overtaking the city. Publicly, the police were appealing for calm and talking tough on crime, but Magda afforded her a view of a police department that was close to being swamped.

"Really, all you've discovered is that Maksim's death seems more straightforward than we believed at first, that he was colluding with one of the city's criminal gangs, and that he was apparently obsessed with a language school."

"There is no way his death was straightforward," she told him. "Where did you get the original police report you gave me?"

"It was passed on to us by a local stringer."

"Who?"

There was a silence. The avatar on the other side of the table continued to smile gently. Finally, Kaunas said, "It was sent anonymously."

Not Stefan; Stefan wouldn't have bothered. Maybe one of the other local Coureurs? "That report was doctored," she said. "It was put together to make things look as suspicious as possible. You would never have heard he was dead otherwise, and even if you did, why would you care unless you thought it made *Les Coureurs* look bad? Whoever sent you that thing wanted you to investigate, because whatever Maksim was doing here is still happening."

Kaunas thought that over. "You're no closer to knowing what that is," he pointed out.

"No," she admitted. "But there's *something* here."

"So what do you propose? You can't stay there indefinitely, and you already pointed out that the situation is going to restrict your ability to investigate."

"Another week," she said. "If nothing's changed, we can talk again."

The avatar nodded. "Very well," said Kaunas, and he disappeared as the connection was broken. Carey took off her glasses and blinked.

SHE WENT DOWN to the kitchen and perched on a stool at the breakfast bar and wrote it out in longhand, the way one of her lecturers at TTU had taught her years ago.

The earliest confirmed sighting of Maksim they had was the day he signed the lease on the apartment. So that was April 9. They had no idea how long he had already been in the country by then. At some point that afternoon he had walked into the lettings agents' office, having negotiated the lease by phone and email. He had taken a six-month lease and he had paid in cash, which had raised some eyebrows but also, Carey noted, served to make the agents remember him. There had been a big pro-independence march that afternoon, and the street had been full of people wearing dazzle scarves and carrying placards and banners. Magda had pulled a couple of hours of street camera footage from the area, but Carey hadn't been able to spot Maksim in the crowd.

It was the same story at the apartment block. Maksim had moved in the following day, but he didn't appear on any footage from the cameras outside or in the surrounding streets. The neighbours had been unaware that the flat was occupied at all, and Carey wondered if Maksim had ever gone there, or just got someone to dress the place for him.

The only clip they had of him was from the morning of April 11, the day he and Yegor had driven out to the offices of the tractor firm they were supposed to be doing business with, about ninety grainy seconds of footage from a high angle of two men getting out of their car and walking across the car park and into the building. Hard to see their faces, but Carey recognised Maksim's body language. At least, she thought she did. The other man, well, it *could* have been Yegor. During their meeting, the car park camera suffered a malfunction which lasted until a technician came out to fix it late in the afternoon, so they had no footage of the two men leaving the building and driving away.

The car was hired from the Hertz desk at the station, and its tracking data was included in the police report, a series of long and seemingly random trips around town and the neighbouring countryside. On a hunch, Carey asked Magda to try and match traffic camera footage with the tracking report, and the car didn't appear in any of the places it was supposed to have been. The only two times when it was where the tracker said it was were at the tractor firm and on the evening of the crash. Carey made a note of this and wrote *Rocketman* beside it. Jerzy had lied to her about only doing surveillance on the Diana Academy, of course; the odds were that his people had spoofed the car's tracking system for Maksim.

Things got vague after April 11. Witek Mazowiecki didn't know when Maksim had first approached the local Coureurs, and he couldn't remember when their people had started to disappear. He'd been out of town from April 14 to April 17, and by then a gang war had been going on.

Although it was sort of unfair to call it a *war*. Witek Mazowiecki had exaggerated it. A couple of shootings and a car bomb. Things were a lot worse than that now. The first shooting was on April 15, and the car bomb—at a house outside town—had been on April 19, the same night that the Diana Academy had blown up. Late one night, Anatoly had put on a stealth suit, walked into the Old

Town, and stuck a camera onto a shop across the street from the academy, but the building was a burned-out shell, its frontage screened by a high hoarding plastered with warning notices. Nobody seemed to be paying it any attention.

She drew a thick line under what she'd written so far, and another line some distance under that, and she sat looking down at the gap between the two. Somewhere in there, Maksim had been doing *stuff*, doing whatever he had really come to Poland to do. He wasn't necessarily doing it in Gliwice—he might just have established his presence here and then gone off somewhere else—but he'd been doing *something*.

Carey sat up straight and massaged her lower back. Her posture had always been good, but she stiffened up easily these days. She felt old and tired and out of her depth. She rubbed her eyes.

The little paperscreen stuck to the kitchen wall was showing a live news feed from the Polish Parliament, where another debate about Gliwice's independence was going on. She waved up the sound, but it was just shouting. That pretty much summed the world up. Angry white men shouting at each other. She waved the sound back down again.

She took out her phone, dialled a number from memory, and when it was answered she said, "Do you have any interests in Poland?"

"We did when my father was alive," said a man's voice. "I closed them down; they were more trouble than they were worth. And a very good evening to you, too. What are you doing in Poland?"

"Karl-Heinz Lang."

"Oh, you're there. Minor street-thug from Leipzig, arriviste. Nobody's going to miss him very much."

"He was a capo for a gang here."

"Drugs, protection," said Peter. "Low-level stuff. Bottom feeders. Are you okay?"

"Maksim's dead."

There was a silence at the other end of the connection. Peter said, "I hadn't heard that. I'm sorry. What happened?"

"He crashed his car into a tractor."

"Not the way I'd have expected him to go," he said. Peter and Maksim went all the way back to the days when Peter had employed Maksim to jump Marthe Schiller out of her marriage. "I saw him about a year ago; he wanted me to bankroll some mad scheme he was cooking up."

"Did he say what it was?"

"Nah. He was being an asshole. I told him to go away."

"That doesn't sound like Maksim, being an asshole."

He chuckled. "He had the old man with him." Maksim and Yegor, the Tweedledum and Tweedledee of Europe's minor criminal underworld. "I didn't see him, but he was spotted in Roskilde. Was Maksim mixed up with Lang?"

"I don't know. I don't know what he was doing here; I suppose it's at least a possibility." She jotted a note, drew a box round it.

"You need some help?"

"I'll let you know," she said. "But thanks for the offer; I appreciate it."

"You sound tired," he told her. "You're not that far away; you should come over and spend some time when you've finished whatever you're doing there. It's been a while."

"Yeah, I might do that," she said. "I'll be in touch, maybe."

"Okay," he said. "You take care."

"You too, Peter."

They hung up, and Carey put her phone on the breakfast bar in front of her and looked down at her notes again. Anything else?

Wareham had checked out. His public profile was almost *quaintly* public, and Magda had been able to dig behind it without any trouble at all. Carey knew his birthday, the names of his parents, his first school in Dorset, his time at Birmingham University reading English. She knew his reading habits and the details of his online food orders. She'd read articles from his time on one of the last Fleet Street papers to still have a physical edition. She'd read the proceedings of his divorce. She knew he'd held joint Polish-English citizenship for the past twenty years. In a world where most people were unconsciously—almost autonomically—careful about identity theft, he was an open book, and she'd felt a little guilty about reading it. Of course, none of it made him any more or less trustworthy. She wrote his name down, then drew a short line from it and wrote *SIS* at the end of it. On the other side of the page, she wrote *Anatoly* and *Russian Intelligence*.

She looked at the gap on the page, then wrote *April 30*, the date of the crash, underneath.

Here, after three weeks of vagueness, there was an almost embarrassing amount of detail. According to the tracker data, the car had spent most of the day driving from place to place outside the city, but once again there was no sign of it on the traffic cameras.

At seven-fifty that evening, telemetry had logged it travelling at speed away from Gliwice, braking suddenly, and making a right-turn onto the Sierakowice road before accelerating again. It topped a hundred and five kilometres an hour, which was an insane speed on that road. At seven fifty-four, the car's data link had dropped out and not come back.

She wrote *19.54—impact.*

Okay, give the old man at the farm and his son time to react, put on coats and boots, and go outside... She swiped through to the police report downloaded to her phone, and there was the emergency call, logged at five past eight. She wrote *20.05 - Michał's son calls the police.*

It had been a short conversation; by ten past eight the police operator had logged a radio call to any available units in the area and one had responded.

She wrote *20.10—Police on their way*.

Michał had said the police had taken about five minutes to arrive, but the next entry in the log showed them getting to the scene of the crash at twenty-five past eight. *20.25, on-site*, it said. *Unit already in attendance*.

Carey looked at what she'd written. She looked at the log. And back again. *Unit already in attendance*. That was why she'd had a problem with the timing. There were two sets of police. One had responded to the emergency call; the other was already there.

"Oh, you evil *cocksucker*," she said quietly.

2

IT WAS TWENTY-FIVE degrees below zero in Helsinki. She knew that because she could see, from the window of her room, a big digital sign on top of a building diagonally across the square which cycled between the time and the temperature in centigrade and Fahrenheit. A little beyond that, the glass tower of a Hyatt rose above the other buildings, a news ticker wrapped around its top scrolling the headlines in six languages. All of them featured the word *community*.

The hotel was weird, in a way she couldn't quite put her finger on. It was big and old and well-worn, all dark wood and big complicated chandeliers, and it seemed at the moment to be mostly full of Chinese tourists. The lifts were tiny and constantly on the verge of failure. Her room was cosy and compact but she couldn't work out whether the bed was supposed to be a bed or a sofa; it was too deep to be a sofa but it was too hard to be a bed. At least it was long enough for her, which was not always the case with hotel beds. On her first night, she had gone down to the bar, which was tiny and tucked away down a short flight of steps off the foyer, and ordered a Scotch and water. The barman had stared at her for a few moments and then given her a glass of Scotch and a full glass of water.

Ostensibly, she was here to cover the Catalonian trade show, which was occupying a corner of the immense exhibition centre that sat like a Borg cube in the middle of an airport-sized car park on the outskirts of town. Catalan independence was still a fragile thing; relations with Madrid were bad-tempered and the success of the Barcelona Olympics a few years ago hadn't improved matters. The adolescent state had been setting out its stall in various European capitals for about six months and she hadn't been planning to bother with it; all trade shows were alike and she'd written a lot about Catalunya in recent years, but then a crash message had come through for an urgent Situation in Finland, and the show presented itself as a cover.

At least, it had seemed like a crash message. She'd been here four days now, waiting for a contact, and so far all she'd done was wander around the trade show and check out the bars and restaurants in the centre of Helsinki. There were, in all honesty, worse places to be, but there were also warmer ones.

It was an age of wonders. Europe's process of dissolution continued, balkanising itself into an ever-changing patchwork of nations and states and republics and margravates and sanjaks and polities and anarchies. Greater Germany alone—the name became increasingly ironic with every passing year—was at a constant rolling boil, throwing off random statelets and then reabsorbing them on what seemed to be a weekly basis. Through this chaos stitched the Line, wealthy beyond reason, smugly sovereign, and above all territorial squabbling.

As if this were not enough for the Continent's commentators, academics, artists, criminals, tinpot populist politicians, racists and bigots of all stripes, there was *another* Europe; a pocket universe called the Community which existed as a single superstate settled sometime in the eighteenth century by the English. The revelation of the existence of the Community had tipped Europe's friable political landscape in any number of unexpected directions. It was all over the news, all the time. Hardly a week passed without some item about Ambrose Ruston, the Community's amiable, donnish President, signing a treaty with some country one had never even heard of a couple of years before. The US agencies were ravenous for material about the Community; Carey had taken a train there the previous year, when they began running a service from London Paddington to Stanhurst, one of the Community's county towns. She'd thought it was creepy, like being on the set of a Miss Marple adaptation, a sort of concentrated wet-dream of Englishness.

Through it all passed *Les Coureurs*, calmly—and sometimes not so calmly—delivering mail and more valuable items across Europe's bewildering jigsaw of borders and legal jurisdictions. Unlike, say, UPS, which refused to pick up or deliver to the Continent's more repressive states, *Les Coureurs* had no moral scruple. They would move anything, for anyone, keeping alive the spirit of Schengen. They were heroes or terrorists, depending on who you asked. The only thing everyone could agree about them was that they were everywhere, the most non-state of non-state actors.

On her fifth night at the hotel, Carey was sitting having dinner in the restaurant when a man sat down opposite her. He was wearing a good business suit with a foulard tie. He'd put on a lot of weight, and for a moment she didn't recognise him.

"Mr Brookshire," she said. "Imagine meeting you here, of all places."

Brookshire smiled and signalled to the waiter. "You're looking well," he said.

"Just passing through, are we?" she asked, finishing her veal chop and laying down her knife and fork. "How's things in the Texas spy business?"

"I'll just have a coffee, please," he told the waiter. He looked at Carey. "Coffee?" She nodded. "Yeah, make that two Americanos." When the waiter had gone, Brookshire said, "I'm on attachment with the European Police Service."

Carey carefully kept a straight face. EuPol didn't like to be reminded that the geopolitical entity it had been created to police had mostly ceased to exist. She couldn't remember if Finland was outside their jurisdiction or not. "And how's that going for you?"

"Well, it's going just great," he said, settling back in his chair. "Europe's been quite the eye-opener for me. I can see why you like it so much."

"Good," she said. "I'm happy for you."

The waiter returned with their coffees. Brookshire poured an almost homeopathically small amount of cream into his, and stirred it slowly while Carey sat across the table from him, watching. "I never got the chance to tell you how much I admired that move of yours back home," he said.

"I got your note."

"That was ballsy," he allowed, "blackmailing the Texan government."

Carey dropped a sugar cube into her coffee.

"Of course, passports can be withdrawn as easily as issued," he mused. He tried his coffee, set his cup back in its saucer. "Although I have a feeling that wouldn't grieve you too much."

In the modern world, it was quite possible to bump accidentally into someone you vaguely knew from thousands of miles away. This, she thought, was not one of those times.

"I never understood what your objection to intelligence work was," he said. "Citizenship of a country comes with certain obligations to ensure its security."

He sounded as if he'd got that from a high school civics class, or maybe off the back of a cereal packet. "I don't do espionage," she said. "Also, you were trying to blackmail me into it."

"Blackmail?" he said, mock-affronted. "That wasn't blackmail. That was a bit of light suborning. What *you* did, *that* was blackmail."

Carey had a short attention span when it came to whataboutery at the best of times. She said, "Okay, Brookshire, shall we cut to the chase, or are we going to spend the rest of the evening calling each other names?"

He grinned and took a printed photograph from an inside pocket of his jacket and put it down on the table in front of her. "Do you recognise this guy?"

Unwilling to touch it, she looked down. It was a very grainy image of someone who looked like Yegor. Somewhat alarmingly, he appeared to be coming out of Stockmann, the big department store round the corner from the hotel.

She shook her head. "No," she said.

"Sure?"

"Sure." She looked him in the eye.

"Okay," he said, reaching into his pocket again and putting another photo on the table. "How about her?"

She looked down again, and this time she thought she felt a moment of dizziness. It was a printout of the personal details page of an English passport in the name of Kay Philby. The photo in the passport was of someone who looked very much like her.

"It's a joke," Brookshire was saying. "K Philby." When she didn't say anything, he grunted. "You should have taken up espionage. You'd appreciate gags like that."

She picked up the print. The birthdate on the passport was hers. "This isn't mine," she said. Then, because he obviously knew what she was, she added, "I've never had an English passport."

"Yeah," he said. "That's what I told my team. I said, 'I know this girl; she'd never get mixed up in something like this.'"

'My team'. If he was on attachment, he was very much a junior member of any EuPol team. She said, "Mixed up in what?"

"We've been keeping a watch out for Ms Philby for the past three months," Brookshire said, all business now. "We believe she's part of the European end of a human trafficking route out of the Middle East. You know how hard it is for anyone to get into Europe from there."

She nodded, still looking at the photo. Europe had slammed the door to people from the South a long time ago.

"The people they're carrying aren't economic refugees," Brookshire went on. "They're young women and girls, mostly, bound for the sex trade in Hamburg and Antwerp and London and other fun places."

She looked at him.

"They bring them over the border in trucks," Brookshire continued. "They set up a new trucking company for each run, hire new drivers and new premises. They're a small team and they keep moving from country to country and they've been hard to find, but for the last run Ms Philby signed the paperwork so we've been keeping an eye out for her, and a week ago she leased a freight yard here in Helsinki. And then one of my people spotted you in town, and, well," he shrugged. "Here we are."

Yes, Carey thought, Brookshire had seen his chance and here they were.

"What about the old man?" she said. "Who is he, Guy Burgess?"

That actually made Brookshire laugh. It was a surprisingly horrid sound. "You see?" he said. "You do get the joke."

Carey glared stonily at him.

"No," he said. "But he might have known people who knew people who'd met Philby and Burgess, back in the day. He's ex-FSB. Very rarely photographed; we've been looking for *this* guy for a very long time. He's a very bad man."

She was chiefly accustomed to thinking of Yegor as unpleasant rather than bad, but she took the point. She said, "None of this is anything to do with me."

"Oh, I know," Brookshire said cheerfully. "That's what I told everyone."

Brookshire, in common with a depressing number of men she had known, hated to lose. Sometimes, you just had to shrug and accept you'd been beaten, but that wasn't in Brookshire's vocabulary. "What do you want?" she asked. She wasn't really interested; she already knew what he wanted. What *she* wanted, mostly, was Brookshire out of her face for a few hours.

"Well now," he said with a smile, settling back in his chair and clasping his hands across his stomach, "that depends."

Brookshire was going to make an event of this. He'd been made a fool of back in Austin and he wanted to enjoy his revenge, but Carey didn't have time for that. She said, "You'll smooth things out for me. You'll remove my face and biometrics from the EuPol database. And in return I'll agree to spy for Texas."

Brookshire's jaw sagged with disappointment.

"There are only about four countries in Europe where you still have powers of arrest," she said briskly, "but if my face is on watchlists all over the Continent it's going to put a crimp in my work—in *both* my jobs. I might as well give up and go back to Texas. So the answer's yes, Mr Brookshire, I'll be one of your little secret agents." She resisted—just barely—the urge to bat her eyelashes at him. She dropped her napkin on her plate and stood up. "And now I have an appointment I need to keep," she told him.

"I guess you already know which room I'm in. We can work out the details later."

The surprised look on Brookshire's face was giving way to a lazy grin. A win was a win after all, regardless of the circumstances. "I'll be in touch," he told her. "Be seeing you."

Not if I see you first, matey-boy, she thought.

"That's actually quite funny," the pianist said. "Kay Philby."

"Yeah, I had the joke mansplained to me already," she told him.

He glanced at her, a thin, shabby middle-aged man with his greying hair in a short ponytail. His English was extremely good—he might even *be* English, for all Carey knew. "Okay," he said, returning his attention to the cabled-together collection of black boxes, tapboards and little screens on the table in front of him. "Shouldn't be *that* hard to find..."

They were in a safe house out on the northern edge of the city, a flat in a block which seemed to be mostly full of guest workers from other parts of Europe. Someone in the block was playing crush music and the entire frame of the building seemed to vibrate with it.

Giving the watchers Brookshire had stationed at the hotel the slip had been fairly straightforward; in her experience EuPol had a few seasoned operators but the majority of them were just cops who'd been recruited from their various nations and given the one-day course in streetwork. Finding a pianist at what was really a moment's notice had been a lot harder; she'd been lucky to find anyone at all, let alone someone who was any good.

"Here we are," the pianist said. "It's not a freight yard, though. It's a unit in an industrial park out near the airport. Three-year lease signed by K Philby on behalf of Waddenzee Transport." Carey felt her nails dig into her clenched palms. "Signed and notarised on the twelfth of this month; does that sound right?"

"What's the address?" The pianist read it out for her. "How the hell do you spell that?"

"I'll print it."

"No," she said, rummaging in her bag for a pen and a scrap of paper. "No printing. Spell it out for me. And when we're done I want you to purge that search and forget you ever saw me." She put a wad of Swiss francs on the table at his elbow.

He glanced at the money. "Give me some credit for at least a little professionalism," he told her.

"You want some *professional* advice?" she said. "Don't fucking trust anyone."

SHE NEVER GOT within half a mile of the industrial park. The cab was waved to a stop at a police checkpoint—a couple of patrol cars parked across the road—and an officer came over and motioned to the driver to lower his window. There followed a brief conversation in rapid Finnish, while Carey tried to will herself to be invisible in the back seat.

"He says we can't go on," the driver told her. "He says it's a counter-terror operation."

Counter-terror. Sure. She tried to sound irritated but resigned. "Can't we go round?"

"The address you gave me is inside the area of control."

She hadn't asked to be taken to the industrial park but to an address a few streets away, intending to walk the remaining distance. She glanced at the policeman, who was reaching for a flashlight to shine into the back of the taxi. "We'd better go back then," she told the driver.

A few more words in Finnish, then the cop stepped away

and the driver raised his window and performed a U-turn back towards the centre of town. It was past midnight and Carey sat watching the snowy, brightly lit streets go by. They passed a suburban railway station; she let the driver carry on for a little while, then asked him to let her out and walked back to the station. She caught a train to Tampere, and another from there, and it was almost eight o'clock in the morning when she walked stiff-legged, sleep-deprived and ravenously hungry down the platform at Oulu. From Oulu there was another train up to the Swedish border at Haparanda, but it wasn't due to leave for another hour so she marched into a McDonald's on the station concourse, bought herself a burger and fries and a big cup of coffee, and sat in a corner watching the early-morning commuters.

There was a big screen on one wall, and it kept cutting between a newsroom and outside broadcast footage which featured night-time groups of armed police, flashing blue lights on police vehicles, and what looked like a big metal shed. As she watched, the footage cut to a shaky handheld view of the inside of the shed and a big group of police officers crowding round the back of a truck parked there. The rear doors were open and a number of boxes were piled untidily on the concrete floor.

The view came round until it was looking into the back of the truck. The interior was full of boxes, some of which had been unloaded, and at the far end there was a confused scene of police officers and flashlights which resolved, for the briefest moment before the scene cut back to the studio, into a door at the front of the container into another compartment. Someone pulled the door open and there was a glimpse of huddled bodies, tangled lifeless arms and legs.

Some time later, she found herself standing in Copenhagen railway station. She had no clear memory of how she had got there, of crossing into Sweden, or from there into Norway and then across the bridge into Denmark. There were just a lot of confused images of trains and men and women in uniform and railway station platforms and miles and miles of snowy countryside passing by outside a window. She later worked out it had taken her a little over six days. Had she checked into an hotel during that time? She couldn't remember.

She looked down and saw she was holding a business card. It was good quality and all it had printed on it was a number. She reached into her pocket for her phone, brought it out holding a burner phone she couldn't remember buying. When she switched it on, the menu came up in Norwegian. Looking at it brought up a memory of shoving bits of her old phone into a snowdrift outside a rural station. Had she done that? Had it been ringing all the time? She thought it might have been.

She looked at the phone and the card. She dialled the number and when it was answered she said, "We met on a train quite a long time ago." Her voice sounded croaky and unused and as if someone else was using it. "I need your help."

3

THE CENTRE OF Tallinn was a landscape of overturned and burned-out cars, the pavements crunchy underfoot with glass from shattered shop windows. Bits of merchandise lay everywhere, abandoned by looters, and there was still, ever so faintly, a tang of tear gas in the cold air.

Krista had watched it all from a hotel room in Tapa, not quite believing what she was seeing. The Prime Minister and President broadcast appeals for calm, the Russian Ambassador held a solemn press conference. There was a terse communique from the Kremlin itself, which had thus far held back from any comment. Almost a hundred injured, some of them seriously. No one had managed to add up how much damage had been done, but it must run into many hundreds of thousands of kroons. Millions, maybe. The damage to tourism was incalculable. A couple of big cruise ships, due to dock in Tallinn that evening, had instead anchored offshore for several hours before electing to sail down the coast to Riga instead.

Somehow, the Prime Minister did not put the army on the streets. Salumäe had begun his career in the Tallin police, and he'd always been sympathetic to the plight of the cop on the beat. He still had a cop's eye for trouble; a rumour was going round that he'd gone into the centre of town during the night, incognito, to scope the situation out first-hand, and he'd decided that the police could cope without bringing the military into things. Martial law was the very last thing anyone needed.

Trouble was scattered all across Estonia. It was worst in the capital and in some of the towns along the eastern border, but there had been some disturbances elsewhere. In Tapa, someone had thrown a firebomb at a police station and thrown a brick through the windscreen of a parked patrol vehicle. Any other time, that would have been near the top of the news, but that night it barely rated a mention.

The next morning, at breakfast, there was an air of tension. None of the guests or staff spoke much and nobody wanted to sit near the windows. Krista ate quickly, checked out, and drove back towards Tallinn.

She still had no idea what to do, and even if she did, she had no resources with which to do it. Had it not been for the riot, Jakobson would have moved heaven and earth to find and arrest her. As it was, she thought she had a limited amount of leeway to move around, so long as she was careful.

Halfway between Tapa and Tallinn, she turned off the main road into a small town, drove around for a while, then pulled into a car park behind a little block of flats and phoned Kustav.

"Are you okay, boss?" he asked.

"I've been better. How are things there?"

"It was quite a night."

"I saw it on the news. Have IA been in touch with you?"

"Colonel Jakobson called last night, before everything went crazy, and this morning too. She wanted to know if you'd been in contact."

"Did she have any message for me?"

"She didn't sound happy. Mind you, nobody's happy at the moment."

"Okay. When we've finished this conversation, call her and tell her you've spoken to me. Tell her I have no intention of interfering with her investigation, but I'm not going to let my father be dragged through the dirt like this."

"I don't see how that qualifies as not interfering with the investigation, boss, with all due respect."

She smiled. Beyond the windscreen, she saw an old man emerge from one of the doors along the back of the block of flats. He was carrying a black rubbish bag, which he carried along to a dumpster at the end of the block and slung over the side onto a snow-dusted pile of similar bags.

She said, "I'm going out of town for a couple of days. There are some people I want to talk to. I'll be in touch when I get back."

"What are you actually *doing*, boss?"

"I don't know. I'll let you know when I work it out."

SHE PRESUMED LAST night's events had driven her some distance down Jakobson's list of priorities—it would be hard, at the moment, to justify expending manpower on a search for one errant police officer—but it couldn't hurt if the colonel thought she'd left Tallinn rather than returning to it. Anyway, technically Laagri wasn't actually *in* Tallinn; it lay just beyond the outskirts of the city.

It was almost five o'clock in the evening when she reached her destination, a little estate of four-storey apartment blocks arranged around a bleak snowbound square that in the summer was a pleasant garden. She parked the car a few streets away, just in case, and walked back to the flats.

On the top floor of one of the blocks, she walked to a door at the end of the corridor and pressed the button on the entryphone beside the door.

After a few moments a distorted voice emerged from the little speaker. Krista bent down close to the grille and said, "It's me, Uncle Stepan."

In the way—in her experience, anyway—of many elderly people, Stepan kept the flat heated to equatorial levels. It smelled of spices and coffee and cigarette smoke and old books, and the walls that were not covered with hanging rugs were covered with bookshelves.

The general tone of the place was dark. The furniture was dark, the woodblock flooring was stained to a dark oak colour, the heavy curtains—now drawn against the evening—were dark. Stepan tended not to use the ceiling lights, preferring to depend on a couple of table lamps, one in a corner, the other by his favourite chair. It gave the flat a sheltered feeling, as if it was walled off against the insults of outside life. It was, of all the places in her life, the most familiar. She could not remember a time when the flat was not a part of her life.

Stepan made them tea with lemon, in glasses with silver holders that had belonged to his grandmother's family in Moscow, before the revolution. He was a short, fat man with delicate hands and a dancer's sense of balance, and he wore his long white hair in a braid.

Like all the detectives who had unilaterally elected themselves part of her family when her mother died, Stepan was not really her uncle. Unlike them, he really *was* part of her family. Like the flat, Krista couldn't remember a time when she didn't know him.

She stood in the living room reading the spines of the books on the shelves—and many of those had been a part of her life as long as she remembered—while he clattered around in the kitchen. The majority of the books were in Russian or Estonian, but there was a fair scattering of titles in English and French and German. Looking around the room, she felt, for the first time in what seemed a very long while, safe.

Stepan came into the room carrying a battered silver tray—another heirloom—in which sat the tea glasses. He put it on top of a pile of yellowed newspaper cuttings on the coffee table, took one of the glasses, and sat down in his armchair.

"How are you?" he asked.

"I'm living interesting times," she told him.

"Yes," he said. "I tried to call, but your phone was unavailable."

It had probably been stuffed down the back seat of a taxi at the time. "Things have been a bit... nonlinear."

"Sit down," he said. "You look exhausted."

She took her glass and perched herself on the edge of the other armchair. "I need some context," she said.

"And you decided you'd come to your tame Russian?" he chuckled.

"It's not like that," she said. "And you know it. It's just..." she sipped some tea. "I need someone who won't lie to me."

He thought about that. "Well, all right. So, here we are.

Your father has been accused of murder, and Estonia's ethnic Russian minority is up in arms about it. Literally. Those in authority have handled the business badly, resulting in last night's... exuberance. Does that all sound about right?"

She nodded wearily. "Do you think he did it?"

"Of course I don't," he said. "What kind of question is that? Do *you*?"

"I don't know any more," she said. She told him about her conversation with Erik Lill, the complaints which had been filed and then apparently buried.

"It sounds like a fairly incompetent cover-up, as these things go," Stepan said when she'd finished. "Just *ignoring* something doesn't qualify as a cover-up."

"I know. But everything sounds just convincing *enough*. I know there were things my father never told me; he was dealing with a lot of classified stuff, towards the end of his career. We both know he had a temper."

"He was a tough guy, it's true," Stepan mused. "Which is not the same thing as being a murderer." He took a sip of tea and put his glass down on the low table beside his chair. "Shall I tell you a story?"

"Does it have a happy ending?"

"It doesn't have an ending at all, happy or not."

"Okay."

He settled back and clasped his hands in his lap. "This goes back to Pronksiöö," he said. "Bronze Night. Do you remember?"

"I wasn't even born, Uncle Stepan. How could I remember that?"

Stepan nodded and looked around the living room. "It was poorly handled," he said. "On all sides. There's still a lot of resentment."

"It was *decades* ago."

"You think we should all let go of our grudges?" he asked, smiling sadly at her.

"I think they're the only thing keeping some of you going."

He laughed. "That would be true. But you know what happened. Everyone knows."

"Pretend I don't. Pretend I'm a foreigner."

"All young people are foreigners." He watched her face for a moment, but she didn't respond to the joke. "Okay," he said. "Well. The Bronze Soldier. Bronzovyj Soldat. It's a Soviet war memorial out at the military cemetery, but once upon a time it used to be right in the middle of town, in a little park on Tõnismägi, what we used to call 'Liberators' Square'. There were the graves of a dozen or so Russian soldiers and a statue of another soldier in Red Army uniform. Officially it was *The Monument to the Liberators of Tallinn*. You can imagine how that went down with the Estonians." He took a sip of his drink. "This stuff runs very, very deep. After the Soviets took over in 1944, they started destroying monuments to the Estonian War Of Independence, which was not the best way to win over hearts and minds. And then they put up this... *thing*." He sat back and lit a cigarette without bothering to offer one to Krista. "Actually, I'd forgotten, but there was originally another monument on Tõnismägi, a wooden thing with a red star on top of it. A couple of teenage girls blew it up one night."

Krista got up and opened the window a fraction. Stepan watched her come back to her chair with a sad expression on his face.

"So," she said. "Alyosha."

He chuckled. "Yes, people call it that sometimes. Alyosha stood there, through rain and sun and snow, all the way through the years of the Soviet Empire, until 1991, when Estonia's independence was restored. After that, really, Alyosha's days were numbered."

"Why did it take so long?"

"I imagine the authorities had some idea what would happen if they tried to take the monument down," he told her. “People tend to want to put things like that off. Until they’ve left public office, anyway. After independence, Red Army veterans carried on as they always had, coming to the memorial with Soviet flags on Victory Day and Liberation Day and generally pissing off the Estonians. There was a bit of a fuss around Victory Day in 2006—Estonians protesting and threatening to blow the thing up and so on—and that, as the English say, is when it all *kicked off*. Although it had been *kicking off* ever since the end of the war, really.” Stepan stubbed out his cigarette and topped up his glass. He waggled the bottle at Krista, but she shook her head and he put it back on the table.

“April 26, 2007,” she said.

Stepan took a drink. “You see? You do remember. Bronze Night. Yes. There was a lot of low-level unpleasantness and manouvering,” he said. “But to cut to the chase, as it were, the authorities exhumed the graves and set about relocating the monument. There was a mass protest and then there were riots. Water cannon, teargas, cars overturned and set alight, shops looted, vandalism. All that joyous stuff. The official figure was about a thousand arrested, more than a hundred injured. It was a lively couple of nights.”

“Are you trying to tell me this is all about Alyosha?”

“Tangentially, perhaps. You said you wanted context.” He looked into a corner of the room. “Anyway, it all resurfaced again about thirty years ago. The flu was gone and the world was just trying to right itself again. The EU was falling apart and Estonian Russians were starting to call for the creation of a Russian polity, somewhere out near the border, you can imagine how *that* was received. And in the middle of all that a rumour started to go round that the government was planning to pull down Alyosha completely and put up a memorial to the Estonian war dead in his place.”

“I don’t remember that at all,” she said.

“You were about eight years old, and I don’t suppose it’s

taught much in schools any more. It was all a hoax, anyway; people just wanted to forget about it, afterward. But things got *lively* again for a couple of nights."

"What did you do, those two nights?"

He regarded her levelly. "The first night, I was at the monument, protesting its removal." He paused, watching her face. "We're a minority," he went on. "A sizeable minority, but a minority nevertheless. Fighting for our identity." It was the first time Krista had ever heard him say 'we', meaning Estonia's ethnic Russian community. "That's really what it was about. Us and Them. There are those who will tell you that it was whipped up by the Russians—the *Russian* Russians, over the border—and maybe some of it was, but in all honesty it didn't need much whipping. Have you ever been in the middle of a riot?"

"You know I haven't."

"It's..." he struggled to find a word. "It's... *exhilarating*. Can I tell you my theory?"

"Please."

"People are angry all the time. Not about any one thing, just this hot, explosive core of anger waiting to be aimed at something. Doesn't even matter what it is. All you have to do is point them at it and off they go."

"Were you angry?"

He looked at her for so long, considering an answer, that she thought he wasn't going to answer at all. "Did I riot?" he said quietly. "Yes, I did. Did I help overturn cars? Yes, I did. Did I smash windows and throw stones at the police? Yes, I did. Then your father arrested me."

Krista blinked.

"He arrested me, then he dragged me down a side street and told me to fuck off," Stepan went on. "He actually said that, and you know what he was like about bad language. 'Fuck off, Stepan. Go home to Nadia and stay there until this insanity is over one way or another.'"

"And what did you do?"

"I didn't leave the flat for a week." He lit another cigarette, regarded her steadily through the smoke. "I won't kid you that your father caused the scales to fall from my eyes, but I did realise I'd had a lucky escape and he wouldn't be there the next time."

"He never talked about it."

"I don't blame him; neither have I, really. He and I never spoke of it. It wasn't our finest hour. Best forgotten."

"Not everyone feels that way."

"No," he said. "Well, that's politics. I try to stay out of politics, these days."

Krista sighed and sat back in her chair.

"Your father and I grew up together," Stepan said. "Our families were neighbours. We played together, grazed our knees together, broke the odd window together. He was the best man at my wedding, and I at his. If I'd been anyone else I doubt he'd have let me go, but he did. It could have got him into a lot of trouble, if anyone had seen him, but he did it anyway." He stubbed out his cigarette. "It's not evidence that you would want to take into court, but I don't think that's the action of a murderer."

Stepan had a touching faith in human nature. She said, "I don't think that's going to carry a lot of weight, but thank you."

He inclined his head in acknowledgement. "Anyway, as I said, it was all a hoax. The police eventually tracked it down to one blog post by someone who called himself 'Villem The Bear', just one post that had started the rumour. They couldn't touch him because of free speech, so a few of us got together and went to see Villem The Bear. He was this crazy little bastard who lived out in Lahemaa. He said someone paid him to write that post, but he wouldn't tell us who it was."

"What did you do?"

"We were *stern* with him." They laughed, and Stepan shook his head. "Villem The Bear. We couldn't prove anything one way or another, but I always thought maybe the Russians were behind it somehow, causing mischief."

"And you think this is the Russians too."

He nodded. "They would be high on my list of suspects."

"Making mischief," she said bitterly.

"That's what they do." He regarded her sadly. "You know, I'm Estonian. Born here, brought up here; I never felt particularly Russian until the business with Alyosha. Sometimes it's quite easy to convince even the most rational people that someone else is trying to take away something that's theirs. Their money, their property, their rights. The people in Moscow know that; they've been doing stuff like this for years, stirring the pot here and there, seeing what happens. Then you've got the people who are angry all the time and are just waiting for any excuse to express it. There's a lot of those. It's really not that hard to cause a riot, if you know where to push." He sighed. "This doesn't help you at all, of course."

She thought about it. "I'd better go," she said, getting up.

"It would probably be better if you stayed here."

She gave his shoulder a squeeze as she went by towards the door. "Too much to do," she said, although she didn't know what.

BRIGADOON

TEN

1

The following morning, after an extremely bad-tempered vote, the Polish Parliament decided that Gliwice's bid for statehood was over. The city immediately released a statement saying that they would be taking the matter to the United Nations. The government responded by putting Gliwice under martial law, and that, really, was the best indication of just how far out of control the whole thing had gone, because the last time martial law had been declared in Poland was still—just—within living memory. A curfew was announced, and a mobilisation of the army to enforce it. Many of the inhabitants suddenly decided to visit their relatives elsewhere, or succumbed to an urge to stay at their little summerhouses out in the countryside. Roads out of the city were choked with traffic.

Carey sat in the living room and watched it all on the news. Or rather, she sat there while the news was on and stared twin holes in the screen. She'd found a bottle of Żubrówka in the fridge and she set it unopened on the coffee table in front of her, along with a glass.

Anatoly, who had seen her like this before, gave her a wide

berth while keeping a quiet eye on her. Magda, who had not, drifted in from time to time and sat beside her for a little while before reporting on the progress of her investigations. Distantly, Carey wanted to tell her to pack up and go home because the investigation was over, but instead she found herself wondering why the girl seemed to have nowhere else to go. Didn't she have family?

Zimnej Wody received visitors. Boksi turned up with escape passports for all of them, something she'd asked him to do a couple of days ago because it was just good practice. The passports would be indistinguishable from the real thing, and they would be meticulously backstopped, because Boksi and Magda were good. Romek was good, too, and he turned up in the afternoon with another stealth suit for Magda and pair of handguns he'd printed up, ceramic things that weighed about as much as a coffee mug. He rode them into town on his bike, which was quite a brave thing to do because the police, already twitchy because of the continuing gang killings, were on a hair-trigger because of the martial law announcement.

This all took place far away, like lightning flickering just below the horizon, while she went over, again and again, what Maksim had done. Every time she went through it in her head another stray part snapped into place and another question came up, but it all worked. It had internal logic, and more importantly it was very Maksim. At one point, her phone rang; she answered it automatically and the woman's voice asking who she was didn't even annoy her any more; the calls had become part of the wallpaper, just part of the generalised madness. When she put the phone back on the table she noticed that someone had come in and put an omelette and a cup of coffee in front of her, but they were both cold. She wondered if this was what a breakdown felt like, but she knew it wasn't.

As dusk fell, Anatoly put on one of the stealth suits and went out for a look round town. The boy loved the stealth suits, and Carey remembered when she had too, but now they were just tools and a lot of their tech was outdated anyway; there were rumours the Chinese had developed a suit that made you invisible even close-up and blended into ambient background temperature without threatening to bake you in your own trapped body heat.

She remembered feeling a little like this after Byron died. She'd sat in the house all alone, staring into space, somehow angry and sad and lonely and afraid all at once, although she'd spent much of that period blind drunk because she hadn't wanted to be sober when the symptoms began. But the symptoms never did. It turned out she was one of the 0.00001 percent of the population to have a degree of natural immunity to the virus, which had led to more than a year of tests and blood donations. She'd worked out once that she had given almost a gallon of blood to the cause of finding a vaccine. Her samples were studied all over the world. And eventually the virus had undergone an antigen drift which had rendered it no more dangerous than normal seasonal flu, although little hotspots of the original virus kept boiling up for another couple of years. She'd left hospital at the end of that year with a thank you from the doctors and a stern warning about her liver function if she kept drinking the way she did.

The Poles were pretty good at stuff, when they put their minds to it, although she suspected the government had been preparing for this for a while. By the time night fell the army had cut off all roads and rail links in and out of Gliwice, and were in the process of surrounding the city. The message appeared to be *If you want a border, here it is*. Units were coming into the city to enforce the curfew, and there had been firefights with the police and other, unidentified, parties.

"Clusterfuck is the natural state of the world," Carey said out loud, the first thing she'd said all day. "There's no way to fight it."

Anatoly, who had been passing through on his way to the kitchen, said, "We have a saying like that in Russian."

She looked at him. "You do?"

"I don't know. Probably; we have sayings for everything. Are you hungry? I was going to make a sandwich."

"Yeah, a sandwich sounds good." She got stiffly to her feet. Her knees and lower back hurt, and there was a kink in her neck that she got when she sat still for too long. She collected the vodka and followed him into the kitchen and put the bottle back in the fridge.

She heard voices upstairs. "We've got visitors?"

Anatoly was putting slices of bread on plates and buttering them. "Boksi and Romek are here. They waited too long and I thought it wasn't safe for them to go out during the curfew." He arranged slices of smoked pork loin on the bread and started to slice a beefsteak tomato. "Boksi called his parents and told them he's staying with a school friend. Would you like mustard with this?"

"No, thanks. Well, we've got plenty of room for them. But make sure Boksi gets home first thing tomorrow. Go with him if you have to."

"Will do." He added tomato to the sandwiches, topped them with the other slice of bread, cut them in half, and nudged one of the plates across the breakfast bar to her.

"He's not dead," she said.

"Oh, I know," Anatoly said. He took a bite from his sandwich. "I never thought he was. Neither did you."

She shook her head. "Nope. I just couldn't work out how he did it."

"And now you have."

She nodded. "I reckon. I still don't know why, though."

"It also raises the question of whether Kaunas knows."

"Of course he knows. What *else* he knows is anyone's guess."

"Are you going to tell him you worked it out?"

Carey shook her head again. "Nah," she said, and the doorbell rang.

They looked at each other. "Are we expecting anyone?" asked Anatoly.

"We are not." Carey turned and waved at the kitchen paperscreen, logging it into the database Magda had constructed for the house. She heard the kids coming downstairs. On the screen, the image from the front door camera came up. A tall old man was standing on the doorstep wearing a long coat and a broad-brimmed hat.

Anatoly sighed. "I'll go."

"I DON'T SEE what's so funny," his father said when he opened the door.

"It's all a matter of perspective," he said, still smiling as he checked up and down the street. "Come in, please."

Everybody was in the living room. The kids were sitting on the sofa and Carey was standing at the window, looking out into the street.

"I won't bother to make introductions," Anatoly told everybody. "You all know who everyone is."

"*I* don't," said Magda, looking his father up and down. The old man stared at her as if not quite believing what he was seeing.

Without turning from the window, Carey said, "I see seven of your people out there." She craned her neck for a better angle, "and I guess I'm meant to see at least some of them. How many am I missing?"

"There are four more," the general said after a little while. "In cars at either end of the street. And three watching the back of the house."

Carey nodded. "Nice. Are they carrying?"

"What do you think?"

Carey turned and looked at him. "I think I'd like to know

if armed people are outside my house, because that might inform any decisions I make."

The general's face slowly turned a shade of red Anatoly was familiar with. It suddenly occurred to him to wonder how a man so prone to anger had survived so long in the secret world. "They're armed," said the old man.

Carey nodded again. "So," she said finally. "Left it too late to get out, did we?" When there was no answer, she waved at one of the armchairs. "Oh, sit down, for Christ's sake. We're not going to eat you."

Anatoly's father gathered the skirts of his coat about him and perched himself on the edge of the chair. "I have come to suggest a pooling of resources," he said.

"You want me to jump you out of here," Carey translated. He didn't reply, and she said, "Well, that's not going to happen. I don't even have the resources to jump myself and your boy out, and even if I did I'm really not going up against the Polish Army." She wasn't about to mention the stash of stealth suits; she was saving those for a real emergency.

The general looked at Anatoly. "And what do *you* say?"

Anatoly was still smiling. "I don't make the decisions. You used to like it that way."

Carey shook her head. *Families*. She said, "Who are they, outside? Embassy toughs? Local talent?"

"Two from the embassy," the old man told her. "The rest are irregulars."

She nodded. "Yeah, well, you can count them out; they're probably mixed up with the gangs, which means they have other allegiances right now. So you only have two people you can rely on."

"That's more than enough."

"Oh, we can be pretty feisty when we want to be." She turned and looked into the street again, narrowed her eyes and tipped her head to one side for a moment, then turned back. "Okay," she said. "What are you doing in Poland?"

"I brought you a piece of highly classified technology."

"That's an excuse, not a reason. You could have put it in a diplomatic bag and had it delivered by your Rezident at the embassy."

The general looked at Carey, then at Anatoly, then at Carey again. He seemed to withdraw into the folds of his coat.

Carey said, "We're going to dust off and leave you sitting here in the middle of a civil war with two bodyguards you can trust and a bunch of mercenaries who'll try to sell you to the highest bidder. And I wouldn't put any money on the bodyguards, either."

The general said nothing.

Carey grinned broadly, all of a sudden. "Ah, hell," she said. "You're not trapped here at all, are you. You don't get to be a general in Russian Intelligence by being an idiot."

"You'd be surprised," he grumbled.

"You stayed here because you think *we* know where Maksim is."

He made a rude noise. "I'd get better information from the entrails of a chicken."

Carey looked out of the window again. "Okay. Anatoly, go and let them in."

"Who?" he said, and at that moment there was a hammering on the front door. He took out his phone and checked the front door camera. "You're joking."

"They're coming in anyway. Might as well save ourselves the price of a new door." He looked uncertain. "It'll be okay," she told him. "They knocked first."

Anatoly went to the door, and a minute or so later returned. Behind him were two men in military camouflage fatigues. They were carrying modern automatic rifles, but the uniforms looked strangely old-fashioned. They took up position either side of the doorway and a third man stepped through. He was older, maybe in his late sixties or early seventies but in good shape. He was tall and grey-haired and his battledress seemed to have been tailored for him. He walked into the room and looked at Carey and Anatoly and the General. Then he nodded.

"Bring them all," he said. He had a broad West Country accent. "Everyone in the house."

"I am a Russian citizen," Anatoly's father said in a loud voice. "I am travelling under diplomatic protection."

The tall man positively beamed at him. "Are you?" he said pleasantly. "Jolly good."

"Lower your weapons," said a voice from the door.

Everyone turned to look, saw a short, stout woman wearing jeans and a thick jacket standing there holding a pistol.

She looked around the roomful of armed people and held up an ID card printed in a language that used way too many vowels and more umlauts than a death metal festival. In her photograph, her hair was a little shorter and she was doing the staring-into-the-distance thing, and she was wearing a rather fetching uniform. The two guards at the door pointed their rifles at her.

"Colonel Krista Lindmaa, Tallinn Police," she said, making sure everyone got a good look at her ID. "You're all under arrest."

Carey and the tall man exchanged looks that acknowledged the essentially comic nature of the universe. She grinned. He sighed the sigh of a man who has already had a long, complicated day and is now watching it slide into absurdity.

"Bring her too," he told the guards wearily.

There were dozens of soldiers outside in the street; Carey did a quick headcount and thought there were more than thirty of them. Parked in a line outside the house were four military vehicles of a design unfamiliar to her, three of them obviously designed as personnel carriers, the fourth a rugged all-terrain thing that looked like a Humvee built for an Ealing comedy production. No sign of the general's men; if they had the sense they were born with they'd be a long way from here by now.

She watched as the kids were led from the house. She said, "Let them go; they've got nothing to do with this."

"I'm sorry, I can't do that," the tall man told her. "But they won't be harmed, you have my word." She noticed he didn't give a similar undertaking about herself and the other adults.

They all got into the ATV. It was a squeeze and the seats were none too comfortable. The driver was separated from the passenger compartment by a metal bulkhead that looked as if it could be hinged down, but at the moment it was raised and locked.

The tall man handed out thick cloth hoods. "I'm afraid I have to ask you all to wear these," he told them.

"Why?" Carey asked, though she was starting to suspect the answer.

"It won't be for long," he said. "My name is Michael, by the way."

"Carey," said Carey.

"Yes," he said. "I know." He held a hood out to her.

"I have questions."

"Yes," he told her. "So do I. And perhaps we can oblige each other when we reach our destination. Now, please." He held the hood out again.

She hesitated a moment, then took the hood. "Okay," she said to everyone. "Do as Michael tells you. Nobody's going to get hurt." She saw the others put their hoods on. They'd been so good, so capable, that she'd forgotten they were all so young, but they were still the best crew she'd ever worked with and she was proud of them. She gave Michael a last look, then she nodded and put the hood over her head.

* * *

When Michael said they wouldn't be long, he hadn't been kidding. They drove down the street, paused a moment, then drove more or less straight on, which put them on Kłodnica. At the end of the street, they turned left, and Carey felt the vehicle bump over the tram tracks as they went past St Barbara's. Something banged against the side of the vehicle and there was a faint burst of gunfire from behind them, where the carriers were presumably following. She heard Michael swear softly.

They drove a short distance, then made a right turn and a left and another right, which by Carey's judgement put them somewhere in the narrow winding streets of the Old Town behind the market square. She heard the tyres rattle over cobblestones.

They made several more left and right turns, and then the road surface under the vehicle seemed to alter subtly and the driver, as if in relief, accelerated smoothly up a long, slight incline. The echo of the engine noise outside sounded different, as if they were no longer among buildings.

Finally, after about half an hour, Carey felt the tyres crunch on gravel and the vehicle pulled to a stop. The door opened, and an enormous smell of forest blew into the passenger compartment.

"Easy now," said Michael gently. "Easy now." Carey felt the other passengers moving as they were helped one by one from the vehicle, then it was her turn and a firm but gentle hand took her arm and guided her out.

She stood with her hands in her pockets, waiting for whatever happened next. She ground the sole of her shoe gently against the gravel, establishing the surface underfoot. It was—there was no other word for it—*awesomely* quiet, wherever they were. No sounds of distant traffic, no aircraft. Just a huge silence and a cool breeze against her neck where the hood didn't quite cover it, and that smell of leaves and bark and mulch and a sense of endless space. They were, she was fairly certain, no longer in Gliwice, or Poland, or even Europe.

There were the sounds of people moving around, footsteps on the gravel, then someone took her hand and laid it on their arm and led her around the vehicle. "There are two steps up," a voice said beside her in an accent like Michael's but with an intonation she almost recognised. "Almost there. Here."

The steps were not high, but they were deep, stone underfoot worn into shallow depressions. They passed through a doorway and into warmer air. Carey felt a wooden floor under her feet, then they stopped and the person beside her stepped away and she heard a voice say, "You can take your hoods off now."

Carey pulled off her hood, blinked against mellow electric light. They were all standing in what looked like the entrance hall of an English country house, a big wood-panelled space with polished floors and a wide carpeted staircase leading up to the first floor directly in front of them. She did a quick head count; everyone was present. The kids were rubbing their eyes and looking about them in wonder. Anatoly and his father were over to one side, regarding the scene with a careful calm that was so familial it was almost comical. Lindmaa, the Estonian cop, was standing on her own looking furious. She couldn't see Michael.

"Could I have your attention, please?" said a voice. Carey looked over and saw a young man wearing chinos and a blazer over a white shirt. He had long brown hair tied back in a ponytail and his skin was deeply tanned, and for a moment she thought he was from the First Nations, but he had that same not-quite West Country accent she'd heard before. When everyone was looking at him, he said,

"Firstly, welcome. My name's Eric and I suppose you could say I'm your host. We have a meal waiting for you all, but I'd like to tell you a couple of things first. You're guests, not prisoners, and I hope you will all be returned to your homes as soon as possible. Meanwhile, feel free to have a look around the estate, but I have to ask you not to try to leave because you *will* get lost and I can't promise we'll be able to find you. There are wild animals in the forest, and they can be dangerous if you startle them. There are rooms for everyone and there's plenty of hot water, so if you want to have a wash before dinner just ask one of the staff and they'll show you to your room. If you'd prefer to have your meal served in your room, just say and we'll arrange that." He looked at Magda and Boksi and Romek and beamed. "And for our young friends, we've arranged a treasure hunt for tomorrow afternoon." The kids looked at him as if he'd just fallen out of a tree.

"Where are we?" said Lindmaa in the same confident voice with which she'd tried to arrest everybody. "Who are you?"

"You all have questions, and I'm sure they're all good ones," Eric told them. "And I hope that you'll have the majority of them answered soon. But first, please, settle in. Dinner in an hour. I'll ring the gong to let you know." And then he just turned and walked away and left them standing there wondering what to do next.

Anatoly came over, eyebrow raised. "Well," he said, "*this* was unexpected."

"Yes," she said.

"Also faintly absurd."

"The whole world's absurd," she told him. "Didn't you notice yet?" She saw Lindmaa coming towards them, radiating annoyance powerfully enough to char the panelling. "Go and see the kids are all right," she said to Anatoly. "And try to stop your dad wandering off." The general was giving every appearance of gearing himself up for some exploration.

"I wish he would," Anatoly muttered, but he went over to Magda and the others.

"You're *way* out of your jurisdiction," Carey said when Lindmaa reached her.

"We have a treaty with Poland," Lindmaa said.

"But not with Gliwice, which was technically an independent nation when you tried to arrest us."

Lindmaa scowled. "You're very smug."

"I'm an International Woman of Mystery. Of course I'm smug. How did you get in the house? It's got a state-of-the-art security system."

"It does. It's Estonian. I called the manufacturers and they sent me the key-codes. It turns out nobody bothered to reset the factory defaults. I've been hiding in the basement for hours."

Carey scowled. *Can't think of everything.* "Are you the one who was asking questions at the crematorium?"

Lindmaa nodded. "You're working with Maksim Petrauskas."

"I am not. I'm investigating his death. I have a Texas private eye's licence to prove it."

Lindmaa snorted. "He isn't dead."

"Oh, of *course* he's not dead, colonel," Carey said. "He came to Gliwice and he staged a *spectacular*. He'd want to stick around to admire his handiwork. What's your interest?"

Lindmaa considered for a moment. "We have evidence he was involved in a cyberattack on my country four years ago."

Carey glanced across at Anatoly's father, who had opened one of the doors which lined the entrance hall and was looking into the room beyond. "Are you sure? Doesn't sound like his style."

Lindmaa looked about her. "You see, when I say 'we have evidence he was involved', it means that we really do have evidence he was involved, whether it was his style or not."

Carey sighed. "What do you think, as a law enforcement officer? Does this qualify as an international incident?"

"If the Community's started kidnapping people and taking them across the border, I'd say so. You're taking all this very calmly, you know."

"Yeah, well, I was shaking the tree to see what fell out. Didn't expect the whole fucking tree to fall down, though."

The front door was still open, and Lindmaa walked towards it. "What do you think they want?"

Carey went and stood beside her. The car was gone, and she could see a big patch of neatly raked gravel at the front of the house with a driveway curving off at either side. Beyond the gravel the ground seemed to drop away beyond the lights of the house, and beyond that there was only a great dark silence that seemed to encompass the entire world. "Something tells me we're not in Kansas any more," she said, half to herself.

"Actually, I'm afraid you are," said a voice behind them. "Sort of."

She turned to see who had spoken, and of course it was Robert Wareham.

2

It could have worked. It already *had*. They'd been running trucks across the border for almost a year, twenty women in each one, three thousand Swiss francs for each woman. Peter thought they could have made upwards of two million Swiss out of the operation, but Carey detected no note of envy in his voice.

He finally tracked Marthe down to a shabby hotel

in Biarritz and had her brought back to Denmark, and watching their covertly filmed conversations Carey couldn't feel any anger towards her. Life with Peter's father had been, at the end, a nightmare, but it had been a gilded one; she'd had an allowance—a golden handcuff, really—of ten thousand kronor a month, and she'd been cut off from that when she made a run for it. She'd taken a bunch of high-end jewellery and some cash she'd been able to put away with her, but that hadn't lasted for ever, and then she was adrift in Europe. There were organisations—few and far between and badly-funded—that helped women in her position, but she was living under a false identity and she was afraid that if the authorities found out who she really was word would get back to her husband, who would already be looking for her, so she went on. She waitressed. She worked in department stores. She kept moving. She did that for years. Old man Schiller died a couple of years after she left, a series of minor strokes culminating in a single stroke of Biblical proportions, but Marthe knew revenge had a way of outliving the person seeking it and she kept going. Carey thought she might have made a halfway-decent Coureur; all she lacked was the training.

She was working as a chambermaid at a guesthouse in Liege when the little man approached her. He'd arrived a couple of days previously, a pleasant, humble, quiet little man with the aspect of a minor commercial traveller. He kept himself to himself, didn't drink, didn't grope the staff, and his room was always in good order, which in Marthe's experience made a pleasant change.

Then, one morning, she'd gone to service his room and found him sitting there in the one rather run-down armchair. She apologised, saying she hadn't realised he was still here, and made to leave, but he replied, "There's no need to do that, Madame Schiller."

She'd been expecting a moment like this, of course, ever

since she left Henning Schiller—only the circumstances took her by surprise—but she still froze. If they could find her *here*, flight was pointless. Nowhere was safe. She didn't even try to convince him he was mistaken.

The little man sensed all this. He told her she had nothing to worry about, that he had not been sent from her former life. Indeed, he was here to help her, to offer her a job.

He had some friends, he told her. Businessmen. They were trying to set up a network of business locations around Europe, but circumstances demanded that they remain discreet, and they needed a public face, someone who could turn up and sign papers on their behalf. It was a job which would demand, at most, a few days of her time, and in return they were prepared to pay her a sum slightly higher than the one she had originally taken out of Denmark.

Marthe wasn't stupid, she knew this was a criminal enterprise—she assumed it was something to do with drugs—but her life over the past few years had worn her down and desperation was overtaking her, and she couldn't see any other choice, so she agreed.

She flew to Helsinki, and things turned out exactly as the little man had promised. She signed leases on business premises, and that was all. She was handsomely paid. A passport in a brand-new identity was delivered to the hotel where she was staying, and she understood that, whatever was going on, her part in it was over, and she had settled in France. She hadn't heard about the subsequent events in Helsinki. Twenty illegal immigrants asphyxiated in the back of a truck in Finland was hardly major news in Western Europe.

As far as Peter was able to discover from contacts within the Finnish government, the Russians knew all about the trafficking operation and had been waving the trucks through for the sake of mischief. On the Finnish side, the traffickers had suborned an entire border station somewhere out in the sticks. The border crossing was entirely straightforward; what they were worried about was spot-checks on the road between there and Helsinki, which the Finns were very keen on.

The hidden compartments in the trucks were sealed and insulated so they couldn't be spotted by infra-red or dogs. They had water and a chemical potty and the women were only supposed to be in there for a couple of hours. Three hours, tops. There were vents in the bottom of the trucks, for fresh air. They were disguised and baffled to spoof detectors. It was a foul night, wet snow, and the air flow under the truck drove slush up into the baffles. And even that wouldn't have been such a problem if they'd kept moving, but the driver, who had no idea what he was carrying, stopped at a roadhouse. He'd been told to drive on through, but he stopped for a beer or something, and the slush froze and sealed the vents. Twenty people, in a sealed compartment the size of a small bathroom. They suffocated before they even got to Helsinki.

In the end, only the driver went to jail. The trucking company didn't exist, its only identified representative a woman who had vanished without trace. In all the time she stayed with Peter, Carey never mentioned Maksim, not once. There was no evidence that he'd been involved; a grainy photo of an old man in a beret didn't prove Yegor had been in Helsinki, and even if it did, so what? She knew, though. The name of the company was a huge giveaway, as if he wanted her to know. He'd been trying to pull the same stunt he had when he jumped Marthe Schiller from her marriage, for reasons she couldn't fathom. That crash Situation in Helsinki hadn't been a coincidence; he'd wanted her there. Only the unexpected presence of Brookshire, who had seen the chance to finally get her to work for the Texan Foreign Intelligence Bureau, had derailed his plan.

"What's going to happen to Marthe now?" Carey asked.

"I'll take care of her," said Peter. Coming from any other international gang boss, that would have sounded ominous, but Peter meant it. He arranged for a trust fund to be set up in Marthe's name, and invited her to stay on at the family estate by the sea not far from Roskilde for as long as she wanted.

He made Carey the same offer, although he did it more obliquely, but she couldn't stay. Improbably, Brookshire had been true to his word and there seemed to be no alerts out for her anywhere in Europe, and angry though she was, she wanted to get back on the horse. If Marthe, with no training and no support, could go on somehow year after year, so could she.

MAKSIM CAUGHT UP with her in Madrid. There had been weeks of messages on boards and in drops, begging her to talk to him, and she had ignored them all, but one grey drizzly day, coming out of a restaurant on Calle de Velásquez, there he was, waiting on the pavement, hands in his pockets and that bashful schoolboy grin on his face.

"Look," he began.

Her first punch rocked him back. The second broke his jaw. She stomped away through the gathering crowds, changed her address, burned through a couple of false identities, and she went on for a few more years, until she took a job in Hungary and everything fell apart. Maksim never tried to contact her again.

SHE NEVER REALLY got to the bottom of Hungary. On the face of it, it had been a milk-run of a Situation carrying a Package the size of a packet of cigarettes over the wire into Croatia. She had wound up being arrested by Hungarian State Security, then being kidnapped by the local mafia, then being rescued by local Coureurs, then being jumped out of the country by a representative from Central. She'd had Situations go wrong before, everybody did—truth be told, more of them went wrong than went right—but she had found this experience profoundly dislocating. She'd thought, at first, that it was Maksim taking a childish form of revenge for that day on Calle de Velásquez, he was perfectly capable of something like that, but the more she thought about it the more she thought she sensed some kind of espionage going on. Theoretically, Central was apolitical, but in practice you never knew what was in the Package, which was different from proactively getting mixed up in spying. If Central was doing that, she was out.

She returned to Texas feeling old and tired and bent out of shape by the events of the past couple of years. She had some money—quite a lot, actually, when she finally got a chance to gather her wits—and she had her eye on a plot of land just outside Austin with a derelict old ranch-house on it. She thought she might renovate the house, sit out there and do journalism. The geopolitical landscape in the United States was still fresh and evolving, and she thought she would be able to do a lot of good, valuable work without ever leaving North America again.

But months went by and she remained in her rented apartment in the Texan capital. She ate in restaurants, went for walks, visited friends, went to the theatre, wrote European lifestyle pieces for the magazines for pocket money. Somehow, she never quite got round to contacting the realtor about that plot of land, and the longer she did nothing about it, the more obvious it became that she was never going to do anything about it.

The situation with Brookshire had resolved itself in an unexpected manner. She'd sent him a few bits of low-level intelligence down the years, and he had always, she thought, been singularly ungrateful for them, always wanting something more meaty. He'd been furious that she'd returned to Texas, and wanted her back in Europe at the first possible opportunity.

Then, one day, she got a message from someone who identified himself as her new case officer. Brookshire, it transpired, had been caught passing classified material to federal agents. He'd been tried *in camera*, found guilty, and taken out and shot.

"I thought he was an asshole," she told her new handler. "I never had him pegged as a traitor."

"They're not mutually exclusive," said the handler, who was just an electronically disguised voice on the other end of an encrypted phone link. "Anyway, all his assets are tainted so we're quietly letting them drop, but you're a rather special case."

"Yes," she said tiredly. She had been Brookshire's only asset in Europe; for all she knew, she had been the FIB's only asset there. Texas wanted to be a grown-up country and that meant spying on other countries.

"We were wondering how you'd feel about continuing to work for us," said the voice.

"Dude," she told him patiently, "I never wanted to work for you in the *first* place."

"Hm," he said. "Yeah, I kind of got that impression. I should tell you Brookshire had a bunch of blackmail material on you."

She sighed. She'd been expecting this ever since the call began. "You could at least try to be original."

"Oh," he said. "No, I don't plan on using it, he'd lodged it with his attorney with instructions to be released to us and EuPol if anything ever happened to him. I guess he was worried you'd try to whack him."

"I'm flattered."

"Anyway, when he had his little *aberation* his attorney turned everything over to us. Guy wants to stay on our good side, I guess, whatever the Bar Association feels about it. I wondered if you wanted to see it before I have it destroyed."

"Why would you do that?"

"We can force you to work for us," he said, "but let's face it, where's the percentage in that? You'll just get resentful and send us chickenfeed and then we'll get resentful and honestly, life's too short."

She took the phone from her ear, looked at it, put it back against her head. "What's your name?"

There was a dry chuckle at the other end of the connection, rendered robotic by the voice-camouflage software. "Sorry, can't tell you."

She thought about it. "Did any of it go anywhere else?"

"Not so far as we can tell, no."

"Then just get rid of it," she told him.

"Nothing easier," he said. "There's also a note from the Ambassador in Budapest. Something about an arrest by Hungarian security services."

She snorted. "If you can get that useless bitch reassigned to the Damascus embassy I might think about working for you."

"We don't have an embassy in Damascus," he pointed out. "Nobody does."

"Well, she's damn-all use where she is."

"I don't suppose you'd consider telling me what that was all about?"

"I don't even know myself."

"Right. Okay, so, all that remains is for me to remind you that we never had this conversation. Good luck with whatever you decide to do, and if you ever change your mind, just get in touch and we'll talk about it." He paused, then said, "You know, a lot of us think what you guys do over there is pretty cool. At least it looks that way on the shows. Is it really like that?"

"No," she said. "Usually it's really boring, and then something goes wrong."

SHE WAS AWARE that she was a relative rarity. The Coureurs had never gained much of a foothold in the US—she suspected the competition from home-grown smuggling organisations, some of them almost a century old, was just too fierce—but they maintained a presence, here and there. On her return, she had been given a contact routine for a liaison/recruiter who called himself Benedikt, an old man with a professorial air and the faintest remnants of a German accent. She had, of course, no idea who Benedikt was in his private or professional life, but in his Coureur life he was—or presented as, anyway, she'd learned to be cautious about what people pretended to be—a stringer, a sort of all-purpose gofer. In her case, he represented a link to aftercare, should she require it, which she had not.

"I must confess a little surprise at hearing from you after so long," he told her after they'd gone through the call-and-response routine and met in the café of the Elisabet Ney Museum. "I thought you'd really shaken off the Life."

"No one really shakes off the Life," she said, attacking her Danish pastry with a fork.

He inclined his head in assent, a tall, bald, pinch-faced man with the long sensitive fingers of a master safecracker. Today he was dressed in chinos and a grey shirt and a blue blazer, a muted grey and carmine cravat round his neck. "You had quite a scare, though. Nobody would think the worse of you if you chose not to go back."

"I'm not afraid," she told him, although she had been. "I'm *annoyed*. Someone used me as a patsy over there. I can't prove it, but I know they did, and that's irksome."

Benedickt nodded. "I'm not of course allowed to know

what happened to you, or even where it happened, and even if I asked I wouldn't be told. But I can sympathise."

Carey wagged her fork at him. "I don't want sympathy," she said. "I want answers."

"I was under the impression that you had been given answers."

"I was given the brush-off," she said. "I was given a bonus. I was given *you*. I was not given answers."

He considered his coffee cup, picked it up, took a sip, returned it to its saucer. "Perhaps there are no answers to give," he said. "Life is not a thriller, where everything is neatly tied up at the end."

She was probably the very last person in the world who needed to be told that. She looked at him for a few moments longer, then went back to her pastry. "I didn't come down with the last fall of snow."

"Indeed not. You've proven yourself efficient and capable in all manner of Situations."

"Stop *handling* me, Benedikt," she snapped.

He shrugged. "It's part of my job." He sighed, a little. "You're bored, and that's to be expected. Give yourself some more time. Let yourself settle."

She shook her head. "I want to go back."

Benedikt thought about that. "If you think, by going back, you'll find out what happened to you, I'm afraid you should prepare yourself for disappointment."

Carey laid down her fork. She had managed, without noticing, to reduce her pastry to a pile of sticky crumbs, but she couldn't recall tasting it. She clasped her hands on the table in front of her and leaned towards him slightly, her voice low and conversational. "I'll move stuff," she said. "I won't move people. I won't do Central Europe. If I get the slightest sniff of espionage, I'm on the next flight back here. And I won't set foot in Hungary."

Benedikt considered for a while. "We don't usually have

people setting *conditions*," he said. "But it would be useful to have someone with your track record back in the field. Things have been a little strange in Europe, of late."

Carey snorted. Ever since the emergence of the Community, 'strange' had been Europe's default setting. And it hadn't exactly been normal to begin with.

Benedikt thought about it a little longer, then he nodded. "It's outside my remit to make a decision, but I'll pass this along. Check your boxes. If you haven't heard anything in a week, assume that wiser heads than mine have decided to turn down your request." He stood, and picked up his gorgeously tooled leather knapsack from the floor beside his chair. "That won't be any reflection on your abilities, by the way."

Carey looked sourly at him as he walked away. It was the last time she ever saw him.

SHE'D NEVER REALLY explained, to herself or anyone else, why she wanted to go back into the field. She'd more or less given up trying to explain it to herself after the first few days. She wasn't bored, but there was a certain *restlessness* she recognised. She was *home*, but she didn't feel *at home*. There was probably a word for it in German, something long and obscure and hard to pronounce.

Underlying it all, of course, was the simmering anger at what had happened to her—what had been *done* to her—in Hungary. Her life had been driven off the rails and for the first time in a very, very long time she had become a passenger. For several days she'd had no agency at all, and that was offensive to her. It reminded her of her younger days, when for a little while she had been entirely out of control.

On her return to Austin, she'd set up a dozen or so dead drops around the city, almost without thinking about it. It was a reflex, something one did when one arrived in a new place. It was only later that she wondered why she'd bothered, when she didn't expect to receive any communication, even though she'd told Benedikt about them. And it was only much later that she wondered whether, even then, she hadn't been planning to go back, preparing the ground, keeping her instincts running.

She kept an eye out for surveillance, but it seemed the security services meant what they said and were leaving her alone. Even if they hadn't, there was hardly any peril for a woman of a certain age wandering about her home town, sitting on a certain bench or visiting a certain library or walking through a certain park where there was a certain stunted tree with a handy hole in its trunk just above head height. Nobody cared. She was invisible.

She spent the week following her meeting with Benedikt in a long, slow tour of her boxes. Then she did it again the next week, and the week after that. But they were bare of the marks which would have indicated that they had been filled, and when she checked, they were empty. There was, of course, no apology, no explanation. She'd simply been turned down, as if she'd been found unsuitable for a clerical job.

A series of storm fronts swept over the Hill Country, scribing twisters across rural parts of Travis County and dumping sheets of rain into downtown. She stood at her window watching the gutters overflowing and bits of debris—some of it worryingly large, she'd been in Europe long enough to find tornado weather alarming—blowing down the street. One morning she looked out and saw a column of National Guard storm vehicles, wide heavy tracked personnel carriers with low centres of gravity, parked outside. As she watched, their engines started up with puffs of dirty smoke, and they moved off, ploughing up bow waves in the standing water on the street. What they'd been doing there, and where they were going, she never found out.

When the weather cleared, she drifted. She found herself checking her boxes again, even though she knew by now that there would be no message. She couldn't quite get a handle on how she felt. It wasn't anger or disappointment, but somehow both of these combined into a weightless sense of loss. She'd been a Coureur a little over half her life—almost as long as she'd been a journalist. She hadn't done anything spectacular in that time, but the work had mostly kept ticking over, and she'd been well-paid for it. The thought that it might be over, through no fault of her own, was unacceptable. "Rules are for losers," Maksim had told her, more than once. "You want to be a loser? Follow the rules."

MEANWHILE, EUROPE WAS getting weird again without her. Part of West London and part of the Community had somehow become transposed. Was it an outrage? Was it a miracle? Nobody knew. Almost the entire population of the Line, along with all its rolling stock, vanished overnight, some said into yet another pocket universe, this one of its own making, although there was also a sturdy subset of conspiracy theorists who claimed to have documentary evidence that it was the largest alien abduction event in history. That old sense that someone, somewhere, needed her help began to nag at her again.

Even so, she thought, sitting in a Waffle House concession in the departure area of Austin-Bergstrom, keeping one eye on the board for her flight to be called, what was she trying to prove? That she couldn't be beaten? That brought her uncomfortably close to Brookshire territory. A century or so ago, she would have been regarded as an old lady; she'd earned her retirement, but she wasn't ready yet. She had a sense of unfinished business, of stuff yet to do. If she let it all just roll over her—the flu, Maksim, Hungary—she might as well just walk under a bus.

* * *

SHE ARRIVED IN Madrid on her old Verónica Hernández passport, with a commission from a high-end society magazine in her pocket. Verónica and her wonky Texas Spanish were well-known around town, and it would have been awkward if she'd bumped into people she knew while she was using another identity. She didn't stand a chance of affording the property prices in the centre of town, but she managed to find an apartment in Alcobendas, not far from La Granja Metro station, and she gradually worked her way into the city's calendar of gallery openings and charity balls and theatre events.

She did that for eight months or so, settling in, readjusting to the rhythms of the city, making herself a familiar face at society functions. In time, she ranged further afield, a film festival in Barcelona, a fashion show in Toulouse, putting some miles under her feet and getting people used to her occasional absences. When she thought she was ready, she started to put out feelers.

One evening, at a private viewing at the Museo de Arte Contemporáneo, someone came up beside her and said, "Thought-provoking, isn't it?"

They were standing in front of an enormous canvas painted white and studded with the decapitated heads of dolls. "I have no idea," Carey said. "I can't get my mind round this stuff any more. Maybe I'm just getting old."

"If you are, it suits you."

She turned her head and smiled. "Hello, Luis," she said.

Luis seemed to have quietly fossilised rather than growing old; he had the smooth density of a statue. He must be in his eighties by now. He was wearing a gorgeously cut suit and a cream silk collarless shirt. His bald scalp was crisscrossed with old scars and he was carrying a black lacquered walking cane with a silver knob in the shape of a skull. Carey suspected the whole ensemble was hired; Luis had always been more comfortable in jeans and a tee shirt. "You wanted to talk," he said amiably, pitching his voice just below the hubbub of guests in the gallery.

"I need to scare up some work," she told him.

Luis looked at the canvas again. "I heard you'd retired."

He hadn't heard any such thing, of course. When he'd received her contact request he'd done some digging to see what she was up to. She said, "And now I'm unretired."

"Congratulations," he said, moving on to the next painting. "I'm sure Central will cater for all your needs, workwise."

The next piece was a blank, unpainted canvas which someone had slashed randomly with a knife. Carey couldn't decide if it was art or just vandalism. She said, "I'm going freelance."

Luis raised an eyebrow, whether at the canvas or at what she'd just said, she couldn't tell. "You're setting up in competition with Central."

"It doesn't have to be like that. I'm just one person; what difference does it make?"

"You're *just one person*," he said, "then another *just one person* goes solo. Then another, then another, and before we know it there are a thousand *just one persons* competing with *Les Coureurs* for work. There's a lot less than there used to be, you know."

She knew; these days, a lot of Central's bread-and-butter business was passing through the Community, where there were no troublesome borders to impede it. It wasn't terribly fast—everything had to go by steam train on the other side, which could take a little while if you were trying to send a parcel from, say, Madrid to Helsinki—but it was reliable.

"There's always been wannabes," she said. "Either they give up after a while or Central absorbs them."

"Neither of which would apply to you."

"Bless you, you *have* been talking to the mother ship."

"There *is* no mother ship," Luis insisted. "But I have picked some brains." He turned away from the wall, looked at a sculpture consisting of a couple of dozen rusty AK-47s piled haphazardly on the gallery floor, and shook his head. "How much is this?"

Carey pointed at the little red dot stuck to the floor beside the guns. "It's been sold."

"Jesus," he said. "Who would have such a thing in their home?" He looked at her. "How old are you?"

"I'm fifty-nine next birthday," she told him. "And I'll view any ageist crack you're about to make very dimly."

He shrugged. "Fifty-nine is the new thirty."

"It was the new forty when I was younger."

"It's late in life to start again," he said. "Especially on your own."

"Did they tell you to say that?"

"*They* suggested I use my initiative. Which I'm doing." He leaned on his cane. "I'll help you if you insist, and if I can, but seriously, give it up and go home. There are monsters out there. I've seen them."

Yeah, well, so have I, she thought.

3

SHE SPENT THE night in another hotel. There was no news but the news of the riot. For a miracle, the unrest had subsided to a slow simmer and there had been no repeats of actual mass violence, but the atmosphere in Tallinn was officially described as 'tense'. All police leave had been cancelled, and the army remained on standby. Prime Minister Salumäe had spent all night in an emergency committee, and when he made a brief statement at breakfast time it showed. He praised the role the police and other emergency services had played during the disturbance and denied that it had been sparked off by police heavy-handedness. He ended with a plea for Estonians—all Estonians—to band together in fraternity. All he would say about the investigation into the death of Sergii N was that it was still ongoing.

Krista breakfasted late, after a sleepless night of her own. She was drinking a second cup of coffee when a tall man dressed in jeans and a fleece sat down opposite her. Krista looked at him, looked around the dining room. It was almost empty; the waiting staff were tidying up to get ready for the lunch service.

"Hello, major," said the man. He was middle-aged, brown-haired, pale-eyed. "My name is Kristjan Alver. Do you mind if I join you?"

"You seem to have joined me already," Krista said.

"Quite." Alver raised a hand to attract the attention of one of the waitresses. "Could I have a cup of coffee, please?" he asked her.

"It's serve yourself, sir," the girl said, indicating a coffee machine sitting on a table piled up with cups and saucers.

"Yes," Alver said with what turned out to be a devastatingly charming smile. "But could I have a cup, please?"

The waitress deadpanned him for a moment before turning and heading off to the coffee machine with a barely suppressed sigh.

"That was cheeky of me," Alver confided to Krista. "I'm not even a guest."

Krista sipped her own coffee. She'd checked in using her own ID, but she'd paid cash in advance for the night's stay. Unless Jakobson had put a bulletin out to every hotel in the country, she should have been invisible. "You're with KaPo," she said.

Alver favoured her with a dialled-down version of the smile he'd used on the waitress. "I'm afraid not. Although we do work a lot with Internal Security. Ah, thank you." This last to the waitress. "Is there any sugar?"

The waitress half-turned, swiped a pot full of sugar sachets from the neighbouring table, and set it down in front of Alver with a delicacy which suggested she really wanted to slam it entirely through the tabletop. "Will that be all, sir?" she asked.

Alver beamed. "It will, thank you."

When the waitress had stomped off, Alver said, "So, no. Not KaPo."

"Do you have any way of identifying yourself as working for Not KaPo?"

"Gods no." He gave a theatrical shudder. "That would defeat the whole object."

"How do you identify each other then? Secret handshakes? Funny walks?"

He leaned forward slightly and said in a stage whisper, "We have a company song."

Despite everything, that made Krista smile. "Very good, Mr Alver. I presume this is about my father? Unless my life has *really* broken free of its moorings?"

He nodded. "I'm here to reassure you that your father is almost certainly innocent."

"There's no 'almost' about it."

"Just so. We'll be notifying the rather splendid Colonel Jakobson of this..." he checked his watch. "Well, it's been done already. So." He beamed at her. "You can go home. There will be no black marks on your career; in fact I think your superiors will be rather apologetic, although I can't promise that. People are unpredictable."

They sat looking at each other for quite a while. Then Krista said, "No, Mr Alver. That won't do. You're not going to walk into my life, tell me everything is suddenly magically all right, and then just walk away again without telling me what's going on." And even as she said it, she knew something more was going on. Alver and Not KaPo could simply have passed their message on to the police; she would never have had to know they existed.

He thought about it, while he tore the ends off three of the sugar sachets and dumped their contents in his cup. "What do you think of," he asked, picking up his spoon and stirring his coffee, "when you hear the word 'disinformation'?"

"Deception. Black propaganda. Fake news."

Alver took a sip of his coffee, frowned at the cup, put it back on its saucer. "The nature of disinformation has changed slightly, down the years. At one time, it was just about spreading lies, and you'll have to believe me when I tell you those were simpler, better times. These days, it's all about making people unsure *what* to believe. If all news is fake, what is real? How is one to decide? In an environment like that, even the most implausible lies can seem true. To a large enough number of people to make a difference, anyway. Even when they're proved to be lies, people will still insist they're the truth. In a sense, 'truth' no longer matters. Truth is what the largest percentage of the population believes." He picked his cup up to take another sip, decided against it, put the cup down again.

He meant her father. Even if he were proved innocent, there would be those who would still believe he was guilty. The accusation would never go away; it would drift around the internet, attracting conspiracy nuts and malcontents, and every time a Russian was hurt during an interaction with the Tallinn police it would be taken out and dusted off and it would gain a few more followers. It would never end.

"You're certain the Russians did this," she said, thinking of what Stepan had said.

"They would be our chief suspects, yes. Although proving it will be tricky; it always is. We believe they engineered the blackout before Christmas as a cover to insert certain items into certain servers and databases, and to make it appear they had been there for some considerable time. And really, you can't fault their ambition. For most people, blacking out an entire city would be enough of an achievement."

"The complaint about Sergii N's death."

"Indeed. They put it, and some supporting material, in various places, and then they sat back and waited for someone to notice it. Sometimes these things work, sometimes they don't. I think this time they worked rather well."

"But Sergii died twenty years ago. They can't have planned that far ahead."

"I think you'd be surprised just how far ahead some things are planned. But no, you're right. They looked for a Russian who had died in uncertain circumstances, long enough ago to make it plausible that witnesses had died or dropped out of touch and memories had become unclear, and they wrote the whole scenario around him. It's rather elegant, really."

"How do you know all this?"

Alver shook his head. "Can't tell you. Sorry."

"Then why should I believe any of it?"

"Because you want to? It rather proves my point, doesn't it? A complete stranger comes up to you in a hotel dining room and spins you a *most* unlikely story. Is it true, or is it not? It confirms what you want to believe, therefore it's true." He sat back and crossed his arms.

Krista looked around the dining room. They had the place to themselves; even the waiting staff had gone. "They've destroyed my father's reputation, just to discredit the police and embarrass the government."

"It's not a game, I'm afraid, major. And it's actually quite an achievement; frankly, we'd be over the moon if we managed to pull something like this off. And we're not at all certain it's over yet. No offence, but it's rather a lot of trouble to go to just to blacken the name of one policeman and cause a riot. We're waiting to see if another shoe drops."

"So what am I supposed to do now? Go home, pretend it never happened?"

Alver looked levelly at her. "I told you, major. It's not a game. It's not a book you can close and put back on the shelf. Your life will never be the same as it was last week, and I won't insult your intelligence by telling you it will be."

"None of this is remotely reassuring."

"We're going to wait a few days before we make this public—operational reasons, I can't tell you why. We'll say the Russians deliberately set out to blacken your father's name. The Russians will issue a shocked denial. People will believe us, or they'll believe them. I imagine at some point there will be some trumped-up outrage for them to accuse us of and us to deny. And it will go on. In the meantime," he added, taking a printed photograph from his pocket and putting it on the table, "there are these."

The image featured two men walking side by side down a street. One of them was old—well over seventy, she thought—with a Russian face. The other was younger and fair-haired. Looking at the background, she realised with a start that they were walking past Raekoja plats police station, *her* police station. She looked at Alver.

"We believe that these men, along with others, were responsible for the blackout," he said.

"So do something about it."

"Ah, but we have no legal powers of arrest," he said. "Imagine that. A modern, progressive democracy limiting the powers of its secret police. Scandalous." He smiled and nodded at the photo. "A gift, if you like. A small way of making amends for what you've been put through."

"Who are they?"

"There's a list of some of their aliases on the back." Krista turned the photo over, saw two columns of tiny printing.

"And that's all I'm allowed to tell you, really. There are some rather strict demarcations between your service and mine; my superiors would be quite cross if they knew I'd shared this with you." He stood up. "For what it's worth, my advice would be to take some leave, I'm sure you have some saved up. Let your colleagues pick up the pieces for a little while, then come back fresh. And congratulations on your promotion." He smiled and walked away.

"IT MUST HAVE been terrible," said the Russian girl.

"It was," Lenna said.

"Have you any idea how it started?"

"Excuse me? Started?"

The girl was a Russian Russian, not an Estonian of Russian ethnicity. She'd flown in from Moscow the moment the airport opened again, and sitting on Lenna's sofa she was as exotic as a borzoi. Her clothes were stylishly expensive, her makeup flawless, her long brown hair streaked blonde and pomegranate. She looked as if she'd stepped down from a catwalk, not from a cab directly from the airport.

"The attack on your people by the police."

"The police are saying some of the protesters threw stones at them."

The girl nodded. There was a strange air of watchful listlessness about her, as if she had written her story already and was only here to get some colour to fill it in. "Of course they would say that," she mused. "I understand your Prime Minister was once a police officer."

"Salumäe? Yes, I think he was, for a while, after he left university. It obviously didn't agree with him."

The Russian smiled politely. "So you might reasonably expect him to be sympathetic to the needs of the police?"

"Oh, absolutely." Lenna remembered a speech Salumäe had made during the last election, vowing to support the police and the work they did, but every politician did that during elections.

"To the extent of helping to cover up this crime committed against Sergii N?"

"You think *Salumäe's* involved in this?" Lenna asked.

The Russian girl shrugged. "It would make sense, wouldn't it? The former policeman protecting his own."

Lenna thought about it. "I suppose it would," she said.

The girl smiled. "Good. Now, you gave up a good career in journalism to take up this campaign. That must have been quite a decision."

"Not at all," Lenna said. "A great injustice has been committed. It doesn't matter whether it's against an Estonian or a Russian."

The girl's smile dimmed a little. "Well, you wouldn't imagine such a thing happening to an Estonian, would you?"

Lenna had no idea. "I guess not."

"Good. So, let's recap. Sergii N was murdered by the police and the police refused to investigate. That would be your campaign's point of view, yes?"

"That's right."

"And you yourself have suffered at the hands of the police while trying to publicise this injustice."

"That's right. I've been arrested. Twice."

"Were the police aggressive towards you?"

"Oh yes. There's one called Jakobson. She's a total bitch."

The Russian glanced at her phone to make sure it was still recording the conversation. "You've been very brave."

"I don't think I've been brave at all," Lenna said, unable to suppress a smile. "Anyone would have done what I've done."

"Against state violence?"

"Well, no one's been *violent* towards me, exactly..."

"But you were arrested!" the girl said. "And the police were aggressive."

"Well, yes, they were. They tagged me. Look." She pulled up her sleeve and held her arm up to let the Russian girl see the mildly inflamed lump where the locator tag had been injected under her skin. "I think I'm having an allergic reaction."

The girl shook her head sadly. "It's a scandal. It's as if you are still in jail."

"*Yes*," Lenna said. "Yes, it's *exactly* like that."

"This is authoritarianism of the worst kind," the girl told her. "It would not be allowed in my country."

"Really?" Lenna had heard different.

"But of course not! Such a thing is not civilised, don't you agree?"

Lenna scratched her arm absent-mindedly. "I don't think I can argue about that."

"Good. So here you are, a crusader for the truth, standing up for the rights of a man whose life was cruelly taken by those he should have expected to protect him." She shook her head. "Just between us, and off the record, I admire you."

"I don't think I've done anything admirable," Lenna said, blushing. "I'm just trying to do what's right."

"That's a wonderful line," the girl said. "And so typically humble of you. You're a lone woman standing up against the forces of authoritarianism. Why, they could have killed *you*."

"I'm not really alone," Lenna said. "There's Mr Reinsalu..."

The girl waved Mr Reinsalu away, as well she might. Mr Reinsalu had been unavailable for some time now. All of his phone numbers were dead. "A lone woman," she said again. She looked as if she was working herself up to some serious fangirling, which was slightly alarming but also quite gratifying, but instead she became all business again and took a fat envelope from a shoulder bag which was probably worth more than Lenna's old annual salary at the news agency. She held the envelope out. "As discussed, here are your travel documents and a Russian passport. We should leave soon; before very long your police are going to come looking for you again."

"Yeah," Lenna said, taking the envelope. "We don't want *that* to happen."

The girl beamed. "You're going to be a *star* in my country."

A FUNERAL WAS going on at Rahumäe when she got there—quite a large one, judging by the number of cars. There was nowhere to park and she wound up leaving the car over on the other side of the cemetery and walking the rest of the way.

The sun had come out, finally, and the light reflecting off the snowy ground was almost blinding. If she closed her eyes and tilted her face to the sky, she thought she could feel the warmth of the sunlight on her cheeks, although her breath still plumed in the chill air. A few kilometres away, across Ülemiste järv, she could hear the engines of jets taking off and landing at the city's airport.

The grave was marked with an unassuming plain stone of black marble, unadorned save for her parents' names and dates. Not even her father's rank. No way to know who they were, what they had done in life. Krista brushed a cap of crusty snow from the top of the stone and stood there with her hands in her pockets.

It was a while since she'd been out here, even though it was only a couple of kilometres from her home. After her father's funeral she'd come every weekend, but work started to intrude and then the Tamburlaine thing had come along and she was spending seven days a week on that, and… well, her father would have understood. Her mother, maybe not so much.

She'd been twelve when her mother died, eaten alive by

an aggressive brain tumour which had been inoperable even before the headaches announced its presence. Her father had never remarried, although there had been a few woman friends down the years, some of whom Krista got on better with than others. They had all turned up at the funeral, six intense-looking women standing in a tight little group. Krista had found herself watching them, trying to see if her father had had a 'type', but the women, short and tall, slim and stout, dark and fair, had nothing in common except the man they were there to mourn. None of them resembled her mother.

Her father had been an outstanding police officer, but nobody could have accused him of being a natural parent. A great chunk of her upbringing had been outsourced to a loose network of aunts from both sides of her family, and there had been rows. She thought her father had been deeply relieved when she went to university, and then to the police school, because it meant he could finally speak to her as an equal. She found she didn't resent any of this; it was just the way their life had been. She didn't even regret the arguments, although she wished she had managed to win more of them.

He had never told her what he thought about her decision to become a police officer. In another family that would have seemed strange, but for her it was perfectly normal. They hadn't even discussed it beforehand; she had just gone ahead and applied. He'd always been there for advice, if she asked for it, and they occasionally talked over cases, but that was it. How he felt about having a daughter in the police force remained a mystery.

None of this meant that they didn't care very much about each other. Every now and again her aunts—her mother's sisters—would profess themselves scandalised by her father's lack of parenting skills, but they didn't understand him the way she did. He would, she had always been sure, have taken a bullet for her, and she for him.

And now it was all moot anyway. He was gone and she was who she was, for good or ill.

She turned from the grave and walked back down the wide path through the wooded cemetery towards the car. A large number of Tallinn's notable citizens were buried here; she passed the graves of politicians and writers and painters and rock stars. Scattered among them were names of Russian origin. She'd never really noticed them before; they were all, in her mind at least, Estonians. That, in the light of recent events, was probably naïve of her. It was going to take some years for the wounds of the past week to heal, if they ever did.

On the way out of the cemetery she passed the grave of 'Iron Man', the legendary rocker Gunnar Graps. Graps had once been arrested trying to cross the Swedish border carrying anabolic steroids. He said his two months in a Swedish jail wasn't so bad; the jail was better than most Estonian restaurants. Krista had never liked Graps's music, but that line about the jail made her smile. She'd visited a prison in Norrköping once, to pick up a suspect who was being extradited to Estonia, and all she could say was that Estonian restaurants must have been pretty terrible back in Graps's day.

Back in the car, she started the engine and let it run while the heater thawed out the interior. She had, she considered, achieved precisely nothing. She hadn't broken the case and proved her father innocent; Alver and Not KaPo had appeared out of thin air and done that while she had been driving around the country wondering what to do next. It was hardly a shining performance. On the other hand, Alver had access to all the resources of the state security apparatus, while all she'd had was a cheap phone. And now she had a photograph and a list of names. Maybe it all balanced out in the end.

The car was finally warm enough for her to drive without

shivering violently. She put it in gear and drove towards the centre of town.

Not all the news was bad. At some point while Estonia was in chaos, Tamburlaine had dropped dead of a heart attack while shopping with his wife in Bremen. Deprived of their leader, his lieutenants had taken to squabbling among themselves for the right to inherit his empire, and the streets of Hamburg were briefly a bloodbath. The situation would bear watching, but it was generally agreed that expansion into Estonia was low down on their list of priorities at the moment.

Also, as Alver had said, she was not reprimanded for her behaviour during the crisis. Indeed, she was now a colonel, and she didn't know what to think about that. She thought her father would have been pleased, in a non-demonstrative sort of way.

News of the Russian cyberattack seemed to have drawn the poison, to some extent. Mostly, people appeared embarrassed about the riot, as if they had been shown footage of themselves during a drunken stag party. The Russian response to the accusation boiled down to *Well, they would say that, wouldn't they,* and the Russian Ambassador had called it 'a fairytale for little children'. As Alver had said, there was still a vocal minority who believed her father in particular and the police in general were guilty and there was nothing she could do about that. Relations between Estonia and Rus remained frosty, but that was hardly a new experience.

Meanwhile, she had bridges of her own to repair. Markus understood why she'd taken off on her own, but he was still aggrieved at being kept so far out of the loop. She had a fairly good understanding of the fragility of the male ego, so she took Alver's advice and booked them a few days in Amsterdam. She'd set in motion a search for the two men in the photograph, but according to the timestamp it had been taken months ago, three weeks before the blackout, and the trail was cold. She wasn't expecting any immediate results.

And it was good, when it came down to it, to get out of Tallinn. She hadn't realised just how wound up she'd been. They visited the Rijksmuseum and stood in the crowd in front of *The Night Watch*, wandered in the Vondelpark, hired bicycles and rode out into the countryside and ate lunch at a little bar in an almost-deserted village.

One evening they dined at a little restaurant off Dam Square, walked back to their hotel hand in hand. They were almost there when her phone rang.

"Have you seen the news, boss?" Kustav asked when she answered.

"News about what?" she said with a sinking sensation.

"You're going to want to see this," he told her.

Back in their room, she called up an Estonian news service on the entertainment set, sat on the end of the bed scrolling through the headlines while Markus took a shower.

She watched the headline item three times, was watching it a fourth when Markus came out of the bathroom wearing in one of the hotel's thick white dressing gowns and towelling his hair.

"What is it?" he asked, sitting down beside her.

"Trouble," she said, starting the news item again.

The footage was jerky and grainy, a night-time scene of a group of figures in Estonian police uniform standing swigging from bottles in some open space. They were joking and laughing and shoving each other, unsteady on their feet. The studio narration informed the audience that the video had recently come to light as a result of an investigation into the Tallinn police and was currently being studied to establish its authenticity.

Whoever had filmed the footage was clearly drunk; the viewpoint swooped and yawed, spending as much time focused on the ground as on the little group of men. Suddenly, one of them lurched to the side and the camera followed him as he stood in front of a statue of a soldier in Red Army uniform, unzipped himself, and began to piss on it. There was laughter, tinny and flat, on the soundtrack.

The police officer finished, zipped himself up, and for a moment he turned grinning at the camera, and the footage froze on the face of Maart Salumäe. He was a lot younger, his hair shorter, but there was no mistaking that face.

The scene cut to a woman in her thirties. She was pretty, but she had the look of a drinker. A caption identified her as Lenna Rüütel, an 'expert on Estonian affairs' for a Russian news channel. She was telling the interviewer that the video was an outrage, an insult to all the dead of the Second World War, not just the Soviet dead. She said it surprised her not at all that the Tallinn police had behaved in this way, but she was saddened and disappointed that the Prime Minister, in his younger days, had shown such disrespect, and she called for him to step down.

The news item ended with a statement from the Prime Minister's office, in the strongest possible terms, that the video was fake and the whole thing was clearly a Russian attempt to undermine Salumäe and his government in the run-up to next month's elections.

"It's got to be a fake," Markus said.

Krista shook her head. "It doesn't matter." She thought this was what Alver had meant when he said he and his colleagues were waiting for another shoe to drop. "Enough people will believe it." Estonia's largest opposition party had lobbied vigorously against joining a Baltic federation, it was the hottest topic in the election campaign. Was that what this was all about? Putting a depth-charge under the federation?

"I'm sorry," she told Markus.

He gave her a hug. "I'll go and pack. See if you can get us a flight home."

ELEVEN

1

DINNER WAS AN exquisite chicken broth, followed by roast venison, sweet potato, and what looked an awful lot like succotash, which Carey regarded with interest. It was followed by apple pie and a selection of ice creams. At the beginning of the meal Magda revealed herself to be vegetarian, and without a moment's hesitation her plate was removed and replaced with another featuring some kind of nut loaf, and Carey found that interesting too.

The kids sat together at the end of the table looking apprehensive, and Carey tried to appear upbeat on their behalf, but she also spent some time glaring across the table at Wareham and experimenting with trying to set him alight by force of anger alone.

The food was pretty good, but nobody could have pretended the meal was any great success on a social level. Anatoly and his father sat next to each other looking miserable, Krista Lindmaa had wound up sitting between Anatoly and Magda, when it was obvious the only person she wanted to speak to was Carey. As host at the head of the table, Eric managed to keep a form of small talk going without answering anyone's questions, which was a good trick. Michael sat looking unruffled and not terribly impressed by the food.

"Excuse me?" Magda said at one point. "Who are you and where are we?"

Eric and Michael smiled a little; Carey noticed that Wareham did not. Eric said, "All questions will be answered in good time. Meanwhile, how's your meal?"

The girl looked at the remains of her apple pie and ice cream. Beside her, Boksi's dessert was almost untouched; he'd hardly eaten anything. Magda gave Eric a hard look. "You're frightening my cousin," she said in a dangerous voice.

Eric looked at the boy and beamed. "Well now," he told him, "there's nothing to be afraid of. This is a place of safety. In fact, that's what it's for. Nothing bad's going to happen here."

"His parents will be worried about him."

Eric's smile didn't waver. "You'll all be back long before anyone misses you," he promised. "Now, would anyone like coffee?"

Carey took her napkin from her lap, dropped it on her plate, got up, and left the dining room.

Her room was in one of the wings of the house, down a long corridor lined with locked doors. Her door wasn't locked; she hadn't been given a key. The room was about three times the size of any hotel room she'd ever stayed in before. It had two en-suite bedrooms, a sitting room, and a little dining area. No tea or coffee making facilities, though, no entertainment centre, and no trouser press. The walls were panelled in dark wood, and behind heavy curtains two big locked windows looked out on unbroken darkness. There were clothes in the heavy wardrobe and chest of drawers, and they were in her size and in roughly what an attentive observer would have decided was her personal style, and the implications of that gave her pause.

There was a knock on the door. When she opened it, Wareham was standing outside in the corridor looking bashful. "May I come in?" he asked.

"You may not," she said, blocking the doorway. "You can stand out there until hell freezes over."

"I know you must be angry—"

"You have no *idea*."

He sighed and said, "Look," in a reasonable voice, and she had a sudden powerful flash of muscle memory of the day she'd floored Maksim in Madrid. Maybe he saw it on her face, because he stopped and started again. "Eric was telling the truth. Nobody's going to be hurt and you'll all be returned to Gliwice soon. You have my word on that."

"Your word," she snorted. The sound of muffled footsteps on the corridor carpeting announced the arrival of Krista, carrying an opened bottle of wine and two glasses. Carey looked at Wareham. "Fuck off, Robert," she said, and she stepped aside to let Krista into the room and then closed the door in his face.

"You okay?" asked Krista.

"Yeah." Carey turned to look at her. "Just sick of being lied to."

"I'll drink to that," Krista said, waggling the bottle.

Carey shook her head. "I don't drink," she said. "Although the temptation is strong right now. But you go ahead." She walked over to one of the room's heavy chintzy armchairs and sat down and rubbed her eyes.

Krista poured herself a glass of wine, put the bottle and the other glass on a side table, sat in the other armchair. "Where do you think we are?"

"I don't know, the Community's a big place. Out in the country somewhere. It's interesting there's a border crossing in Gliwice, though; I never heard about that before."

"I heard they could open and close crossings wherever they wanted, whenever they wanted to."

"Yeah, I heard that too. I heard a lot of things about them. Never heard of them snatching people off the street, though."

"No," said Krista. She took a sip of wine, then looked at the glass as if pleasantly surprised. "So, Maksim Petrauskas."

"Are we really going to fail the Bechdel Test?" Carey said. "We were doing so well, too."

Krista chuckled. "What's your interest in him?"

"My former bosses called me in and asked me to investigate his death."

"His death which never happened."

"That would be the one, yes. What about you? You said something about a cyberattack."

Krista nodded. "Long story short, he caused a blackout in Estonia four years ago, and under the cover of that he put some incriminating data on some computer systems to discredit the Tallinn police in general and more particularly my father."

Carey shook her head. "Like I said, I can't see him doing that. Sure, it's the kind of thing he'd *admire*, but it's outside his competencies."

Krista took a photo from her pocket and handed it over. Maksim and Yegor, walking down a busy street. Carey nodded. "That's him."

"Who's the other one? We've never been able to get a good identification of him, just some aliases that went nowhere."

"Yegor. At least, that's how I've always known him. Ex-Russian security services, from way back in the day." She saw a sour look cross Krista's face. "I heard about that thing with your Prime Minister a few years ago. Was that something to do with this?"

"The consensus of opinion is that it was part of the same operation. Petrauskas helped bring my government down."

Well, something like that had always been on Maksim's bucket list. "I can't help you," she said. "I don't know where he is. I wish I did, because I want to tear one of his legs off and beat him to death with it."

"You think this is all something to do with him too?" Krista gestured with her glass to encompass the room, the house, the world beyond.

"I would bet every penny I have on it, although for the life of me I can't work out how."

Krista thought about it. "What are we going to do?"

"I don't know. We can't bust out of here because we don't even know where here is. They took your sidearm, right?"

"The soldiers did, but I found it on the table in my room." She shifted in the chair to show Carey the holster clipped to her belt under her sweater.

"Now that's intriguing," Carey said, looking at the gun and wondering whether it was a hopeful sign or not. "That was ballsy, by the way, coming in and trying to arrest everyone like that. Kind of crazy, but ballsy. Did you have any backup?"

Krista shook her head. "Nobody's going to miss me until the morning."

Carey nodded. "I guess we'll just have to roll with it and wait till we find out what they want."

"What if we don't like what they want?"

"Oh, I think that's pretty much guaranteed. I don't like it already."

THE NEXT MORNING, she pulled back the curtains and found herself looking out over a gently undulating sea of forest. It dropped steeply away from the house and then swept away into the distance, mist rising gently from it in the heat of the sun. Here and there, she could see thicker twists of fog she presumed marked the courses of rivers and streams.

It went all the way to the horizon—*over* the horizon—in every direction she could see.

She showered quickly—all the shower gels and soaps and moisturisers were in unmarked packaging but were definitely high-end—and dressed and went downstairs. The front door was open, and she stepped outside.

Anatoly was already there, standing at the edge of the gravel circle at the front of the house, hands in the pockets of a green waxed jacket and staring into the distance.

"This is quite something, isn't it?" he said when she came up and stood beside him.

"It really is," she said, looking around her. She turned and looked up at the house. It was a no-nonsense English country house, built of tawny stone, the parapet around its lichen-spotted slate roof crenellated but plain. The central portion was a simple cube with three rows of windows. The two wings looked as if they might be slightly later additions; one was fronted by a dozen windows, the other had a pair of big windows on the ground floor, and two rows of smaller ones on the upper floors. Carey thought it was sort of ugly. Maybe ivy would have improved things, but she didn't think so.

"I looked out of my window last night," he told her, "and I thought I saw a glow in the sky over..." he looked at the house, trying to locate his bedroom window and orient himself, "...there." He pointed off to one side. "It might have been some kind of settlement, just the other side of the horizon, but it was very faint. I could have been imagining it."

"That could be useful to know."

"I'm not sure how we'd get there, though," he said. "We're on top of a hill, with forest all around us." He gestured off to one side of the gravel, where a driveway curved away down the hill through steep lawns dotted with low bushes. "That's the only way out, as far as I can see.

It goes down about a kilometre to a gate in a high wall topped with some sort of countermeasure, I'm not sure what. Three strands of wire, anyway, all the way along. The other side of the gate, there's a proper paved road, but I can't see where it goes. It's over there." He pointed in another direction.

She looked at him. "How long have you been up?"

He shrugged. "I didn't sleep well."

Against all expectations, Carey had slept like a log. "Where's your dad?"

"Inside, poking around. He won't come to any harm. And even if he does, so what?"

Indeed. "The kids?"

"Having breakfast. Breakfast's *really* good. The Estonian woman's in there too."

"Mm. I had a chat with her last night. Maksim was a very naughty boy in Estonia a few years ago." Carey looked up into the sky. There was a little high cloud, but no contrails. The air smelled wonderful, not a hint of pollution. "Where do you suppose we are?"

"I don't know a lot about the geography of the Community," he said. "Only what I see on the news, and I doubt they're letting us see everything. I will tell you something, though. When I was looking through the gate I thought I saw a bear crossing the road some distance away."

"A bear?"

He nodded. "It looked like a bear, anyway."

"What kind of bear?"

"I don't know what kind. A bear bear."

"I'd have thought a *Russian* would be able to tell bears apart."

"I'm from Moscow," he told her. "No bears in Moscow." He looked off into the distance again. "It was brown. A brown bear."

Okay. Scratch hiking out of here, if it had ever been a serious possibility. No way was she going wandering around a strange forest full of bears. She looked out over the endless canopy. "How far do you think you can see from up here? Fifty, sixty miles?"

"It's a big forest," he said. "There's room for a lot of bears."

THE ROOM WHERE they'd eaten their evening meal had been reconfigured for breakfast by moving the dining table to one side, under the windows, and setting out half a dozen smaller circular tables with four chairs each. Krista had gone by the time Carey walked in, but the kids were still there, sitting at a table in a corner with plates and cups in front of them. Magda and Romek had showered and were in fresh clothes—and it was weird to see Magda, makeup-less, in jeans and a baggy grey shirt, Carey barely recognised her—but Boksi looked as if he'd barely slept and he was still in his school uniform because nobody had adequately explained to him that whatever clothes he found in his room were his to wear.

"My mum's going to kill me," he said miserably as Carey sat down at their table.

"Your mum thinks you're at Tomek's," Magda told him soothingly. "It'll be fine."

"The phones don't work here," he said, which was something Carey had noticed. "If she can't call me she'll call Tomek's mum, and she'll tell her I'm not there. She'll kill me."

Magda looked at Carey, and Carey told him, "It's going to be okay, honey. We're going to make it okay."

He looked at her as if she'd just broken into a show tune. "*How*?"

"I don't know yet, but I'm working on it." She reached out

and held his hand and looked at the others. "I don't think they want to hurt us; if they did they could have done that already. I think they just want to talk."

"Is this the Community?" said Romek.

She nodded. "Yeah, I think so. And that's quite exciting because normally it costs a lot of money for a ticket and they don't give visas to everybody, so you should take a look around while you get the chance." None of them looked particularly excited.

"What do they want to talk about?" Magda said. "Is this something to do with Maksim?"

"He'd be my first suspect, yes." She glanced up. Anatoly's father, looking dapper in chinos and a blazer over a blue shirt and a cravat, was standing in the doorway. He turned and walked away. "Look," she told the kids. "I don't think there's anything to worry about. Seriously. If I did, I'd be doing some stuff, but I want to know what this is about as much as you do, and the best way to do that is to play along. They'll take us back soon. In the meantime, try not to get stressed. I know that's a hard call, but I need you all at the top of your game. You're my crew and I'm relying on you to keep things together."

Magda and Romek looked as if they thought this was bullshit, although it was, to a greater or lesser extent, perfectly true. Boksi managed a brave smile. The three of them got up and went out of the dining room, and Carey was suddenly struck by how much they looked like a young family, notwithstanding that Boksi was only about four years younger than Magda and Romek. She sighed and got up and went over to the dining table.

Here, there was at least a more cheering sight. The table had been covered with a thick tablecloth, and on this was arrayed a breakfast to lighten the hearts of the most jaded international businessfolk. There were three different types of cereal and muesli, cold milk, fruit, four fruit juices, croissants and pains au chocolat, five kinds of bread roll, some seeded, some not, still warm from the oven, sliced meats and cheeses, warming dishes with bacon, eggs—scrambled and fried—sausages, hash browns, fried potatoes, grilled tomatoes, baked beans, a shiny four-slice toaster sitting beside packs of sliced white and brown bread, and all the jams and marmalades and sauces and condiments anyone could ever want. Carey loaded up a plate, put it on an unused table, got herself a mug of coffee from a new-looking Braun coffeemaker that sat on a little side table, and sat down to eat, and she'd only taken a couple of bites when Michael walked in.

"Do you mind if I join you?" he asked.

Carey gestured at the empty chairs with her knife and fork, and he went and collected a coffee and came back and sat opposite her. "We didn't have a chance for introductions last night," he said.

"Yeah," she told him, not looking up from her food. "You were too busy kidnapping us."

He nodded. "That was a little more… intense than one would have hoped for." He'd changed his combat fatigues for a really excellent double-breasted suit and a silk tie with a discreet stripe. The sharp points of a starched and ironed handkerchief peeked out of his breast pocket.

"Did you really have to take us all?" she asked. "Really?"

"I had to make a quick decision. It seemed best."

"The kids have got nothing to do with this," she said. "One of them's a sixteen-year-old boy, for Christ's sake."

"That sixteen-year-old boy is one of the most talented forgers I've ever seen," he told her. "I've seen his work. I'm tempted to hire him myself."

Carey laid her knife and fork down and looked Michael in the eye. "Lay one finger on him," she said, "and I'll completely ruin your life. For ever."

Michael held her gaze for a moment, then looked away and took a sip of coffee. "Understood."

She picked up her cutlery again and resumed her breakfast. "Is this about Maksim?"

"Yes," he said. "I'm rather afraid it is. We'll be discussing that shortly."

"Who are you?"

"Oh, a civil servant. Your average plodder. One gets sent hither and yon to resolve the occasional *problem*. Never a thank-you from one's superiors, of course, but one doesn't do it for praise."

"I'll be contacting my government about this."

"And my government will no doubt quake in its boots," he agreed. They both knew that the Texan government would be the very last place Carey would go for help, even under normal circumstances. He sipped some more coffee. "Do you think you'll be mentioning it to your superiors?"

"*The Austin Intelligencer*? Why would they care?"

Michael gave her a let's-not-play-games look.

"That would have to be a judgement call," she told him. "Central asked me to look into the circumstances of Maksim's death, see if I could find out what he was up to in Gliwice. Until I know what that has to do with all this," she waved her knife to take in the dining room and everything surrounding it, "I can't say."

Michael sat back. "I knew a Coureur once," he said. "Resourceful chap. Bit of a pain in the neck, really."

"Yeah, well, that's us. Resourceful and a pain in the neck."

He gave her a long, level look. "One doesn't like to sound *dramatic*," he said, "but there are forces at work in the world of which you're quite unaware, and you should be grateful for that. Some of these forces can't be reasoned with or bargained with. All we can do is try not to disturb them."

"What, like Cthulhu or something?"

He smiled. He had a nice smile; she suspected he'd

practiced it a lot, when he was younger, to get it right. "You're angry," he said, "and I understand that. In your position, I would be angry too. But what you must keep in mind is that I'm—we *all* are—trying to prevent a bad situation becoming much, much worse, and we're afraid it may already be too late." And with that, he got up from the table. "I'm glad we've had the chance to have this little chat. I'll see you at three o'clock. Room four in the east wing."

She watched him go. "'Trying to prevent a bad situation from becoming much, much worse,'" she muttered in a cod-West Country accent. "Blah blah." She looked down at the remains of her breakfast and sighed.

Breakfast had given her a clue, but the east wing confirmed it. This place was more of an hotel or a conference centre than a country house. The ground floor of the east wing was divided into two big rooms, one of them empty, the other set with rows of chairs and with a dais and a lectern at one end. The smaller rooms had boardroom tables and chairs covered with dust-sheets. Room four was tiny; it had seats for five people, which was a problem because Carey turned up at three o'clock with her motley crew in tow.

"I'm afraid it's just you and Colonel Lindmaa," Eric told her apologetically at the door.

"I don't have any secrets from my people," Carey said.

"And that's absolutely splendid," Eric agreed. "But we *do*, you see."

Carey turned to the others. "I guess you'd better go off and amuse yourselves," she told them. "Smash stuff up. Set some furniture on fire or something." Boksi's eyes widened in alarm. "Just kidding." She looked at Anatoly. "Why don't you all go for a hike in the grounds? Maybe you'll see a bear." He narrowed his eyes at her, but he started to herd everyone back along the corridor. His father hung back for a few moments. He *really* wanted to be in that room, and it lifted Carey's heart to see the look on his face as Eric closed the door on him.

Michael and Wareham were already seated, and the only spare chairs were either side of Wareham. Carey sat down without bothering to look at him. There was a little sheet of polished glass in front of each place setting, and beside each one was a small stack of loose notepaper and three sharpened pencils. In the middle of the table was a group of water carafes and some glasses. Carey took one of each and poured herself some water. The room was windowless, lit by sconces around the walls, and it had a bit of a bite of air conditioning.

Eric seated himself and looked at them all. He was wearing a tweedy three-piece suit. For a moment, Carey heard a familiar mosquito-whine, and then it had risen beyond the range of her hearing. "Well," Eric said, "normally I'd be thanking you all for coming, but under the circumstances that would probably be inappropriate, so perhaps I could just thank you for your cooperation, however unwilling." This last addressed to Carey, who just looked at him. "So. We're here because we all have something in common. We're all looking for Maksim Petrauskas."

"I'm not," Carey interrupted.

"I do beg your pardon," Eric said.

"I'm not looking for him. I never want to see him again. I was just sent to investigate the circumstances of his death." She looked round the table. "Can I go now?"

Eric gave her a long-suffering smile. "I was going to go round the table, but since you've spoken up first, perhaps you'd like to explain to us your involvement in this matter."

"I'm not involved," she said. "I just told you."

"I'm afraid you are," said Michael. "All of us know part of the story. Could you tell us yours?"

"Anatoly's dad's looking for Maksim too, I think," she said. "Why isn't he here?"

"We'd really rather like to keep the Russian security services at arm's length at the moment," Michael told her. "Also, I don't like him."

She looked at them and sighed. "This all starts four years ago, right?" She saw Krista nod. "The Russians blacked out Tallinn and used that as cover to edit some databases to discredit the Estonian police force and eventually force the Prime Minister to resign."

"There was talk of the Baltic nations forming a federation," Krista added. "The Russians didn't like that. After Salumäe quit and his party lost the election we pulled out of the talks and the whole thing just fell apart."

"Maksim was involved in the original cyberattack somehow," Carey said. "What he was doing between then and now, I don't know, but a couple of months ago he turned up in Gliwice making a lot of noise, making himself *obvious*. He rubbed the local Coureurs up the wrong way, did some business with some local gangs, then he died in a car crash,"

"Except he didn't," said Wareham.

She turned her head and glared at him. The angle was awkward, sitting right beside him, but she thought she could still get off a good punch.

"That's interesting," Eric said. "Why would you think he's not dead?"

"He was using his own name," she said. "If he'd been in a Situation or running some kind of caper he'd have used false papers and nobody would have known he was there. He wanted people to know."

"And that's it?" said Michael. "That's the only thing you have to base your suspicion on?"

Carey rubbed her eyes. "Okay. Okay. Can I assume that everyone in the room knows the circumstances of the accident?" Nods, around the table. "Okay. Well, the whole thing was staged. They brought the tractor up on some kind of cargo trolley, something with big fat tyres and electric motors, because they didn't want the people who live at the farm by the intersection to hear anything before they were ready. The ground got all churned up a ways down the road and somebody tried to disguise it but they missed a couple of tyre marks. I took some photos.

"Meanwhile, they've got the roads blocked off at three points by road repair crews so nobody comes along and disturbs them while they position the tractor at the intersection and they bring up the car, which they've had hidden in the woods somewhere until they need it. They'd got someone to hack its transponder so it looked as if it had been driving around all day and then suddenly taken off down the Sierakowice road at over a hundred kph, but they'd also hacked its electronics so it could be driven remotely, although that stretch of road is so straight it hardly mattered; all they had to do was keep its nose pointed in the right direction and floor it.

"So, the car crashes into the tractor and the people at the farm come running out. It's dark and it's raining and there's bodies and bits of vehicles all over the road. One of them calls the police, and somebody's monitoring his phone and when they hear the call they signal a couple of fake police cars with some fake police who're hidden somewhere nearby, and the fake police count to a hundred and then drive up to the intersection and take charge of the scene." Wareham was nodding. Maybe she could just stab him in the neck with a pencil.

"Timing's important here," she went on. "The fake police only have about ten minutes to do their thing and split, and they didn't get it quite right and that bugged me for the longest time. They moved too soon; the people at the farm thought it was odd that they hadn't taken longer to arrive."

"That's true," Wareham said. "We all thought that."

"I'm telling this story," she said coldly without looking at him. She looked at Eric. "Does this guy have to be here?"

"I'm afraid so," Eric said in a kindly voice. "Please. Go on. This is fascinating."

"What they wanted was to take charge, make sure the witnesses knew what they thought had happened, make sure the scene was credible and nobody had left anything incriminating behind. They took statements from the witnesses and told them to go back inside, and that was about when the real police turned up. Like I say, it's dark and raining and everything's chaotic and the real police don't realise that they don't know the fake police, they just think someone else got there first, and that's when the handover happens. The fake police stooge about for a minute or two, lending a hand. They share the witness statements with the real police. Then they get an urgent call or something, I don't know, and they leave the scene to the real police." She shrugged. "Sleight of hand."

"There were bodies," Michael said.

"It's not hard to get bodies, if you're that way minded," she told him. "The tractor driver was a drifter; he lived in a squat in town, had no friends or family, nobody to miss him. The other guy, I don't know. Somebody roughly Maksim's age and build. Someone else that nobody would miss, probably. I'd guess they were killed just before they staged the accident, maybe just a few minutes. They made sure the other guy's head was more or less destroyed. At around the same time, Maksim's wingman's making a call of his own to the police. Oh dear, Maksim's upset about a business deal that's gone bad, he's been drinking a lot, he's gone off in the car and I'm worried he might get hurt. A little later he's called in to make an ID and he says yes, that's him. Maybe he wipes a tear from his eye. The police write it all up, release the body to Yegor, he has it cremated, and that's all she wrote."

There was a silence in the room. Krista had been making notes and she was catching up on the last few sentences. Michael said, "It's all very *Mission Impossible*, isn't it?"

"It's very Maksim."

"And the road repair workers pack up and leave before the real police arrive," Krista said, still writing.

Carey nodded and took a drink of water.

"I like it," Eric said. "But surely, if he wanted to disappear, there are less elaborate ways of faking one's own death?"

She shook her head. "He wanted it to be elaborate. He wanted people to pay attention. He wanted someone to come along and *witness* it."

"He wanted you," Wareham murmured, and there was another silence in the room.

"Yeah," she sighed finally. "Yeah."

Eric and Michael and Wareham exchanged glances. Michael said, "He couldn't know you'd come."

"He did, though," she said. "He told Rocketman's boss I would be coming, before I even knew myself. He made a fuss with the local Coureurs because he knew they'd complain to Central. He knew Central would want to know what the fuck was going on in Gliwice, and he knew they'd ask me to look into it because I knew him so well." And may the gods help her, he knew she'd agree eventually.

Krista said, "But why would he want you to investigate his death? If he had everything else planned out he must have known there was a possibility you'd see through the whole thing."

Carey had wondered about that. At first she'd thought maybe his idea was that her presence would lend the whole thing credibility. Then, for a little while, she'd thought it was revenge, final payback for that broken jaw in Madrid before he departed for fresh pastures with a new name and probably a new face, but now she wasn't so sure.

She said, "He knows I wouldn't have come willingly, and he knows that if the accident was a hundred percent convincing I'd just wrap it up and go home. He wants me to find him."

"Why?" said Michael.

"I don't know. Maybe he thinks I'll let bygones be bygones and we'll fly off into the wide blue yonder together."

"What's to stop you just going to the police with all this?" Krista asked.

Helsinki, that's what. Somewhere, in spite of Brookshire erasing anything that might incriminate her, there would be material linking her to the trafficking operation, carefully put away in case of need. "It's a crazy story. The car and the tractor have probably been scrapped and the fake Maksim's sitting in an urn in Gliwice. All the evidence is gone. Nobody would believe it."

"*We* believe it," Eric said.

"Yeah, well, you live in a parallel universe; you've got a head start on them in the crazy department."

"Speaking as a professional, I would probably arrest you if you came to me with a story like that," said Krista.

"Thank you."

"You're welcome."

The men were exchanging glances again. Carey said, "Anyway, enough about me. Your turn, boys."

"Oh, I don't think we have anything that can top that," Eric said. "Michael?"

Michael nodded. "I agree; it's almost embarrassingly mundane, really. Petrauskas and his friends caused a certain amount of mischief for us. While we thought he was dead, we considered the matter closed. Now he seems to be alive, we're interested in him again, which is why we brought you here."

"So, what do you want?" said Carey. "Revenge?"

"Petrauskas goes back to Estonia with me to stand trial,"

said Krista. Everyone looked at her. "I just wanted to make sure that was understood. It's not negotiable."

"So long as our involvement in the matter was never mentioned, I think we could settle for that," Michael said. Eric nodded.

Krista looked at Carey. "How about you?"

"Hell, *I* don't want him."

"Fine," Krista said, and she made another note.

"What did he do to you?" Carey asked.

Michael shook his head. "I'm afraid the whole point of this exercise is to make sure as few people know about it as possible."

"If we told you, we'd have to kill you," Eric said. He smiled, to make sure everyone knew it was a joke, but Carey was fairly certain he meant *we'd have to kill you* too.

"So," Michael said, "how do you propose to continue?"

Carey shrugged. "If he wants me to find him, he'll have left some way for me to work out where he is."

"Like what?" asked Eric.

"I don't know. It probably wouldn't be obvious to anyone else. I guess I'll know it when I see it."

Eric nodded. "Just so. You'll keep Robert informed, and he'll keep us up to speed."

Carey turned her head and looked at Wareham. "Yeah," she said, "Okay."

"Good." Eric beamed at them all. "Well, this has been very constructive. Thank you, all. I'll make arrangements to have you returned to Gliwice but I hope you won't mind being our guests here for one more night."

"Why can't we go right now?" Krista asked.

"The border crossing was closed behind us when we came here," Michael told her. "Reopening it takes a little while."

"I'd quite like to see that," said Carey.

Michael chuckled. "I'm afraid there's not a lot to see. It's rather dull."

I'll bet. How do you do it? Sacrifice a chicken? Bury a hanged man at a crossroads at midnight? Sing a jolly song? "That's a shame."

"Yes." Michael and Eric stood, and a moment later so did Wareham. Eric opened the door and the men left the room. Carey and Krista remained sitting where they were. Finally, Carey got up and went over to the door and looked out. The corridor was empty. She looked at Krista, who was still sitting down.

"Those guys are going to try to fuck us over so badly," Carey said quietly.

"I know," said Krista.

2

DINNER THAT NIGHT was tomato soup, followed by roast beef, roast potatoes, Yorkshire pudding, and a medley of vegetables. The roast beef was terrific. Looking round the table, Carey thought the kids looked more relaxed. As usual, Anatoly and his father looked as if they were unwillingly taking a break from an argument.

"We saw a bear!" Boksi told her. "Down by the gate." True to their word, the house's owners had laid on a treasure hunt for the kids. Nobody had found any treasure, which Carey thought was an important life lesson.

Eric nodded and said, "We have bears, deer, beaver, many different animals. It's very wild out here."

"Where are we?" Krista asked. "I don't recognise it from the photos I've seen of the Community."

Michael smiled. "I'm afraid we haven't shown you pictures of *everything*."

"Yeah, I said that," said Carey.

"This is intolerable!" Anatoly's father blurted out, all but throwing his cutlery down on his plate. "I am a Russian citizen, abducted and brought here against my will and told *nothing*. And you just sit there talking about *bears*!"

"Serves you right for meddling in other countries' affairs," Krista said.

"I have done no such thing," the old man protested.

"I know who you are," Krista told him. "I know what you did." And then, all of a sudden, they were yelling at each other in Russian.

The kids watched them, open-mouthed. Eric, Michael and Wareham were very *English* and just ignored them and went on eating as if nothing was happening. Anatoly gave her a weary look and she shrugged.

After a minute or so—and it felt like a very long minute—they either got tired or ran out of invective. The general sat there red-faced and glaring. Krista primly finished her meal.

"Excellent," Eric said after a moment or so. He looked round the table and smiled brightly. "Ice cream, anyone?"

LATER THAT NIGHT, unable to sleep, Carey snapped the hook off one of the hangers in her wardrobe, took one of the pencils she'd stolen from the conference room, and went for a wander.

The two wings of the house were connected, on the first floor, by a corridor that ran the whole length of the building. Carey walked unhurriedly along it, trying doors as she went. According to the grandfather clock in the hall, it had been just after half past eleven when she went up to bed, so it must be past two in the morning by now, but as she went across the landing at the top of the stairs she heard quiet voices down below in the lounge. Maybe some of the staff.

In the east wing, she started trying doors again. All the conference rooms on this floor were unlocked, and there was nothing in them but chairs and tables. She carried on to the end of the corridor and went up the stairs to the next floor.

Here were locked doors, which was more interesting. She picked the lock of the first one and found herself looking into a storage cupboard. Shelves of cleaning products, dusters, a mop and bucket. She locked the door and moved on. The next door opened onto a storeroom. Chairs and tables were stacked around the walls and a pile of dustsheets sat on a table in the middle of the floor.

She was unlocking the next door when she stopped and frowned. She went back to the previous door, picked its lock again, and went in, switching on the light.

On one wall, above a stack of chairs, was a framed map of North America with Canada, Alaska and Mexico lopped off. The landmass it represented was the same shape as North America, but there all resemblance ended. This was not a map of the US. For a start, none of the states were marked. Much of the continent seemed to be forest, broken up by rivers and lakes. Roughly where the Rockies should have been, there was a spine of what looked like low hills, curving all the way down from what would have been the Canadian border to the Mexican border. A line of dots outlined the east coast, all of them named. She moved closer and read them. *Clopbury. Aldbury. Leeward. Hatten. Marbury.* There was no way to tell if they were megacities or one-horse towns, they were just dots on the map. On the West Coast, there was a cluster of dots around San Francisco Bay. *Newminster. Linebury*. Further down the coast, Los Angeles and San Diego were missing.

"This is what you meant about us being in Kansas, isn't it," she said without looking away from the map. "I thought you were kidding."

Standing in the doorway, Wareham sighed.

"What is this?" she said. "Something the Community never told us about?"

"In a manner of speaking," he said. "This isn't the Community."

She looked at him. He was in his stocking feet, holding his shoes in one hand, no doubt to creep soundlessly along the corridor, but she'd seen his reflection in the glass over the map when he moved into the doorway.

"Do you know how the Community came to be created?" he asked.

"There's a rumour it was a family of English magicians."

"Not magicians. Mapmakers. The Whitton-Whites." He came into the room, took a chair off a pile, sat down, and started to put his shoes on and lace them up. "One of them came to North America on the *Mayflower*. We don't know why; perhaps there was a family argument." He finished tying one shoe, started on the other. "Anyway, the place didn't agree with him. The weather was awful, the animals were strange, there were incomprehensible natives living in the forest." He sat up. "So he decided to make something a little more *convivial*."

She looked at the map again. The word *ARCADIA* was printed across the top. "One guy did all this?"

"Oh, it was quite small to start with," Wareham said. "A square mile across, if that. But it was safe, it was a little pocket of England, somewhere to take refuge when the New World got a bit too much. And it kept growing. And eventually he moved over full-time, and took some people with him, and they settled here."

"That's... wild," she said.

"Only a few dozen people know about us," he said. "In your world and in the Community. We never had the large-scale immigration that the United States had; we're relatively few in number and we'd like to keep ourselves to ourselves. For a long time, the only contact we had was with the Community, and even that was very cautious. We built this place as a sort of embassy, neutral territory where we can meet."

"Does that make Eric the ambassador?"

Wareham smiled. "He's the head of our security service. My boss."

"And Michael?"

"Head of the Community's security service. Neither of us entirely trusts the other, of course, but that's hardly unusual."

Basically like sharing a country hotel with the director of the CIA and the D-G of MI6. "What did Maksim *do* to you?"

He shook his head. "It's really better you don't know. Safer for you."

"Michael was talking about Cthulhu."

Wareham raised an eyebrow.

"Dark forces," she said. "Ancient powers best left undisturbed."

"Oh. He probably meant Crispin."

"Who's Crispin?"

"Crispin is..." he began. "A long story. Too complicated. Let's just say nobody wants him getting involved in this."

They looked at each other for quite a while. "You lied to me," she said.

"Technically, I just didn't tell you the truth."

"That sounds a lot like lying to me."

"Everything I told you about myself is true. I did come to Poland just after the flu, and I have been there ever since, and, mostly, I have worked as a journalist."

"And that stuff about being an MI6 stringer?"

"Oh yes, that's quite true. I do slip them the odd bit of intelligence now and then. They have no idea where I'm really from, of course."

"Your legend's pretty good. I didn't spot anything."

"Thank you. Yes, we did work quite hard on that. I should

point out that I'm not there on some long-term operation. I'm just there to watch and report back to my service. Just more journalism, really. And until Maksim came along it was completely uneventful."

"Are you going to report back to your service about this?" She waved a hand to indicate the room and the map.

He thought about it. "No," he said. "I don't think that's necessary. But you must promise not to tell anyone about it, not even your companions."

"You'll keep a secret if I do?"

He smiled. "Something like that, yes."

She gave that some thought. "Okay."

"Good." He stood up. "And now, it's late and I need some sleep, so if you'd like to lock up I'll see you in the morning."

She turned the light off and they went into the corridor and she used the wire hook and the pencil to lock the door. Wareham watched her. "That's really rather clever," he said. "Could you teach me to do that?"

"Sorry," she told him, walking away down the corridor. "Trade secret."

SHE COULDN'T SLEEP. She dozed, woke up, dozed again. As dawn broke, light began to outline the curtains. Outside, an ocean of birds began to sing.

She got out of bed and used the bathroom. She went to the window and pulled the curtain back and gazed out over the great vista of forest steaming gently in the growing light. She thought about those first English settlers, about the First Nations people who must have strayed accidentally across the border and found themselves in a strange new world. She thought about those little dots straggling down the east coast.

Turning from the window, she let the curtain drop back,

and as she walked back over to the bed she felt rather than heard a low, steady humming sound from outside. She went back to the window and held back the curtain and looked out over the forest again, but she couldn't make out the source of the sound. It seemed to be coming from everywhere, and now she thought about it, it seemed she had been hearing it for quite some time before consciously noticing it.

A flash of motion caught her eye, and when she looked she saw that an enormous shape was moving across the sky. It was so large that for a moment she couldn't work out what she was seeing. Its engines were the size of locomotives, and the *Hindenberg* could have fitted comfortably six or seven times inside its envelope. A line of huge gondolas hung along its belly, windows catching the first rays of the sun. Carey felt her jaw drop.

It was some distance north, and heading west, which meant that after a minute or so it passed out of sight behind the house. If she wanted to see it again she'd have to go outside, and she wasn't sure that was a good idea. It was, what, half past four? Five o'clock? Anyone with any sense was fast asleep, and the sound of the airship's engines, while quite noticeable, was not intrusive. It wasn't like an executive jet flying overhead. Maybe it wasn't supposed to be seen. And then she wondered why, if nobody wanted anyone to see it, it had flown over so close to the house. Had it been meant for her after all? A message that, while Arcadia might be lightly populated and shy, it was not primitive?

3

NOBODY MENTIONED THE airship over breakfast, from which Carey gathered she had been the only one to see it. She decided to keep it to herself, and she sat, bleary-eyed and stiff and grumpy, and worked her way through a plate of bacon, egg, sausage, hash browns and beans, which she kept washing down with coffee until she felt vaguely human again. Wareham came in looking absurdly chipper and well-rested, took one look at her, and made the sensible decision to just nod good morning and take his porridge to another table.

Carey remembered when she could go without sleep for a couple of days at a time, drink a lot, cross half a dozen borders, maybe get into a fight or two. She and Maksim had gone from one end of Europe to the other and back again, Situation after Situation after Situation, a landscape of hotels and safe houses and jumps and dustoffs. Now look at her, an old lady who could barely function without her eight hours' sleep. She felt *incapable*.

Back then, Europe had seemed strange and new and vibrant and full of *possibility*. Now it just felt weird, and somewhere in the back of her mind Carey thought the disappearance of the Line had a lot to do with that, as if it had been the only thing holding the Continent together.

The abandoned infrastructure of the Line had proved too much of a temptation for some. One night, a couple of years after Carey returned to Europe, someone had driven a truck bomb into a road tunnel under the tracks and detonated it.

The tunnel was deep in the French countryside, on a little-used local road connecting two villages kilometres apart, and a handful of locals reported hearing a distant peal of thunder which they had not really given a second thought. Certainly, none of them called the authorities.

The explosion collapsed the tunnel, in its turn bringing down a section of fencing and disabling many border countermeasures, and a small army of scrap metal merchants swarmed onto the Line's territory intent on stealing rails and cabling and any technology they could get their hands on.

When the police did finally turn up, around breakfast time the next morning, they discovered almost two hundred bodies, some of them armed, scattered around the site. None of them showed any signs of violence—some of the conspiracy boards, which sometimes (just by the law of averages) turned up a corner of the truth, talked darkly of batrachotoxin—but the remains of a drone armed with a dart gun, brought down by a lucky shot, suggested that the Line was not quite as dead as people assumed.

Some days later, while contractors appeared from who knew where to repair the damage, someone fired an anti-tank missile at a blockhouse on a level crossing near the Belgian border, killing the caretaking staff who had been patiently maintaining the crossing.

Almost a year passed, and then a wave of killings and disappearances swept through the Balkan underworld. Local authorities reasoned that it was one of those gang wars which occasionally erupt and just as suddenly subside, and as all the victims belonged to the criminal classes they were content to keep an eye on it and let it burn itself out. When it was over, two entire identifiable criminal groups had been wiped out, from the lowliest foot soldier to the loftiest kingpin. No one ever, officially at least, connected the killings with events in France, but so far, apart from vandalism and the occasional act of petty thievery, nobody had tried to rob the Line again.

There was a lot of stuff like that in Europe these days, and you didn't have to look very hard for some of it. Carey thought the place was getting old and tired, that the hopefulness of the early days after the flu, when things had seemed new and people tried to rebuild their shattered lives and all things had seemed possible because they had just survived an apocalypse, had burned itself out. Now, she thought, Europe expressed itself like those annoying leg-jerks you sometimes got just as you were falling asleep, and maybe this whole business with Maksim was part of that. Just random noise as the system ground to a halt.

She looked out of the window and saw Anatoly's father, wearing a thick sweater and a waxed jacket, walking along the terrace outside. Of course the Russians wanted Maksim; he was a loose end in their Tallinn operation that needed tidying up. Everyone knew who had caused the blackout and brought down the government, but knowing it was one thing and having a living, breathing witness giving evidence in court and appearing on chat shows was something else. He must have known what would happen if he got mixed up in an op like that, and she wondered what on earth had possessed him.

Krista wanted Maksim because she wanted him in that Tallinn courtroom. She wanted to see justice done for a crime against her country. It was also the final step in the exoneration of her father, someone literally standing up and admitting it was all false.

Carey was the only person who didn't want Maksim, and ironically it seemed that she was the only person he wanted involved. On the run from the Russians and the Estonians and, presumably, the Arcadians and the Community, he had effectively wandered out into the open in the middle of Central Europe and started jumping up and down and waving his hands over his head, which was crazy even by his standards. He might reasonably have expected to fool the police with his little extravaganza out on the Sierakowice road, but he couldn't have hoped to fool the various actors who were pursuing him.

She looked around the dining room. There was Wareham, stirring honey into his porridge. There were Michael and Eric, conspiring over a pot of tea and a plate of scones. There was Krista, cup of coffee at her elbow, going through the notes she'd made the previous day. There was the general, pacing back and forth on the terrace. All the players in one place.

Logically—and it could be hazardous to apply logic to Maksim—he hadn't been trying to fool them at all. He'd been trying to flush them out, and he'd wanted her there to witness it.

So, what am I supposed to be seeing, and why is it so important that I see it?

DINNER THAT EVENING was subdued. Anatoly's father had chosen to eat in his room, which was hardly a loss, and apparently Michael and Wareham had departed at some point during the afternoon, although Carey hadn't noticed any vehicles pulling up. Eric did his best to keep a conversation going, but nobody was really interested. Carey wanted to chip in with a question about Arcadia's security services, but she wasn't supposed to know about that so she concentrated on the meal instead; spatchcocked poussin with duchesse potatoes and green beans and a chestnut puree she wasn't very keen on.

"We'll be taking you home later," Eric told them when they'd finished the medley of sorbets which had been served as dessert. "If you could assemble in the hall at eleven that would make everything much easier for us. And please, take any clothes you've found here with you, with our blessing."

Carey, who was planning to wash any clothes she took out of here—whether she'd arrived in them or not—on an insanely hot program and then give them to the nearest charity shop in case the Arcadians had tagged them with trackers or worse, nodded along with the others. Boksi had shown signs after yesterday's treasure hunt of finally getting into being here, but now he started to look worried again as he realised he was soon going to have to explain to his parents where he'd been for the past two days. Krista leaned over and hugged him and said something which made him stare at her wide-eyed.

Later, Carey went up to her suite and went slowly through the rooms, not checking if she'd left anything behind—she hadn't brought anything with her except her phone and the clothes she stood up in—but just looking. She took some photos, just to prove to herself that the past two days hadn't been an hallucination. It was just the latest in the long, long line of temporary spaces she'd passed through since she left Texas for Madrid all those years ago. Some of them she'd stayed in for longer than others—several years, sometimes—but in the end she didn't actually live *anywhere*. She just moved around, place to place. The last time she'd thought of anything as permanent was when she was living with Pru and Byron.

She had once—admittedly for a period so brief you'd have needed an atomic clock to measure it properly—thought she'd wind up settling down with Maksim, which was so hopelessly naïve that sometimes, when she thought about it, she wanted to call an ambulance for her younger self. Even if Maksim hadn't been who he was—and, she supposed, she hadn't been who *she* was—their lives wouldn't have sustained it. He was off somewhere when she wasn't busy, she was off somewhere when he had downtime. They didn't see each other for months at a time—almost an entire year, once. They were not faithful to each other—at least, she wasn't, and she was certain the same was true for him—but when they were together there was a very strong sense, for her, of coming home, like returning to an old familiar house where you knew which stair creaked underfoot, which door needed a little extra shove to open it because it stuck, and that had been important to her. And then it had turned out she had been living in the wrong house all along.

She turned all the lights out and went to the window and opened the curtains. By pressing the side of her face to the glass, she could look in the direction Anatoly had indicated yesterday. Was there a glow on the other side of the horizon? The faintest lightening on the underside of the clouds? Maybe, maybe not, it was hard to be certain. At this distance, if it was a town, if she wasn't imagining it, it must be quite a size.

She heard the sound of engines on the other side of the house; the vehicles arriving to take them back to Europe. She closed the curtains and turned away from the window.

HOODED AGAIN AND sandwiched between Anatoly and Krista, Carey tried to build a picture of where they were going. There was the downhill drive to the gate, which someone must have opened as they approached because they didn't even slow down. Then the echo of the engine outside changed as they drove along the road into the forest. They accelerated a little for a while, then they slowed almost to a crawl and made a sharp left turn and the echo changed again and they were back among buildings. That was it. That was the border. Carey concentrated, trying to remember the turns so she could reconstruct the route, but it was hopeless. Gliwice's one-way system meant that they had to go back through the town a different way to the way they'd come. They kept stopping, and a couple of times they backed up and tried another street, and she lost track. She thought she heard gunfire very faintly in the distance, which wasn't good. *Jesus, is that still going on?*

Eventually, they stopped and the doors opened and hands helped them out of the vehicle and took off their hoods, and they were back outside the house on Zimnej Wody and Carey could smell burning in the air. She looked around her, but there was no one else about. The neighbours in the blocks back along the street would all be keeping their heads down. If military-sounding vehicles came down the street, so what? So long as they weren't coming for them.

Without a word, the soldiers got back in their vehicles and they got themselves turned round and drove back towards the centre of town and left Carey and the others standing on the pavement. Anatoly unlocked the front door and they went inside.

In the house, nothing seemed to have changed, but that didn't mean things were the same. "Sweep the place," Carey told Magda. "Top to bottom, attic and basement too." They'd checked the house for surveillance devices when they first moved in, but it had been empty for two days now and the Arcadians and the Community and anybody else who knew the factory defaults for the security system could have been industriously bugging it the whole time. To the others she said, "Watch what you say until we're sure we're secure."

Everyone sort of drifted in different directions away from the hallway. Carey went into the living room and waved up the screen to check the news. The same anchorpersons were sitting in the same studio, periodically narrating jerky phone-camera footage of burning buildings and groups of angry people. Her phone, reconnected to the network, kept vibrating in her pocket as it received backed-up messages. She put it on the coffee table and sat on the sofa and waited for the news to cycle to a roundup.

Anatoly came in holding his own phone. "What time is it?" he said.

Wondering why he couldn't see the clock on his own phone, Carey looked down at hers. "It's half past three," she said. And then she looked at the date.

She looked at him, and he gave a very expressive shrug. *Beats the hell out of me.*

Carey pointed at the screen and swiped through the news channels until she found one that had a ticker at the bottom with the time and date. And then she sat back and stared.

They'd been gone six hours.

At some time early in the morning, Gliwice's provisional government, realising that the situation was hopeless and fearing arrest, fled the city. By breakfast, they were sitting in front of the cameras in Breslau and making angry statements about the actions of the Polish government and threatening to take the whole thing to a UN Special Court, while the Polish government tried to get them extradited. Carey wondered how they'd got past the cordon around the city, wondered if she detected the hand of Stefan and his people. If it was, she might have underestimated them: going up against the Polish Army was the kind of thing that turned your average Coureur into a legend.

And at some point in the morning, Anatoly's father had slipped away. He didn't bother to say goodbye and nobody saw him go, and nobody, in truth, was sorry that he wasn't there any more, but Carey did wonder where he'd gone, and what he thought about the time difference.

Breakfast time also brought a knock on the door. A check of the door cam revealed a somewhat grimy and battered police car parked outside and a weary-looking policeman in a riot suit standing on the doorstep.

"It's okay," Krista said, "he's here for Boksi."

Whatever was going on, she and the boy had obviously discussed it already, because he was standing in the hall, face washed and hair combed. Anatoly answered the door, and the policeman said he was here to take Boksi home.

Carey went over to the boy and gave him a hug. "You are the smartest, bravest boy I ever worked with," she told him. "We're going to be leaving soon, but I'll be in touch. You stay out of trouble, you hear? In a couple of years, when you're old enough, I'm going to send a friend of mine to have a word with you. Maybe my friend Luis. Luis looks sad all the time, but he's an absolute star and he'll teach you how to be a Coureur, if you still want." Boksi looked at her and his eyes were shining and he hugged her back.

Romek had decided to go with Boksi, and she hugged him as well. "You too," she said. "Keep your nose clean; I'm going to start putting work your way as soon as I get this thing sorted out."

All of a sudden, Anatoly decided to go too. He grabbed his coat. "I'll walk back," he said. "See what's going on in town."

"Don't take any risks," she said, and then she turned and Magda and Romek were in the middle of a long and extremely heartfelt kiss. Carey wondered when that had started, and why she hadn't spotted it.

She and Krista and Magda stood on the steps and watched them all get into the police car and drive off. Magda and Romek waved to each other until the car was out of sight.

"How did you swing that?" Carey asked, watching the car go.

"Someone I know back home," said Krista. "He's not exactly a colleague, he's kind of outside the command structure, but he owes me a favour. He called someone who called someone who called someone who called the local police. The cop's going to tell Boksi's parents he was at police headquarters all night. He helped pull an old man out of a crashed car and get him to safety and they couldn't get him home because of the riot and he didn't want to worry his parents so he told them he was at his friend's. He's going to get some kind of award."

Carey looked at her and smiled. "Thank you."

Krista nodded. "You said we're leaving."

"As soon as we can strike the tents and the army open up the roads again." She glanced at Magda. "You're coming too; I'm going to need you." The girl looked sad, obviously thinking about being parted from Romek. "It won't be for long. He'll wait."

"Why do we have to go?" she said.

"We need a circuit break," Carey told her.

THE UNREST ON the streets petered out; everyone seemed tired and sort of shell-shocked and unwilling to carry on breaking things. Even the gangs appeared to have come to some fragile accord. The army pulled out after a few days, and a couple of days after that so did Carey and her crew.

They hired a car and drove to Hindenberg, Carey and Anatoly and Magda on the escape papers Boksi had made for them and Krista on some kind of nuclear-strength diplomatic passport which seemed to give her access to the entire Continent without the need for irritating formalities like visas and customs checks.

From Hindenberg, they crossed into Greater Germany and drove up towards Rostock. Krista and Anatoly shared the driving. Magda and Carey sat in the back with a bunch of mobile tech.

Curious, Carey reviewed the footage she'd downloaded to a pad at Zimnej Wody before sending kill-commands to the cameras she'd stuck around the house. The vehicles which had abducted them must have been carrying some kind of jammer, because around the time Michael and his men turned up all the cameras started to broadcast static, which cleared when they drove off. One camera glued to a balcony halfway up the polytechnic building showed a grainy view of the vehicles' tail-lights as they reached the end of the street. Then there was six hours of not very much happening at all, at the end of which the camera on the balcony picked up an image of headlights turning onto Zimnej Wody for a moment before the static came back. Incredible to spool through those six hours of footage and know that, for her, two days had passed. There were rumours that time in the Community passed at a different rate to time here, but this was wild. Arcadia must be thousands of years old. Granted, if Wareham had been telling the truth, their population had grown agonisingly slowly, and it must have taken them many hundreds of years to get to a point where they could even think of an industrial economy, but still, what must they be capable of now?

She stared out of the window at the rainy landscape of northern Germany beyond the transparent panels that screened nearby farms and houses from the noise of the autobahn. Again, assuming Wareham had been telling the truth and he really had been here for thirty-odd years, everyone he'd known when he'd set out on his mission was long dead. It was a lonely life being an agent-in-place, but Wareham must have been more cut off than any intelligence officer in human history, and she felt a pang of sympathy.

On a hunch, she checked the footage from the camera Anatoly had stuck to the wall in the Old Town, opposite the burned-out shell of the Diana Academy. Sure enough, the feed filled with static around the time they had been abducted, which suggested the vehicles had driven by. She spooled forward three hours, waiting for the static to reappear, but instead she found herself watching the three vehicles seemingly driving out of a solid wall.

She watched the footage over and over again. It was just a few seconds, before whoever was responsible for the jammer belatedly remembered to turn it on and static filled the screen, but it was enough. The vehicles behaved as if they were just turning from one street into another, but an optical illusion made it seem that the street they were coming from wasn't there. That was the border crossing, and it was right next door to the Diana Academy. The border must run right through the building.

Carey thought about that a lot, as they reached Rostock and took the ferry to Gedser. The Arcadians were smart, technologically advanced to an unknown degree, and they planned in terms of centuries. Not one single thing about that was remotely reassuring.

Carey had done some advance research, and in Roskilde she'd found them an hotel that had a dining room, room service, full breakfast and a Michelin star. It was ten minutes' walk from the station, and the day after they arrived she took the short train journey to the campus of the university.

The weather here was much better than it had been on the drive to Rostock. The sky was blue and the sun was warm, and the campus was full of students. She walked unhurriedly from the station, down the hill and across the bridge over the main road. A little further down the hill, there were a couple of lakes set in parkland with a cluster of buildings over to one side.

Some picnic tables had been installed outside one of the buildings, and she seated herself at one of these and sat watching a kayaker disturbing the ducks on the lake. A few dozen students were sitting in little group on blankets on the hill overlooking the lake, equipped with beer coolers and food. A few yards away to her right, under a stand of trees, another small groups of students appeared to be rehearsing some kind of play while one of their number filmed them. Carey smiled and closed her eyes and tipped her face to the sun.

In time, someone came and sat beside her. About ten minutes passed. It was a nice day to just sit and not think about things for a while before trying to go on.

She said, "Thank you for coming."

"I invited you, remember?" Peter said. She opened her eyes and looked at him. His hair and beard were streaked with grey now, but he still had gentle, calm, amused eyes. He was wearing jeans and a NATO surplus combat jacket. "How are you?"

"I need a favour."

"Sure," he said cheerfully. "Always happy to help."

"You haven't heard what it is yet."

He looked at her for a few moments without speaking. "Are you okay?"

"I need a place to stay for a little while," she said. "Me and three other people. Somewhere we won't be bothered."

He shrugged. "Come and stay at the house. Nobody will bother you there."

"One of us is a cop."

He grinned. "You've started keeping bad company."

"It was inevitable," she agreed, "sooner or later."

Peter thought about it. "Well, I don't mind if he doesn't. What's his jurisdiction?"

"*She's* Estonian, but she seems to have some weird sort of ticket to ride, I can't quite figure it out. Something governmental. I don't know what arrest powers she has."

He looked at the lake. "Estonia," he said in a thoughtful voice. "Well, I'm sure everything will be fine, so long as she doesn't get *adventurous*. Is this something to do with Maksim?"

"Maksim?"

"You were asking about him last time we spoke."

"I can't tell you, Peter. I'm sorry, it's really better for you if I don't. One day maybe, when this is all over—*if* it's ever over—but not right now."

He thought some more. "Listen," he said, "your friend's only making himself look conspicuous. Why don't you call him over?"

She looked over at where Anatoly was sitting at a picnic

table a few yards away trying to wrestle a printed newspaper against the breeze, and she shook her head. Sometimes he had some of the best moves she'd ever seen—she'd watched him escape from a house in London in the middle of a police raid—and sometimes he was just a complete putz. She waved to get his attention, and beckoned him over.

While he was still out of earshot, she said, "I'm going to need a line of credit, too."

Peter frowned at her, but he nodded. "That also is doable. Hello." This last to Anatoly, who sat down on the end of the bench.

"Peter, Anatoly," Carey said. "Anatoly, Peter. The two men shook hands and she said, "Peter's an old friend, from my roaring days."

"You had roaring days?" Anatoly said, deadpan. "I'm sorry I missed *those*."

"Anatoly's a Russian hood," she told Peter, and smiled at the pained look which crossed Anatoly's face. "But he saw the light."

"I don't recall having a lot of choice," he said.

Peter was giving Anatoly a look of professional interest which she recognised. She said, to Anatoly, "Peter's going to put us up for a while."

"Okay," said Anatoly. He said, "Thank you," to Peter.

Peter inclined his head slightly. He said, "If this thing is as bad as it sounds, you should have some personnel too."

Peter was the last, desperate port in a storm, but there were some things she couldn't accept from him. "I think I have all the personnel I need," she told him. "Besides, I'm going to be travelling. It could get complicated."

He watched her face. "You look tired."

"Yeah, I am," she said.

He stood up and said, "I'd appreciate hearing what this is about, when you're able to talk about it."

Information might be worthless; it might be the most

precious thing in the world. The only thing you could be certain of was that you never had enough of it. "I'll let you know what I understand, although at the moment I can't promise that'll be much."

"Doesn't matter." He reached down and squeezed her hand. "It's good to see you. I'll send someone to pick you up from the hotel later. Seven o'clock?"

"That would be great, yes."

"Okay. See you soon." And he turned and walked away along the shore of the lake.

"Are you going to explain it all to *me* when you're able to talk about it?" Anatoly asked.

"It'll do you good to work it out for yourself," she said, watching the canoeist paddle his kayak to the edge of the lake and clamber onto the bank. Up on the hill, all the picnickers were getting up and folding their blankets and packing their coolers. The students under the trees were putting away their recording gear and walking away. In a couple of minutes everyone was gone, apart from a lone cyclist on the other side of the lake and a middle-aged man walking a mean-looking schnauzer along the path.

On the way back to the station, Krista and Magda fell into step beside them. While Peter and his people had been watching Anatoly ostentatiously making himself obvious, they had been sitting in a little pizza restaurant watching the meet, theoretically unobserved.

"You're not serious," Krista said.

"That's right, honey," Carey told her. "We drove all this way just for the lulz."

"There's no way I can get involved with him," Krista told her. "That's just crazy."

"Oh, stop being such a fucking *cop* for a while," Carey said. "He's helping us."

"Who is he?" asked Magda. She'd spent the morning in Roskilde's shops and she'd rebuilt her goth look; she was wearing a long black velvet dress with a narrow black ribbon around her throat and she was in full makeup. In some places she'd have looked like a student, except here the student look seemed to run to work boots and jeans and chunky sweaters.

"Peter Schiller," Krista told her. "Nobody's ever seen him in the flesh. *I* only know him from old photos. And she just phones him and he turns up."

"That was Peter Schiller?" said Anatoly, and Carey grimaced. "We're allying ourselves with the Mafiye now?"

"Don't get all sanctimonious," Krista told him crisply. "The Mafia runs your country."

"It's been some time since anyone knew for certain *who* runs my country."

"He looked sort of cute," Magda said.

"Peter's going to help us," Carey said again, stomping along as if trying to leave them and their questions behind. "And no, you can't ask why."

TWELVE

1

THE DRIVER WHO came to pick them up was a cheerful but not particularly talkative young woman in a grey suit who introduced herself as Astrid and then didn't say another word as she drove them towards the coast in a discreetly expensive electric Audi.

The Schiller estate stretched for almost a mile along the curve of a little bay north of Roskilde, behind high walls topped at intervals by the protective weather domes of small railguns. As the car approached the main gate Krista felt herself automatically hunching her shoulders up around her ears to foil the police surveillance she knew must be watching the place. *19:25—car arrives with four passengers, one positively identified as Colonel Krista Lindmaa, Tallinn police. WTAF?* She imagined her father looking on disapprovingly. He'd had contact, now and again, with some of Tallinn's gang bosses—there were occasions when diplomacy was preferable to, and more effective than, brute-force policing—but he had never lost sight of them as adversaries and he had never taken any help from them. What she was doing now was quite different.

Of course, her father had never faced a situation like this, so there was that. The police department had behaved perfectly properly over the investigation of her father—she was the one who had behaved unprofessionally—but she thought it was faintly embarrassed about the way it had treated her and was inclined to cut her more slack than it might otherwise have done. Still, becoming the house guest of a major organised crime figure was going to take quite some explaining.

Beyond the gate, the drive wound through parkland and low formal gardens towards where the house perched overlooking the bay. The house itself was a big irregular glass and stone prism that looked as if it had fallen from a colossal tiara and half-buried itself in the grass. Carey thought it looked like the headquarters of a tech conglomerate or the lair of a megalomaniac supervillain, and she supposed that both of these, at one time, had been true.

Peter was waiting to greet them. He didn't have to do that, the house was easily big enough for him never to see them at all, but that wasn't Peter's style, and Carey suspected he wanted to get a look at the cop she was bringing with her anyway. He'd made an effort to smarten himself up, a grey casual suit with an open necked white shirt, and he hugged Carey and shook hands amiably—Peter was going to be amiable no matter what clothes you put him in—with everyone else. Carey thought he and Krista held their handshake and looked into each other's eyes for just a fraction too long, but that might have been her imagination.

Peter's housekeeper was a frighteningly efficient Englishwoman named Mrs Potter. As if she was aggressively trying to depart from the archetype of an English housekeeper, she was toned and tanned and had an expensive hairdo and wore a top-of-the-range bespoke business suit—no off-the-peg Jesse Dunne for her. She seemed not to have changed at all in the decade or so since Carey had last stayed at the estate. She showed them to their rooms, issued key-cards, told them there was a buffet in the dining room, and managed to convey by body language that their presence was disrupting the smooth running of her house. Then she left, presumably to harass the staff for a while.

Carey wound up back in her old room. It was large and neat and Scandi-modern, pale wood and rough-woven rugs on the floor and a big window looking out over the bay. The window glass was more than an inch thick and bronzed on the outside, to protect from any snipers who took it into their minds to take a boat out and use the back of the house for target practice. For attackers with greater ambitions, there were more railguns in pods on the roof, and an anti-missile system buried under the lawn sloping down to the beach which would pop up and bring down approaching projectiles with a stream of depleted uranium splinters. It was apparently capable of splashing anything up to and including a cruise missile. It had never, to Carey's knowledge, been deployed in anger, but local environmental groups, alarmed at the prospect of toxic metal raining down into the bay's ecosystem, had been hitting the estate with lawsuits at a rate of roughly one a year ever since the system had been installed. This was the way the super-rich—and not just the criminally super-rich—lived these days, walled off behind concentric lines of defence in case anyone came to take away what was theirs or simply decided to kill them because they had more than anybody else. It was not, Carey considered, not for the first time, much of a life.

There was a quiet knock at the door, and when she opened it Peter was standing there. "You okay?" he asked.

She walked back into the room. "I was thinking about those guys," she said. "The ones who keep suing you about the missile defence."

Following her to the window, Peter chuckled. "They drove the old man mad," he said. "He wanted to snatch a couple of them and send them back to their families in pieces."

"Well, I'm glad one of us can giggle about that, at least."

He shrugged. "That was the old man. These days their lawyers and our lawyers meet every now and then and have a nice lunch and go through the whole thing all over again and that satisfies everybody's honour for the next year or so."

"Sounds like they need better lawyers."

"They've got the best lawyers money can buy; I should know, I'm paying for them."

She looked at him and pursed her lips.

"Oh, they don't know that," he said, "and neither do the lawyers. I just set up an anonymous charitable trust, and that makes regular donations to environmental causes, including their legal fund." He looked out of the window. "At least they've got professional representation now. You should have seen some of the lawyers they used to have."

"How's Marthe?"

"She's fine. She's in New York right now; Fashion Week. So you won't bump into her." Peter had always been faintly amused by what he saw as Carey's almost superstitious dread of meeting his former stepmother; she'd found it hard to explain to him how weird it would feel to sit across a dining table from someone you'd spent a couple of days impersonating.

She said, "Do you use outside contractors much?"

He shook his head. "It's safer to keep everything in-house. But I've got some contacts. I thought you didn't want any more personnel."

"I don't, but there are some people I might need tracking down."

"If I can help, I will."

This was the second time she'd crashed into his life asking for help, and the second time he'd given it without question. Carey knew he was grateful to her and Maksim for helping Marthe escape from his father, but it had always seemed to her that this went beyond gratitude, and she couldn't work out why. Maybe it was as simple as the need for a friendship—he'd never shown any romantic interest in her. They'd never talked about it, and now she thought they never would; that moment had passed. This was just the way they were now; he would drop everything to help her, and she would do the same for him.

"Anyway," he said, "I'm feeling peckish. Did Mrs Potter tell you about the buffet?"

"That woman doesn't like me."

"Mrs Potter likes things to be tidy," he told her. "You're… not."

"I'm *differently* tidy," she said, and he laughed.

THE HOUSE WENT quite a long way below ground. There were offices and comms centres and panic rooms and an armoury and a little nuclear generator which would have given the environmentalists a fit of the vapours. Right at the bottom there was a room as big as an Olympic-size swimming pool. Suspended from wires in the centre of this was a big white box, and suspended inside *that* was another, smaller box containing an oval mahogany conference table and a dozen comfy chairs. In Schiller family nomenclature, this was called 'the Bug', for reasons nobody could explain.

The morning after their arrival at the estate, Carey sat everyone down in the Bug, closed the doors, and waited for the space between the two suspended rooms to be pumped empty of air. By the door, a row of little green lights indicated that the electronic countermeasures were operating. The room's life support package clicked on. Peter said his father had liked having meetings in the Bug because there was only an hour's life support and if the meetings ran on longer than that everyone would suffocate. Carey didn't like it; the room made her feel uncomfortable, but when it was sealed and everything was switched on it was one of the most secure spaces in Europe.

"I guess you figured out we weren't in the Community," she said, sitting down.

Anatoly nodded. "The time difference."

"Nobody knows for sure what the physics of the Community are," Magda said. "If you accept the existence of a pocket universe in the first place, why not zones where time runs at different rates?"

"It doesn't matter," Carey said, "because Wareham told me it wasn't the Community. It's a version of the US, and they call it *Arcadia*."

"We were in America?" Anatoly said. "I thought border crossings had to be in roughly the same place in both universes."

"I don't understand that and maybe one day we can find a mathematician who'll be happy to explain it to us, but right now it's not important," Carey said. "Except that the border crossing is right next to the Diana Academy."

"Oh," said Anatoly, who had done some digging into the academy's background, without a lot of success. "They had a foothold."

"A building people could go in and out of all day and not attract attention, staffed by a bunch of tutors and admin people who are now nowhere to be found," said Carey. "And someone blew it up."

"I wonder what they're up to," he said.

"Yeah, you and me both. The house over there is some sort of meeting place, somewhere the Community and Arcadia can get together and thrash stuff out. Eric's the boss of Arcadia's security services, and Michael runs the Community's."

"So Maksim somehow managed to upset the Community *and* this Arcadia?" Anatoly said with an edge of wonder in his voice.

"They wouldn't tell us what it was," Krista said. "They just wanted to see him out of circulation."

"They want us to lead them to him so they can kill him," said Carey.

"They said that?" said Anatoly.

"Not in so many words," Krista said. "But I agree with Carey, the subtext was there. They must have realised we'd spot it."

"I don't know," Carey said. "I got the impression they didn't think we were any too bright. Also we're women. They were patronising us the whole time. I think they thought they'd pulled the wool over our eyes."

"That's what you meant about a circuit break," Magda said. "We had to drop out of sight somewhere you knew they wouldn't have any influence."

Carey nodded. "We're safer here than anywhere else in Europe."

"You're sure about that?" Krista said. "You trust Peter Schiller that much?"

"Yes," Carey told her evenly. "I do."

Krista shook her head.

"So," said Anatoly, "what's the plan?"

"We find Maksim and Krista takes him back to stand trial," Carey told him.

"That's not a plan," he said. "That's an *objective*. How do we find him? If there's any indication of where he is, it'll be in Gliwice."

Carey took from her pocket the little Wadden Islands postcard she'd found in Maksim's flat. "Not necessarily," she said.

* * *

2

"So," said Krista, "this will be in the way of being a *hunch*, then."

"Oh, this is how we do everything," said Anatoly from the back seat.

Carey ignored him and concentrated on the stretch of causeway between Juist and Borkum. It was a bright, cloudless day and the sea on either side of the high dyke on which the causeway ran was calm and blue-grey. To the left, on the sheltered surface of the Wadden Sea, hundreds of sailboats flocked across the water. A sparse line of traffic stretched ahead of them into the distance, heading in the direction of Texel. Every now and again, they passed a pumping station or a set of floodgates, or crossed a bascule bridge, big brutalist structures streaked by years of North Sea weather.

For their departure from Roskilde, Peter had laid on something of a spectacular, throwing a big dinner party for friends and business associates.

"We do it a couple of times a year," he told Carey, "so it's nothing out of the ordinary."

Police interest in the estate had been more or less constant when Henning Schiller was alive, routine surveillance usually involving a van parked nearby with a view of the gates, and another parked a little way off with a view of the bay, to keep an eye on comings and goings by land and water. It had spiked when Peter took over, lines of cars parked on the road and drones flying overhead and police boats stooging about offshore and, for all Peter knew, satellite surveillance too, although that was fantastically expensive and the kind of thing only governments could organise. Peter had endured it, and eventually it had dropped off again, until now there were just the two vans again. It was a game. Peter knew they were there, and they knew he knew. Now and again, he sent meals out to the officers who spent long boring hours watching the house. Carey wasn't so worried about the police—at least she knew they were there, and they were more interested in Peter's business than hers. It was other, less obvious surveillance, by unknown actors, that bothered her. She had to presume that they'd been traced to Roskilde—it wouldn't be difficult, their hire car had a tracker and anyway it had been pointless trying to sneak out of Gliwice—and from there to the estate. The slightly tricky bit was leaving again without anyone realising.

In the end, though, it all went smoothly. Thirty guests turned up for the party, in a variety of vehicles, from black SUVs with smoked or mirrored windows to little electric sports cars. They arrived, singly or in twos and threes, and waited at the gates to be admitted, helpfully allowing the police and anyone else who might be watching to photograph their licence plates and, if possible, their drivers and passengers. The underground garage to one side of the estate filled up.

Apparently, the dinner was a great success—Carey and the others ate in their rooms, like naughty children—and at ten o'clock on the dot the guests started to leave. Carey and her crew walked through the tunnel from the house to the garage, climbed into one of the mirror-windowed SUVs, and were driven out of the estate with the other departing cars. The police could have set up a road block and stopped and searched the cars as they left, but that would have caused the equivalent of a diplomatic incident; Peter could make an awful lot of trouble in Denmark, if the mood took him. As it was, they didn't have the resources to follow all the cars, and if Arcadia and the Community and the Russians were here in sufficient numbers to tail them all Carey thought she might as well give up.

The car drove them out into the countryside, where they transferred to another SUV, and that took them across the causeway to Nyborg, past the blinking navigation lights of a forest of wind turbines. In Nyborg, there was another underground garage and another car waiting, this one a nondescript old electric Accord, and Carey drove them to Esbjerg and the bridge over to Fanø and the Wadden Islands Federation. Once they were through passport and customs checks in Nordby, it was a matter of ferry-hopping from island to island until they got to Wangerooge and the far end of the causeway. It was hardly the worst dustoff Carey had ever had.

They reached Texel late in the afternoon, and Carey was pleasantly surprised to discover that, when it wasn't being lashed by horizontal gales of hail and sleet, the island was rather lovely, a low-lying landscape of grassy dunes and fields and little villages and townships crisscrossed by cycleways. It was market day in Den Burg, and the little square was full of stalls. Carey parked behind the hotel and they checked in separately, Peter having made individual reservations for each of them via a different—and quite legitimate—shell company so the hotel's register wouldn't show a group of four turning up. Considering what they had to work with, and what they had to do, it was about as secure as they could make it.

The hotel seemed not to have changed at all. Even the décor and the furniture were the way Carey remembered, and that felt a bit spooky. At least she wasn't in her old room.

They had dinner that evening at a vegetarian restaurant a couple of minutes' walk from the hotel, just the other side of the square, and afterward took a stroll along the town's little pedestrianised shopping street.

"One of these," Carey said casually as they passed a row of half a dozen houses sandwiched between the shops.

Magda, who was still mildly annoyed at having to dress down—Carey having decided a goth wandering around a small place like this would just stand out too much—

glanced at them, memorising the numbers. They had narrow frontages but seemed to go quite a long way back, and their brightly painted front doors opened directly onto the street. It had been a long time ago and the angle had been poor; Carey couldn't remember which door she'd thought she'd seen Yegor emerging from. They'd have to check all the houses. "All right," she said.

"This does seem a bit of a long shot," Krista said as they walked on. "If you don't mind me saying."

"Nothing is accidental," Carey said. Maksim had left that card as a bookmark in *Moby-Dick* because he knew it would nudge her memory, and she thought, now, that she had been *meant* to see Yegor—if it had been him—stepping out of one of the houses. Why had he done that? So she'd know he had a safe house on Texel, just in case?

"This is nice," Magda said, looking about her. "I think I'll live here."

"What about Romek?" Carey asked.

"Romek will live here too," the girl answered, and Carey wouldn't have bet against her pulling that off.

They walked unhurriedly for about twenty minutes, then turned back towards the hotel along a street which ran along the rear of the buildings. When they reached the houses, Anatoly gave them a casual once-over as they passed. Their backyards were all hidden behind tall wooden fences, some of them with little trees poking their heads over the top, but Anatoly seemed satisfied by what he saw.

Back at the hotel, Krista went for a shower and Magda went up to her room to set up the cloth laptop—which had never left her sight, even in Arcadia—and get to work on the houses they'd looked at. Carey and Anatoly sat in the bar, Anatoly with a glass of Amstel and Carey with a coffee, and watched the other guests. The hotel was pretty much full, and the bar was busy, but the clientele was different from the last time Carey had been here, older people, retirees come for a few days' cycling holiday, no young Euro-folk among them.

"My father will have worked out where we were," Anatoly said. "Whatever else he is, he isn't stupid. He'll know there's another pocket universe out there."

"They wanted us to know," said Carey. "They could have taken us into the Community. They could have taken us somewhere else in Gliwice and chained us to a radiator and slapped us about until we told them what they wanted to know. But they wanted us to work it out. Michael said something's happening."

"Like what?"

"I don't know. Dark forces, things better left undisturbed. I thought he was just babbling." She sipped her coffee. "Do you think your father will do something stupid?"

He thought about it. "I don't know," he said finally. "It's hard to know where the boundaries of *stupid* are, any more. What were you thinking?"

"Go running to his bosses. Blab everything."

Anatoly shrugged. "Difficult to say. He's got a lot of autonomy. He'll be working out how best to turn it to his own advantage."

She nodded sourly. "Remember the good old days when all we were doing was trying to find out how Maksim died?"

"A golden age," he agreed, lifting his glass in a toast.

"I've been thinking about retiring, once all this is over," she said.

He raised an eyebrow. "Really?"

"I really am too old for this shit now, Tolya."

Anatoly thought about it. "What would you do?"

She glanced at him. "You know, I was kind of hoping you'd say something like 'You're not old', something like that," and they smiled at each other. "Ah, hell, I don't know. Maybe I could retire to Montana and farm dental floss."

He raised both eyebrows.

"You never listened to Zappa?" she said.

He shook his head.

"Really?"

"Really."

"Kids." Her coffee had come with a little almond biscuit. She unwrapped it and dunked it in her cup. "I've been doing this almost as long as you've been alive," she said. "There's got to be some point where you say *stop*." She bit the sodden biscuit in half.

"You may not get a choice."

"How do you mean?"

He drank some beer. "I've been thinking this might be one of those situations that are never over. You might not be able to pick up the ball and just walk away."

That had crossed her mind. "What would you do?"

"Me? I wouldn't have got involved in the first place."

"Says the man who got involved in the first place."

"You asked me to come and lend a hand."

"You want out?"

He shook his head.

"Because you can go any time you want."

"You need someone around to keep you out of trouble," he told her.

"Well, you've done a piss-poor job of *that* so far."

They sat there in silence for a little while. Anatoly said, "Are you really going to give him to Colonel Lindmaa?" For some reason, he couldn't bring himself to refer to her by her first name.

"I don't see what I can do to stop her, apart from maybe darting her and taping her to a chair. She's been chasing Maksim for four years; she's not going to let me get in her way." She looked at him. "You think we shouldn't let her have him?"

"I can think of circumstances where it might be useful to have him as a bargaining chip."

"Yeah, well, I can think of circumstances where he gets us all killed; you, me, the kids, everybody." She shook her head. "Krista's the only person in this whole mess who had the manners to come straight out and tell me what she wanted, so she wins Maksim." She popped the rest of the biscuit in her mouth. "And she's welcome to him."

Of the six houses, three were owner-occupied. One was jointly owned by two families from Amersvoort. "One of the owners died two months ago and their estate's still in probate," Magda said, "so nobody can use the house for the moment." Which left number thirty and number thirty-four. "Number thirty's been empty for a year now. The owner's suffering from dementia and her son put her in a nursing home on the mainland. Number thirty-four was bought twenty years ago through a law firm in Amsterdam; their name's on all the paperwork. It's been used as a business let, corporate teambuilding weekends, that sort of thing. The last time it was occupied was ten weeks ago."

Maksim and his crew, getting together for one last briefing before they split up and headed for Gliwice. "Good work," Carey said. "And it's empty now?"

"Gas and electricity records don't show any usage. If anyone's there, they're not cooking or using the lights."

"Okay. Security system?"

"All the homes and businesses on that street subscribe to the same security company. They have emergency codes for all the systems, in case of fire or something; I pulled the one for number thirty-four. I spent last night recording six hours of footage from the street cameras, front and back. I'll loop that back into the system tonight and the security people won't see you."

Carey squeezed her shoulder. "Genuinely excellent work," she said. She looked at Krista and Anatoly, who were standing beside her looking at the display Magda had plugged the cloth laptop into. "Anything else?"

"We can't all go," Krista said.

"Not unless we really want to attract attention, no. I would say it's best if I do it on my own, but I suppose you want to go too."

"That's right."

"You do realise this counts as breaking and entering?"

"I just spent nearly a week as the houseguest of one of Europe's more notable mobsters," Krista told her. "I hardly think a little recreational burglary's going to trouble my superiors overmuch."

"Fair point."

"Also, if there is any contact with the local law I might be able to talk us out of it."

Carey glanced at Anatoly, who was looking unconvinced, but he shrugged. "Okay, Colonel," she said. "Welcome to your new life of crime."

Krista snorted.

DEN BURG TURNED in early. There were some bars in the town that stayed open until midnight, but by then only a few people were out and about, and by one in the morning the streets were deserted. Carey and Krista left the hotel at half one and strolled casually down the side of the market square in the direction of the town's little bus terminus, then turned off and walked along the back of the shopping street, counting houses as they went. At the back of number thirty-four, they paused. The gate in the back fence had a mechanical lock, but it was straightforward to pick, and they slipped into the backyard and went to the back door of the house. Carey touched her phone to the door, heard the lock click open, and they went inside.

They were in a little utility room; a washer and drier side

by side, a rack with a couple of waterproof jackets hanging from it. Beyond, in the light from a streetlamp at the back of the house, they could see the marble and metal surfaces of a kitchen. Beyond that was a short hallway with a dining room off to one side, and then a living room at the front of the house, with stairs up to the first floor over to one side.

The house smelled musty and cold and unused, and there wasn't very much in it. The living room furniture consisted of a threadbare sofa that smelled of mould, and a pair of lumpy armchairs, and a bookcase with a dozen or so paperbacks on its shelves. No entertainment set, not even prints on the walls.

They went cautiously through the house, not searching yet, just getting a feel for the layout. In the three bedrooms, the beds had been stripped. The shower room was bare, and there wasn't even a roll of toilet paper in the lavatory.

"This is a bust," Krista said, her voice barely a whisper. "There's nothing here."

"We'll see," Carey murmured.

Torchlight wasn't the ideal way to search a house, but they did their best, room by room, looking in cupboards and wardrobes and chests of drawers, lifting rugs, checking for loose floorboards, checking the walls to see if some hiding place had been freshly painted over. Apart from pots and pans and crockery, the kitchen was completely empty. The cooker was spotless. Carey took out the insert of the cutlery drawer and looked inside.

"It'll be getting light soon," Krista said around twenty past four. "We should go."

Carey looked around the living room. Had the postcard just been a coincidence? Was she looking for patterns where there were none? Was the whole thing just one of Maksim's little jokes, sending her running pointlessly around Europe while he was somewhere else? Were they actually in the wrong house? She looked at the bookcase, shone her torch on the few books on its shelves. "You checked these?" she said.

"Yes," Krista said patiently. "No notes, no inserts, no bookmarks, no underlinings. Not even a dog-ear."

Where did that leave them? Secret writing? Microdots? She tipped her head to one side. One of the books was a battered old Dutch edition of *Moby-Dick*. She took it down, and, holding her torch between her teeth, she rifled through its pages. Nothing fell out. It didn't fall open naturally at a certain place. Granted, it was one of Maksim's favourite books, but why was he wandering around with editions in different languages? She rifled it again, and this time something caught her eye. She paged back slowly, then stopped and shone the torch on the page. There was a tiny little pencil mark under the page number.

Flicking through more slowly, she found more numbers marked. She closed the book and put it in her pocket. "Let's get out of here," she said. She went over to the window and lifted the curtain to check the street, and found herself looking at the back of Robert Wareham's head. He was standing outside, not three feet away, looking at the screen of a phone.

Carey let the curtain fall gently and backed away from the window. She turned Krista round and steered her into the utility room. "Did you tell anyone where we were?"

"Only my superior," Krista said, "Why?"

"Wareham's outside."

"No," Krista said. "No, that's impossible."

"Anatoly wouldn't tell anyone," Carey said, taking out her phone. "And Magda's too into all this not to do as she's told. Your boss sold us out." She speed-dialled Anatoly's number and when he answered she said, "We're blown. Get out now. I'll see you at the dustoff. If we're not there, go without us." She hung up and gave Krista a hard stare.

"Tamm wouldn't," Krista said. "I've known him for years."

Carey stared at her for a few more seconds, then she opened the back door and led her out into the garden. They walked to the gate and stood listening for a while, opened it cautiously and looked out. There was no one to be seen. They stepped out and walked away from the house. The eastern sky was just beginning to lighten.

WAREHAM HAD BEEN a coincidence. Even if the Arcadians knew that Carey was looking for something in a house in Den Burg, they couldn't know which house. Krista had only told her superior where she was, not what she was doing there. Wareham had just happened to be standing outside when she lifted the curtain and looked out. Maybe he'd only just arrived. Maybe he was taking advantage of the early hours to scope the place out. Maybe he was alone. Probably he wasn't.

It was almost seven in the morning when Carey and Krista arrived, somewhat footsore, at Oost, on the eastern side of the island. Apart from the occasional car and, once, a bus, they hadn't seen another person since leaving Den Burg, but that didn't mean they weren't being watched by a drone, high up in the overcast sky, or some piece of unknown technology the Arcadians had brought over the border. There wasn't anything Carey could do about that.

They walked along the dyke overlooking the Wadden Sea until they came to a little dock and a row of boathouses. Tied up to the dock was a traditional Frisian lemsteraak, and sitting on board were Anatoly and Magda and a tall, lanky man wearing a smock and jeans.

"Hello, Wim," Carey said as they approached. "Permission to come aboard?"

"Please do," said Wim, grinning. He had a head of thick, untidy grey hair and his face was tanned and seamed.

Carey and Krista climbed onto the boat. "How did you get here so quickly?" Carey asked Anatoly.

"Stole a couple of bicycles," he said. "Dumped them in a drainage channel a couple of kilometres away."

"I've been giving this young man a piece of my mind about vandalism and ecological awareness," Wim told her.

"And quite right, too," Carey told him, although she should have thought of bicycles herself. She felt very tired. "I should do that more often. Could we go now, please?"

"Sure. Give me a minute." He went off to cast off the ropes securing the boat to the dock.

"I hope this was worth it," Anatoly said as Carey sat next to him on an equipment locker.

She felt the book in her pocket and looked across at Krista, who was watching the land as if she expected Wareham and a posse of Arcadians to come screeching up the coast road in armoured vehicles. "We got *something*, anyway, I think," she said. "Not sure what, yet."

Wim came back to the cockpit and fiddled about with the engine control panel, and a moment later the engine coughed into life and he backed the boat away from the dock, then he turned it east in a wide half-circle and as they put-putted across the Wadden Sea in the direction of the Frisland coast the sun came out from behind the clouds.

3

There was a boat moored a few hundred metres offshore of the estate. Or possibly, Carey had thought, seeing it from a distance on walks in the gardens, a ship. It looked as if it might have started life in someone's navy, a minesweeper or something. Now all things military had been stripped away. It had been given a helipad on the rear deck, a winch from which hung the full-size cabin cruiser it used as a water taxi, and a blinding-white paint job.

It didn't belong to Peter. It belonged to his friend Latzis, who everyone called Loppi. Loppi was so tanned that it was impossible to be certain of his age. He had a magnificent head of snow-white hair and a huge white moustache that was stained yellow by the enormous cigars he smoked. He habitually wore white cotton trousers, deck shoes without socks, and a white linen shirt open to the waist so one could see his plenitude of white chest hair and the tiny gold cross hanging on a chain there. *I'm a bit of a rogue,* it said, *but I'm still devout*. Sometimes he wore a captain's hat, complete with gold braid, but he was self-aware enough to know it made him look ridiculous so he wore it to amuse people by making fun of himself. Carey thought he wouldn't be quite so relaxed about anybody else making fun of him.

One evening, Carey asked Loppi what he did, and it turned out that Loppi just went to places. Gstaad, Paris, Madrid, Gibraltar, Miami, London. He was like a swift; he spent his entire life in motion.

"He's not a crook," Staci said with the tone of someone who was still a little surprised by the fact. "He *knows* crooks, for sure, but most of them are kind and rather sad, really. It's the politicians you have to watch out for."

Staci was Loppi's girlfriend, a tall, slim brunette woman about half his age who wore plain white kaftans and no underwear. They were staying at the house when Carey and the others returned from the long, miserable and dull dustoff from Texel. Peter said they were old friends but didn't elaborate. What the police made of the arrival of a minesweeper in the bay was anyone's guess.

Krista had wanted to carry on to Tallinn and tear her superior a new asshole, and it had not been easy to talk her down. Carey had to take her to one side and remind her that they were no longer operating to cop rules, that this was something bigger and much more complicated, and sometimes it was better to leave things in place, even things which were deeply hurtful and offensive. Krista's boss would be a useful conduit for disinformation; at the very least they could present to the Arcadians and the

Community the impression that they didn't know what they were doing.

Not that *that* was much of a stretch. Magda's opinion was that they were dealing with some kind of book code, with the marked pages providing a key. She scanned the edition of *Moby-Dick* and fed it into the cloth laptop and let it run. "This is actually what it's *for*," she told them. A week after returning to the estate, it had still not come up with anything. "Of course, the code could refer to *another* book," said Magda.

"Excellent," Carey deadpanned, "I'll just pop back and get the rest for you."

Magda looked at her uncertainly.

Krista, still angry about what had happened on Texel, *did* want to go back, with a mob of Estonian forensic specialists, and take the house to pieces, and the hell with what information got passed back to the Arcadians. Anatoly thought they were dealing with microdots, and had put out discreet feelers to try and find an expert they could bring in. At odd moments, Carey found herself holding the book open under a hot lightbulb, just in case there was secret writing somewhere on the pages. They were floundering. It was a fiasco. She thought of Maksim leaving a trail of clues for her to follow, and her being too stupid to follow them, and him laughing.

"He wants you to find him," Peter said one evening over dinner. "Although I can't work out why. He wouldn't have made it impossible for you to figure it out."

"Maybe he just underestimated how stupid I am," she said moodily.

"Perhaps the book itself is the clue," he mused. "You said there was a copy in Poland, yes? That must be significant."

"You think maybe he's gone to New England and signed aboard a whaler?" They both grinned. "He's trolling me, Peter. He knows how much I hate that book."

"It's hardly a situation for levity," he pointed out.

"You know what he's like. There's nothing so bad that you can't get a laugh out of it somehow."

"Yes," he said. "Yes, that was always one of the most irritating things about him."

"This is just one of those times. He's enjoying making me run around."

Peter shook his head. "It's very shabby. You don't deserve to be treated like this."

"Nobody ever *deserves* Maksim," she said. "You just sort of hang on and hope things will get better one day."

"Have you discussed the situation with Central?"

She shook her head. Ever since leaving Arcadia, she'd been getting messages from Kaunas. She hadn't replied to any of them and she'd long ago stopped even opening them. "I can only cope with one snafu at a time, Peter. Whatever game Central's playing, it's only a distraction."

"Maybe they found him."

"If they did they wouldn't be telling me." She poured herself a glass of water. "I'm sick of being everybody's little messenger girl. Kaunas is sitting in some ritzy hotel suite somewhere waiting for me to do his work for him, the Community and the Arcadians are waiting for me to do the same, and all Maksim's doing is playing fucking stupid games. Sick of it."

"You could refuse to have anything more to do with it," he suggested. "Leave the field, walk away. Let the principals sort it out for themselves."

She remembered having a similar conversation with Anatoly, except that had been about retirement. She said, "I can't let it go. He staged everything in Gliwice just to get me there, and he's laid a trail of breadcrumbs for me. I'm responsible for all this."

Peter looked levelly at her. "You are *not* responsible."

There was a knock at the door and Anatoly looked into

the dining room. "Sorry to bother you," he said, "but we think we've figured it out. We think the page numbers are GPS coordinates."

"To where?" she asked.

"You're not going to like it," he said.

"WE THOUGHT MAYBE we were just making everything too complicated," Magda said, typing on the cloth laptop's tapboard. "Codes and microdots and stuff. If Maksim wanted you to go to him, he'd make it obvious, not something you'd need special equipment to read."

"So we wrote out the page numbers as a series of digits and tried splitting them up into phone numbers or online addresses," Anatoly said, "to see if anything came up."

"He had the idea of GPS," Magda went on. "Cutie, he's not as stupid as he looks. We had to juggle the numbers around a bit until we got coordinates that made sense. It's not exact, down to the last metre, but we've got a ballpark latitude and longitude and he says it means something to you."

"Okay, okay," Carey said. "You're both superstars and I don't pay you enough. Where is it?"

Magda finished typing and a map filled the display. She pointed. "About there," she said.

Carey looked at the map and felt her skin crawl. "Fuck," she said.

GETTING THERE, AND getting there covertly, was not as straightforward as it had been for Texel. Air and rail were out of the question, and it was a long drive with multiple border crossings.

"Loppi can take you," Peter suggested. "He's going that way."

She looked at him. "Sometimes I wonder what goes on behind that beard."

"He doesn't have to know what your final destination is, or why you're going."

"Can we trust him?"

"Loppi? Gods, yes. Don't let that captain's hat fool you, he's a smart guy."

"Because it would be embarrassing to be boarded in the middle of the Baltic by a boat full of Russians or Arcadians or mimes or whoever the fuck else is mixed up in this circus."

"A lot of... *discreet* people have travelled on that boat," he said. "And nobody's been arrested yet. And anyway, I thought the whole point was for you to get there; they're not going to stop you."

"We're also supposed to be trying to keep the miserable fucker alive long enough to go to jail; if those guys tag along I don't give much for his chances." She'd already spent the morning trying to talk Krista out of causing an international incident by having the Estonian Army come riding over the horizon. It felt like a very long time since the morning she'd walked out of Hotel Barbara on her way to meet Kaunas. "Did you have any luck with contractors?"

"Yes," he said. "Yes, actually that went very well. I should have some good news soon."

"I'll take any good news I can get."

"We don't go into the Med any more," Staci said. "Because of the pirates."

She meant refugee boats, desperate enough to reach the southern edge of Europe that they had started to arm themselves with all manner of surplus artillery from the war zones in North Africa. The favoured tactic was to swarm an unsuspecting ship, board it, kill the crew, and use it to make port under cover of darkness. This had fooled port authorities the first couple of times, but the wealthier countries around the Mediterranean had cottoned on quickly and taken steps to defend themselves from the invading hordes. Monaco had built a couple of platforms a mile or so offshore and mounted on them railguns so powerful that they could bombard Corsica, or so Carey had heard. Now, if the urge took Loppi and Staci to visit Cannes or Nice or Cap Ferrat, *Karolina Nova* had to dock in Lisbon and they had to fly the rest of the way in one of Loppi's private jets, which was apparently a bit of a faff. In her mind, Carey unlimbered a tiny violin and played a sad tune for them.

She put her head back and looked straight up into a sky full of stars. It was a warm, calm night and they were sitting in deckchairs on the helipad at the rear of the ship with a little table between them supporting bottles and glasses. Far off to the right—she couldn't be bothered to learn which was port and which was starboard—were the lights of a town. Klaipėda, she thought, on the Lithuanian coast. 'Memel-as-was', Maksim used to call it darkly, for reasons she'd never discovered. *Karolina Nova* wasn't exactly setting any water-speed records. They'd already been at sea for the best part of a week, and it would be another couple of days before they entered the Gulf of Finland. Of course, nobody who realised they were on board would believe they were going anywhere important at such a leisurely pace.

"He's not a bad man," Staci said. They'd been discussing Loppi and Staci's migratory lifestyle. "He doesn't even bother me much for... *that* these days, you know." Which was rather more information, strictly speaking, than Carey needed. "I think he just likes having company."

They had been sneaked onto the boat the evening before its departure by the simple expedient of taking the place of four crew members ferrying supplies from the estate. All anyone watching from a distance would have seen was a steady procession of inflatables taking food and drink and bits of gear out to *Karolina Nova*. After that, it was just a matter of sitting around and waiting for them to actually get to their destination.

Which was not, when all was said and done, such an imposition. *Karolina Nova* was richly fitted-out, its rooms and companionways wood-panelled and its stairways carpeted. There was a lot of art on the walls; Loppi seemed to have a special passion for English landscapes, and Carey thought she recognised at least one Constable. It was either a good forgery or it was the original, she couldn't tell and she didn't suppose it really mattered.

The staterooms were large and luxurious, the food was excellent, and the weather was good. Magda in particular seemed to be enjoying herself, especially when they sailed up the Polish coast and she could stand on deck and watch her home pass by in the distance. Carey had taken her aside and had a quiet word about the importance of maintaining radio silence. No lovey-dovey phone calls to Romek about her little cruise. Krista had been a little harder to convince; she was still seething about the near-fiasco on Texel and was angry about not being allowed to do anything about it. Carey sympathised—this whole thing had started with the Russians trying to undermine the Tallinn police, and the discovery that at least one of them was passing information to the Arcadians must have been a blow—but she didn't want to get where they were going and find Michael and Wareham and probably Anatoly's father as well waiting for them, innocently eager to lend a hand. "What? Kill him? Us? No, we just want to help." Eventually, she and Krista came to a compromise, but it wasn't one that made either of them particularly happy.

"What if he's not there?" Anatoly asked, watching the lights of Helsinki grow closer as *Karolina Nova* drew to the end of her Baltic cruise. "What if we get there and there's just another postcard or a note or *fuck you* sprayed on a wall?"

"We carry on, I guess," Carey said.

"For how long?"

Carey turned away from the railing. "As long as I have to."

THIRTEEN

SHE FOUND THAT she had come to think of Maksim as existing in some kind of Schrödinger state, neither dead nor alive, real or unreal. He might have been a nightmare, a figment of her imagination, someone she had read about in a book. It seemed absurd that she had ever known him, let alone shared a significant part of her life with him.

Of course, if you laid the days they'd spent in each other's company end to end they probably wouldn't add up to much more than a couple of years. They'd grown used to snatching a week here, a month there, then going their separate ways and picking up again months later, and she thought perhaps that Maksim had become something of a mythical figure to her, that the long periods they spent apart masked what an utterly average man he really was. If they'd actually spent those two years together their relationship would probably have ended long before Helsinki and she wouldn't be here now.

Wouldn't have missed this *for the world*, she thought, looking about her. It was a couple of hours after sundown, and the evening was still warm. The sky was clear, and a full moon shone down on the road and the thick forest of birches and pines on either side. Standing very still, she could hear something moving around in the darkness under the trees: probably some kind of animal, she had no idea what. Wild boar, maybe. Did they have wild boar in Finland? Probably. Wild boar were everywhere; you saw them on the streets in Warsaw sometimes.

Someone had once told her that the Finns—the ones who lived in the south, at any rate—thought of themselves as a Baltic people rather than a Scandinavian one. She didn't know if that was true or not; the same person had denied that Denmark was a Scandinavian country—"It's just North Germany"—which she thought might be a tough opinion to sell in Copenhagen.

Scandinavian or not, it was a long way from anywhere. You even felt it in Helsinki, something in the air, a sense of being on the far northeastern edge of Europe, tucked away at the top end of the Gulf of Finland. After you got here, all that was left to do was to turn north, where the only things standing between you and the Arctic Circle were reindeer and Santa Claus.

Thing was, now she was here she *really* didn't want to do it. To see him, real and alive, would be to confront the failure of her life, the weight she had carried for a decade. Peter had said that it wasn't her fault, but it was. If she'd never met Maksim, he'd have found someone else and it would be their problem, but she *had* met him. She was as responsible for those dead people in the truck as he was, and she'd never faced that. She'd run away and Peter had given her sanctuary and she'd *put it behind her*. She'd hated Maksim for what he had done, and never faced the fact that she could have stopped him if only she'd paid more attention.

Anatoly had thought she was crazy, when she'd told him about the truck one evening back in Gliwice. She wasn't involved in what Maksim was doing, didn't even know he was doing it. She wasn't responsible. Thing was, she *had* known he was doing something. She remembered Maksim suddenly having a lot of money, a lot more than he would have had from Coureur work; it should have been obvious he'd found some other kind of scam. She could have asked him where it was coming from, and when he brushed her off—charming his way around the question, as he usually did with difficult subjects—she could have made an effort to find out, put her ear to the ground, tracked down Oskari or Raphael and leaned on them to find out what they knew. But she hadn't.

"You're going to judge yourself into your grave, I think," Anatoly had told her sadly.

She looked along the road that led down to the border station, and thought about all these things, and cursed herself for thinking about them. Then, out of habit, she cursed everything else. Maksim, Central, Hungary. She had never managed to discover what had happened in Hungary—and she *had* tried, there. It was a black hole, a blind spot. She'd even reached out to a couple of Coureurs in Esztergom, and they had no idea what she was talking about. It was as if she'd never been there.

The road to the border ran slightly downhill, curving off a little to the right so she couldn't see the control post from where she stood. There was nothing else out here; the nearest habitation was about five miles away, and in the still moonlight she felt as if she had finally, after all those years of running, reached the edge of the world. This spot where she stood was actually slightly closer to St Petersburg than Helsinki.

The border station was an anomaly. There was no real reason for it to be here at all; it was hidden away down a side road off a minor road, nothing like the huge acreages of lorry parks and multiple traffic lanes at the larger crossings further up and down the border. It was like something out of a 1960s spy movie. Michael Caine should have been here, wearing a big furry hat, instead of her. Anatoly theorised that it was a local arrangement, something that had come into being over decades by the agreement of people on either side of the border. That seemed unlikely; Finland had been in varying degrees of alert because of the presence of its colossal and troublesome neighbour for longer than Carey had been alive.

But here the station was, and it had been ideal for Maksim's purposes. It had only had a complement of about a dozen border officers, and somehow he had managed to bribe or blackmail every single one of them. The scandal had echoed around the Finnish Parliament for years.

Coming around the curve in the road, she thought the place looked temporary and thrown-together, a shabby compound surrounded by high wire fences. There was a big paved area to one side, its asphalt cracked and choked with weeds now, which had been used for cars and trucks waiting to cross the border at busy times. If there ever *had* been busy times. There was a toilet block, a couple of one-storey concrete admin buildings, another area of asphalt for official vehicles, a cafeteria building, and a small filling station with a row of hydrogen dispensers and charging points and—off to one side as if in shame—a single petrol pump.

Maksim had actually managed to cause a minor international incident. In the wake of the scandal, the Finns had accused the Russians of being complicit in human trafficking by letting the trucks through, and the Russians had denied knowing anything about it, and eventually the Finns had closed the crossing point and sealed it.

Carey stopped at the entrance to the compound. The gates stood open. It looked as if they had been open for quite some time; weeds and grass had grown up and twined through them almost as high as her head. Everything was quiet and still. Beyond the buildings was a double line of tank traps, huge four-pointed concrete objects scattered on the ground, and beyond those was a high triple fence of densely woven smartwire mesh topped with enough razor-ribbon to cut an army to bits, blocking the road's progress to the border. On the other side of the fence was a strip of land perhaps a hundred feet deep cleared of trees and undergrowth and sown with listening devices and sensors and countermeasures, and then there was the border itself, the line on the map. And beyond *that* was Rus. *Here be monsters.* Carey had been crisscrossing Europe for more than half her life, but standing here looking at this abandoned little post it seemed the first time that she had actually *felt* as if she was at a border.

She couldn't understand why the Finns had just left this place here, rather than demolishing it and letting the forest reclaim it. Was it just too much trouble, or was there some long-forgotten contingency plan to reopen it one day? She had a sense that there had been some maintenance, at least in the past, because though it was shabby and overgrown it wasn't as overgrown as you'd have expected after ten years of neglect.

She couldn't see vehicles or anyone moving about, but there was the flat white glow of a pinpoint lamp from the windows of the cafeteria, and she stood by the gate looking at that for a long time before walking slowly over to the building and opening the door. It was on a strong spring and she had to put her back into it.

The pinpoint was stuck to one of the walls, a globe the size of a grapefruit illuminating a big room laid out with rows of tables and bench seating. Running along the back was a metal counter with a couple of serving hatches behind it and a swing-door to one side that probably led into the kitchen. The air in here was cooler than outside, and it smelled of mould and old grease and something musty and musky as if animals had got in and taken up residence.

He was sitting at a table right in the middle of the room, a bottle of beer in front of him. For a moment, she was almost overcome by a powerful urge to turn round and push the door open and walk back up the road, but she forced herself forward, and he sat back in his seat and watched her pick her way stiff-legged between the tables. She could almost see him trying to decide how to pitch it. Be serious? Be the old laughing, joking Maksim? How best to get away with this?

She stopped by the table and looked down at him. The photo in his passport must have been a few years old, because he'd put on a lot more weight since then. His face was heavy and puffy and unshaven, his hair untidy. He was wearing a coat and a sweater and he looked as if he'd been sleeping rough for a while.

He reached out and picked up the bottle in front of him. "Beer?" he asked.

"No." She slid into the seat opposite him and clasped her hands on the table.

He took a mouthful of beer and examined her face, and she wondered what he saw there, the years that had passed. She wondered if he was thinking about what she'd been through since that night in Helsinki, but she knew it never even crossed his mind. He was trying to gauge the changes in her, working out how he could play them to his best advantage. She'd seen him do that before, and at the time it had seemed like something of a superpower, but now she thought it was just a cheap conjuring trick.

"You took your time," he said finally. "I've been here for weeks."

The thought of him camping out here in the middle of nowhere while she sailed leisurely up the Baltic with Loppi and Staci was very fine. Little victories. She sat staring at him and didn't say anything. There had been a time when she had loved him, or at least had felt something for him that she rationalised as love, and now that seemed like something she'd seen in a movie.

He said, "I came to see you a few months ago, in Madrid, but you weren't there."

She'd been busy earlier in the year, and then she'd been in Catalunya for almost a month before she got Kaunas's crash message. Her first instinct had been to ignore it. She regretted not doing that, not just for herself but for all the others whose lives had been uprooted by this business.

"I guess you wouldn't have wanted to talk to me, even if you *had* been at home," he went on.

He was winding himself up to blame her for the whole thing. *None of this would have happened if only you'd talked to me*. She wasn't going to let him do that. She said, "Jaw healed up, then," and that shut him up. She saw him trying to decide whether to glare at her or laugh it off. "Where are the Coureurs?"

His eyebrows went up. "The what?"

"The Coureurs from Gliwice. The ones you went off with."

"Oh." He relaxed a fraction. "Estoril," he said. "They're in a place down the street from Admiral Horthy's old house. I've got Luis Sanchez babysitting them, you remember Luis? They think they're setting up for a big Situation, but Luis has just got them running about doing stringer stuff. He'll send them home in a week or so."

He looked proud of himself, and he expected her to be proud too. *Look how smart I am*. She just glared stonily at him. She thought, really, she should have been pursuing him through the Vienna sewers, but instead she was sitting across a table from him in a disused cafeteria on the edge of Finland. Real life was always disappointing and complicated and shabby and not very exciting, and it constantly amazed her that people were surprised by that.

"Is that all you wanted to ask?" he said finally. "About a bunch of Polish Coureurs?"

It occurred to her there were some ends that she might have liked tying up about Helsinki, but she had that mostly straight in her head; he'd brought her there as a patsy, a decoy. If things went wrong, he would anonymously have given the police the address of where she'd been staying and she'd have been arrested. After a little while it would have become obvious to the police that they had the wrong woman and they'd have released her with an apology, and that would have bought him time to get clear. But Brookshire had got to her first and she'd already been in motion when the catastrophe happened. She didn't think there was anything more he could tell her about it that wouldn't enrage her. He'd killed twenty women, and she didn't want to sit here listening to him trying to justify it. Besides, she'd ended that particular conversation that day in Madrid.

He tipped his head to one side. Maybe he was thinking she'd changed more than he had expected. But maybe she hadn't changed all that much; she was here, after all. She just sat looking at him, wondering who he was, who he had been all the time she'd known him. Coureur work, at the level she and Maksim had done it, was a constantly-changing landscape of false names and papers; she had, on occasion, tired and harassed, needed to pause for a moment and try to reestablish for herself who she was supposed to be. But Maksim had always been like that, she thought. He'd been like that before he even became a Coureur.

He said, "About five years ago, Yegor comes to me and says, 'Maksim Ilyich, my dearest friend, I have met a man who has proof that the Community are running an intelligence operation in Europe, a big one. Infiltration, subversion, bribery, you name it. It's been going on for years.'" Carey sighed inwardly. He was going to turn this into an epic saga. "You know Yegor, he's been doing this for so long that everything's an intelligence op. We don't get involved in espionage, right? What's it to do with us? 'Ah, Maksim, Maksim, every intelligence op needs to be *funded*, and this one happens to be funded through a black bank in Tallinn. Now, it also happens that I hear from my former brethren that they're planning an operation of their own in Estonia in the not-too-distant future, and it occurs to me that two smart men might sail in under the cover of that and take this Community money, put a crimp in their operation, and incidentally make themselves rich.'"

"You weren't involved in the Russian op?" she asked. "Not directly?"

He shook his head. "Nah. Yegor might have been; he's still connected in the Russian intelligence community, some of those guys worship the ground he walks on. I didn't even know what they were going to pull."

There was no way Krista was ever going to believe that. Carey blinked slowly at him. She wondered how desperate he'd have to be, to get mixed up in something like that. On the other hand, she was disinclined to believe a single word that came out of his mouth.

"You met this guy? Yegor's friend?"

"*Rupert*. Sure I met with him, I'm not stupid. Old guy, but hard as fucking nails, like Yegor. I got the impression he was ex-English Intelligence."

I got the impression. He'd been *that* desperate. She said, "How much?"

He looked at her for a moment, then embarked on a low-level comedy routine as he patted himself down looking for a pen and something to write on. He finally came up with a crumpled bit of paper, smoothed it out on the table, and wrote 27. Then he spent quite a long time adding zeroes. He turned it round and showed the figure to her.

"I hope that's not in US dollars," she said.

"Swiss francs."

"That's a big intelligence op," she mused.

He crumpled the piece of paper up again and stuffed it in his pocket. "So Yegor and I are in Tallinn," he said. "We go out to this business park and find the right building and we wait, and bang on cue the power goes out. The whole city's blacked out. We get into the building and it's deserted. No security at all. It's got an emergency generator so its internal systems are all running, but it's completely cut off from the outside world. We find a terminal and we input the passwords Rupert's given us, and there it is, all the bank codes to the money, along with some other stuff.

"I copy everything, and I'm about to leave when I realise Yegor's not there any more. Then I hear him shouting, down the corridor, and when I go to find him he's in the server room, sticking thermite charges to everything. '*Now* we tell them!' he's shouting. '*Now* we tell them!' like he's gone crazy.

"I don't know what he's doing, but there's no point standing there arguing with him; we only had a window of an hour to do everything and get clear, so I leave him there and get out. The streetlights came back on as I left the business park, and the data networks came back up a minute or so later and I moved the money to the O'Keefe Brothers."

The O'Keefes were Carey's accountants, a pair of immensely aged Malay gentlemen. They were not Irish, and they were not brothers, but they were very, very good at what they did.

"The brothers washed the money and split it up and sent it to accounts in Liechtenstein and Luxembourg and Grand Cayman and they sent me the codes for those accounts. They took a cut and so did the banks, but I figure there's still twenty billion or so left. I was in Latvia three hours later." He sat back and took another swallow of beer.

End of Part One, she thought. *Maksim Pulls Off the Crime of the Century. The audience will now pause to be properly admiring*. Well, fuck that.

She said, "What went wrong?"

He raised an eyebrow.

"You don't have the money, otherwise you'd be sitting on a beach somewhere with a banana daiquiri in your hand. What went wrong?"

He didn't answer immediately. He looked across the room, to where a line of windows gave diners a scenic view of the toilet block on the other side of the compound. He said, "My phone was stolen."

"Excuse me?"

"I was in a bar in Antwerp last year and some kid picked my pocket and took my phone. I never even felt it go, didn't realise it was gone until I got outside and tried to call someone. Yegor got hold of the security footage from the bar and tracked the kid down but he'd already sold the phone on to somebody, didn't have a name or anything. Yegor wanted to kill him, but he was just a kid, stole the phone for some quick cash to pay for a fix or something. The phone was gone."

"So?"

He put his forearms on the table and leaned forward. "There's a thing the NSA developed years ago, it's to hide stuff that might be embarrassing. Emails, bank details, tax returns, that sort of thing. You input your data and it breaks it down into little pieces and sort of scatters it *everywhere*, one piece on one server somewhere, another piece on another server somewhere else, it's impossible to find them all and reconstruct them. In some places, the data doesn't even exist legally any more. At intervals, it'll gather the bits together again on some random server and reassemble the data and contact you to see if you want to do anything with it. If you don't, or if you don't respond, it breaks up the data and hides it again."

It sounded like one of the stupidest things Carey had ever heard, like something dreamed up by a second-rate spy novelist. There were less *baroque* ways to hide data, but that was how you sold stuff like this. People still thought that if something was weird and complicated it must be good. Still, she felt the first distant stirrings of a faint disquiet.

"It'll keep doing that for a while," he went on. "Then if you still don't respond it'll switch to an alternate contact. If that doesn't respond, it'll try another one, and on down its list. If it gets no joy from any of them, it scatters the data one last time and shuts down and then it's *really* gone. For ever."

"You gave it my number," she said, feeling a cold sensation prickling the back of her neck. No matter which phone she'd had, down the years, she'd kept the same number for work, the one she gave all her press contacts.

"You were down at the bottom of the list," he said. "Yegor and Oskari and a couple of other people came first, but I never expected to need them because I never expected to lose the phone."

"So you wait a year and this thing calls Yegor and you're back in contact, so what?"

He looked her in the eye. "It's voice recognition."

For a moment, she was completely at a loss. Then the pieces clicked together in her head. She thought of Peter saying, *Perhaps the book itself is a clue*. "*Moby-Dick*," she said.

He shrugged.

He'd cut together the voiceprint recognition strings using the audio files she'd sent him of her reading the book. "You *motherfucker*."

He looked at the windows again.

"Didn't you keep a backup?"

He shook his head. "Just one copy. On my phone."

If she hadn't seen the books recently, it would never have occurred to her. She sat back. "Well," she said, "shit."

"Half for me, half for you," he said. "All you have to do

is wait here until it calls, and say the magic words, then we can go our separate ways."

"You faked your own death just to get me here to answer the phone for you."

"You wouldn't have come otherwise," he said. "If I'd called you and told you all this you'd just have hung up."

"Don't you *dare* try to blame me for this, you evil cocksucker." She wanted to leap over the table and pull his ears off. "What about the people you killed? The tractor driver and the guy who was supposed to be you?"

Maksim shook his head. "Yegor handled all that."

"You're out of your *fucking* mind, Maksim Ilyich."

"Twenty billion Swiss," he reminded her.

"What about all the other stuff? The gang war, was that you?"

He shook his head. "I figure that was just some guys taking advantage of the general batshit craziness to settle some scores, although the Community did have a shopfront in Gliwice for a while."

"Which you blew up."

"Actually, no. I've got no idea who did that. I had some people keeping an eye on it, but it's been empty for months."

"Fuck you, Maksim," she said. "Just fuck you."

He gave her a level look. "You do this thing, you never see me again."

"I was already doing that pretty well by myself." He had absolutely no idea what he'd blundered into. He didn't know about Arcadia, didn't know they had diplomatic relations with the Community, didn't realise that whatever this was, it was bigger than money. "You absolute *dick*, Maksim Ilyich."

Her phone rang.

They looked at each other. The phone kept ringing. Maksim said calmly, "Put it on speaker. It wants to know what to call you."

She almost left it. Eventually the software would stop calling her, and the money and whatever else he'd stolen in Tallinn would be gone for ever.

She took the phone out of her pocket, set it to speaker, and thumbed *answer*. "Hello?"

"Who are you?" the familiar woman's voice said.

Carey didn't reply.

"Who are you?" the voice asked again. Carey didn't say anything. She watched a little bead of sweat, even in the coolness of the cafeteria, run down the side of Maksim's face.

"Who are you?" the voice asked patiently.

Without taking her eyes off Maksim, she said, "Call me Ishmael."

"Hi, Ishmael," said the software. "What's your number?"

She raised an eyebrow at him and he said, "It's the date on my—" and she held up her hand. Of course it was; the bastard had *shown her* the password. She swiped up the photos she'd taken of the urn at the crematorium in Gliwice and read out the date on the little plaque digit by digit.

"Thanks, Ishmael," the voice said. "Do you want to continue or do you want to start download?"

Maksim was sitting very still.

"Download," Carey said.

"Okay," said the voice. "Under way. Anything else I can help you with?"

Can you make my ex die horribly right in front of me? "Not right now, thanks."

"Okay. Talk to you soon." The connection was cut, and then the phone began to vibrate as it started to receive messages. She swiped one open and saw bank codes. Another looked like the image of a page of mathematical notation. So did the next. And the next. Hundreds of pages of maths. GPS coordinates. Columns of figures and numerals in five-figure groups. Then more bank codes.

Maksim said, "So, I'll take that now," and reached for the phone. Without looking up from the screen, she took one of the ceramic guns that Romek had printed for her from her pocket and pointed it at his head. He regarded the muzzle. "That thing looks as if it'll go off in your hand if you pull the trigger."

"My hand, your face," she told him. He sat back and rubbed his eyes. Then he dropped his hands into his lap and sat looking at her, and she felt her heart break all over again. They looked at each other for quite a long time before he glanced towards the windows.

"The sniper's not there," she told him coldly. "None of your contractors are. They pulled out when I arrived; Peter Schiller bought them out from under you."

He stared at her.

"There's nowhere to go, Maksim Ilyich," she went on. "You've got your back to the wire and you don't have anyone left. Nobody wants anything to do with you unless you pay them. I bet you put every penny you had into setting this whole thing up and all you've done is make a fool of yourself."

He leaned forward again a little. "This friend of Yegor's? Rupert? He said the Community caused the pandemic."

Well, it wasn't the first time she'd heard *that* theory. But she'd also heard the flu blamed on the Chinese, the Americans, the Russians, the Illuminati, the Anunnaki, and a race of Nazis who lived inside the Earth. "Did *Rupert* have any proof of that?" she asked, glancing at the phone again.

He lunged forward suddenly, kicking his chair away behind him, and made a grab for the phone, and she shot him in the chest, bowling him backward.

Carey sat where she was for a few moments, then she zipped the phone up in an inside pocket of her coat and got up and went around the table and stood over him where he lay on the floor. His coat had fallen open and there was a hole in his sweater, low down on the left. She'd been aiming at his heart, but he'd been moving. She examined her feelings and found it wasn't enough, so she shot him again.

"Will you stop *doing* that?" he shouted.

"You tried to have *me* shot," she pointed out.

"You couldn't be sure I was wearing a vest," he said, grimacing.

"No," she agreed. "I couldn't. Imagine my disappointment." Modern ballistic armour looked like a thick sleeveless tee shirt; it protected the wearer from gunshots by absorbing the impact and spreading it over its entire surface and then radiating the kinetic energy out as heat. If she shot him a few more times in swift succession, his clothes would probably catch fire, which did appeal. "Get up, let's go,"

Grunting with pain, he managed to roll himself over and get himself up on hands and knees, and then stood agonisingly slowly until he was facing her, hunched over with one arm wrapped around his chest. "I've broken some ribs," he said.

"Technically, *I* broke them," she told him. His torso was also going to be one huge bruise in a little while. What a shame. She stepped away and gestured towards the door. "You first."

Breathing shallowly and clutching his side, Maksim shuffled to the door and shoved it open by leaning all his weight on it. Then he lurched forward and let it swing back. Carey was too close; the door came back hard on its heavy spring and knocked the gun out of her hand. By the time she'd scooped it up and got the door open, Maksim was loping across the compound, not quite as injured as he'd pretended. She stood by the door and watched him.

"Where are you going to go?" she called. "The Finns

and the Estonians want to put you in jail, and people you never even imagined existed want to kill you. You've got nowhere to run to."

He didn't pay any attention. He'd made it between the tank traps. He seemed to gather himself, then he took a step forward towards the fence, two steps to the left, one to the right, one forward.

"Oh, *seriously*," she said in a loud voice, raising the gun.

Two steps forward, one to the right. Maksim was standing right in front of the fence by now. He half-turned, flipped her the finger, and seemed to step *through* the wire.

Carey stood where she was for quite a long time, watching the place where he'd vanished. She lowered the gun, made it safe, put it in her pocket. She walked across the compound, thinking. This must have been how he got the trucks across the border; they'd all thought the Russians had been in on it, but he must have brought them through the Community somehow. Or maybe, it occurred to her, through somewhere else. If there could be another Community, why not a third? A fourth? She stood where he'd been standing, tried to repeat his footsteps, but it was hopeless. Nothing happened. Obviously, he hadn't quite run out of people prepared to help him yet. She wondered what would happen when he told them he didn't have the money.

She turned away and walked back to the gates, continued on up the road beyond the compound. Every few steps she felt the phone in her pocket vibrating against her chest as it received another set of bank codes. She wondered if Magda would be able to make any sense of the pages of mathematics, or if she knew someone who could. All she could be sure of, for the moment at least, was that nobody knew she had what Maksim had stolen. She took out the gun, unloaded it, and without breaking stride half-turned and pitched it hard into the trees. It went a surprisingly long way before she heard it rustle into the undergrowth. She put the clip in her pocket as she came round the curve of the road.

She lifted her arms and put them straight out on either side as she walked, hands open and palms forward. "I'm alone and unarmed," she called out, and all of a sudden rows of headlights came on on vehicles parked a little way further up the road, first two, then four, then eight, then she was walking towards a wall of light with figures moving in it like the end of *Close Encounters*. Krista had wanted to call out the police and armed services of every country around the Baltic, which would have been like sending up a flare. She'd unwillingly agreed to settle for arranging Finnish police backup at very short notice. Hopefully, other watchful eyes might not have noticed, and if they had, it was too late for them to do anything about it. Carey squinted her eyes and kept going.

She reached a line of waist-high barriers set across the road in front of the vehicles, and stopped. Krista and Anatoly came forward and pushed one of the barriers aside.

"Where is he?" asked Krista. She was wearing a full combat suit; Anatoly was wearing a Kevlar tabard over a hoodie.

"He's gone," Carey said. "There's a border crossing into the Community or somewhere back there. He took a couple of shots at me and he ran for it."

"Shit!" Krista motioned to a tall young policeman who was also wearing a combat suit but with a weird orange knitted hat on his head. He unholstered a sidearm and set off at a trot down the road, followed by a couple of dozen Finnish police. "You were down there a long time."

"I did spend a while cussing him."

"Fucksake. Did he say what this was all about?"

Carey shook her head. "We didn't get to that. He got angry and started shooting. Can I put my arms down now?"

Krista nodded. "We'll talk about this," she said. "Don't go far." And she set off after the others towards the border station. Carey lowered her arms and watched her go. The phone vibrated one last time in her pocket, then stopped.

"What happened?" Anatoly asked.

She remembered Byron, years ago, telling her that, for the very rich, it was quite possible to live to at least a hundred and twenty. And that had been a long time ago; who knew how long you could live now, if you were wealthy enough? She'd thought her life had been on its final lap, but now it seemed possible that it was barely even half over.

She looked at him. "The bad guy got away," she said, and she stepped past him, a tall Texan woman of a certain age with a temper and twenty billion Swiss francs in her pocket, and walked into the light.

ABOUT THE AUTHOR

Dave Hutchinson is the multi-award winning author of the critically acclaimed *Fractured Europe* series for Solaris: *Europe it Autumn*, *Europe at Midnight*, *Europe in Winter* and *Europe at Dawn*.

FIND US ONLINE!

www.rebellionpublishing.com

/rebellionpub

/rebellionpublishing

/rebellionpublishing

SIGN UP TO OUR NEWSLETTER!

rebellionpublishing.com/newsletter

YOUR REVIEWS MATTER!

Enjoy this book? Got something to say?

Leave a review on Amazon, Goodreads or with your favourite bookseller and let the world know!

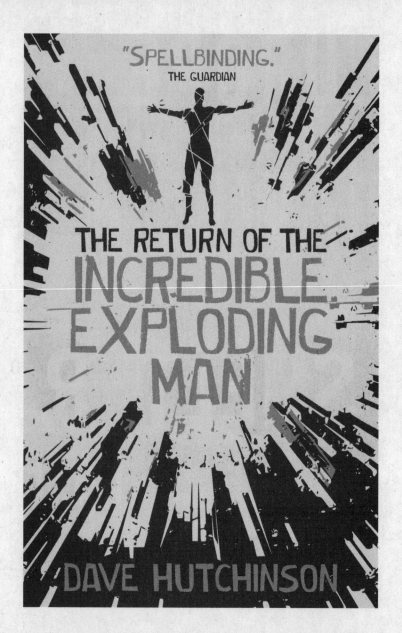